Signed First Edition

DREAM COUNT

BY CHIMAMANDA NGOZI ADICHIE

Dream Count

Mama's Sleeping Scarf

Notes on Grief

Dear Ijeawele, or A Feminist Manifesto in Fifteen Suggestions

We Should All Be Feminists

Americanah

The Thing Around Your Neck

Half of a Yellow Sun

Purple Hibiscus

DREAM COUNT

A NOVEL

Chimamanda Ngozi Adichie

4th ESTATE • *London*

4th Estate
An imprint of HarperCollins*Publishers*
1 London Bridge Street
London SE1 9GF

www.4thestate.co.uk

HarperCollins*Publishers*
Macken House, 39/40 Mayor Street Upper
Dublin 1, D01 C9W8, Ireland

First published in Great Britain in 2025 by 4th Estate
First published in the US in 2025 by Alfred A. Knopf

1

ISBN 978-0-00-868573-7 (Hardback)
ISBN 978-0-00-868574-4 (Trade paperback)

Designed by Anna B. Knighton
Cover design by Jo Thomson

This novel is entirely a work of fiction. The names, characters
and incidents portrayed in it are the work of the author's imagination.
Any resemblance to actual persons, living or dead, events or
localities is entirely coincidental.

In memory of my beautiful, beloved mother,

Grace Ifeoma Adichie (née Odigwe)

NOVEMBER 29, 1942–MARCH 1, 2021

Uwa m uwa ozo, i ga-abu nne m

DREAM COUNT

Chiamaka

ONE

I have always longed to be known, truly known, by another human being. Sometimes we live for years with yearnings that we cannot name. Until a crack appears in the sky and widens and reveals us to ourselves, as the pandemic did, because it was during lockdown that I began to sift through my life and give names to things long unnamed. I vowed at first to make the most of this collective sequestering: if I had no choice but to stay indoors, then I would oil my thinning edges every day, drink eight tall glasses of water, jog on the treadmill, sleep long, luxurious hours, and pat rich serums on my skin. I would write new travel pieces from old unused notes, and if lockdown lasted long enough, I might finally have the heft I needed for a book. But only days in, and I was spiralling inside a bottomless well. Words and warnings swirled and spun, and I felt as if all human progress was swiftly reversing to an ancient stage of confusion that should by now have been extinct. Don't touch your face; wash your hands; don't go outside; spray disinfectant; wash your hands; don't go outside; don't touch your face. Did washing my face count as touching? I always used a face towel, but one morning my palm grazed my cheek and I froze, the tap water still running. It couldn't matter, surely, since I never even stepped outside, but what did 'don't touch your face' and 'wash your hands' mean when nobody knew how this had started, when it would end, or what even it was? I woke up daily assailed by anxiety, my heart stirring itself into a race, without my permission, and sometimes I pressed my palm to my chest and held it there. I was alone in my house in Maryland, in suburban silence, the eerie roads bordered by trees that themselves seemed stilled by the quiet. No cars drove past. I looked out and saw a herd of deer striding across the clearing of my front yard. About ten deer, or maybe fifteen, nothing like the lone deer I would see from time to time chewing shyly in the grass. I felt frightened of them, their unusual boldness, as though my world was about to be overrun not just by deer, but by other lurking creatures I could not imagine. Sometimes I barely ate, wandering into the pantry to nibble on crackers, and other times I dug out forgotten bags of frozen vegetables and cooked spicy beans that reminded me of childhood. The formless days bled into one another and I had the sensation of time turning inward. My joints throbbed, and the muscles of my back, and the sides of my neck, as if my body knew too well that we are not made to live like this. I did not write because I could not write. I never turned on my treadmill. On Zoom calls, everyone echoed, reaching but not touching, the distance between us all further hollowed out.

MY BEST FRIEND, Zikora, nearby in DC, called one afternoon and said she was at Walmart buying toilet paper.

'You went out!' I said, almost shouting.

'I'm double-masked and I'm wearing gloves,' she said. 'The police are here organizing the line for toilet paper – can you imagine?' Zikora switched to Igbo and continued, 'People are shouting at each other. I'm really afraid someone will soon pull a gun. This White man in front of me is suspect; he came in a massive truck and he's wearing a red hat.'

We never spoke pure Igbo–English words always littered our sentences – but Zikora had vigilantly shed all English in case strangers overheard, and now she sounded contrived, like a bad TV drama about precolonial times. *A man riding a big land boat and wearing a hat the colour of blood.* I began to laugh and she began to laugh, and I felt briefly released, restored.

'Honestly, Zikor, you shouldn't have gone out.'

'But we need toilet paper.'

'I think it's finally time for us to start washing our bums,' I said, and in the next moment Zikora and I chorused, 'You are not clean!'

I had told the story so many times over the years, about Abdul, our gateman in Enugu – willowy Abdul in his long jellabiya, walking one evening to the latrine in the back, holding his plastic kettle of water, and then turning to calmly tell me, 'You Christians use tissue after toilet. You are not clean.'

ON OUR FAMILY ZOOM CALL, I said, 'The greatest crime you can commit in America today is to disrupt the long lines of people waiting to buy toilet paper in supermarkets. The police are now very busy guarding toilet-paper lines all across the country.'

I hoped everyone would laugh – we used to laugh so much – but only my father did. My twin brothers were on the cusp of yet another argument.

My mother said, 'I've never understood why Americans call it paper. Toilet paper. It sounds rough. Why not toilet tissue or toilet roll?'

We spoke on Zoom every other day – my parents in Enugu, my brother Afam in Lagos, and his twin, Bunachi, in London. Each call was like an overcast day, bleak and burdened with the latest bad news.

My parents talked of death, of the dying and the dead, and my brothers were brazenly barbed with each other, no longer bothering to shield my parents from their hostility. It was as if we could no longer be ourselves because the world was not itself. We talked about the rising numbers of Nigerian cases, changing day by day, state by state, in a macabre competition. Lagos had the most for now, and then Cross River was next. Afam sent us a video of an ambulance in his estate, screaming its way down his street, and captioned it 'one down'. Bunachi said doctors in the UK wouldn't be getting any protective gowns soon, because the people who made them in China were dead. I always joined the call last, and I pretended I had been on other calls with editors, when in fact I was just staring at my phone, bracing myself to click 'Join'. My parents had returned to Nigeria from Paris just before lockdown and my mother often said, 'Imagine if we had been stranded in Europe. This thing is killing our age-mates there like flies.'

'Imagine the disaster if we had Europe's death rates,' my father said.

'God is saving Nigeria; there is no other explanation,' Afam said.

'There's magic,' Bunachi said waspishly. Then he added, 'Europe is just honest at recording coronavirus deaths.'

'No, no, no,' my father said. 'If we had high death rates, we wouldn't be able to hide it. We're too disorganized; we're not China.'

'Jesus, Mary and Joseph. All these numbers are people, people,' my mother said, her face turned away, watching TV.

'I took a spoon to an ATM this morning,' Afam said.

'A spoon?' my mother asked, fully frontal again.

'I just didn't want to touch that machine, so I pressed in my pass-code with the spoon and then threw the spoon away,' Afam said.

'You didn't wear gloves?' my mother asked.

'I did, but who knows if coronavirus can pass through gloves?' Afam said.

'The virus dies in seconds on solid surfaces. You just wasted a spoon,' Bunachi said, all-knowing as ever. A few days before, he had declared that ventilators were not the right treatment for coronavirus. He was an accountant.

'But you should not have gone out in the first place, Afam,' my father said. 'What are you doing with cash, anyway? You people stocked up well.'

'I need cash. Lagos is very tense,' Afam said.

'Tense how?' Bunachi asked, and Afam ignored him until my father asked, 'What do you mean by tense?'

'Mobs are gathering at estates all over The Island, asking for money and food. You know many people earn their living day-to-day; they don't have anything to fall back on. All these hawkers on the road. I saw a video where somebody in a mob was saying they don't want lockdown, that it's the rich who go abroad and catch coronavirus, and since they washed our clothes and pumped our car tyres before lockdown, we should now feed them. To be fair, there's a kind of logic to it.'

'There's no logic to it. They're just criminals,' Bunachi said.

'They're hungry,' Afam said. 'I even walked to the ATM. I heard that if you dare drive out in an expensive car, they chase you with sticks.'

He lived in an estate of hulking houses where visitors needed unique passcodes at the electronic entrance gates. The next day, he said the mob had beaten the guards, and were banging at the gates, trying to deactivate the security system.

'They've started a fire just by the entrance,' he said. 'I've never seen our WhatsApp group so active. We're all contributing money, trying to work out how best to get it to them.'

'Do you still think they are harmless?' Bunachi taunted.

'I never said they were harmless. I said they were hungry,' Afam said.

On his screen, we saw grey smoke rising into the evening sky. He looked fragile and untested, standing there by a tall potted plant in his marble balcony. The plant was so verdant, leaves so lushly full, that it startled me to remember when life was ordinary and my brother master of his days, running his businesses, a young Lagos Big Man with power in his pockets. Now he was standing there while his wife barricaded their two children in the kitchen because the kitchen had the sturdiest door. He was trying to look unafraid, which only made him look afraid, and I thought how breakable we all are, and how easily we forget how breakable we are. A loud bang split the air, and I jumped, unsure for a moment whether it had come from Afam's screen or from outside my window.

'Did you hear that?' Afam said. 'Some kind of explosion at the gate.'

'It's nothing serious,' my father said. 'They must have thrown a can of insecticide into the fire.'

'Afam, go inside and lock all the doors,' my mother said.

To change the subject, I said high-dose vitamin C was sold out everywhere online. Bunachi, of course, knew it all and said vitamin C didn't prevent the virus, and he would send us the recipe for an infusion made with fresh basil, which we should inhale daily.

'Nobody has fresh basil,' Afam snapped.

Bunachi began to recite the latest statistics on deaths by country and I said, 'My battery is dying', and hung up. I sent Afam a text, ending with a line of red heart emojis: *Hang in there, bro, you'll all be fine.*

MY COUSIN OMELOGOR said nothing of the sort was happening in Abuja, Abuja was milder than Lagos, as always, it was like a Lagos bleached by sun, nutrients leaking away.

'People are dying and people are having birthday parties,' she said.

'What?'

'The president's chief of staff died yesterday of coronavirus and this morning Ejiro invited me to her birthday party. I told her that if I want to risk death, I will choose a better way than her birthday party.'

It jarred to hear Omelogor say 'died' and 'death'; she rarely spoke of symptoms or numbers of the dead. She talked of resealing cartons of Indomie noodles with strong Sellotape before leaving them at the gate of a motherless baby's home; or of the surge, since lockdown, of web traffic on her website, For Men Only, more unique visitors from more countries, many asking her to make a video and finally reveal herself. 'It almost feels intimate, asking me to make a video,' Omelogor said with laughter in her voice. Of all the people I loved, Omelogor was the most like herself still, undefeated by this communal unknown; she always looked awake and showered and alive with plans. 'Chia, this thing will pass. Human beings have survived many plagues throughout history,' she said often, sensing my sagging spirits, and her tone bolstered me, even though 'plague' reminded me, for some reason, of blood leeches.

'Don't call it a plague,' I said.

Sometimes we didn't talk, propping our phones on a book, or a mug, sharing our silences and our background sounds. Only with

Omelogor was silence tolerable. On Zoom calls with friends, quiet felt like failure, and so I talked and talked, thinking how quickly we adapt, or pretend to adapt, to a life reduced to screen and sound. Zikora said she liked working from home, in her bed, because she could hear Chidera's high-pitched crying from the living room, and the low tones of her mother's soothing voice. Chidera was crying so much, asking to go to the playground, that she had finally let him watch cartoons for the first time in his life, and he had looked scared when the first show started, but now he sat, hypnotized, in front of the TV and wailed when her mother turned it off. LaShawn, in Philadelphia, was making sourdough bread and leaving plates of fried chicken on the landing for her mother, who was quarantined upstairs because they weren't taking chances. Hlonipha, in Johannesburg, said she had unplugged her Wi-Fi and was painting watercolours, but they made her sad because they seemed too watery, too faded. Lavanya, in London, was always drinking red wine, raising the bottle to her screen as she refilled her glass. Her neighbour had died of coronavirus, an old lady who lived alone with her dog, and nobody had taken the dog, and she could hear it barking and it broke her heart, but she didn't know if dogs got coronavirus too.

Soon the Zoom calls became a mélange of hallucinatory images. At the end of each call, I felt lonelier than before, not because the call had ended but that it had been made at all. To talk was to remember all that was lost. I longed to hear another person breathing close by. I dreamed of hugging my mother in the anteroom of our home in Enugu, and I woke up surprised because I had not consciously thought of hugging her. I wished I was not alone. If only Kadiatou had agreed to bring Binta and quarantine with me. But I understood her wanting to be in her apartment, even as I worried so much about her. A few days before lockdown, she had said, 'I wait in my apartment.' Wait. We really were all waiting. Lockdown was an unknown waiting for an unknown end, and Kadiatou's was heightened by untamed pain. I called her daily, and when she didn't pick up, I called Binta to make sure she was fine. We spoke on WhatsApp video because she didn't have Zoom. 'How are you, Kadi?' I would ask, and she would respond, 'We are okay, we thank God.' Sometimes she said, 'Miss Chia, don't worry about me', her voice quiet, unwilling to make a fuss. And yet only weeks before, that same voice, raised in panic, was shouting on the phone, 'He will send people to kill me! He will send people to kill me!' She had refused therapy, shaking her head, saying, 'I cannot talk to stranger, I cannot talk to stranger.' All she wanted was for the trial to be over, but court cases were suspended now, and I worried that, stuck in lockdown's limbo, she might succumb to darkness.

'How will I get a job again after this? How will I get a job again?' she asked me, and she sounded so despondent that I wanted to weep.

'You can open your restaurant after the trial is over, Kadi,' I said.

'Nobody will go to restaurant again after corona,' she said flatly.

On one call, a flash of aggression from Kadiatou startled me. 'Don't send money again, Miss Chia. You give me enough already.' She had never spoken in that tone to me before. Hushed tension settled across distance, between screens.

'Okay, Kadi,' I said, finally. She hung up without saying goodbye, and I waited a few days before calling her again. Whenever I asked Binta, 'How is your mom doing?' her reply was the same: 'She cries at night.'

Nobody will go to restaurant again. I could not imagine this new isolated existence, where people no longer went out to eat, because I needed to believe that the world could still be an enchanted place again.

THE SILENCE OUTSIDE frightened me. The news frightened me. I read of old men and old women dying alone, as if unloved, while the people who loved them stood weeping behind glass screens. On television, I saw bodies carried out like stiff mannequins wrapped in white, and I mourned the loss of strangers. I scoured Twitter for coronavirus hashtags, and on Google Translate I pasted the tweets of Italian doctors who seemed to know what they were talking about. Which wasn't much, because in the end, everybody knew so little, all feeling their way in the dark. Each new symptom I learned about, I imagined that I had, and the symptoms kept changing – every day a new surprise, from face rashes to foot sores, like a freewheeling apocalypse with no sign of an end. An itch in my toe or a hoarse morning throat and I would panic, and tell myself, 'Breathe, breathe', mimicking the meditation apps that I never took seriously before.

Often I felt a dull torpor numbing its way through me, and then sometimes the rising heat of restlessness. Zoom calls became strained with the effort of good cheer, especially the group calls with friends in which everyone brandished a glass of wine. I began to avoid them, and to avoid our family calls. I ignored even Omelogor's calls, and nobody was closer to me than Omelogor, but talking to her became an effort because talking at all was an effort. I lay in bed and did nothing, and I felt bad for doing nothing, but still I did nothing. I sent texts to friends to say I was writing, and because I was lying, I gave too many details, instead of keeping the messages short. To lessen my sense of doom, I decided to stop following the news. I ignored the Internet and television and read Agatha Christie mysteries, gladly escaping into their genteel improbability. Then the news swallowed me whole again. I drank ginger in warm water and added lemon juice from a fissured old bottle sitting in the back of my fridge, and from my spice cabinet, cayenne pepper and garlic and ground turmeric, until the mixture made me nauseous. Every morning, I was hesitant to rise, because to get out of bed was to approach again the possibility of sorrow.

In this new suspended life, I one day found a grey hair on my head. It appeared overnight, near my temple, tightly coiled, and in the bathroom mirror I first thought it was a piece of lint. A single grey hair with a slight sheen to it. I unfurled it to its full length, let it go, and then unfurled it again. I didn't pull it out. I thought: I'm growing old. I'm growing old and the world has changed and I have never been truly known. A rush of raw melancholy brought tears to my eyes. This is all there is, this fragile breathing in and out. Where have all the years gone, and have I made the most of life? But what is the final measure for making the most of life, and how would I know if I have?

TO LOOK BACK at the past was to be flooded by regret. I don't know which came first – whether I began to nurse regrets and then Googled the men in my past, or whether Googling the men in my past left me swamped with regrets. I thought of all the beginnings, and the lightness of being that comes with beginnings. I grieved the time lost in hoping that whatever I had would turn to wonder. I grieved what I did not even know to be true, that there was someone out there who had passed me by, who might not just have loved me but truly known me.

There was a Korean boy in a music class I took in freshman year, so long ago, my first year in America when everything was still new. Introduction to Music. The small White professor was enthusiastic, fast-talking, and the stream of her American English, with a strong regional accent, was so strange, like an unending burring sound, that I often felt lost. One day I looked across at the student next to me, to see if he had caught her last words, and on his page were not letters I recognized but delicate images, made of the briefest, most elusive of lines. I stared, fascinated by the beautiful calligraphy of Korean, impressed that he could write such a thing and make meaning of it. In my memory, this is how I first noticed him, but our memories lie. How did I know it was Korean, since I didn't know the difference between Japanese and Chinese and Korean? I don't know how I knew but I did, and I knew, too, that if he was writing in Korean, then he must have come from Korea; he was not an American, we were similar, and so his days, like mine, must be owned by loneliness. I willed his attention but did nothing to attract it. He was handsome, stocky and solid, his hair cut to a spiky shortness that felt to me like a marvellous defiance. He always walked into class with his face lowered, as if shy or preoccupied, shrugging his backpack to the floor before he sat down. I imagined us holding hands and sitting on the lawn where American students ate their sandwiches in the sun. We would be like those students who took trips to the beach in a car, coming back to park in front of the dorm, tipsy, carefree, dripping sand and salt water. Each Wednesday and Friday before music class, I planned to write my phone number on a piece of paper; it felt daring and exciting, something people did in films, people who knew how things were done. For weeks I sat next to him in class, his nearness an electric pulse in the air, but I didn't write the number until the week before finals. I added, *Do you want to meet later?* Then I tore it up, and as we settled in for our exam, I wrote just my name and number on the back of a café receipt. I never gave it to him. I handed in my blue book and walked away. I never saw him again, my handsome spiky-haired Korean. I scanned classes and hallways throughout the next semester, and once or twice I saw an Asian with angular features, and I looked until I saw that it wasn't him. Perhaps he went back to Korea. Might we be together now, my Korean and I, with a child or two children, visiting Seoul and Lagos, and living in New York City? I don't like New York City. Its air has a tart edge; its anonymity singes. It makes me feel unmoored, like a pebble rattling in a large indifferent gourd. I lived there for a year, just after college, in a one-bedroom on 42nd and Lex, after convincing my father that aspiring writers needed to live in New York. What was it about the city that brought the urge to hide, so that I spent days cowering in my apartment, ordering delivery, and avoiding eye contact with the pleasant doorman. When I gave up on trying to write a novel, I got a job in advertising and moved away, never wanting to return. Yet New York City often featured in my imagined lives, maybe because it is the city that is supposed to feature in imagined lives. Paris featured too, another city I do not care for. Paris wears its badge of specialness too heavily, and therefore gracelessly; Paris assumes it will charm you merely because it is charming. And Black Parisians look grey, as if the cordial contempt that France reserves for Black French people had formed ash on their skin. This description of Black Parisians came from a man I thought I loved for three years of my life. No, a man I loved for three years; but after it ended, I wished I had not loved him. Darnell. His name was Darnell.

'They look grey and washed out. The French treat their Black folk like shit, but if you're African American, you kind of get a pass,' he said.

He told me a story of stepping out of a train in Paris, where uniformed men swooped in and began to ask only the Black people for their papers – *Les papiers! Les papiers!* A quick glance at his blue

American passport and they waved him by, and he looked back to see four Black Frenchmen humiliated and huddled by the pillar of the train station while other French people walked unconcernedly by. I wanted Darnell to say he was moved or heartbroken or angered by this, but he said it was the reification of the subjective neo-racial paradigm. Or something like that.

Two

We met at a birthday dinner. My friend LaShawn said people called him the Denzel Washington of academia and his art history classes had long waiting lists, and starry students stalked his office hours. He didn't look like Denzel, but of course Denzel was just a metaphor for men like him, men of coiled beauty. I looked at him and gravity loosened and slipped. The pull I felt was immediate, consuming, elemental, every granular part of me suddenly rushing towards him. In that moment, something was not so much lost as surrendered. He was dark and dark-browed. A few times our eyes met and held, but he glanced away and then barely paid attention to me. There was a nonchalant slouch in his manner, in how he wore his power; he knew he didn't have to try too hard, with the world yielding so easily to his light. When he spoke, everyone at the table seemed rapt as if they were sitting at his feet, waiting for crumbs of extraordinary insight to fall their way.

'He opposed civil rights and supported apartheid in South Africa, and I'm supposed to mourn him?' he said, very slowly, as if he felt his listeners should have known better than to even bring up the subject. 'We've forgotten his "states' rights" campaign speech? I'm not even talking about his disastrous war on drugs. Man, Reaganomics destroyed us.'

I had never heard the word 'Reaganomics' before, and for years afterwards, whenever I heard it, an emotion both wistful and bittersweet consumed me. Dinner was over and everyone was saying goodbye, and still he made no move. I wished I was brave enough, like Omelogor, to make the move myself, but I didn't know how to be that kind of woman with men, the one who initiated things. Finally, he asked for my number, not eagerly, but as if he could do with it or not, and yet I felt triumphant.

I have never lied in my life as often as I lied to Darnell. I lied to please him, to be the person he wanted me to be, and sometimes I lied to wrest wretched scraps of reassurance from him. *I'm sick,* I would write, to force a reply, after days of sending him unanswered texts. Sometimes he replied right away, and other times he waited a day or two. *Feel better,* was all he would write; not a question that opened the door for more, not *How are you feeling now?* or *What's going on?* My days passed as emptiness until I saw him again. My phone lay always beside me on my desk, never on silent, for fear I might miss his call. When it beeped with a text message, I snatched it up and felt annoyed with whoever had texted, as if by texting they had taken up the space meant for him. His silences astonished me; how could my force of feeling not cause in him a similar obsession? I imagined him looking through boxes of papers in the bowels of the library, sneezing from the dust, and not thinking of me, while my every moment was mined in thoughts of him. I was trying again to write a novel and already failing again, but in his silences I failed more. I kept starting and restarting, making tenuous connections to Darnell in everything I read, and lingering over sentences that had to do with love, or men, or relationships, as if they might shine a light on the mystery of Darnell.

'I WAS WORRIED about you,' I would say when he finally re-emerged.

'But I'm deep in the archives every minute I get, and you're working on your novel.'

'We can still check on each other every day, can't we? Even if just a quick "hi" text before you teach your class, or when you take a bathroom break,' I would say, feeling desperate, and unable to quell my desperation. He would respond only with a look, that withering look, so eloquent in its lordly disappointment, that said 'your needs are so ordinary'. I wanted love, old-fashioned love. I wanted my dreams afloat with his. To be faithful, to share our truest selves, to fight and be briefly bereft, always knowing that the sweetness of reconciliation was afoot. But it was pedestrian, he said, this idea of love, bourgeois juvenilia that Hollywood had been feeding people for years. He wanted me to be unusual, interesting, and it took a while before I understood what that meant.

'What *nasty* things have you done?' he would ask. 'Tell me.'

I told him of things that had never happened, rich detailed stories plucked from the air: the massage therapist with supple hands who paused in the middle of my massage to unwrap a dildo from a roll of silver cloth. Sex, that primitive interlacing of bodies, to me has always been about hope for connection, meaning, beauty, even bliss. But I lied to Darnell, because he wanted the unusual more than he wanted the true. With each story, he watched me, as though assessing its worth. Sometimes he wanted me to retell the stories he liked, and each time I did, I added small embellishments. I always had the sensation of something about to slip through my fingers. We were two adults, and Darnell made a living from teaching adults, but there was a terrible childishness in my lies and in his expectations. He told me his ex-girlfriend had carved blood-filled rifts on her thighs with razor blades. A Somali woman called Sagal. Even the name alone. Sagal. I imagined her, lithe and lissom, moving liquidly through a room. He said she was brilliant and adventurous, but didn't say what he meant by adventurous. I did not want to ask what became of her. She was a ghost that existed only to make me feel insecure.

ONCE, HE APPEARED after a week-long silence to say he had been in Alabama, looking at lithographs of African American art.

'What? I had no idea,' I said.

'Well.' He shrugged, leaning back on his chair, as if already bored with our conversation, his eyes scanning the people in line at the café counter. He seemed to me not a full knowable person but a mystery deepening by the day.

'I mean, I thought you would let me know if you were going to be out of state,' I said.

'What difference would it make? I could have just been in the library.'

But it did make a difference. What if there had been a plane crash, a tornado, a hurricane? Or nothing had happened and I just wanted, no, deserved to know that he was not on campus as usual, a few miles away from me. I deserved to know if he had even just driven somewhere outside Philadelphia – but to go out of state, all the way down south, a thousand miles to Alabama, while ignoring me for a week? Tears pooled in my eyes.

'What are we doing? Am I your girlfriend?' I asked. I heard, and hated, the nasal tone in my voice.

'What are we doing?' he repeated, with that quick one-sided twitch of his mouth. Sometimes it showed irritation, other times contempt. 'That's a hackneyed question lifted from the contemporary morass that is pop culture. That kind of language is the enemy of thought.'

I looked away, to try and blink back my tears. On the café wall were cheerful drawings: a bendy wineglass with a strawberry on its rim, a lollipop stuck in a coffee mug.

'The important thing is that I'm here,' he said, his face briefly softening, and under the table he pressed his leg against mine.

'I love you,' I said. He didn't respond, of course, and so I said, 'Darnell, I want to hear you say, "I love you."'

'I wouldn't be here if I didn't.'

'But say it, please. I want to hear it.'

'I love you,' he said. A mumble, but to me a victory. I was a beggar without shame.

'I'd love to hear that in bed,' I said.

'What?'

'When you say, "Shit shit shit", it feels so unromantic.'

'Girl, you're hormonal.'

I laughed. I was always so quick to laugh falsely. I had told him how a doctor finally gave me a name for a horror I'd lived with for years, suffering, really suffering, a few days every month, my mind mute with self-loathing, my bloated body drained of energy and hope – premenstrual dysphoric disorder.

'How's that different from premenstrual syndrome?' was all Darnell asked me, sounding clinical, as if I were a case study without a soul. Whenever I laid intimacies before him, he responded in detached tones, or with a breezy mockery that stung. But I hid my hurt in laughter, because hurt would seem needy and he said neediness was boring. My love for him was a thing bled dry of reason. Even the physical was no consolation. For a man drawn to stories of the unusual, he was singular, habitual, oblivious to needs outside his, and near ecstasy, when he said, 'Shit, shit, shit', I closed my mind to his words, which in turn made my body shutter itself. Love can be self-damage, if in fact it is love. Do we need another name for this state of queasy euphoria? This ardent absence of contentment. I looked him up online and read things I had read before and studied photos I had seen before. I set up fake email accounts and sent him messages pretending to be students in love with him, and I was relieved when he did not respond to them but anxious that he still might. It baffles me to think now of the madness of my emotions.

EVERY YEAR, my father took us all to Portugal on holiday, to Lisbon and to Porto and then to Madeira, the only time he ever lavishly spent money. He said it was to show his gratitude to Portugal for helping Biafra during the war. Just as in the World Cup he would shift his support to Portugal as soon as the Black African teams were out. Through the years I saw Lisbon change. We used to be the only Africans shopping on Avenida da Liberdade, and shopkeepers would switch to English as soon as we walked in. Then came Angola's oil boom and the street was filled with Angolans in Gucci and Prada buying more Gucci and Prada, and shopkeepers began to speak to us in Portuguese, assuming that we, too, were Angolan.

'History as irony, Angola is saving the Portuguese economy,' my brother Bunachi said as we watched a Portuguese salesperson bend on one knee to help an elegant Angolan woman try on a pair of designer shoes. I took stealthy photos of the Angolan woman, her permed hair pulled back, her eyes haughtily half-closed as the shoes were slipped on. I sent Omelogor the photos with the quip *Portugal on its knees,* and she replied, *So funny, you should suspend the novel and try travel writing.* It was a joke, but it brought me a dawning. So much tourism was about the past, but what about the present? Restaurants and nightlife said more about a place than museums and old castles did. I quit my job, heady with my new anticipation, and already I imagined my articles, and a cover letter that said, 'Light-hearted Observations from an African Perspective'.

I travelled in comfort, chartered taxis, shopped and walked alone. I wrote of eating a salty omelette in a famous hotel in Paris, attending a rave club in Budapest with some women also travelling alone, and counting the number of clothes hanging out to dry on lines across the cobblestone streets of Rome's Trastevere. All the travel magazines rejected my articles. One magazine sent back the cover letter page, across which was written, in capital letters, the word 'NO', followed by an exclamation mark. The exclamation mark unnerved me. So aggressive, that line and dot. I read my article again, looking for clues to explain why it deserved this slap. A simple 'no' would have sufficed, even if writing such large – and capital – letters across the page was still excessive. Other magazines sent a slim piece of paper, a quarter of a sheet, with two generic lines that said this article is not right for us.

I asked on a travel-writing web group if anybody else had received a 'no' with an exclamation mark. None had. But they shared stories of their own rejections, one about an editor who said yes, only to say no after the final revision. Somebody said the exclamation mark could have been a typing error. No, I replied, it was handwritten. Another said submissions are becoming electronic and very soon, nobody will get rude handwritten responses from some editor having a bad day. One wrote, *Editorial judgements about your work are never permanent. This exclamation mark editor might very well like and publish your next piece.*

Thank you, I replied. In the jungle of the Internet, there still existed the kindness of strangers. I found tips and ideas on those web groups, and made Internet friends of people who had published in real travel magazines, and sometimes I travelled to places where they had gone too.

On my flights back I felt energized, my mind pulsating, my note-book pages filled. Ideas swam in my head, but when I sat in my study and tried to plait them into sentences, they skittered away, stubbornly separate, refusing to meld. And in a haze of frustration, I wrote sentences that were not quite what I wanted to say, and I felt that my true words were close, achingly close, and yet I could never reach them.

'It is now travel writing?' my mother asked. 'You've become an explorer of foreign lands?'

'No, more like a watcher of people and a taster of food in foreign lands,' I said, smiling.

My mother looked skywards and clapped her hands – wonders shall never end! I did not begrudge her leeriness. Here I was with another new hubris, after floating in and out of minor jobs since graduation, instead of returning home to join the family business with my father and Afam.

'You don't earn any money until your article is published? How will you pay for all this watching and tasting?'

'With my own money.'

'You mean with your father's money, which he puts in your account.'

'Mummy, if somebody puts money in your account, isn't it now your money?'

'You did not earn it.'

She didn't earn any money, either, and she spent more of my father's money than he did. But I would never say that, of course. Later, I heard my parents talking, and I knew from my mother's theatrical tone that she wanted me to overhear.

'First novel writing, now travel writing. What if we couldn't afford to fund all these things she keeps doing?'

'But we can.'

'You need to stop this last-born-spoiling. It's not good for her; she has always been too soft and you are not helping her.'

My father hummed, a neutral, peace-seeking sound. Somewhere underneath his shrewd, cautious nature, a part of him dreamed, and recognized dreaming, and let others dream. My mother protected me the only way she knew how, with blunt slabs of pragmatic sense, tried and true, the norm. Often I saw her watching me, eyes dimmed in bewilderment, her baby, her only girl, refusing to come home, drifting about like a dried leaf chased by wind. I lacked the kind of ambition familiar to her, and for this she blamed America. It took years before she stopped asking when I would move to Nigeria, as if my life here was mere prelude. America was like a party whose host has prepared for any eventuality, any at all. I wanted to stay because I could never be too strange here. But I didn't tell her that, because I felt it unfair to expect her to understand.

DARNELL GOOGLED MY FATHER and said, 'Jesus fucking Christ. Is that actually his net worth?'

'You know these things are always exaggerated,' I said.

'No, I don't know. Some of us have folks who don't even know what "net worth" is. I mean, I knew you were a princess, this fancy-ass apartment in Center City, and you just up and quit your job to focus on travel writing,' he said, his forefingers curving in air quotes as he said 'travel writing'. 'But this? Jesus.'

After that he joked often about my family's wealth, his teasing always studded with thorns. His friend was filing immigration papers pro bono for an African family in New Jersey, he said, and added, 'A real African family, not like yours', as if affluence made Africans impurely African.

With alcohol his acid humour, which was not quite humour, flared and filled the room. After a few drinks with his friends, he liked to say, 'You know Chia's people probably sold my people? She comes from old Igbo money going back centuries. It wasn't just palm fruit they sold to the White folks on that West African coast.'

His friends would stiffen into expressions of in-between, as if they could not laugh but could not not laugh. At first, I said jokingly, 'The Biafran war wiped out old Igbo money, so it's all spanking new now.' But the joke fell flat, and so after that I just smiled a smile full of the promise of remorse. Anything to calm the simmering in Darnell. It was a strange kind of resentment, because it had admiration at its edges. At a fundraising gala his friend invited us to in New York, he said, boastfully, to the WASPy White man who had paid for our table, 'The fancy soap your New York ancestors ordered from London in the 1880s was made with the palm oil that Chia's family exported from Igboland.'

'That's wonderful,' the man said, while nodding non-stop, red-faced from alcohol, and struggling to hide his confusion.

It unsettled me, but I told myself it was at least not as bad as the international counsellor at college who asked her colleague, while I stood there waiting to fill out a form, 'So how dirty is her family's money?'

I was shocked into silence. Only after I left, walking down the hallway, did I think of a reply I would never have had the courage to give anyway: 'My family's wealth is cleaner than your body will ever be.'

I POSTPONED MY FIRST TRIP to India because Darnell suddenly emerged from his silence. He appeared at my apartment door, after days of unanswered texts, his black bag slung across his front. As soon as I saw him, the sky aligned with the earth and all was well. My excitement made me as jittery as when I had too much caffeine. I fluttered about, asking what he wanted to do, should I order dinner or should we go out, and his hoodie had a stain down the front and did he want me to pop it in the washer? He was lounging on my couch, and I sat beside him and tenderly touched his cheek. I did not usually touch him unless he touched me first, because my weakness for touch might be yet another flaw. He pressed my palm against his face, and for a moment I felt that we knew each other and our future loomed secure. Later, I asked if he would look at my article. I had never asked before, because I knew not to ask, but the day felt special and suffused with hope. The article was called 'How We Nigerians Travel Before We Actually Travel', about the obstacles my passport brought, the visa denials, the extra wait times, the glowering suspicion of the visa officer at the Indian Embassy. Nigerian passport as object of distrust.

'It's a bit different. I want to know what you think,' I said.

'You need somebody objective,' he said. He didn't look at the open laptop I had pushed to him. Saying I needed somebody objective was his way of saying no.

'But you peer-review your friends' work,' I said.

'That's different,' he said shortly.

I never asked again, just as I didn't take my anxieties to him, to protect him from the burden that I could be.

I was rebooking my hotel in Delhi when he asked, 'Is it travel writing if you're travelling in luxury?'

'It's not really luxury.'

'Maybe not to you. Folks backpack and do hostels and shit.'

'But there are people who travel like me. I don't think travel writing is only about budget travel.'

'Reader, know thy class! The high-and-mighty have ordained!' he mocked.

'If you read my pieces, you would know it's not like that.'

He glanced at me, and I realized he thought my response was defiant, which I had not meant it to be.

'I meant a general "you", not *you* you,' I said, and laughed. 'I mean that if anybody reads what I write, they'll see I'm not all high-and-mighty.'

'Okay, okay,' he said, with that side twitch of his mouth that shredded my self-esteem. I began worrying about being patronizing. I went back to my last article and cut the paragraph about hiring a taxi to drive for hours through the countryside around Zurich. It might be high-and-mighty to rent a taxi instead of taking a tour bus. But it was true, so why pretend? I pasted the paragraph back, and then deleted it again. I felt a bewilderment similar to what I had felt in senior year, on a trip to Mexico with a group of friends for spring break. Some girl I didn't know well asked me, 'You're taking a taxi to Tulum? Who does that? The fare costs enough to feed the kids up in the mountains for a year.' I remembered her pale eyebrows, her face alight with accusation, as if I had somehow seized the money meant for feeding children in the mountains. I didn't even know which mountains she was talking about. But I cancelled the taxi and took the bus with everyone else. Later LaShawn said, 'Why did you do that? We totally wanted to get in the taxi with you.'

I wished I had stood my ground then. I put back the paragraph about driving outside Zurich for almost seven hours, with my warm chatty driver who came from a family of farmers in Vnà and spoke Romansh, a language I did not know existed until then. Was it patronizing to write about him too? Finally, I deleted the paragraph again.

DARNELL'S FRIENDS WERE the kind of people who believed they knew things. Their conversations were always greased with complaints; everything was 'problematic', even the things of which they approved. They were tribal, but anxiously so, always circling each other, watching each other, to sniff out a fault, a failing, a budding sabotage. They were ironic about liking what they liked, for fear of liking what they were not supposed to like, and they were unable to feel admiration, and so criticized people they could simply have admired. *Nobody gets grant funding that fast unless they're fucking some bald White guy. Half of that book was totally stolen from a postdoc. He finished that shit too fast, it's not real research, he's a lightweight.*

With them, I felt hopelessly lacking. A rich man's daughter who had published two articles in an online magazine that nobody had ever heard of. If only I wrote complicated articles in prestigious journals.

'Darnell says you've travelled in Central and South America,' Shannon said, the Black woman who taught American Studies. She seemed fresher and much younger than the rest, always in graphic T-shirts, her pretty coppery Sisterlocks held up in two girlish buns.

'Yes,' I said.

She looked at me, waiting for more.

'I discovered how mixed many Latin American countries are,' I said, and immediately thought I sounded idiotic.

'It's interesting to think about the ways in which the Black diaspora is invisible in Latin America,' Shannon said. She said 'the ways in which' very often. They all did.

I thought about my Brazil article comparing two restaurants: 'Be carefree in Rio or self-important in São Paulo.' I had thought the sentence clever but now saw how lightweight the whole article was. Shannon would never read an unknown online magazine based in New Zealand anyway.

'I couldn't believe that half the population in Brazil is Black. There are never Black people in popular images of Brazil,' I said, and hoped this was more substantial.

Darnell shifted and pursed his lips; I could tell he was unimpressed, maybe irritated. If only I knew how to talk like his friends.

'It's a structural erasure, a symbolic genocide, because if you're not seen, then you don't exist,' he said.

'Exactly. Except that the genocide isn't merely symbolic,' Charlotte said, the White woman who taught sociology.

'I survived the genocide,' Thompson said drily, the Garifuna man from Belize, a visual artist, his beard like a black map painted on his chin. I laughed, gratefully, because Thompson always dimmed their harsh glare.

The first time we met, he asked if 'Chia' was short for something, and then repeated 'Chiamaka' in a way that made me feel like a person who could be interesting.

'Speaking of travel writing,' he intoned, 'would it be offensive to say you're too beautiful to be a travel writer, Chia? You could have been an actress.'

I glanced at Darnell. He looked amused, so I laughed and said, 'I can't act to save my life.'

'Neither can many actors,' Thompson said.

'Newsflash, Thompson. A woman can be beautiful and have an occupation unrelated to her looks,' Shannon said, quite seriously, as though Thompson hadn't been joking. 'Besides, we need more women travel writers. Travelling as a woman has its unique challenges.'

'True,' Thompson said.

'Travel writing is a self-indulgent genre,' Charlotte proclaimed, looking at me. She was small and slight, with the pinched, humourless face of a person who thrived on grievances.

'I see what you mean,' I said quickly. 'But I'm hoping mine isn't too self-indulgent. I've just come back from Comoros, and it's such an interesting place.'

'A friend of mine at Brown did some work there,' Charlotte said.

'Oh really,' I said. She spoke of Africa only as a place where her friends had 'worked' – so-and-so did some work in Tanzania, in Ghana, in Senegal, in Uganda – and I imagined her Africa full of White people all toiling unthanked in the blazing sun. It was hilarious, but I always tried to look alert and interested.

'Nice shirt,' Thompson said to Shannon.

'This old thing,' Shannon said, looking down at her T-shirt, at the print of a behatted Mary J. Blige, her face partially in shadow.

'Is it me, or is Mary J.'s beauty not acknowledged enough? A subject worthy of inquiry,' Thompson said.

'What is it with your misogynistic obsession with beauty today?' Shannon asked.

'Why is it misogynistic?' Thompson replied.

'The question should be: Why isn't Mary J. Blige's talent acknowledged enough?' Charlotte said.

'Her talent is not in dispute. She's beautiful, but it's obvious the music industry doesn't reward looks in certain kinds of Black women,' Thompson said.

'With the collaboration of the rewarded women,' Charlotte said, as though she disapproved not just of women being objectified but of women being attractive at all. She had to be sending me a message, that beauty's appeal was beneath her, beauty itself problematic, and beauty, apparently, was my only draw. She looked at me and I looked away and cut into my well-done steak. I cut carefully, slowed by my sinking confidence.

'I can't believe I sold out and got an iPhone. Apple is so problematic,' Shannon said, cradling the phone in her palm like a reluctant offering.

'Apple's project is to homogenize our thoughts and actions. It's not about unleashing creativity or solving problems; it's a plan for mass conformity and mass banality. There's a way in which it runs parallel to heteronormativity,' Charlotte said. Then she turned to me and said, 'You're eating death.'

I tried frantically to make the connection between Apple, my eating, and death.

'Oh. You mean my steak. Well, I guess it's tasty death,' I said, and out came my bright false smile. I wanted Darnell to defend me – he ate meat, too, even if he had ordered a bulgur salad – but he said nothing.

Charlotte was not done with me. 'If only people could see how much meat just hangs around in their intestines undigested. It's disgusting. Never mind that eating meat has deadly consequences for the global south, especially Africa.'

'Charlotte, Charlotte, Charlotte,' Thompson said. 'This isn't how we'll win recruits to the climate cause. We'll need better messaging than that.'

'Appeasement is never a good look,' Charlotte said, and Thompson, smiling, reached out and gave her a quick side hug.

'Have you written about Belize, Chia? You should go. I'll take you,' he said, and winked an exaggerated wink.

'Hey, Thompson. Who says my woman needs you to take her anywhere?' Darnell asked.

Darnell's possessiveness, playful as it was, gave me a rush of happiness. My *woman*. I loved hearing it and he said it so rarely. Sometimes he was so detached from me in public, I feared he was only waiting for the evening's end to tell me it was over.

'We could go this summer, when Darnell is doing his fieldwork with sharecropper sculptors or whatever,' Thompson said, and laughed his hearty laugh.

'Actually, Chia is going to be in writing seclusion this summer,' Darnell said. 'In her house in Maryland. Her father bought her a house in suburban Maryland because she wanted a quiet place to write that book. Just sit and write in this house with an original fireplace and a housekeeper.'

'Wow,' Thompson said. 'That's the life I want!'

'There's a violence to the wealthy buying homes that are only occupied for part of the year while there's a housing crisis,' Charlotte said.

'It's really a family home. My parents stay there when they visit,' I said. It sounded too defensive, and so I tried a joke – 'Darnell forgot to say the housekeeper doesn't actually come with the house' – which of course fell flat. A soft contempt glowed in Charlotte's eyes. I chewed my meat, loathing her and longing for her approval. I'd seen photos Darnell took at her parents' summerhouse, showing fluffy dogs and the washed-out shabby décor of New England wealth. I wondered if that house, too, was a 'violence', or maybe violence was done only when people who were unlike her owned second homes. I would never say this, of course, because I was not brave like Omelogor. Instead, I smiled my hopeless-hapless smile. Later I told Omelogor, 'Charlotte doesn't like me, but if I were a poor African, she would dislike me less.'

'Nonsense, you don't need her to like you,' Omelogor said promptly. 'They can't stand rich people from poor countries, because it means they can't feel sorry for you.'

'Charlotte's not really like that,' I said, knowing I was shielding not Charlotte but Darnell. Our close friends are small glimpses into us, after all, we choose them, they are not grants from nature like relatives are, and being close to Charlotte said something about Darnell. Omelogor could be so cutting about people who were ignorant of Africa, and I didn't want Darnell caught in the snare of her scorn. I already softened and edited the stories I told her about Darnell, with a knot of worry that she could tell, because she knew me so well. Once I said that since I'd met Darnell, I was getting nicer responses from editors, and she said, 'Thanks to Darnell's magical essence?'

It was easier on the phone, at least she wasn't watching me steadily with her head tilted – and nobody's gaze pierced more than hers. She saw people, through people. Only two years older but she had always hovered vigilantly, ready to jump in and protect me from myself. I told Darnell how brilliant and fearless she was, gleaming wherever she went, a star from birth doing starry things as a banker in Abuja.

'You talk about her like a myth,' Darnell said.

'I do?'

'Yep. Like she can do no wrong. Her dad rich too?'

'Oh no. He's just a lecturer,' I said quickly, and as soon as I did, shame spread slowly over me. Why had I spoken like that about my beloved Uncle Nwoye? Yes, he wasn't rich, and wealth didn't matter to him at all, but saying he was 'just a lecturer' in that tone was an unnecessary belittling, to please Darnell, and not to tell the truth of my uncle.

'He's a pioneer professor and he went to Cambridge; he's globally famous in his field,' I added. 'My mom's brother. He's lovely, very kind and also vague about lots of things. We like to say he's the only professor who doesn't know how to use a TV remote control.'

AN EDITOR AT *Out Wonder* wrote to say he liked my Copenhagen piece and wanted to see a revised version with a little more moxie. A real editor, not a one-person outfit working from a home office in Auckland. *Out Wonder*, a magazine with an editorial board, that paid in money, not in copies. I closed my eyes and saw the table of contents, real writers' names spread across a page, and somewhere among them, my own name, me. Naturally, one published piece should open doors to more, and to commissions, and to book publishers in search of fresh faces. This might be my book's origin story: it began with an article about Copenhagen. A novel was above me but this travel book I could do, a collection of light-footed essays, the title already secured in my mind: *The Non-Adventurous Adventures of One African Woman*. I would become the real deal. My mother finally a believer, holding my book and flipping through, sending copies to all her traducers, both real and imagined. I reread the Copenhagen piece as though I hadn't written it, to tease out the magic of *Out Wonder*'s interest.

An elegant woman on a bicycle nearly ran me over this morning because I was staring distractedly across the road at some elegant women cycling to work. In nice shoes, too, not sneakers. Do they not sweat? And why was everyone in my hotel speaking English, while I wanted to hear Danish? Was my boutique hotel making some kind of patriotic statement with that extraordinary range of liquorice in my minibar? Such were the questions I grappled with. I had hunger pangs at night and really wanted candy, sweet candy, not little things in different colours, each tasting more medicinal than the last.

I didn't know what having more moxie meant, but I would go back to Copenhagen and find that moxie, and rewrite the article there. In my excitement, I was buoyed and I bounced. I told Omelogor and Zikora about *Out Wonder*, but I didn't tell Darnell, because I was afraid of his indifference and how it would maim my spirits. Still, I wanted him to travel with me, as I wanted him to do everything with me.

'Did you know that Denmark traded in African slaves?' I asked him.

'Of course,' he said, archly, as if everybody knew but me.

'I'm just reading about the Danish slave fort in Ghana,' I said. I wasn't interested in Denmark's slave-trade but I wanted him to think I was; it was a sombre subject, and weighty enough. 'I'm thinking of doing Denmark again. Copenhagen and Aarhus. Will you come? Your classes don't start for another two weeks.'

'Man, I don't know about this "kept boy" thing. Thinking about what you paid for the Mauritius trip still makes me sweat.'

'I have awards tickets this time, so it's technically free,' I said, which was untrue.

'I don't know,' he said doubtfully, but I knew he would come. He just needed, first, to perform his ritual of reluctance. He always said no when I paid for things, although I knew he wanted me to pay. Sometimes he delayed in bringing out his wallet, even for the smallest of things, like a late-night pack of beer at Walgreens. On his birthday, he tore apart the bronze-toned paper in which I had wrapped a MacBook and an iPhone and said, 'Thanks, babe, but come on, it's too much, it's almost vulgar.'

'Your phone is cracked and you keep saying your laptop is so slow.'

'Yes, but still. You could have picked one,' he said. Yet he kept them both. And when I sheepishly slipped a first-class ticket between the pages of a book he was reading, he said, 'Hey. You trying to buy me?'

I laughed. But I was, in a way. I paid for bottles of good wine, massages, restaurant meals, a cleaner for his apartment: life changes he mocked himself for liking, experiences he would have only if he stayed with me. It was a kind of buying. He was moody throughout that birthday trip, as though resentful of what he had accepted, and I was watchful and tentative, eggshell-careful not to offend. 'Jesus fucking Christ. An actual opulent spa shower inside an airport,' he said, in the first-class lounge, and I almost said, 'I'm sorry.' In Mauritius, everything irritated him, nothing was deserving of praise. He wanted to cancel the boat ride; he didn't care to see the waterfall; he had so much student work to catch up on anyway. Maybe his crabbiness was an act of atonement: it was problematic to like luxurious trips and now the least he could do was not enjoy it. Mo, the shrivelled Indian-looking man driving us around on winding roads, pointed animatedly as he drove. *The mother of my wife lives here. This place before was all wild trees.*

I talked to Mo and wished Darnell would talk to him too, but Darnell stared out of the window and spoke only to say he had an itchy bug bite on his neck. Mo kept looking at Darnell in the rearview mirror, hoping for a reaction, man to man. 'So interesting!' I said, chipper and overbright, to make up for Darnell's coldness. At the airport on the day we left, I opened my wallet to give Mo a tip in American dollars. I had a few twenties and a hundred. I folded the hundred and pressed it into his hand.

'Thank you,' he said, turning to leave. 'Safe journey! See you next time!' Moments later he came running back. 'You gave me . . . ,' he started and stopped. 'Did you mean to give this to me? Maybe a mistake?'

'No, it's not a mistake, Mo. Thank you very much,' I said.

'Thank you, thank you,' he said, bowing, lowering himself.

I stopped to watch him hurry away, until his small figure disappeared through the airport exit. Then I erupted in sobs. It was all too much, Darnell's iciness that, try as I might, I could not thaw, the subservience in Mauritius, as if people were inhaling and exhaling not air but fumes of servility. Omelogor once said she was happy Nigeria wasn't a tourist country because 'people become props, and countries become performances instead of places'. I had thought she was being a little intense, as usual, but she could not have been more right. Suddenly everything was doomed, beyond rescue. My lower back was aching and my temples throbbed. I stood there crying.

'What?' Darnell asked, impatient, pulling his carry-on and mine.

'Tourism in poor countries does something to people that just breaks my heart.'

'You're hormonal,' Darnell said.

It was true. Two days to my period and I felt bloated, and constantly, tremulously close to tears. But he said 'You're hormonal' so carelessly, like flinging a stone at me, and I cried even more, fumbling in my backpack for a tissue to wipe my runny nose.

'Chia, pull yourself together. These folks think I've done something to make you cry,' Darnell said.

ON THE FLIGHT BACK, I curled inward, tired and unwell, saying little but enough to let him know I was only seeking survival, and not shutting him out. My bloated body was taut, sore, close to bursting. I felt the sudden urge to talk about Darnell, really talk about Darnell, not in my usual careful way, but with the protective wrapping yanked off. I started writing Omelogor a text and then I stopped. Many times in my life, just talking to Omelogor had brought out a backbone I didn't know I had, her words always so searing and sure. But now I did not want strength to be asked of me. I wanted only to complain about my weakness and then retreat, back into my weakness. There was no point being trussed in Omelogor's high expectations, I was not seeking help to leave Darnell, I was not leaving Darnell, I wanted only to talk. It was better to talk to Zikora instead. About being in a relationship but never feeling at home, about being unsure, and never made to feel that I could one day be less so. With Darnell, I was like a small animal, newly born and hairless, innately incapable and always falling. I would say these things to Zikora just to say them, not seeking solutions or resolution. I immediately felt better merely for making this decision. As soon as I was alone in my apartment, I called Zikora.

'ZIKOR,' I said and she burst into tears. Zikora was not a crier. Somebody must have died, or was close to dying. My hands began trembling violently and I wished I had not called, to delay hearing whatever bad news this was.

'Zikor, *o gini?* What's wrong?' I asked.

'I'm thirty-one years old,' she managed to say, her sobs distorting her voice. I felt the swift incision of fear, that *she* had been diagnosed with a serious illness, that it wasn't someone else who was close to dying.

'I'm thirty-one years old. I thought I would be married by thirty-one, with my first baby.'

'Oh,' I said, so incredulous and so painfully relieved that I feared I might start laughing.

'Thirty-one with no prospects,' Zikora said.

'But your birthday is still two weeks away,' I said, stupidly, as if she might find a man and get married in two weeks.

'My friend Nkechi's wedding is on Saturday in New Jersey. People will be wondering and whispering. You know how "Is she married?" is what everyone asks about each other these days?'

I hadn't noticed, but Zikora's circle was mostly Nigerian, unlike mine, her friends a little older, their concerns a little different.

It was my mother and aunties who talked to me of marriage; last Christmas an aunty in the village said, 'Chiamaka, I am very thirsty for wine. I have been wine-thirsty for too long.' I looked blankly at her, and then smiled when I understood she meant my wine-carrying ceremony. I gave her the standard response that made them leave you alone: 'I am praying, Aunty. It is in God's hands.'

I wasn't sure which would comfort Zikora more, downplaying marriage or telling her to be positive and believe it would happen soon. So I said, 'You don't have to go to the wedding. Tell Nkechi you'll be in Hong Kong or London for work, since you have a great job in a great DC law firm, and then buy the most expensive thing in her gift register.'

At least Zikora laughed, briefly.

Our call left me with a lingering unrest, an agitation of spirit. Zikora crying because she was not married at thirty-one – crying so much she had to blow her nose a few times, choking on her tears, heaving as she spoke – felt like something that happened somewhere else, with other people who were not my closest friend. She had broken it off with her past two boyfriends because they avoided all talk of the future, but each time she had revived herself, her eyes always forward-looking. She seemed fine, not at all vulnerable to being hijacked by other people's expectations. Besides, this kind of collapsing happened on turning thirty, or forty, simply for the symbolism; rounded figures caused panic because they felt like an ending. Thirty-one was premature, too premature, and more worrying for not being a rounded figure. When did Zikora take on this despair? From birth an unquestioned hand had written marriage into our life's plans, and it became a time-bound dream, but when did she go from waiting to raging despair? Burnished successful lawyer Zikora; organized, buttoned-up, ambitious Zikora; Zikora with her manner of always refusing ruin. I wondered if I had missed a shift, a crack in the certainty of our lives being as we planned. Would I cry if I was not married in two years? I wouldn't. I didn't think of marriage as shaped by time – how could the merging of two souls be shaped by time? With Darnell, I dreamed not of marriage but of how we might become truly intertwined, how the fear might disappear. More than marriage, I was looking for what I then did not know as the resplendence of being truly known.

That weekend, I took the train to DC and surprised Zikora. We had dinner at Busboys and Poets; a poetry reading was just starting, and so we sat and listened to the singsong reading of the woman whose big Afro was dyed burgundy. Afterwards we walked along U Street, holding hands and laughing at jokes we had told each other many times before. Tending to Zikora shifted my unrest, and soon, my body no longer in my hormones' wrecking hold, I returned to talking of Darnell as before.

MY PARENTS WERE VISITING that summer, but only for a week before going on to London, because my mother didn't like to spend time in America. 'This country is not civilized. Everything is "Do It Yourself". Everything is too casual. Look at their airlines, their first class is rubbish. They don't know how to provide service with finesse. Even the way they talk. "Let's go and grab lunch." How can you be grabbing your lunch?' She always found a way to say this, or something similar, and then my father's rejoinder would follow, like a well-oiled duet, or a call-and-response song.

'America is great because they have the best people from every part of the world,' he would say. Or sometimes he said, 'America is great because it is the only country that believes in being egalitarian in theory, even if not in practice.'

He liked America and would have spent more time here but for her; he always indulged her, without resentment, as if feeding rich treats to an already-fed pet, and luxuriating in the pet's purring pleasure. I liked to watch them, my mother talking and talking, complaining about something, while he made agreeing sounds, not fully present but fully content. He, born into wealth, hardly grumbled, while my mother acted as if the life she married into had always been her birthright. But her complaints were slapstick comedy, sweeping and superficial, delivered with the trace of a vanishing smile, as if she, too, knew how difficult it was to take her seriously.

I was looking forward to seeing them. I enjoyed their short visits, our time together overlaid always with languorous satisfaction, unlike my Nigerian visits, in which nothing was ever still or slow – the house alive with drivers and househelps, trays of drinks carted in and out of the parlour for visitors; my mother complaining about the vultures out to take advantage of my father; my father working late and coming home tired and apologetic; my mother hosting gossipy meetings of her club in the living room, with the scent of Guinness stout in the air. For the week of their visit, I would regress and become their little girl again. Their only girl. Their last-born. My mother and I would go shopping in DC, and she would buy me expensive handbags or jewellery that I didn't need, and we would eat lunch in a hotel while I half-listened to her entertaining talk. *I now pay Emmanuel's salary into his wife's bank account because that Emmanuel is just irresponsible and I want to make sure his children are eating. I'm going to confront Aunty Njide this Christmas, I'm tired of all these stories she is spreading about me. I don't know what this man your cousin wants to marry actu-*

ally does for a living. I don't like his face, he looks like a ritualist. Your
father is allowing these villagers to manipulate him again. He has already
done so much for them. Our people are so ungrateful.

I TOLD DARNELL my parents were visiting, hoping he would
say he wanted to meet them, but he said, 'Oh, okay.'

So I gathered all the pieces of my courage to my tongue and said,
'I'd love for you to come to Maryland while my parents are here.'

'Not sure that's a good idea. You need your quality time with the
parents. I don't want any pressure on you,' he said.

Who said anything about pressure? I was asking him to meet
my parents and he was backing away, casting his withdrawal as a
thoughtful act, and all I could say was 'Okay.'

'I could come the week after,' he said.

I did not know what else to say. Stevie Wonder was playing in the
background.

'Okay,' I said again, and then I mustered my light-heartedness and
said, 'Well, at least you'll finally meet Kadiatou when you visit!'

'Your housekeeper?'

'Well, yes, but you know she's like family.'

'There's some scholarship where folks argue that slaves and slave
owners were like family, with Mammy raising the white babies and
all,' he said.

'That isn't fair, Darnell,' I said.

'I'm kidding, come on.'

MY PARENTS HAD hardly settled in before my mother asked,
'Chia, so have you and Dr Ojukwu's son decided on a wedding date?'

A perpetual joke, Dr Ojukwu's son was socially awkward, a brilliant engineer who brought his face too close to people when he
spoke to them. For years he had sent me tortured love letters.

'Mummy!'

'When is the Black American coming to greet us?'

I now wished I had not, in a rare reckless moment, told her about Darnell.

'He was going to come but he's doing a lot of research, he's writing a book, he's a rising star in academic circles.' I regretted my words as soon as I said them. Too many words desperate to be believed. I should have said we were no longer seeing each other, to save me from more questions.

'What is his discipline?' my mother asked.

'Art history.'

'Art history.' A sniff. It wasn't engineering or medicine.

'He's in high demand. Different universities want to poach him.'

'He's writing a book on art history, and that is why he didn't come to Maryland to greet your parents? Aren't you writing a book too?'

'No, Mummy, it's not like that.' I stopped, flustered, and felt as if a crime was about to be uncovered.

'My child, my sunshine, is everything okay?' she asked, her eyes wary with worry. Underneath her faultless ability to find faults lay a deep apprehension. She wanted the world to be perfect for the deserving, and the deserving were those she loved.

'Everything is fine,' I said. I hugged her, pressed my face into the strong floral scent of her neck. Whenever I walked past airport duty-free, a waft of any florid perfume would bring pangs of nostalgia so intense they almost hurt – for childhood, when my mother and I would sit at her enormous dressing table while she held my hair in bunny-tails, never too tight, all the time song-praising me: *Omalicha m, nwa m mulu n'afo, anyanwu ututu m.* My beautiful one. Child of my womb. My sunshine in the morning.

MY MOTHER HAD wanted my father to buy a different house for me, because she worried about the dense grove of protected trees at the back. 'Why should they say we cannot cut down some of those trees? Why do these White people like to live in dangerous forests? One day snakes and wild animals will kill somebody,' she would mumble in Igbo each time they visited. As she did before we went out, standing at the sliding glass doors that led to the deck and looking almost accusingly at the trees.

I watched her, sleek wig grazing her chin, asking imperious questions in the shops in CityCenter, then loudly saying, 'We should have gone to New York.' At lunch I watched her, swirling her wine, napkin floating down on her lap. She enjoyed it all, and I enjoyed her enjoyment.

'Oh, there's nothing in the house for your father to eat,' she said.

'Kadi said she will stay and cook.'

'Kadiatou's cooking, is that even food?' my mother snorted. 'Why would anybody eat cassava leaves that is goat food? *Tufia.*'

I laughed. Any African food that wasn't Igbo met the same fate at her hands. All she said after a trip to Nairobi with my father was 'Did nobody teach Kenyans about seasoning and spices?'

When we finally got back home, my father was sunk on the sofa, legs propped on a stool, watching the news, the volume a little too loud.

'We abandoned you. I was worried about what you would eat,' my mother said.

'Kadiatou served me something nice before she left, rice and a sauce.'

'You ate that Guinean food?'

My father smiled sheepishly, slow to admit he liked Kadiatou's cooking.

'Can the driver go?' my mother asked. 'We don't need him until tomorrow?'

'Yes.'

She drooped, as if our shopping had exhausted her. But I knew it energized her; she came alive in front of displayed things. The drooping was a cue for my father, and he sprang up, saying, 'Sit down. I'll tell the driver.'

He went outside to the black SUV in the driveway. They used the same car service and always requested the same driver, Amir from Jordan. But Amir was unavailable and the driver was a South Asian who my mother said was dangerous because he stepped too forcefully on the brakes. Back inside, my father asked her, 'Did you eat something good?'

'Yes.'

She showed him the shopping bags, she always did that – *look at this one, that one was the last they had, I've been looking for this exact colour for years* – while he looked perfunctorily at them.

'That Dior shop was tiny. We should have gone to New York,' she said.

'London and Paris are waiting for you,' he teased.

She pulled off her wig and put it on a side table, relaxing deeper on the couch next to my father. Sans wig, her cornrows lifted her face, slanting the wide-set almond jewels of her eyes. I was eight when I first saw my mother as others did. We were in the village for Christmas, our house a whirl, as always, people streaming in and out, and the air smoky from many firewood fires across the village. My mother was standing by the fountain near the colonnaded entrance, surrounded by a crowd of small children, handing naira notes to each child and then saying briskly, 'I have given you, now go!' I was skulking by the front door, and next to me was a cluster of benches with villagers who had wandered in for Christmas rice. Two women, shovelling jollof rice into their mouths with plastic spoons, were watching my mother.

'O dika ife akpulu akpu,' one of them said. To look like sculpture, like art, was to be unusually beautiful, and I was startled, because until then I hadn't thought of my mother as a distinct person, separate from merely being my mother. After that, I felt a flash of sadness as if in hearing strangers admire her, a unique privacy between us was now lost. I learned later of how rare that admirer's tone was, because my mother trailed envy and bitterness, even hatred, in her wake.

Fate had been too kind to her – beauty, wealth, an adoring husband who never looked outside – and she sailed through her days as if she deserved it all. People wanted humility from her, to prove that no woman deserved so much. She was guilty of being not only a peacock, but also an unmoving boulder in the path to my father.

He never gave out one kobo, the story went, without first getting her permission. Of her band of detractors, the loudest were disgruntled men whose improbable business plans my father had refused to fund.

'Will you drink tea?' my mother asked my father.

'Yes. Chia, I hope you bought decaf.'

I got up to make the tea. Another childhood ritual, my parents drinking Lipton after dinner, the squeezed shrunken tea bags placed together on my mother's saucer. This was the kind of evening when my father talked about the Biafran war, and as he spoke he would seem to me like a blessed sorcerer, summoning solid things from bare air. My brothers and I called it 'Daddy's Bank of British West Africa talk'.

'I started from zero after the war, zero,' he would say. 'The Nigerian government stole my houses and warehouses in Lagos, in Port Harcourt, in Kaduna. During the war, the banks confiscated our business accounts, and after the war, the same banks refused to give me loans. Every Igbo person got twenty pounds, twenty pounds, for all the money they had before the war. All the money in my private accounts, the money I made and the money I inherited, all gone. My great-grandfather traded pepper with the Portuguese and built the first modern mansion in Port Harcourt. My grandfather was one of the biggest traders with the British. He was the first Igbo man to open an account with Bank of British West Africa. The first! My father worked hard, multiplied what he inherited from my grandfather. And then just like that, during the war, gone! The government stole everything, everything!'

As he said 'everything' his hands drew an arc in the air. He never raised his voice, his face held its usual calm, but in that wave of his hands I understood so much of him, his cautiousness, his low-burning paranoia. He always had a small, packed bag under his bed and an envelope full of never-touched cash in a safe whose code we all knew. The war ended before I was born but it left him forever in the shadow of Just in Case, never fully relaxed, always in a muted crouch of preparedness, saying Igbo people could be attacked en masse again at any time, as happened in the nineteen forties and fifties and sixties. He pushed us three to study business, even when I kept failing economics, saying, 'My children must carry on. When I die, I want to know the business will continue growing.'

Once I asked him, teasing, 'Why would it matter, Daddy, if you're not here?'

'We want what we've made to stay long after we're gone. That is how we seek immortality,' he said, and because he hardly spoke in this solemn way about a future without him, I felt tearful at those words 'seek immortality'.

I LISTENED WHEN Darnell's friends talked about books they had read – never novels, always academic books with colons in their titles – and I ordered them without telling Darnell, and tried to read them, but they were like the sacred texts of an exclusive sect whose code I did not know. Each one that I gave up on, I dumped behind a pouf in my study, and now I hurried to hide them in the basement so he wouldn't see them.

'What time he's coming?' Kadiatou asked.

'He lands at BWI at seven. I'm picking him up.'

Please like him, Kadi, I thought. Please like him. If she liked him, it would be a good omen. Kadiatou, with her calm face and wise eyes, her faltering English and her contagious dignity. Sometimes, rarely, you meet a person who blends into your life as if the designers of destiny had long made room for her. Something about her drew me from the beginning, a clarity of spirit. At first she braided my hair in her relative's braiding shop in Laurel, then in my living room, an easy silence always between us. She cleaned up the hair attachments after each braiding and then she cleaned the kitchen, and the whole house, until I said we must agree on a fee, not just her 'Give me anything, Miss Chia, you help me a lot already.' The loving, territorial attention she paid to the house reminded me of well-meaning relatives in Nigeria. A tear in the window netting by the deck, a dead bulb downstairs – I said I would call Pedro and she snorted and climbed on a ladder and changed the bulb. 'In Conakry I take care of very big house,' she said. She always stood by, watching quietly, when someone came in to service the heater or fix a pipe. Now that Zikora had helped her get a job at the George Plaza in DC, she came in on her days off. Sometimes she brought her daughter, Binta, whose skin was like glistening blueberries. Binta's earnestness, her lack of teenage sass, surprised me. She seemed older than her American age-mates. At first, Kadiatou said, 'Don't disturb Miss Chia', and made Binta sit in the foyer or vacuum the stairs, and I would say, 'Kadi, leave her alone.' Binta asked about my travels, reverently examining my collection of carvings and sculptures, especially the tiny seated black doll from Colombia; a black woman in a market in Cartagena had lovingly thrust it in my hand after I said I was from Nigeria.

'Aunty Chia, I will be a travel writer too,' she said in her utterly American voice, so unlike her mother's.

'Don't let your mother hear you! I think she wants you to be a nurse.'

And we laughed a conspiratorial laugh.

'Binta is saying what?' Kadiatou asked.

Kadiatou was not a talker, even in Pular. I heard her on the phone sometimes, all silences and humming, her words always sparse. She spoke rarely about her past. I knew she had been married off young and her husband had died. I knew her grandmother once slapped their cow for not producing milk, the cow itself as bony and under-nourished as everyone.

'What will poor cow do?' she asked after she told me the anecdote, saying nothing else. Very often, as if they were punctuations, she said, 'I'm so happy to come to this country, so Binta can have this country.'

One day I stood up and saw that I had left a large bloodstain on the kitchen barstool; my heavy period defying my double padding. Kadiatou was beside me, and her eyes darted from blood to me.

'Oh,' I said, almost ashamed. My mother had raised me to hide all incarnations of my female body, burn used pads in the evening at the back of the house with nobody else around, wash any bloodstains furtively, so nobody noticed.

'I clean it,' Kadiatou said.

'No, Kadi, I'll do it.'

She was already marshalling detergent and scrubber from the cabinet beneath the sink.

'I have fibroids,' I said, to apologize, explain, or even absolve.

'You have fibroids?' she repeated in a strangled tone, staring at me, her eyes clouded over, but she didn't say more and I didn't ask. Maybe fibroids prevented her having other children; maybe large tumours had sprouted from the walls of her uterus, invading the hallowed space where a baby should have been. I waited to know if she would tell me about the fibroids, but she didn't, and I resolved not to bring up fibroids again, so as not to poke at whatever pain she was guarding.

WHEN KADIATOU OPENED the door, I noticed she had powdered her face. How heartwarming that she had done the African thing of 'looking presentable' for a guest, and this for Darnell.

'Darnell, this is Kadiatou; Kadi, my boyfriend, Darnell.'

Darnell barely glanced at her, saying something like 'How you doing?' before he walked over to a painting in the foyer. Sometimes I wondered if he even knew that his casual rudeness was rude.

'Welcome,' Kadiatou said to Darnell's back, her expression serene, while Darnell stood with his legs wide apart, staring at the painting.

'It's Ben Enwonwu,' I said.

'I know.'

He was in a bad mood and already I felt as if I had done something wrong, or would do something wrong, and this knowledge seemed inevitable, the weight of it crippling me.

'I didn't realize how massive this place was. Your neighbour has a pool. How come you don't? You certainly have the grounds.'

I made a sound, a half-laugh. There was simply no right answer to the question 'Why don't you have a pool?' Especially not now, with his darkening mood.

'Remember the fellowship I applied for?' he asked.

'The Europe one? In Germany?'

'I didn't get it.'

'Oh no,' I said, and disappointment surged through me as if my body had drawn it from his.

'Third time certainly wasn't the charm. There's got to be somebody in the selection committee who hates me,' he said.

'I'm so sorry, Darnell.'

His reasoning seemed childish to me: somebody who hates me. Maybe he was right, and his rejection was indeed personal. I wanted to help him but didn't know how. Whenever his mood smouldered like this, I stumbled clumsily for what to say or do, always worried about worsening it. I asked if he wanted to go out to eat. He said he wasn't hungry. While he showered, I sat on the bed, fiddling and uncertain, thinking of what I could do to lift his spirits. His phone buzzed next to me and I saw on the screen the words *You'll have to use your imagination.* Another buzz and I told myself not to look, but I couldn't help it. *Was going to send a visual aid but I better not.*

I stared at it, confused, surprised. I almost jumped when he came out of the bathroom, a towel round his waist, and took the phone. 'Might as well do some work emails while sitting on the throne,' he said.

I wouldn't ask him about the text messages. Not today. But when would I ask and what would I ask? I didn't know what rights I had, or if I had any rights at all. He would say his phone was his private business, or it was juvenile or melodramatic, or something about pop culture; or he might say my behaviour was the semiotics of something or other. That night he didn't touch me. He turned away and said he was tired, and I lay awake for hours, thinking I might have been too generous with the organic pillow spray. The next day he said he was leaving because he needed some space.

'What's wrong?' I asked.

'What's wrong?' he repeated.

Before he could say more, I said, 'I'm sorry. I don't mean to be insensitive. Please stay. Let's do something together to cheer you up.'

He was calling a taxi.

'Darnell, please.'

Still, he left. A taxi drove up and parked by the garage and Darnell got in and left. As the taxi drove away, I saw his head bend towards his phone, as if I was already dismissed, forgotten, his mind miles away.

I HEARD KADIATOU let herself in, and moments later she was at my bedroom door. 'You don't eat for three days,' she said.

'I ate. I'm okay, Kadi.'

'Nothing in fridge, no plate in dishwasher, nothing in kitchen trash.'

'I ate peanuts,' I said.

She left and returned with a plate of scrambled eggs and toast. The oily eggs would be too salty.

'Miss Chia. Please eat,' she said.

I smiled and felt false to be smiling falsely at Kadi. I didn't want to smile. Darnell was not answering my calls or texts, and I didn't know why.

'Daniel did something?' she asked.

'Darnell. Not Daniel. He just left and now he's not calling or texting.'

She was looking at me with an expression I could not read.

'Something inside you, not the heart. The spirit. The spirit cannot break, even if your heart break. Your spirit stay strong,' she said.

'Kadi, it's not that serious!' I said sharply. She was making assumptions, flirting with the unbearable possibility of finality; a broken heart, even a breaking heart, meant an ending.

'You want rice?' she asked.

'No, Kadi. Thank you.'

Omelogor sent a text to ask if I had heard from Darnell. No, I said. Call him again, she said. Call him back-to-back twenty times. The least he owes you is a response. She sounded irritated, and I sensed with me as much as with Darnell. She thought everyone was born strong and bold like her, and even if they weren't, she believed they could easily become so. How wrong she was. I didn't call him back-to-back twenty times because I worried it would annoy him. Finally, he called me a week later and never said a thing about leaving so abruptly. He would come back to Maryland to visit, he said, if it was okay. I said, 'Yes.'

I thought often of Kadiatou's words: *The spirit cannot break, even if your heart breaks.* It had irritated me, but my irritation might have been the reflexive refusal of an unwanted truth. She was comforting me and maybe warning me. Don't let your spirit be destroyed, even if he breaks your heart. Your heart can break while your spirit remains whole. But what of when a spirit breaks?

He will send people to kill me! He will send people to kill me!

Years later, when Kadiatou was staying in my house with Binta, to avoid the alarming crush of journalists chasing after her, I walked into the guest room without knocking, to coax her to eat, and there she was rolling on the floor from side to side. No, not rolling. Punishing. Those rough jerky movements uncaring of her body.

'They call me prostitute!' she said. 'Prostitute. My father in paradise can hear them. They call me prostitute!'

How primally African she looked, supine on the ground, as if reproaching her ancestors while also begging them, saying 'Help me', and saying 'How could you let this happen?' She was moaning, drawn-out guttural primal sounds, her pain so great that to bear it quietly was to dishonour it. I lowered myself to the floor, to touch her without restraining her, to tell her she was not alone, and all the time thinking: Have they broken her spirit?

I ALWAYS SPENT Christmas in Nigeria, but I told Omelogor I wasn't sure this time, because I was hoping Darnell would say 'Let's spend Christmas together'. I expected a bracing response from Omelogor, like I should not let Darnell dictate my life, which I didn't want to hear. But all she said was 'I want to get us VIP tickets to go to the Heineken concert in Lagos, before we leave for the village. I'll still get them, in case Darnell forgets to ask you.'

Darnell didn't ask to spend Christmas together. He asked when I would be back from Nigeria, and I hadn't even left yet. If only he knew I wanted to spend Christmas wherever he wanted. I wished he would show some interest in visiting Nigeria, say something about wanting to see it, so that I could say, 'Why don't you come and visit?' His hard walls would soften if he met my parents and saw that they weren't about 'net worth'. But I was wary of just inviting him; I feared he might turn me down with cutting words.

OMELOGOR WAS IN America for a conference and my stomach clenched and unclenched thinking of her meeting Darnell. I was afraid of what she would see. Best to have dinner at home and light some candles and pour some wine, and we would have a nice time, me, Omelogor and Darnell. Maybe Zikora, too, to neutralize things. And maybe LaShawn to balance things a bit, but LaShawn was away on a trip to Italy, and how ridiculous to fret so much about a simple dinner. Zikora and Omelogor would be perfect, my closest friend and my closest cousin, even though a fog always hung between them, the air never entirely clear. But it wasn't dislike. They simply didn't understand each other, being so different, and because I was the glue, the reason they even knew each other, I felt responsible.

Once Zikora said, 'Omelogor is a bully', and I said, 'She really isn't; it's just that her passion can be too much.' But I understood why Zikora said that. Omelogor saw others so clearly and yet was blind to herself – how her certainties could intimidate, how her words scalded even if she didn't mean them to. And maybe she wore her brilliance a little too easily. Sometimes people reacted to Omelogor as if her magnificence was not neutral but a conspiracy to force an inferior status on them. Zikora always hated to be wrong, but especially if Omelogor was there. With Omelogor she talked only of her victories, never her vulnerabilities. When she was studying for law school, Zikora had stopped answering my calls and so, worried, I went over and banged on her apartment door. She opened the door, her eyes glassy, wearing a dirty, slack T-shirt, her cornrows matted. She had not showered in days. She smiled and began talking to me about brutalist architecture, or something like that. I was too startled to really listen. I found the bottle of pinkish pills she had bought online, with 'all night study aid' written on the label in unserious-looking graffiti font. There were two other bottles of white pills.

'Zikora! What have you taken?'

She was still talking, and for a moment I worried that she didn't even know who I was, until she said, 'Chia, I've been up since Sunday. What's today?'

'Wednesday.'

I called our family friend Dr Maduka, who was a surgeon in Connecticut. 'Is she making sense?' he asked, and I said, 'I think so, well yes, but what she's saying has nothing to do with what she's supposed to be studying for.'

He told me to make sure she drank a lot of water, to darken the room and put her books away and make her lie down. Zikora agreed to lie down, just for five minutes, still talking – 'Raw concrete dominates, and patterns are made using boardmaking,' she said a few times, until those words wormed their way into my ears, and for years afterwards the word 'boardmaking' brought to mind that frantic evening.

She was lying down but she was twitchy and shivery, unable to be still, and so I filled a bowl with ice and water and dumped it on her head. 'Chia!' she shouted, but the shout sounded less robotic and she accepted the towel I gave her and dried herself. Before, finally, she slept it off, she mumbled, 'Chia, I have to get into Georgetown Law.'

I stayed until she was stable, and I took the pills with me but felt reluctant to throw them away, as if I needed proof of the strangeness of that day. Those pill bottles remained at the back of my drawer for years. 'Don't tell Omelogor' was all Zikora said, and we never spoke of it again. Don't tell Omelogor. Maybe because she knew Omelogor would easily get into Georgetown Law and never consider study-aid pills.

THE DINNER WAS GOING WELL. Two candles lit. Red wine poured. Kadiatou served the catered food, chicken and asparagus delivered oven-ready from DC in elegant foil pouches. It was going well, yes, but Omelogor was praising me excessively, and I remembered a novel about an unattractive Indian bride with an unimpressive dowry whose desperate family recited her virtues to potential grooms while she stood in the corner, looking down at her feet.

'Our relatives are always talking about how brave Chia is for deciding to do her own thing,' Omelogor said, which was a lie. Omelogor lied only for reasons she thought worthwhile. Why was she lying? Zikora glanced at her with narrowed eyes that said, 'What is she up to now?' Darnell was opening a second bottle of wine, saying how good it was. Zikora and Darnell were joking about music, something I didn't understand, but they were laughing and I loved to see Darnell laugh. Omelogor asked Darnell about his work, and he was surprised she knew about African American art.

'As soon as I could afford to buy myself a ticket to America, I wanted to visit MoMA, just to see Jacob Lawrence's work,' Omelogor said, and I could see Darnell liked that.

Kadiatou came in to clear things away and Zikora said, 'Kadi, your fonio is better than this food, hands down.'

'This kind of food, I don't eat. No taste,' Kadiatou said with her quiet smile.

'So when you're away, she's here in the house?' Darnell asked me after Kadiatou left.

'She comes and goes. She takes care of everything, she's so trustworthy and dependable and lovely,' I said.

'It's because she's a Muslim,' Omelogor said.

'What?' Darnell looked at her.

'She's trustworthy because she's a Muslim. Like my Muslim gateman in Abuja. I trust him one hundred per cent.'

'She's trustworthy because she's a Muslim?' Darnell's words came out slowly to emphasize his incredulity.

'All over Africa, a Muslim believer is more likely than a churchgoer to be honest in everyday life. Go and ask any Nigerian employer who they trust with money, their Christian houseboy or their Muslim gateman.'

I felt tight with discomfort. This conversation would be normal at a dinner in Lagos or Abuja, and everyone would talk like Omelogor, bold and baroque declarations topping one another. But here her words bruised the air. She didn't know how to wear different selves like I did. I heightened my voice in Nigeria, and I swallowed more speech here. I was afraid to look at Darnell's face.

'So it's all about religious stereotypes, huh,' Darnell said.

'Stereotypes are an exaggeration of reality,' Omelogor said, stressing 'reality', and reached over to refill Darnell's glass.

'Interesting,' Darnell said.

'Muslims are trustworthy until they start rioting and killing you because of a cartoon published in Denmark,' Zikora said.

Goodness, not Zikora too. She was Americanized enough to know not to speak like this, but she was reacting to Omelogor; that prickliness between them again.

Omelogor looked at me, her eyes shaded, and I knew 'rioting and killing' had reminded her of our Uncle Hezekiah. I hoped she would not bring him up, I hoped she would let the shadow pass. And as if she heard me, her face brightened and she shrugged off Zikora's caustic tone with a quick laugh.

'You can hedge that. My friend Ejiro pays her gateman extra every month; she calls it an information allowance, so the gateman will give them notice whenever Muslims are about to riot!'

'All this talk of servants,' Darnell said.

'Tough life,' Omelogor said, and I wished she wouldn't joke about domestic help, as there was no telling what might offend Darnell.

'So how are you and Chia related again?' Darnell asked. 'Because you know Chia's people probably sold my people? All that old Igbo money going back centuries. They sold more than palm fruit on that West African coast, because they certainly made a killing.'

There was a pause. Darnell's favourite drunken quip didn't fit here, at my dining table with two lit candles melting down.

'That is such a lazy thing to say,' Omelogor said, so coldly it was hard to believe laughter had only just come from her.

'Why is it a lazy thing to say?' Darnell's slouchy cool had stiffened, unused to reproach. 'You're going to tell me the Romans practised slavery and shit, so nobody can blame Africans?'

Omelogor was staring at him in that full-on way of hers, head tilted.

'It's lazy because it's simplistic nonsense,' she said.

'Slavery has existed throughout human history,' I said, and instantly felt stupid. Why I had said that I did not know. I wanted only to return to safe waters.

Omelogor shot me an impatient glance, and then said slowly, 'If your ancestor was a slave in Igboland a hundred years ago, nobody would know that today. You would have been absorbed into the family of your enslavers.'

'Jesus,' Darnell said. 'We're doing a hierarchy of slavery here.'

'Of course there's a hierarchy: one system was much more barbaric than the other. That's a fact. Igbo slave traders could never have imagined the transatlantic slave trade, because it was nothing like the slavery they knew. The Europeans and Americans industrialized slavery. They turned people into things, like bits of wood. A piece of wood can never be part of your family. A piece of wood can never be human. In Igboland a slave was still human.'

'What page of the slavery apologist compendium is that?' Darnell asked, pushing back his chair, but he didn't get up.

'You know why else it's lazy? Because you forget that Africans were also victims. You think the people sold into slavery weren't missed and mourned? You think they weren't loved? My grandfather was almost sold as a boy. In Igboland it was men from Aro who were the slave raiders. People were terrified of them. They appeared on my great-grandfather's farm and kidnapped my grandfather and his brother, who were in the middle of harvesting cocoyams. My grandfather had a bad sore on his leg and so after a day's walk, they set him free, saying nobody would buy him because of his sore. He refused to leave his brother, but they beat him badly. His brother was sold. My grandfather made his way back home from the coast, a boy who was saved by his sore but had lost his brother. He grieved his brother for the rest of his life. He named his first son after his lost brother. He never ate cocoyams, which is why today my mother's onugbu soup is different, because she doesn't use cocoyams. My mother was born very late in his life, but she says even then he always spoke of his lost brother.'

We were all still, as if stunned, even Omelogor. I felt close to tears.

I had forgotten this story of her maternal grandfather. Aunty Chinwe told it one Christmas Eve. Everyone had gathered in our house before midnight Mass, and as Aunty Chinwe talked, my mother had shifted and sighed to show she didn't care for this slavery story.

'Look, all I'm saying is Africans have a hard time with accountability, some Africans,' Darnell said finally.

'And all I'm saying is don't forget it's a shared pain,' Omelogor said.

'Hopefully the lecture is over now,' Zikora said.

'By the way, I believe that the most remarkable ethnic group in the world is the Black American tribe. Look at them, cheated of so much, but their culture dominates the world,' Omelogor said. My mad cousin who just did not know when to stop. I wished she would at least say 'African American', to sound current, and why would she say 'them' like that, as if excluding Darnell, who was seated across from her. Darnell was staring at her, uncertain about just what to make of this. Seeing him look so nakedly unsure felt new.

'Should we play cards?' I asked.

'Yes, and maybe we can learn some accountability with Uno,' Omelogor said, and laughed, and Darnell's expression relaxed into a faint, almost reluctant grin.

'YOU HIDE YOUR worth with him,' Omelogor told me later.

'I'm happy.'

'Chia, it's almost idolatrous,' Omelogor said.

'What?'

'Your love for him.'

'Idolatrous. Talk like normal people, please.'

'Remember your half-caste boyfriend in primary school? Eric?'

'Yes?'

'Remember how your sneaker laces came undone during interhouse sports, and you were about to retie them and he said, "No, wait", and he bent down and retied them for you?'

'You weren't even there. I told you the story.'

'That's what you deserve, Chia, to be adored.'

'It's different, but I'm happy.'

'Don't decide that this is it. This person is not the love of your life.'

'Who said anything about being the love of my life?'

'I mean, apart from Nnamdi, of course,' Omelogor said, gently; she knew how tender it still was, so many years after. Nnamdi, who died in a car accident when I was seventeen. Nnamdi, who on blustery harmattan mornings would drape his red and black sweater over my shoulders at morning assembly in secondary school. Nnamdi, the trembling delicious wetness of my life's first kiss, both of us standing pressed together beneath the eave outside our kitchen. Nnamdi. Would we have stayed together? Would life have separated us? At seventeen, I was so sure. I had picked out the names of our two children – Richard and Daphne – this was before I became sophisticated enough to reject English names. *I will love you forever*, I wrote on his last birthday card, just weeks before he died. He was the love of my life, if anyone was.

DARNELL WASN'T HOPEFUL about the other fellowship that brought American academics to Paris for a year. The German fellowship was easier, and since he didn't get that, no way would Paris happen. Which was why, after glancing at his phone one crisp autumn morning, he jumped up and pumped his fist in the air and hugged me. For once I saw a glimpse of him free of poison, his armour lowered, his face beautiful uncaged.

He said casually, 'You should come, Chia. They're giving me an apartment. Certainly not up to your standards, but hopefully you can cope.'

He was asking me to live with him. Three years and he had never mentioned living together. Once, after I stayed the night, I left my sweater slung across his sofa, and the next day he had it folded on the table. 'You forgot that.' I immediately put the sweater in my handbag. I understood what he meant, that I could lay no claims. But of Paris, he said, 'You should come', and so I eagerly bought a ticket. I felt a weightlessness, the ascent of hope. In Paris, I would finally blur his edges. I would pull him into the light. I would cure his insomnia and gently show him that we could need each other without losing ourselves. My illusions were so radiant then. At Charles de Gaulle airport, the young Black man who stamped my passport said, 'Your eyes, very beautiful', and pulled his eyes, up and slanted, to show that he meant the almond shape of my eyes.

'Thank you!' I said, delighted by the surprise that was this man, his twinkle of mischief, his cinnamon skin, sitting in the glass booth stamping passports. His compliment had to be an augury of my new life with Darnell in Paris: a life glazed with excitement and free of silences.

As we left immigration, Darnell said, 'That was common.'

'Common?' I asked. 'How?'

'You were too obvious with him.'

'A compliment was the last thing I expected, with my sleepy mess of a face. It was just a nice surprise because I don't feel beautiful at all. I don't feel beautiful most of the time.'

'Always so interesting to hear a beautiful person moan about not feeling beautiful.'

'Darnell, I'm just trying to explain.'

'Doesn't make it any less common.'

I wasn't sure what he meant, but I agreed and felt chastised. I would have delighted in Darnell's jealousy, but it wasn't jealousy, because he knew I was blind to everything but him. It was control, a rationing of what I was allowed. He squashed my smallest pleasures, and I helped him flatten them, sinking myself into the mean crevices of his will. I look back now and see my weakness in such sharp relief, being pliant and docile in exchange for nothing; the clarity of hindsight is bewildering. If only we could see our failings while we are still failing.

DARNELL LOVED PARIS because of James Baldwin; Heaven forbid he should love it for any of the conventional reasons. For him, a thing had value simply by being obscure; a man of the people who hated what the people liked. We broke up in Paris. We broke up because I ordered a mimosa in Paris. If there is a soundtrack to our ending, it is his Senegalese friend Mamadou's voice saying, 'Voltaire's heart is in the Bibliothèque.'

Hélène, Mamadou's friend, invited us to drinks because she wanted to meet Darnell. Darnell said she was 'Parisian culture royalty', working on an exhibition of American artists, and she probably wanted to offer him a 'gig'.

'Mamadou says there's a pile of family cash behind her,' Darnell said, his tone disapproving and admiring; he had fussed with his clothes and changed shirts twice. We were in an elegant hotel bar and the waiter arrived, notepad in hand. Mamadou ordered something in a stream of rapid French. Hélène asked for a Perrier, Darnell a red wine. I drank red wine, like Darnell, because of Darnell. But I had a sudden craving. 'Can I have a mimosa, please,' I said, the first to speak English.

'Mimosa?' asked the perplexed waiter. 'What is this, mimosa?'

'Don't take her seriously,' Darnell said in his Americanized French, which I would not have so easily understood if it had been better. 'A mimosa is a vulgar drink. She'll have the same as me.'

'Ah,' the waiter said, with the expression of a person who did not get the joke.

'Okay, yes,' I said. 'I'll have the same Bordeaux, thank you.'

Something shifted in the air. A lethal chill came from Darnell and unsettled me. I had done something wrong but did not know what. Mamadou was saying, 'Voltaire's heart is in the Bibliothèque.'

'His actual heart?' I asked.

'His actual heart. It is shrivelled and black. The French removed his heart as a tribute to his greatness and put it in a library. If we Africans did this, they would call it uncivilized voodoo.'

Darnell laughed, his body now angled away from me.

'I didn't know Voltaire was so heartless,' I said, desperate to be funny, to salvage an unknown wrong.

Mamadou and Hélène laughed. Darnell did not.

'Chia, your face has such symmetry, so beautiful,' Hélène said kindly.

'Thank you,' I said.

'There is a continual flow, and there's a way in which that is formally significant, but the beauty is in the restlessness. Aesthetic success comes with not conforming, being offbeat, a tad askew,' Darnell said, picking up the photos Hélène had brought, as though he was talking about the art installations. When I first looked at the photos, slices of metal hung on jagged ropes, I thought them cold and ugly.

'I agree, they're gorgeous,' I said, and Hélène cast me a pitying glance, but without contempt, as if she recognized women like me. For the rest of the evening, Darnell talked easily without ever looking at me, and a few times he flirted with Hélène. I sipped my wine, my stomach tightly knotted. Darnell's words flowed – cosmopolitanism in African American painting and archival theory of African American modernisms and African American visuality or something. I didn't speak. I didn't know what to say, and I feared speaking at all might worsen whatever ruinous thing I had done. That Darnell did not look at me, not once, was wounding. I might as well have been a statue, a pillar of salt, empty air.

Back in his apartment, he waited until we had both showered, like a school headmaster delaying punishment, before he asked, 'You ordered a mimosa at the Hotel Montalembert? Like it's your favourite chain brunch spot in DC? Seriously?'

'What's wrong with that?'

'That's some Ugly American shit right there. It's not like you haven't travelled the world.'

His beard oil glimmered in the light. An itchy rash had broken out on my cheeks when he first started growing his beard. I told him I was allergic to the oil and he said, 'You're probably hormonal.' He never changed the beard oil, and each time after sex he watched me get up to wash my face. I hated his beard oil. It smelled of mildew. My fingers were trembling. Something in me long submerged had burst out growing claws.

'You're angry because I ordered a mimosa? I don't understand.'

'Pointing out something to you is not being angry.'

'I like mimosas. I don't have to perform whatever you think Paris is supposed to be, just because you want to impress some Frenchwoman.'

'Okay, that's patronizing classist shit.'

'How?' For a moment, I wondered if I was wrong, but didn't know how I was wrong. He made me doubt my right to anger. 'How?'

He walked away and I heard the click as he locked the bedroom door. He locked the door, to fend me off, to keep away this person darkly guilty of ordering a mimosa in Paris. I slept on the thin sofa and awoke early in a kind of cold light. While he silently made coffee, I looked online for flight tickets to Washington, DC.

I sent Omelogor a message to say I was leaving Paris today and it was over. Her response was *Love you. Call once in the taxi.*

It was done. Telling Omelogor made it real, and I heard in my head the sound of breaking spells. I had held on for so long, and now, letting go, it surprised me how quickly mystery dissolves to dust. There was no wavering will, no fear. We are in love and then we are not in love. Where does love go when we stop loving?

THREE

In January, when the world knew of the virus brewing in China but lockdown was still unimaginable, Aunty Jane came to our house in the village and asked to see me. My mother's sister and manic shadow, who made everybody's business hers. I was packing for my return to America. I was bloated from too much Christmas chin-chin. I didn't feel like seeing Aunty Jane; I already knew what she wanted to talk about, but I had never learned to disobey relatives older than me.

'Chia, you're running out of time!' she said, as soon as I stepped into the living room. 'Your only option now is IVF. I know somebody that just had twins at forty-five. But you have to hurry up if you want to use your own eggs. Stop travelling up and down, and find a man to do IVF with. Or you can use donor sperm. All this travel, one day you will be tired, and without a child, your life will just feel empty and meaningless.'

It might have sounded cruel, but it wasn't; she was only being benignly blunt, as Nigerians are wont. I was forty-four and I did not have a husband and I did not have a child, a calamity more confounding because it was not for lack of suitors.

'So a husband is no longer necessary, Aunty? You should have told me this ten years ago,' I said, laughing.

The stipulations from my mother and my aunts, maternal and paternal, had started in my mid-twenties, firm and fine-edged, and repeated often: He must be Catholic and Igbo, have a university degree, and be able to maintain you. 'Maintain you', always said in English. Such a strange expression, as though you were a machine needing frequent oiling. In my mid-thirties, the conditions began to wilt at the edges, my life by then rooted in America. A Christian was fine, of any denomination; a Nigerian of any ethnicity; or an African; or just a Black man; or, well, a man. Now, in my mid-forties, with my female eggs in an unforgiving rush to uselessness, marriage had become secondary. Have a child, by whatever means. My mother, on Christmas Day, had said while looking at the Nativity scene set out for the village children, 'A child is more important than marriage.'

How slippery moralities are, how they circle and thin and change with circumstance. Imagine if I had decided to have a baby ten years ago, without a husband. Imagine my mother's exploding horror.

'Aunty, I am still praying for a husband,' I said.

Aunty Jane looked sceptical, assessing me as if to divine what exactly was off. I did want a husband and child, but not under any circumstances. I didn't want to be single, but being single was not intolerable. Much worse was the prospect of a marriage that wasn't a merging of souls, a baby not intensely born from love. Even friends barely understood. They thought all my talk of wanting the truest love was a false pose, a defensive sleight, because what else was I going to say, having failed to find a husband? Who lived in a fairy tale? A secondary-school classmate wrote on our class's WhatsApp group: *Who would have thought that Chia, rich man's daughter, with all her beauty, is still unmarried while some of us, our children are finishing school?* I skulked silently in the group, and tried to remember who the poster was, but she looked unfamiliar in her profile photo. It was easier to pretend that I was as broken by singleness as I was expected to be. People did not easily believe that you longed for the unusual. I always said what women confronted by the crime of singleness said: I am praying, please pray for me, my own will come by God's grace.

'Chia, what really happened with Chuka?' Aunty Jane asked.

'We just didn't make a good match.'

'But you were engaged.'

In response to my silent shrug, Aunty Jane prodded: 'Did you discover something?'

'No. It just didn't work out,' I said firmly, and hoped she would leave it alone. If I had said he beat me, or he's not actually divorced, or he is seeing another woman, Aunty Jane would have understood. Real meaty reasons, with sympathy poured on me, and opprobrium on him. But she would never have understood the truth, that I broke up with Chuka because I could no longer ignore that exquisite ache of wanting to love a lovely person that you do not love.

WE MET AT a Nigerian wedding in Indiana. I hadn't wanted to go, but my mother said they couldn't come and I would have to represent them. Febechi told me, 'There's somebody here that is perfect for you. You people fit each other, children of Big Men.'

I didn't know Febechi well; we were classmates in secondary school, and even then she always joked about my father with a slyness that felt too close to spite.

'Febechi, please let me eat my rice in peace, *biko*.'

Nigerian wedding introductions were so lacking in wonder, so predictable, so planned, and they could not end with marriage as I believed marriage should be, a merging of two souls. And what slim sad pickings: wearied men in search of a Nigerian wife, any Nigerian wife, but preferably a nurse, because somebody somewhere had convinced Nigerians in America that nurses made good money and that men could not be nurses. Once, at a wedding in Houston, I overheard a man ask, 'Are you willing to train as a nurse if we go ahead?'

Febechi ignored my groaning and brought Chuka to our table. He was umber-skinned, built as if he played rugby, his moustache linked to his short beard by a thin groomed line, his bald head shining in the ballroom's chandelier light. There was a leonine quality to him. You noticed him; he subdued space. It surprised me that he needed to be introduced to anybody at all. He had an unusual self-possession, as though he would face emergencies with genuine calm. He was nine years older than me but seemed even older; not aged but vividly grown up, like an adult archetype, so courteous and proper, so sensible. He must have been a prefect in secondary school, the kind liked by both students and teachers, who could quiet a rowdy classroom but would also sneak out of school with friends for beer and cigarettes.

'It's nice we both live in the DMV area,' he said that first day, with quiet anticipation, and I smiled and said, 'Yes.'

His living room in his house in Northern Virginia reminded me of our house in Enugu: tan leather sofas, a tan coffee table and heavy tasselled tan curtains. I felt, for a moment, the strange sensation of being pursued by the past.

'Everything matches,' I said in dismay, without meaning to sound so dismayed.

'Is that bad?' he asked.

'No, no, of course not.'

'You can change whatever you want to change.'

He signalled to permanence almost right away. 'Chia, I'm too old to play games. I saw your picture on Febechi's Facebook page and told her I wanted to meet you. My intention is marriage,' he said, and I said nothing, knowing he would hear acquiescence in my silence. I had always imagined my choice of husband would be like my travel writing: unusual, but not so much as to alienate my parents. Somebody foreign, with poetry in his soul. Not a successful Igbo engineer who still shined his shoes with the Kiwi polish that everybody's father in Nigeria had used. Where did he even buy the tin? His manners were those of a person with good 'home-training', he was interested in my family, my friends, the people who mattered to me. He wanted to say hi to Afam and Bunachi when they called; he wanted to meet Omelogor; he came with me to see Zikora after she had her baby.

'Is your friend always this hostile?' he asked as we left Zikora's.

She had been sitting on a sofa, looking worn out and drawn, holding the baby. As Chuka came towards them, to bend and look at the baby, Zikora suddenly shifted, giving him her back, and shielded the baby with her body. In the awkwardness that followed, Chuka turned and sat away from her, next to her mother. Until we left, Zikora never looked at him. But her mother held our visit aloft, talking easily with Chuka, telling him about the two schools she owned in Enugu.

'It's not personal. Zikor is dealing with a lot,' I said.

'It felt personal, as if she knows of something bad I did in the past,' Chuka said.

Because I wanted to guard Zikora's story, I jokingly asked, 'So what bad thing did you do in the past?'

Later, Zikora said Chuka's 'good man' air had set her off, and even she was surprised at the tumbling hostility she felt, which meant the true depth of her damage was still unknown to her. I told her I understood and that Chuka understood, even though he didn't. He was always watchful with her afterwards, even after I told him her story, as if he expected an outburst of strange behaviour from her at any time.

'She's not an easy character' was all he would say. But about Omelogor he said, 'I like your cousin!' He overheard my video-call conversation with Omelogor, no, with the warped person Omelogor became in graduate school in America. 'Why do these Americans say "enjoy" instead of "eat"? "I enjoy it with cheese. I think you should enjoy it with a side salad." How do you know I'm going to enjoy it? It's so presumptuous; it's from an entitlement worldview.'

'She has a point!' Chuka said, amused, but I didn't feel amused, because I was worried about her. It baffled me how, so quickly after she started graduate school, Omelogor changed and became leached of her light. One day she called me crying. I had seen her cry so few times that shock overwhelmed me, as if she was somehow built differently, without the crying gene. I remembered her weeping, properly weeping, only once, many years ago when a man was beheaded in the North, after Uncle Hezekiah's death. She was in university then. But that was different; her distress was honed, focused on its cause, unlike this formless crumbling.

'Omelogor, Omelogor, o zugo, don't cry,' I said helplessly.

When she didn't cry, she burned with a serrated anger, unlike her usual clear-thinking rage where she would argue in sharp slices. This anger was jagged, as if it impaired her, as if she was lost. She complained about things worth complaining about and things that were trivial and things I did not understand at all.

'I didn't know "centre" had become a verb,' she said, with a bitterness that did not match the subject. 'They're always talking of "centring minorities". It's bad enough Americans turned "impact" into a verb, but now "centre" too?'

'I think "centre" was always a verb,' I said.

'Not in the way they use it. You can use a preposition like "centred around" but not "centre indigenous people".'

'Okay.'

'It's like that absurd American word "share", and now the whole world uses it – "Share the document with her; oh, she shared that she won't be at the meeting" – so nonsensical.'

I didn't quite understand why 'share' was nonsensical.

'Start a conversation with Americans and before you know it, they're saying, "It's kind of like that movie." Always a stupid American film.'

Mostly I listened to her, silent and perplexed. Her grievances felt like balloons overfilled with air, unnecessary, that could only end in a pop. One day, she said, 'Chia, the American', the closest she had ever come to sneering at me. And sneering was not her style, nor was spite. 'The problem with Zikora is that she has always had a surfeit of that trait women are blessed with – the ability to tolerate nonsense from men,' she said when I told her about Zikora's situation, in a tone unlike her, her words shaped like weapons. I decided I would no longer discuss Zikora with her, at least until she became herself again. When she told me, 'America makes more sense when you're looking in from outside', I thought: She should have stayed looking in from outside. She was depressed. She was depressed, but it enraged her to hear me say so. She should not have left her life in banking to come to graduate school in America to study pornography. 'I want to do something that actually helps people,' she had said, as if to atone for her success in banking.

'By studying pornography?' I asked, amused. I thought it was just

Omelogor being Omelogor, but she convinced me. Pornography was a teacher for so many people, and it was a terrible teacher, and she wanted to study how the industry was built, so she could learn how its influence could be undone. Even that thesis she had given up, saying her adviser hated her, and 'She hates me' was not a sentence I thought I would ever hear from Omelogor. Now she was writing on her website, For Men Only, and sometimes she called to ask me questions like 'What do you think of choking?'

CHUKA FOUND HER website and read two posts aloud, laughing, and I thought about how rarely I saw him laugh like that, with abandon, unrestrained by his constant seriousness.

> Dear men,
>   You know that she knows you love her. Maybe she knows, but she wants to hear you say it every day, just like you need to oil your beard every day to keep it groomed. (Do you have a beard? No? Okay, then your hair or your armpit or whatever you tend to every day.) See, love needs tending.
>   Tell her 'I love you so much.' If you can carry off some creativity, tell her 'I love how you walk or talk or smile. I love hearing what you think of movies. I love that crazy look you have when you're half asleep. I love it when you're happy and laughing. I love you.'
>   I know, it's a lot. Saying one or two extra sentences can be exhausting. But try it and see the benefits you'll reap. Remember, I am on your side, dear men.

When Chuka read another post, he looked up and asked, 'I hope you don't have this problem with me.'

> Dear men, solutions to three different permutations of the same general conundrum.
>   You told her 'I'm sorry if I hurt you' and she got even angrier. I know you didn't mean any harm, but next time

don't say 'if'. 'If' means something may or may not have happened. To you, the 'if' is harmless. To her, it feels dismissive, as if you don't really mean your apology. Try again without the 'if'.

You sometimes do nice things for her after a fight, and it's your way of saying sorry, but the best way to say sorry is to say sorry. Not to pretend that all is well and do nice things for her. It's nice that you're doing nice things, but doing nice things is not saying sorry. Saying sorry is saying sorry.

She said you're ignoring the issue even though you've said sorry. I know you mean no harm when you say sorry. But to be effective and reduce resentment, always be specific when you apologize. Don't just say 'I'm sorry.' Say 'I'm sorry I didn't do X. I should have done X. It was just wrong.'

I know talking is a drag. I get it, I really do. Remember, I'm on your side, dear men.

Chuka's loudest laughter came after he read the last post.

Dear men,

Women do not always hear what you say, they hear what they want to hear. So please be very clear. If you're not interested, don't say you're busy, say you're not interested. I understand you want to be nice and protect her feelings, but that's what got you into this problem. You told her you were busy when she asked for a second date and she then sent you a long stinker of a text about how you string women along. If you're too nice to say you're not interested, then invent a girlfriend or a wife. If you're not interested, don't leave the smallest space for doubt, because in the single and searching secret society of women, you will be burned at the stake as a wizard. Remember, I'm on your side, dear men.

———

EACH DAY WITH CHUKA I encountered his otherness. He made his bed as soon as he got up, sheets pulled taut and straight, and wore his shirts neatly tucked in, even on weekends. Nigerian boarding-school values. In his closet, his socks were curled in neat rows. He read books I did not think of as real books, about leadership and project management. He wrote his name on the title pages, at the top right corner, in a geometric hand, *Chuka Aniegboka*, which brought to me an odd rush of nostalgia, because I had last done that in primary school. He listened to the BBC World News every morning. He liked films that bored me, formulaic thrillers, and he watched them with intense focus. If I spoke, he would pause it and say, 'I don't want to miss anything.'

'But we already know what will happen!' I would tease.

He was strong, he lifted weights in his basement, his toolboxes were tidily arranged in his garage, and he closed the jam jar so tight that I could not undo the lid myself. One day, watching him replace a door handle on his deck, I thought guiltily that he was like that door: sturdy, reassuring, uncreative. He always ordered a well-done steak at restaurants, never anything else, and back home he would promptly microwave a portion of jollof rice, which came in flimsy plastic containers from a Nigerian caterer in Baltimore, saying restaurant food never filled him. He crossed himself before he ate, and I thought how I had stopped crossing myself years ago because it felt unnecessary and showy. I planned a trip to Broadway, where he fell asleep in the middle of the play. I nudged him awake, and he said, 'Sorry, I should have had coffee at the hotel', as if it was caffeine rather than interest that could keep him awake. He suggested brunch at The Four Seasons and I suggested something less stuffy.

'Okay,' he said to my suggestion, doubtful but willing. 'It's just that The Four Seasons is a trusted brand.' His was a life of faith in trusted brands. He flew only airlines that were 'mainstream', even if it meant multiple connections, and he looked astounded that I never flew British Airways. He agreed the airline was pompous and, yes, a kind of petty pleasure always lit up the flight attendants' faces as they demeaned Nigerian passengers, but was that reason enough to make me fly airlines that nobody really knew? Whenever I travelled, he dropped me off or picked me up at the airport, asking only if my trip went well, seeking no details of my adventures. He did not understand, he could not possibly understand. I imagined him saying, 'You have a degree from a good school, why not get a proper job? You can still do your writing on weekends.' He didn't say this, he never did, but I imagined the words burning to roll off his tongue. He read my articles and always said, 'Nice', as after tasting a tolerable food that still does not appeal.

> San Blas Islands. Yes, the ocean really was clear as glass and I looked down from the canoe and saw starfish, but all that secluded tradition gets boring very quickly. After a while the other people on the canoe looked bored too and started swiping through photos on their phones. My highlight was a drink I had after we got off the canoe. Someone cut open a fresh coconut and splashed rum generously into it, stuck a straw in and handed it to me. It was so delicious because it was dirty. The knife looked suspicious. The rum was cheap. The guy didn't wash his hands anywhere. And I want to go back just to drink it again.

'You liked it because it was dirty?' Chuka asked, giving me the look you gave to Westerners who did foolish Westerner things, like not greeting their elders. He read my article about Greece, which began with 'How do other tourists tolerate the smell of donkey shit in Santorini?' Afterwards he said, vaguely, 'Very nice.' Not just his usual 'Nice', but 'Very nice', which must mean the donkey shit offended the properness at his core.

'I liked the other islands,' I said, in penance. 'We should go together when you're on vacation.'

'We should go to Dubai,' he said. 'It's a miracle of engineering and political will. Really what Nigeria should be.'

I thought Dubai all sterile kitsch, but it did not surprise me that Chuka liked Dubai, because Nigerians liked Dubai. He was a harking back to my Nigerian life, familiar but now made exotic by the wide gorge that separated me from it, like a fond anachronism. He told me, 'I don't want to rush you', as boys said to girls they were serious about; it made you special, exempt from the sex-haste reserved for less deserving girls. I wasn't even sure I wanted to sleep with him at all. It took months before I let him undress me in his bedroom, not really wanting to, but feeling I should because I did like him and I was by most measures his girlfriend now and he somehow deserved it, being so proper and attentive. It would be predictable, I was sure, even perfunctory, but at least not unpleasant. How unutterably wrong I turned out to be. Chuka startled me with new and unexpected pleasures; doors never opened were suddenly flung apart, our bodies in riot and all the old laws undone. 'You're so sweet, you're so sweet,' he said, forceful and urgent, until I was heady with earthly power. I felt for the first time in my life an intensity of forgetting, those brief raw moments of bodily transport, of physical oblivion. Afterwards I lay dazed. 'I love you,' he said, and I said, 'What did you just do to me?' Already I wanted a repeat. Already I wanted and wanted.

I WAS TELLING CHUKA a story about primary school, how the other children called me Milk Butter, because my hands were soft.

'I was maybe nine, and another school had come to ours for a debate competition. We were asked to shake hands and one of the boys let go of my hand very quickly, as if my palm was hot, and he said, "Your hand is too soft!" I remember the debate topic: "Doctors are more important than lawyers." Our school won. I think that boy was just angry about losing, and so he started taunting me – "Softy-softy hands, you don't do any work at home, you're not strong, you just eat milk and butter" – and soon the other children were calling me Milk and Butter, which then morphed to Milk Butter.'

'Milk Butter,' Chuka repeated, and reached for my hand. 'So soft. That boy wasn't wrong.' He was running his thumb over my palm and I was thinking of his tongue. My life had become a scattering of unexpected eroticism.

'You have the hands of a labourer,' I teased. 'So rough.'

'Oh my father did not play, I could change a car tyre by the age of eight. When I moved to Lagos for university, I was so shocked to see men getting manicures in salons.'

'You should come with me to get a manicure.'

'I'll do anything for you, but manicure in a salon? *Mba.*' I loved his saying no to a manicure, and I loved it only from him. From other men it would be laughably backward. But Chuka was my old-fashioned fantasy, a manly man, he could sweep me into his arms, pick me up as if I weighed nothing, carry me, protect me. Refusing a manicure fit just right.

I would watch him immersed in the mundane and see only sensuality: Chuka cleaning his kitchen counter, thorough and broad-shouldered; Chuka paying for groceries at Whole Foods; Chuka driving, eyes trained on the road. Even his reticence with his friends felt sensual.

I watched him at barbecues in his friends' yards during that summer's lovely languid days. I liked to sit and listen to the loud Nigerian voices, sheltering in their presence, enjoying the newness of it, because I did not often go to Nigerian gatherings.

'Take her out of that public school now before she comes home and starts twerking,' somebody said.

'Imagine, one White patient came into my consulting room and asked me where the doctor is, in this state of Maryland!' another said.

'There is somebody in Bowie who can organize a goat for you,' somebody else said.

His closest friends in America, Enyinnaya and Ifeyinwa, hosted Saturday gatherings in their house in Bethesda. Ifeyinwa was the kind of Igbo woman who intimidated me: sure-footed, bristling with capability, always able to handle things, and contemptuous of any foolishness. She had a big county job and I imagined her dogged climb up the ranks, while raising children and getting a master's degree or two. She was tall and wore a short side-part wig that was uninterested in looking realistic. I desperately wanted her to like me.

I brought bottles of wine when we visited. I sprang up to help her serve puff-puff and meat pies.

'Thank you, my dear, but please just sit down and relax,' she said.

She wasn't unfriendly, but the coolness of her tone created distance. One Saturday, Chuka said Ifeyinwa's sister was visiting from Nigeria, but I didn't see her until late in the day, when the other guests had gone. She walked into the kitchen, in a cloud of heavy perfume. Upon seeing a beautiful woman, animosity erupts unprompted in some women. I knew from experience how to diagnose it. At first, I thought Ifeyinwa's sister was afflicted with it, how she radiated hostility, not acknowledging me in a way that made clear she was not acknowledging me. She filled a glass of water at the dispenser, and then I realized that it wasn't me. It was Chuka. The flounce in her manner. She was ignoring Chuka. That stir of defiance, even vengefulness, was for Chuka. They had a history. Or more than a history. What was their story? I felt a breathless stab of jealousy. Her long lustrous weave fell in waves to her shoulders. Her designer jeans were slightly pinched at the crotch. To douse the sudden charged air after her sister left with the glass of water, Ifeyinwa said, 'Chuka, *biko* come and help me open this thing.'

Witnessing Chuka's effect on Ifeyinwa's sister left me shaken. I saw him anew and admired him anew, his vitality, the controlled, sustained energy of him. When he went to the living room, I got up and followed him. I sat by his side. Until we left, I kept him always in my line of sight, my jealousy mounting, climbing, enveloping me.

'Ifeyinwa's sister was not very sociable,' I said in the car, and then wished I had simply asked what their story was.

Chuka sighed and said Ifeyinwa had introduced her sister to him just after his divorce and they met once and he wasn't interested. He had never given her any hope, never played games. He didn't understand why she was so angry.

'Because she wants you,' I said, suddenly light from relief. 'Who wouldn't want you?'

His smile was barely there, as if he didn't quite know what to do with compliments.

———

I OVERHEARD IFEYINWA say to a friend, with laughter, 'Any Igbo man from Anambra State will cheat with a woman if she cooks ukwa for him. That's why I married from Imo State. I didn't want to lose my husband to ukwa.'

Chuka and I were always last to leave, and so in the waning evening, I went to the sink and began to rinse glasses and load the dishwasher.

'Oh, no . . .' she started to protest.

'Sister Ify, I've been looking for ukwa to cook for Chuka,' I said, a lie I had not planned on until it came floating out of my mouth. I hated the mealy oiliness of ukwa, I was the only one in my family who did, and I had no idea how it was cooked.

Ifeyinwa squinted slightly at me, surprised, no doubt thinking this Big Man's daughter, with her 'travel writing' frippery of a job, was still solid enough to want to make ukwa for her man. It made me redeemable. She told me to try the African market in Catonsville. Days later, from the back of the store with its musty smell of stockfish, I sent her a text saying, *Just bought ukwa, thank you!*

At the counter, as the cashier rang me up, an African American woman in line behind me peered at the register and said, 'Whatever that is better be worth it!'

I smiled at her. 'It is. It's a delicacy from the southeastern part of Nigeria. Breadfruit. I'm making it for my fiancé.'

'My fiancé.' More words sailing unplanned out of my mouth. How was I slipping on this new persona like a T-shirt? I cooked from a YouTube video and laid out a surprise dinner for Chuka on my dining table.

'Chia!' he said, lifting the lid of the Dutch oven. 'Ahn-ahn! Where is this from? You can make ukwa? Baby, thank you, thank you so much,' he said. Something about his expression made me teary. How easily he was made happy, how uncomplicated his conditions for fulfilment.

Soon after, Ifeyinwa began teasing Chuka about our getting married. Her approval felt like an accomplishment and warmed me like a compliment.

'Why are you wasting time, Chuka? See Chia's pointed nose. Your children will win beauty contests.'

'Chia is the cause of the delay,' Chuka said.

'Don't mind him!' I said, to appear eager for marriage, as she would expect.

Enyinnaya looked up from his phone screen.

'Look at this young Nigerian writer. She's doing very well, we're proud of her, but I heard she is married and decided to keep her maiden name. Why is she confusing young girls? If something is not broken, don't fix it.' He looked at me slyly, as though I, too, might commit this crime.

He was a small soft-bellied man, a neurosurgeon. On our first visit, he had thrust into my hand a hospital magazine from a pile on the coffee table which had his photo on the cover, and then hovered, waiting, until I awkwardly opened to the page filled with his face. 'Congratulations,' I said, unsure of what else to say, and he nodded, a monarch accepting his due adulation. How could this be Chuka's closest friend? Their television was always turned to Fox News.

'The truth of the matter is that illegal immigration is killing this country! Democrats don't want to admit it,' Enyinnaya said.

'Your brother is an illegal immigrant in Texas looking for somebody to marry for papers,' Ifeyinwa said briskly, and I wondered what they talked about when they were alone, if they talked at all.

Chuka laughed and told Enyinnaya, 'Keep supporting people that don't even want you.'

He was at the counter twisting a wine opener and fluidly removing the cork. Just hours before he had been lying in bed in his boxer shorts, wide-chested, saying, 'Chia, I'm waiting for you.' He didn't strain to sound suggestive, it wasn't his style; he simply said, 'Chia, I'm waiting for you', and the evenness of his tone riotously lit my longing.

Ifeyinwa was saying something to him and he said, sensible as always, 'They should send you the invoice first.'

She could not possibly guess how, with passion, his nature changed so wildly as to become someone else. A person's surface was never the full story, or even the story. That I had this knowledge of Chuka, this shared secret, brought its own frisson. Suddenly I could not wait to go back to his house. I got up and whispered in his ear, 'I want you.' He smiled and briefly squeezed my hand, another tame gesture that said nothing about the latent fires. Later, we burned, and after we burned, we lay in slaked and sweaty silence, and I thought about how desire can live beside love without becoming love.

'Do you sometimes want to escape and find another life?' I asked him.

'Find another life?' He propped himself up to look at me, waiting for more details, but some things resist explanation; it takes instinct, intuition, a knowing at your centre that is either there or isn't. From the moment I saw his dutiful living room, its matching furniture, I knew there were large swathes of me that he would never understand.

THEN CAME A MOMENT of splendour. A Friday evening, and Chuka and I planned to go into the city later for some live music. An editor named Katie emailed me to ask if she could call – a proper publisher in New York finally interested in my book proposal. Finally. Before I took the call, I washed my face and put my braids in a bun to look presentable, as if Katie could see me. On the phone, Katie was talking about my title, actually talking about my title, with serious interest; no hazy words and no 'We'll see'. Her voice was soothing, all creamy educated tones. She punctuated her sentences with the word 'right.' She said *The Non-Adventurous Adventures of One African Woman* was wonderful, but perhaps *Black Woman in Transit* was stronger, because 'African' was limiting and 'Black' opened it up more. I thought 'Black' too wide-ranging; 'Black' didn't explain the humiliations of my Nigerian passport, the rejected visas, the embassies leery of a Nigerian travelling just to explore. But I said, yes, it was a wonderful idea, I was happy with *Black Woman in Transit*. I said thank you, thank you, too many times. I said I was excited and wanted to make the book playful and personal. Yes, of course, she said, and then more gently added that she was wondering if maybe I should write a different book first, with more relevance, to create real debut buzz, right? I said maybe my piece 'Dining in the Three Guineas' should open the book, because Conakry, Malabo and Bissau were not well-known at all and visiting restaurants there made for interesting reading. She was still talking about a book with relevance, and I realized with a curdling anxiety that we were not talking about the same thing at all.

'Do you mind my asking what you mean by relevance?' I asked, and she said, 'I saw a news story about Congo, what women there are going through, right? The horrific rapes. It's been going on for years. I'm not saying you have to travel there, we would need to be clear about where is safe to go, but a book on Congo and the struggles of the people there would really resonate right now.'

As soon as she said 'struggles', the word lengthened piously, enunciated earnestly, I knew she saw me as an interpreter of struggles. She was saying, 'Somalia or Sudan could work too. A more general introduction to what's going on there. People will buy it even if they don't actually read it; they'll buy it to show they care, right?'

A soft underbelly of cynicism ran through her words. She was asking if I would think about it and let her know, and I said yes, of course, and I hung up quickly before my tears betrayed me. In the shortest moment, self-doubt can swoop down and swallow you whole, leaving nothing behind. It was pointless, all of this. It suddenly felt delusional to think anybody would publish a light and quirky travel book by a Black Nigerian woman; don't forget the wealthy family, no struggle story, and her love of the nice parts of cities. Maybe I needed to go back and work for the family as my parents wanted. If nothing else, I could write reports, as spreadsheets would always be incomprehensible puzzles to me. My confidence, ounce by ounce, squeezed itself dry. I cried and stopped and started again.

I sent Chuka a text to say I didn't feel up to our evening and he called right away. I said I felt a bit unwell and he said my voice sounded off. 'I'm fine,' I said, no point in telling him, because he wouldn't understand. He didn't tell me he was already getting in his car as we spoke, but when my doorbell rang, I knew it was him. I opened the door. Tears hijacked me. I hadn't expected to cry, but at the first glance of Chuka at the door, in jeans and a button-down shirt, tucked in as ever, stable and steadfast, I burst into tears. He held me, enveloped in his musk, silent for long moments, as if to say whatever it was could be solved.

'What's wrong?'

I told him. At least he would listen and maybe I needed that. 'How can she want me to write about war in Sudan? War in Sudan!'

Chuka said nothing.

'I mean, don't you see?' I asked, desperate to make him understand. 'I want to write light, funny takes on travel, and to her I'm just an African who should write about struggles.'

'The problem is that many of these White people don't think we also dream,' he said.

I stared at him, astonished. 'Yes,' I said. 'Yes, exactly.'

'Chia, you'll find the right editor. There is definitely somebody in publishing who will understand. Just keep trying.'

My tears changed in tenor. I sobbed and sobbed, hugging him with a long exhalation of my body's breath. He did understand me. He saw all the places where I shone and all the places where I could shine.

'You get it,' I said, almost in wonder.

'Of course I do.'

'You never said anything.'

'You know I'm not a talker.'

Bolstered by the moment, the rapture of being known, our future together took shape for the first time. I told my mother about him, that he was divorced, no children, an engineer, Catholic, and not just Igbo but from Anambra State too. For a moment my mother was silent, stunned, because what were the odds – her free-range daughter untethered from the life expected of her, now ending up with just the right man from next door. A daughter almost forty years old too. In what world did a successful childless Igbo man marry a woman who was thirty-nine years old? My mother broke into song – *Abu m onye n'uwa, Chineke na-echelu m echiche oma* – which made me misty, because in my childhood, it was the church song she always sang in the face of joy. Chuka said his father was already making plans for the *iku aka* ceremony, and I thought how beautiful it sounded, the first stage of an Igbo marriage: *iku aka*, to knock on the door, to seek permission, to hope.

TO OUR PASSION, hope was now added. Our relationship a soft riverbed, my feet easily sinking and rising. We spoke Igbo in public, and made fun of Americans in restaurants, and it was like crawling together into a delightful secret tent. Chuka read about the publishing industry and said it made no sense how they kept publishing writers who were only recently teenagers. What could they know, when they hadn't lived life?

I enthusiastically agreed. I was always seeking out stories of writers who published their first books later in life. A new editor in New York, a woman named Molly who grew up in London, said, 'I understand what you want to do, but what you have here won't hold up for a book. You need more heft.'

'Then you'll get more heft,' Chuka said when I told him. 'Chia, this is progress. You're committed to this thing. You'll get there.'

'Yes,' I said. There is no elixir more potent than the genuine encouragement of a lovely person.

HE CALLED ME BABY, in a tone that reminded me of an older person from an older time. At the high-school graduation party of Enyinnaya's son, he called out 'Baby!' and at least five women looked up. They, too, were Baby. I had joined a cadre of women called Baby. I got up and went to him, smiling, thinking that the picture I carried in my mind of the life I wanted was not one in which I was called Baby. Babe or Babes, maybe, but not Baby.

We had arrived early for the party. My halter top began unravelling as I climbed out of the car. Chuka, amused, asked if we needed to go home so I could change, and hadn't he said those ropes looked impractical? He took my handbag while I retied the top more tightly behind my neck.

I didn't know Enyinnaya had walked up behind us until he said, 'Ahn-ahn, Chuka, why are you holding her handbag like her house-boy?' His first words. No greetings. It was an odd, tense moment, Enyinnaya stern and unsmiling, looking truly appalled. As if Chuka holding my bag was an existential failure. A sudden outsize tension hung between us on the driveway, the hum of arriving guests drowned by our silence. And this because of a handbag? All I wanted was to go back to a graduation party on a carefree summer day. I reached for the bag, but Chuka brushed me away.

'I am holding her handbag because I want to hold her handbag,' Chuka said steadily. Enyinnaya shrugged and moved ahead. Chuka looked softly at me and said, 'Sorry, sometimes Enyinnaya acts as if a nut in his head is loose, but he doesn't mean harm.' We walked into the house, Chuka still firmly holding my bag, and in my eyes, he swelled and became a hulking glorious god. Later, I told him I didn't understand how Enyinnaya was his closest friend; there was nothing wrong with Enyinnaya, of course, I added hastily, but they were so dissimilar.

'He stood by me when I was at my lowest,' Chuka said.

I looked at him and thought: He's mine. This solid-gold hunk of a man is mine. This man who chooses his side and stays steadfast. This breathing paean to loyalty. I was content, sated. I was where I was supposed to be.

Yet in quiet moments, alone, I feared that my contentment was a kind of resignation.

CHUKA SAID HIS FAMILY would go and see mine at the end of the month.

'I think we should compress as much as we can, do all the traditional ceremonies in one day, and then focus on the wedding, to save time,' he said. By saving time I knew he meant my age. At thirty-nine, there was a shrinking stretch for the two children he so wanted to have.

'A smaller ceremony here is fine with me but you know they'll want the wedding to be back home,' he said.

I stared at him. The wedding. I had never visualized a wedding. It existed only as a vague awareness somewhere in the back of my mind.

I thought of my mother saying 'Why did she use local printers?' about Mrs Okoye's daughter's wedding invitation, while gleefully examining the deficient card. She and Mrs Okoye detested each other and called each other friends. I imagined the wedding invitations my mother would print in London, two *C*s tastefully intertwined on champagne-pale paper. Soft tissue inside the envelope. *Chiamaka & Chukwuka* in sophisticated font. At the wedding, she would wear a blouse with dramatic puffed sleeves, the glittery stones on her George wrapper flashing as she walked. She would make sure Mrs Okoye got two or three of the lavish gift bags. Our parents would give us generous gifts: maybe a flat in London from Chuka's parents, maybe a bigger house in Maryland from mine. I would fold into a life no longer lived alone, have a baby, find a Jamaican nanny, and try for a second baby. Febechi, I knew, had her second at forty-three. I saw the attentive, patient father Chuka would be, bent over guarding our toddler on a tricycle, or on the floor with her, building a Lego house. So attractive, this vision, like photography in flattering light. But I felt only a gathering dread, a turmoil in my stomach, to face a truth I wished were not true: I did not want what I wanted to want.

'No,' I said quietly.

'What?'

'I'm not sure I'm ready,' I said.

He looked confused. I said 'ready' because 'ready' was softer, and I knew it was cowardly of me, because 'ready' could be taken to mean a delay rather than a conclusion.

'What?' he asked.

'I don't want your people to go and see my people,' I said.

There was a quickening in him, a flare of his nostrils.

'What do you mean, Chia? I told you my intention from day one.'

Later I thought of that word 'intention'. Women all over Nigeria haunted by that word, 'intention', fathers smouldering silently, mothers and aunties asking, 'What is his intention?' By asking and asking, they meant you had failed to make an intention happen, as intentions had often to be prodded and simpered and manipulated into being.

'I'm sorry, Chuka,' I said. 'I'm sorry.'

'Sorry about what?' He looked incredulous. 'Is there someone else?'

'No,' I said.

'Chiamaka, what are you talking about? What nonsense is this?'

His anger surprised me. He was so angry, angry that I had rejected him, or maybe his hurt had, as hurt often does, folded itself into angry shapes. His face was transformed, each plane hardened by rage, and he looked like a different person. A flash of fear shot through me, that he might slap me. But he didn't. He wouldn't. It was not in his nature. 'I don't understand. Tell me why? What do you mean?' he kept asking. But I did not know what to tell him, or even what to tell myself, and for a brief moment I thought of Aunty Chinwe once saying someone in her church was possessed. It was a kind of possession, the incomplete knowledge of ourselves.

'Chia, I was clear from the beginning that I'm not playing games. I want to honour you,' he said.

'I know. I'm sorry. I'm so sorry.' Honour you. I wished I could think of marriage as an honour, a badge bestowed on me. But I couldn't. The thought of marriage to Chuka felt like the truncating of my life to fit a new mould, and I could think only of what would change that I did not want changed.

Later, I sent him text messages saying I was sorry, and he never replied. Even the messages were spineless. What was I sorry for? How do you break a heart and then say you're sorry? Sorry would be acceptable to him, I knew, if I asked for another chance, to please come back. But I didn't. The root of his loving was duty; he loved as an act of dependable duty, and wasn't it childish of me to think this dull, to want an incandescent love, consuming, free of all onus? I stumbled through the following weeks, my mind furred in gloom. I was perplexed by the size of my own uncertainty. I woke with lucid visions of our passion, his urgency, my clothing drawn and pulled aside. What had I done, I asked myself, this wanton waste, this loss I had created for myself? But something was missing; it was there in the echo after sex, the silence we slipped into, which was not uncomfortable but empty. Did dreams serve a purpose and was it real to imagine what I wanted, and did it even exist? Febechi called me a few times, leaving curt 'please call me' messages; the peevish match-maker whose project had failed. When I finally returned her call, she said, 'Chia, this man is a catch. There isn't anything better out there. Life is not a novel.'

She could not possibly know that I secretly dreamed of writing a novel, but it felt like an unfair punch, dismissing what I felt, whatever it was, by calling it fiction. Why was a novel a metaphor for unrealistic, anyway? Novels had always felt to me truer to what was real.

'Honestly, you were never grateful that he loved you,' Febechi said with a sigh. For a long time afterwards, I thought of her accusation, because it was an accusation, that I was not grateful to have been loved. What is this gratitude to look like? Is it to be a state of being, to live adrift in gratitude because a man loves you?

Four

Before I met Chuka, I did once say to a man, 'I am grateful for you.' But it was different from Febechi's gratitude. Febechi meant the gratitude of a woman to be loved at all, which was not the same as a woman being loved in a way that made her feel whole. I said those words – 'I am grateful for you' – in a bookshop café in London, to the married Englishman who did not tell me he was married. Around his wrist he wore a thin silver bracelet. Do we like men who wear jewellery? No, but we liked this one. It began online, on a Jan Morris fan site. His thoughtful comments fascinated me, and I plied them with stars, even before I saved his profile photo of a lean-faced handsome White man. I had never saved a profile photo before, but nothing wrong with mild curiosity. He was just so appealing; I felt in reading him that I was learning from a person who wished others well. Anyway, he could be ninety years old using a photo he had plucked off the Internet. It was a few years after Darnell, and I was still coiled, still watchful, unwilling even to date casually. The

Englishman starred my comments too. I wrote, *The real benefit of travel is that you encounter the comforting ordinariness of everyone else.*

And he commented, *Couldn't have said this better.* Soon we were sending each other private messages, musings and links to articles, and when he didn't reply on weekends, I sent the subject line WAITING FOR GODOT.

I'm going to be in London, I wrote to him, a trip I hadn't planned on at all. *Would you like to meet for a cup of tea?* he asked, and suggested an independent bookshop. He told me later that he had slipped off his ring on the tube, just before walking the short distance to the bookshop. The slice of skin on his finger should have been lighter-toned and it wasn't, but I did not even consider his ring finger until the evening, weeks later, when he told me he was married. That first day we drank Earl Grey tea, his with sugar, mine without, and he stirred his for too long. He was nervous, his movements unsmooth. I felt tense, unable to meet his gaze. Exchanging messages had felt so right, and now here was reality, brooding with the unknown. At least he looked like his photo, with light hair falling untended across his face. But he was much taller than I had imagined, and more well-worn, his fingernails rough, his brown leather jacket faded to beige at the elbows. Both our teas were half-finished when he abruptly asked, 'Shall we take a walk?'

'Perfect idea!' I said, feeling a little silly.

As we walked, the awkwardness melted away. He said it had never felt so nice to be in London; he hadn't been in a while, he was hibernating at home writing his book. He said he thought much of poetry was really travel writing and I said much of poetry was poetry and he laughed. He flicked his hair back when he laughed. He looked at me – looked down at me, really, since he was so tall – his eyes tenderly baffled, as if he, too, was stunned to find such pleasure merely in walking the streets of London amid a cooling wind. 'Sorry!' he said to a man he nearly bumped into at a corner.

'You weren't paying attention,' I teased.

'No,' he said, and his 'no' spoke of unfolding mysteries. On a narrow street, he gestured and said this was the remnant of a century past. His arm brushed against mine. With evening fading, I felt a catch in my throat, as if I might burst into tears from a sense of impending loss.

Perhaps I fell in love that day; love happens long before we call it love. In the following weeks we took many long walks. I discovered how a city, because of another person's eyes, can become a glimmering sanctum, everything alight with interest, everything worth exploring. We browsed in Daunt Books, his favourite haunt, and did I know, he asked, that it first specialized in travel writing? We ate at a small basement restaurant on the Strand, pizza at an Italian place in Marylebone, lingered reading menus at restaurant doors. One day he slid a slender manuscript across the café table and told me I was the first person to read it; even his editor hadn't seen it yet. A history of English travel writing; he'd left his job in publishing to write it. I read it carefully, warmed by his trust. He wanted to read something of mine, and at first I baulked. 'It's not very good,' I said when I finally showed him my article about my trip to Qatar. We were walking across a rain-dampened park and he sat on a bench under an oak tree and read it aloud.

'"I have never heard a sound as beautiful as the Muslim call to prayer, at dawn, in Doha." What a marvellous beginning.'

His voice made me like my own words. He read poems aloud from an app on his phone and even when I didn't like the poems, his voice was all that mattered. It was a throwback, his voice, a smoky masculine sound, and listening to him, especially as he read, I felt myself held by brute desire. He read from *Arabian Sands*, a book he loved, and said perhaps we could take a day trip to Oxford sometime to see Wilfred Thesiger's photographs. A trip together.

'Yes, I'd love that,' I said. Newly ebullient, I added, 'I admire the curiosity and courage it took for people to go off to places they didn't know.'

'Isn't it more from disenchantment with their lives than curiosity about other lives?' he asked.

'Maybe both,' I said. I mentioned a famous travel writer, about his age, whose book I had just read. 'I think he has both.'

'Oh, he's rubbish,' he said, and his lips thinned and twisted, and his beauty was briefly lost. It was jealousy without envy's bile. I was disappointed, absurdly, as if he should be above the base instincts in our nature.

'Are you living the life you imagined you would?' I asked.

'No, but who is?'

'I think some people are.'

'Some people think some people are.'

'What do you mean? That nobody is? That's depressing.'

'Is it? I find it quite reassuring.'

'I need to believe some people are. Otherwise, what's the point of it all?'

He looked sober. 'Does it help to know that the world is full of people who are sadder than you?'

'But I'm not sad, I just dream,' I said, and laughed to lighten what suddenly seemed a dark descent. Later I thought of his words, 'Does it help to know that the world is full of people who are sadder than you?', because he said them when I did not know he was married, and after I knew he was married, they took on new meanings.

FOR HIM I ADOPTED a fake English accent. I did not know when I did; so immersed in him, and in our long talks, that soon I was saying 'heah' for 'here', and because I liked myself saying 'heah' I continued to say 'heah'. 'I think I'm starting to sound like you,' I said, and he said he had learned to sound posh at Oxford, but his Essex roots emerged when he said words like 'male'. There was a grandeur to his simplicity, to what he valued: he never used a thesaurus, he finished every book he started, he didn't eat fruit where it was not locally grown. I felt the weight of fate in coincidences, saw signs in our similarities. How could it not mean something, that we both disliked dogs?

'Joyce disliked dogs too,' he said. 'He carried stones in his pocket to throw at dogs.'

I patted playfully at his pocket and he laughed.

'I don't wish them harm,' he said. 'I just want them to stay away from me. I do love animals in the wild.'

'Me too,' I said.

I felt, with him, that I could lay bare all my quiet hungers. I told him I wanted to love lavishly and wanted to be loved lavishly. I felt shy saying this, but I saw in his eyes that he understood. At a tiny restaurant near the V&A, the waitress, whose hair tips were dyed turquoise, said to me, 'Aren't you beautiful!'

'Oh. Thank you,' I said.

'A plainer truth has never been told, and yet you seem surprised,' he said, watching me. 'It's sort of winning a lottery, isn't it, to be so beautiful?'

'How would I know?' I joked, a little awkward.

'I imagine it can bring pressure, too, for a woman.'

I looked at him, grateful for the delicacy of his observation. I told him how when I was little adults forgave me things and allowed me things, and how my mother fretted about pimples on my teenage face, and the evening my Aunty Jane said a TV newscaster was so beautiful and my mother said, 'She is nothing next to my Chiamaka.' My mother was smug with love and pride, but all I kept thinking was that I could not possibly be that beautiful, and what if I was no longer beautiful tomorrow and how could I keep being beautiful?

'I remember something else in my debate club in secondary school, in SS2,' I said.

'SS2?'

'Senior Secondary Two. Year ten here,' I said.

'SS sounded a bit worrying there,' he said and I laughed.

'I was a finalist for the debate prize, along with two boys. One of the boys won. He deserved to, he was better than me, but I was also good, and debate was actually the one thing I was good at. When our club leader talked about all three of us, she praised the boys for being so intelligent, and then she said I was very beautiful. I felt so hurt I went home and cried, but I didn't tell anybody, because I knew they would think I was complaining for nothing. Actually, I've never told anyone.'

'You've told me,' he said, and held my hand on the table. I wanted desperately to kiss him. The waitress returned with our drinks and glanced at our clasped hands and smiled a benevolent-fairy-godmother smile. It had been weeks and we hadn't kissed. We hadn't kissed because he hadn't tried. Each time we parted, we hugged a close, charged hug, pressed together, before he unclasped himself and backed away from me. His backing away had the quality of unheeding haste.

'Let's take things slow,' he said, part question and part statement; he had decided but still needed my assent. An English eccentricity, I thought, almost quaint, which only made him more desirable. Without touching, I breathed him in, soaked him in. I imagined that he lived in a small frayed flat full of books, and I imagined fixing up a flat that I had not seen. He was uninterested in money, and it amused me to think of how my mother would view him, my mother with her Igbo ideals. A man had to have money, preferably, and if he didn't, then 'potential' and 'hard work' could temporarily suffice, but a man uninterested in money? An absolute alien. Already I wanted him to meet my parents. Already I imagined our shared life between countries, England and America. One rainy afternoon, we were sitting in a casual bistro, a margherita pizza between us, and I watched him raise his glass of water to drink, and suddenly realized how happy I was. How very happy I was. From time to time, somebody would enter the restaurant, bringing a blast of cold air and the smell of wet roads.

'In America, this pizza would be twice as big with double the salt,' I said, laughing.

'When I went to America, I was astonished to be served potatoes for breakfast,' he said. 'Potatoes!'

'Well, at least it's made differently from dinner potatoes.'

'Americans have a sort of aggressive lack of sophistication, don't they?' he said.

I knew what he meant, I agreed even, but his words rankled. 'Every country has its philistines,' I said.

'I haven't upset you, have I?' he asked.

'No,' I said.

'By the way, the poem "America" by Claude McKay. Do you know it?' He sounded solicitous, pacifying.

'No.'

'"And see her might and granite wonders,"' he quoted.

'I don't know it,' I said.

He was watching me. 'I have upset you.'

'No, no. I think I just want you to like America, or at least not dislike it too much. Only because it's where I call home, and I'd like you to visit me or maybe just spend some time . . . It's stupid, I know.' Why did I feel so upset, as if a brick was about to slip out from underneath a perfect precarious house? The freight of my feelings for him almost frightened me.

'I don't dislike America, not at all. And now more so than ever. Why would you think that?'

'When we were talking about Jan Morris's American and British covers, you said American publishers tend to fussiness.'

I began to laugh, because I knew how silly I sounded, and he laughed and said, 'We better not talk about book covers, then.' He shifted his glass of water away from the table edge. 'You're not going back very soon?' There was a hesitation about him that might, in different circumstances, be read as weakness.

'Oh, no,' I said.

He leaned back, as if to take the full measure of me. We looked at each other. 'It feels so precious.'

'What?'

'Everything.'

'Yes,' I said. I was falling in love. I had fallen in love.

We took the same tube to the train station and then parted there, he to Essex and me to my parents' house in Buckinghamshire. Weeks passed and we grew closer, but still he hugged me and then backed away. We had taken things slowly enough. Why did we always have to meet in London? Why couldn't he ask me to dinner at his? He lived not far from where he grew up, and he made it sound very far away, a long unreachable distance, but when I checked online it was about forty minutes by train. I began to worry that he was closeted; there was his slightly effeminate manner, after all. He didn't have the kind of unfettered masculinity that thrust itself into the centre of everything. As a little boy he must have shared willingly; his mother would not have had to scold him to share. I told Omelogor that I was in love with the Englishman but things were still platonic. I was confused, reduced to reading unreadable signs.

'My only problem with White people is that they don't shower with soap,' Omelogor said.

'Omelogor!'

'When White people shower in films, have you ever seen them use soap? They just stand in the water for two seconds. They don't scrub the folds and holes. How can somebody be clean after that?' She was laughing her cackling laugh. 'How can we be managing a White man who doesn't use a sponge, and now on top of it, no action?'

I told her to be serious.

'Chia, you've never said that before,' she said softly.

'What?'

'That you're in love. You never said it with Darnell. Not in those words.'

'This is so different. I didn't know love is supposed to be so easy.'

'Maybe he's shy. Take the initiative. If you're too shy to tell him, then show him.'

I channelled Omelogor's courage. When we hugged at the train station, I gently lowered his face to mine and kissed him, all tongue and more tongue, and felt his desire until he drew away.

'I'm waiting for you to ask me to come home with you,' I mumbled.

'Chia,' he said. I looked up at him. Something spread on his face that made me anxious, as if a big engulfing flame were close, and I suddenly did not want him to say whatever it was he wanted to say.

'What's wrong?' I asked.

'I'm married.'

His words came out in a near-whisper, a secret only for me.

I stared blankly. 'What do you mean? You're separated?'

But he wasn't separated, he was married, and she worked long hours in a hospital and he went home each night to her.

'I wanted to tell you, and every day I didn't tell you, it became more impossible.'

My head felt light. I wondered what it said about my ability to see only what I wanted to see: his silence on weekends, his vagueness about the everyday details of his life.

'I was afraid of losing you. I know just how barking mad that sounds, but it's true,' he said.

I said nothing.

'I'm sorry,' he said.

I said nothing.

'I understand if you won't see me any more,' he said.

'No,' I said, because already tomorrow without him felt like exile.

He exhaled, elaborately, from relief, taking my hands in his. 'What are we going to do?' he asked. I pulled my hands free. I felt ambushed, unfairly ensnared in a guilt that was not of my making. 'What are we going to do?' How could he ask me that? Why would he ask me that, so soon after his revelation, as though he had not deceived me? I wanted to say, 'How dare you', and 'This is your doing, not ours', but I knew that because I had not turned and walked away as soon as he said he was married, it had indeed become ours. We went into the last café that was still open, near the escalator, and talked, and I wondered what he would tell his wife about being home so late. I shocked myself by how quickly the idea of a wife had sunk in. How calm I was. He said she was lovely but his marriage was stale. Stale. For a long time afterwards, I could not bear to hear anybody describe bread as stale.

WE MADE LOVE for the first time in my parents' house, on a flowered bedspread, in my room that reminded me of the year I failed my A levels, the year I lived there, mostly alone.

'I have my period,' I said hesitantly, and he said, 'Blood is what we are.'

He got up to get a towel from the bathroom and I touched the coffee-coloured spots splattered on his back. They would become so intimately known to me, those spots. He kissed my collarbone and rested his cheek against mine. So much tenderness. It didn't feel physical. It was a merging of those parts of us that dream, a full unmasking of two human beings. Afterwards he went to the bathroom and returned and began swiftly to get dressed. He sat on a chair, away from me, and I saw in his eyes something like regret, a faraway look. Moments before, hovering above me, he had said, 'I want to look at you', and now there he was upright and remote, his face shuttered, his shirt slightly creased. I wanted to cry. I sensed his withdrawal, this man who was not at ease with lies, who had never cheated on his wife. I would not cry. I would not cry. I should have walked away when he said he was married but I hadn't, and this was my fault. I thought of his question, 'What are we going to do?', and my anger flared. I would wrap myself in anger, my anger would protect me until he left; and then I would cry. He got up and sat on the bed next to me. 'Everything feels so precious,' he said quietly, and all became as it should be in the world.

ON TRAVEL-WRITING WEBSITES his posts were now different. *It might be helpful,* he wrote, *to be more specific when we send guidelines about destinations. Diverse city but what kind of diversity, an open-minded region but open-minded to whom? A village might, for example, be welcoming to Japanese but not Zambian travellers. A Black lesbian and a White lesbian might fare differently in a country we consider friendly to sexual minorities.*

I was proudly amused, and wondered what his readers would think. Would any of them think: He has fallen in love with a Black African woman and now sees the world through different eyes? As for me, I wrote my articles with only him in mind. He was my audience, before even myself. I read that Skopje was the most boring capital in Europe and decided to go, wondering what he would think of an article called 'Being Bored in an Already Boring Place'. I was going for two days, and before I left, we sat on a park bench looking at blog pictures of Skopje, so much unsaid between us, such as that we should have been going together, such as that we should not be as we were.

In Skopje, I sat in a rustic restaurant texting him. They didn't try to make their food decorative; my main was pork and leeks plopped onto a dish. A woman at the next table asked in heavily accented English if she could take a photograph with me. She was polite and

nicely dressed, a silk scarf splashed on her neck, her jacket hem fash-
ionably frayed. I wanted to say I'm not famous, until I realized she
didn't think I was famous. She was asking because I was Black. I said
yes and stood stiffly beside her as a smiling man, maybe her husband,
took the picture. They seemed like locals; it was not a touristy restaurant. I almost wished I were famous, to bring some worth to their
photos. I sent the Englishman a surreptitious picture of the couple
as they went back to their table. This had never happened to me
before, but I knew of Black travellers chased after and photographed,
in central and eastern Europe and in Asia. 'Surely not in today's
world,' the Englishman replied. He was sending me links to articles
about an erupting volcano in Iceland, a forming ash cloud which
meant that planes could not fly. I thought of tiny particles of ash
keeping huge planes down. 'I'm worried,' he wrote. 'I don't want you
stuck there with people taking circus pictures of you.' True enough,
my flights were cancelled, from Skopje to Budapest and from Budapest to London. In the airport I felt the hot flush of panic rise in my
chest, thinking of being trapped here for days or weeks, away from
the Englishman, in this city where I was a curiosity. Every flight was
cancelled, airline staff befuddled at the counters, saying they were
sorry they had no information. I was feeling slightly unwell, my stomach unsteady, the smell of garlic rising from my pores. In London the
Englishman was searching for options online and he called to say I
could take a bus to Germany, a twenty-four-hour drive, and I might
be stuck in Germany, but better that than in Skopje, where people
were photographing me like a bird with unusual feathers. I told him
I didn't really mind the photographing.

'Do you think they would have asked you if I was there with you?'
he asked.

His question surprised me. 'I don't know.'

'I wish I were there. I want to be trapped with you in a place that's
new to both of us.'

WHEN FINALLY I RETURNED to London days later, he held
me in a tight embrace that fell just short of dramatic, as if the ash

cloud could have lasted forever. It must have roiled his balance, because that evening he said in a high voice, trying to convince himself, 'Chia, I am going home to end my marriage.' The next day he said she had nobody – her parents died when she was young, and just last year her sister died of cancer in her arms. And so began a cycle: he would tell her this evening, next weekend, at the end of the month. Then he said he hadn't told her because he couldn't tell her, as she had nobody, and her grief for her sister was still so young. If the ash cloud hadn't happened, all this talk of telling her might not have started. I was sleeping poorly, awake before dawn wondering if he had finally done it. Each time I saw his face, I knew he hadn't and things formerly precious became tawdry and cheapened. I told him I loved him but this wasn't enough. Many times I stopped talking to him and texting him and meeting in my parents' house. Only to start again. I lied to friends and pretended he was single, but I lived always on the edge of panic, that something would slip and somebody would find out. Only Omelogor and Zikora knew he was married.

One day we were walking from the station to my parents' house and he said something about his childhood and crumpets, and I said, 'Crumpets!' and started laughing and he started laughing, and in the middle of my laughter I looked at a patch of dying winter grass and thought: I am sad. There was a softness to my sadness but I was sad. The last time I saw him, at the train station, I said I was returning to America and would not be back. 'Can I come and see you? I'll come and see you, I'll find a way . . .' he said, and let his voice trail off. He held my hand for a long time before he let go. I did not go into that station for many years, and when one day I did, I walked in and memory came at me, swift as a punch. The smell of a busy London train station, coffee and food and perfume and people, display boards blinking their train times, the bright shops and the escalators. My body stalled, by itself, on its own. I stumbled. So visceral, so deep, was the tidal rush of memory and regret, and loss, and longing for what could have been.

Zikora

All through the night, her mother sat near her but never touched her. In the airless hospital room, they were mostly silent. When Zikora screamed, a sudden sound as if torn from her, her mother said calmly in Igbo, 'This is what labour is like.'

Zikora said, 'No shit', but only in her mind, because even in her agony she dared not be disrespectful to her mother. She had prepared for pain, but this was not mere pain. It was something like pain and different from pain, spreading from her back to her thighs and then splitting her apart – vicious, crushing, refusing remorse. It felt like the Old Testament. A plague. Her body forsaken, a primitive storm raging at will. And yet they said she wasn't progressing. Each time Dr K examined her, an invasion of his gloved fingers, he announced, 'You're not progressing', as if it were her fault. What did 'progressing' mean anyway? How could she not be 'progressing' when this torment remained at its highest pitch, hour after hour, a saw wildly hacking away inside her, at her intestines and her spine, bent only on destruction. Her vision blurred. What is he talking about and what am I doing here? She wasn't ready, of course she wasn't ready, her due date was two weeks away. Chia was not yet back from Bolzano and her *New Mom* nightshirt hadn't arrived and her own mother had arrived only the day before. A sense of monstrous unpreparedness overwhelmed her. And now a new wave of pain slashing through her back, her stomach tossed about, her body confused as to which to do, vomit or poop. If only a scrap of respite could come, to make this stop just for long enough to feel like herself again. But waiting was the only cure. Helpless, hapless waiting. She had planned to say the Rosary between contractions, but her chaplet lay crumpled on the table. Prayer, an unreachable fort. She often said, 'I can't believe this', about all kinds of trifles, but only now did those words feel truly apt. Childbirth transcended imagination; if she were not now trapped in this, she could never have imagined the vulgar helplessness of birthing a child. So little felt controllable and so much unbearable: this oppressive tiny room, the feel of cloth against her skin. She yanked off her hospital gown, the flimsy thing with its effete dangling ropes that gaped open at the back, as if designed to humiliate. Naked, she perched on the edge of the bed and retched. The room's lights glared; inflamed with impossibility. She stood up and sat down, searching in vain for a comfortable position, and then she got on her hands and knees, her taut belly hanging in between. The nurse was saying, 'Breathe', or something like that. In her back, clenching cramps came and went like mean-spirited surprises. She wanted to crawl out of her skin; she wanted to shed herself of it all. If this was pain, then nothing she had experienced before in her life deserved to be called pain.

'I need it now!' Zikora shouted. 'I need the epidural now!'

Blood was rushing to her ears and her head, and the nurse's lips were moving but she heard no words.

'I need it now!' Zikora shouted again.

'Let's adjust this, the external uterine monitor, this thing right here on your belly,' the nurse said.

Thick false lashes sprouted from the nurse's upper lids like black feathers, and they made her eyes look heavy-lidded, half-closed, as though she were not as alert as she should be for this job. She moved the pad on Zikora's belly and tugged the belt that held it in place, her movements edged by impatience; she wanted to be done with this labour already. Zikora bristled. They were probably talking about her at the nurses' station, how fussy and ill-tempered she was from the beginning, unable to remain still at triage. Resentment rose like a tart taste in her throat, towards the nurses and towards all the women who soldiered through childbirth like unwounded warriors.

'I'd like to check you, just to be sure,' the nurse said.

Zikora tensed at the thought of being poked and prodded again. The nurse's nails must be sharp talons, to match those ridiculous lashes, and who was to say they wouldn't pierce the gloves and injure her cervix or whatever they were checking?

'Bring your feet up and let your legs fall apart,' the nurse said.

'What?'

'Bring your feet up and let your legs fall apart.'

Let your legs fall apart. How could legs fall apart? Imagine that! Zikora began to laugh. From somewhere outside herself, she heard the frenzied ring of her laughter. The nurse looked at her with the resigned expression of a person who had seen all the forms of madness that overtook birthing women lying on their backs with their bodies open to the world.

ZIKORA WAS TIRED, so tired, and she was floating in a void away from her body. Fatigue came in surges, as if she could not be more tired before a new tiredness crashed in. It felt humid and smothering, the fatigue, but it also promised respite if only she succumbed and let herself go. It frightened her. All the stories she knew of birthing gone wrong grew in sharp relief in her mind. She could die. She could die here, now, today, like Omelogor's cousin Chinyere died in the labour ward of a hospital in Lagos while about to birth her third child. The story was that Chinyere had been walking and breathing through contractions and chatting with the nurses, and then, mid-sentence, she had paused and collapsed and died. Zikora had barely known her but had mourned her. Now her heart was beating fast. Dr K said he would check on her in an hour. She could be dead in an hour, and she didn't trust these nurses to know what to do. But she couldn't die here, surely, not in America, in a good hospital near Washington, DC, paid for by her good health insurance. Chinyere had been in a good hospital – she remembered Chia saying all the rooms had huge flat-screen TVs – but no matter how good the hospital, everyone there was still breathing the mediocrity that was Nigerian air. Still, she had read somewhere that maternal mortality was higher in America than anywhere else in the Western world – or that it was only higher for Black women in America, she was no longer sure. She should have paid more attention. Dying happened here too. If she died in this hospital room, with its rolling table and picture of faded flowers on the wall, she would become just another tiny nameless dot in the data, one more of the forgotten multitudes of women dead from the blessing of pregnancy.

Dr K came in, looking unbearably calm.

'Dr K, I don't feel right, something is wrong,' she said, because something had to be wrong; childbirth could not be this malicious, this gratuitously cruel.

'Nothing is wrong, Zikora, it's all normal.'

'I'm so tired.'

'Epidural is almost here. I know it's uncomfortable, but what you feel is perfectly normal.'

He spoke as if she was being unreasonable and had to be patronized with a pacifying tone.

'You don't know how it feels!' she said. Before today, he was the nice Iranian doctor she had chosen for the compassion in his eyes. Today, he was an obtuse man sermonizing opaquely about an experience he would never have. 'Uncomfortable', indeed; such a mild word, so ill-suited. And what was 'normal', that Nature traded in superfluous pain? *His* intestines weren't aflame; *his* body wasn't caged by horrific waves that curled from back to front.

'Hold yourself together,' her mother said in Igbo, close to a whisper, as if anybody else could understand. *Jikota onwe gi.* Those words so often hissed or muttered or said with a sigh, whenever Zikora did something in a public place where she couldn't be slapped right away. Hold yourself together. It was a warning and a lament, saying don't let things spill out, and if they have, then gather back what you have revealed. Weakness and need, but especially need; her mother despised her showing any kind of need, no matter how benign.

She was nine when her father's second wife, Aunty Nwanneka, had her brother, Ugonna (your half-brother, her mother always said).

To visit the baby, her mother put Zikora's hair in a tight extra-neat bun and asked her to wear a going-out dress, pink and full-skirted, as though for Sunday Mass. Aunty Nwanneka's house smelled deliciously of frying food. The baby was asleep.

'Will you eat plantain and fish, Zikky?' Aunty Nwanneka asked.

Before Zikora could respond, her mother said politely, 'Zikora has eaten, thank you.'

All the while, Zikora was breathing and dreaming plantain and fish; she had eaten lunch at home, but that was irrelevant. She could taste the air, and so heady was it, that she almost got up and walked to the kitchen in a trance. She did get up but it was to pee, and as she came back out to the passage she saw Aunty Nwanneka going to check on the baby, and she told Aunty Nwanneka that she was a little hungry, just a little. Aunty Nwanneka brought her a plate, glistening oval pieces of plantain fried golden yellow and a piece of fish, the tail no less, fried crisp.

'You know children,' Aunty Nwanneka said to Zikora's mother, with a laugh.

Zikora faced the plate and ate without looking at her mother.

'We're actually on our way to Nike Lake,' her mother said abruptly, already standing while Zikora still had plantain pieces left on her plate. Outside, near the car, Zikora felt vertigo, a sensation of surprise rather than pain, as her mother's palm forcefully landed on her cheek.

'Don't disgrace me like that again,' her mother said quietly. Now here she was, disgracing her mother by not facing labour like a wordless stoic. Part of her mother's philosophy was to endure pain with pride, especially the kind of pain that belonged to women alone. When she had cramps as a teenager, her mother would say, 'Bear it, that is what it means to be a woman', and it was years before she knew that other girls took Buscopan for period pain.

THE ANAESTHETIST was full of false cheer, a freckle-faced man with a reddish moustache. He was talking too much, too fast. He reminded Zikora of her associate at work, Brad, also red-haired, chattering non-stop at meetings, his animation a shield for his incompetence.

'I need your help to get this done, okay? I need you to be very still, okay? It'll only take a minute, okay?'

He did not inspire confidence at all. Zikora began to wonder if he was qualified and where he had trained. Didn't women become paralysed from epidurals poorly done?

'That's your mom?' he asked. 'Hi, mom! I'd like you to help us out here, okay? Great. It helps to have family. If you can hold her so she doesn't move . . .'

Her mother, still seated on the armchair, said, 'She can manage.'

'Oh, okay,' he said, flustered.

'Okay,' the nurse repeated, and Zikora's fury flared, because it was an unnecessary comment, made only to taunt, this nurse saying 'Okay' with an eyebrows-raised look of false surprise.

Why make a face because her mother didn't want to hold her?

Did other mothers sit still as a coffin with their faces perfectly powdered and their gold-framed glasses perched just so? So why be surprised?

Maybe the nurse was thinking her baby's father should be here instead of her cold mother, which would show some nerve, because this nurse probably had three children with different absent men, unmannered children she screamed at while she stuck on those lashes in some cramped and overheated apartment in Baltimore. Zikora felt ugly and she felt angry, and she welcomed both like a bitter refuge. The middle of her head was pounding. How petty of childbirth to insist on all forms of pain, even headaches, common headaches. The anaesthetist would not stop talking. 'As still as you can, okay? Don't flinch, okay?' In stony silence, Zikora bent over and hugged the pillow, holding still through the cold smear of liquid and the brief prick of needle on her back. Tears filled her eyes; her anger began to curdle into a darkness close to grief. The medicine was spreading strangeness through her, a phantom sensation, as if half her body were cut off while the other half clung to the memory of that loss. It really should be Kwame here with her, sitting in that chair, finding a way to make a joke about 'nutty'. On an impulse, she reached for her mobile phone and sent him a text: *I'm in labour at East Memorial.* She held on to her phone, checking it again and again, willing Kwame's reply to appear on the screen, until Dr K asked her to push.

Two

They met at a vegan cookbook launch that she almost didn't attend. Stylish people milling about in a rooftop space downtown, while someone at the microphone described the complicated canapés circulating on trays. The author was a private chef, married to her colleague Jon.

'You two know each other?' was how Jon introduced her and Kwame, and Kwame leaned towards her, an act of casual intimacy, surprising but not inappropriate, as though they did know each other but only as good friends.

'When they say something tastes nutty, do we know which nut they mean? Because a walnut tastes nothing like a cashew,' Kwame said.

'I think they mean a texture, not a taste,' she said, and laughed, a little too eagerly, because she hadn't expected to meet anyone at this vegan cookbook launch, and now here was a clean-looking Black man and possibility trilling quietly in the air. On their first date he said, 'You're looking nutty good!' He had a boyish quality, which was not, as in some men, mere cover for immaturity; he was a grown-up who could still reach and touch in himself the wonder and innocence of childhood. 'Nutty' became their word. They used it as an adverb, an endearment, an adjective; and even when it wasn't funny, it was still theirs.

On the day they broke up, he said, looking her over, 'Hey, you nutty gorgeous person'. Neither of them knew they would break up that evening as they arrived at his law firm's gala holding hands, in his dark suit and her emerald dress, an elegant Black couple in Washington, DC, full of glittering starry promise. She had never known a man so attentive and free of restlessness. He volunteered details about his life, and at first his openness confused her because she had dated men who were so guarded they made secrets of simple things. When Kwame saw her, he let his face show its light; he didn't mask his delight or pretend not to care too much. He said 'I love you' before she did. He was supposed to be like other single straight successful Black men in DC: intoxicated by his own rarity, replete with romance opportunities, always holding out for the next better thing. At first she held her breath, waiting for him to change and rupture and reveal the sludgy sinister core. But he remained as he was, and so she unfurled wholly into their life together. She was thirteen months older but sometimes she felt much older, as though she knew better than he how uneven life's seams could be. He was blind to the insincerity in people and the ill will of friends, so often self-evident to her. He said jokingly that she needed to vet his friends, to protect him, a joke with the undertones of truth. 'You would have probably warned me about Maya,' he said once, with a laugh. Maya, the long-term girlfriend from college and into law school, who told him she was done because she was bored, and left him reeling and celibate for years. Zikora knew that when he said he loved how she 'got' him, left unsaid was that Maya hadn't. Or when he said he loved how similar their backgrounds were, he was saying Maya wasn't African, and being African was a plus. It pleased her competitive impulse, to have these advantages over his ex. But his American childhood seemed fraught in ways quite different from her Nigerian one. He had grown up in Northern Virginia with his dreams already dreamed for him. His Ghanaian father's immigrant intensity mixed with his African American mother, who was determined to open for him the many doors that history had slammed shut in her face. He and his younger brother had violin lessons and went to private school in formal uniforms, and every summer his father arranged tutors and pasted reading lists on the refrigerator. He had barely unsealed his undergrad acceptance letter from Cornell before his parents began talking about law school. The first time he took her to Sunday lunch at his parents' house in McLean, she was surprised by their warmth. From his stories, she had expected them to warily welcome her and then spend the meal measuring her worthiness. She hadn't expected to be so at ease with them, but she knew their approval would have been slower had she not had the right bona fides. His mother asked her about Watkins Dunn. 'The mayor's husband was a founding partner before he passed,' she said, which Zikora hadn't even known. His father asked about her father's oil business in Enugu, and Zikora said, 'Well, oil-servicing', a little surprised that Kwame had told them in that much detail about her life. His father listened intently when others spoke, tilting his head of salt-and-pepper hair with the demeanour of a charming diplomat. His mother mothered her, saying you haven't eaten much, you do eat meat, don't you, is the fruit tart okay. After lunch, his mother said they had to show Zikora a special performance and she sat at the piano and began to play, while Kwame groaned and his father sang the Ghanaian national anthem.

'I'm so glad he's finally moved on,' his mother said in her ear as they hugged goodbye.

In the car Kwame said, 'That could have gone a bit better', and she playfully punched his shoulder.

'Yours or mine?' Kwame asked.

'Mine.'

He always asked, even though they spent more time at her apartment; it was bigger than his, with taller windows, the living area flooded with light. He said all that natural light made his video games look better on the screen. Every Sunday he went with her to Mass, and at brunch afterwards he joked about how the Black Baptist church hadn't prepared him for all that Catholic sitting and standing. 'But it's all love,' he said. 'Martin Luther King said Jesus was "an extremist for love".'

He told her that his childhood visits to Ghana had petered out after his father became estranged from his family, over inheritance issues he never fully understood.

'My dad won't even talk about it,' he said.

'It's sad how these things can really divide families,' she said.

'I know. But we'll get me back to my African roots, right?'

'We will,' she said, and kissed his lips.

So this was happiness, to live in the first person plural. *We need milk. How about we do a night in this weekend? We're going to be late to this thing. Are we doing the museum or no?*

—————

THEY WENT TO HIS mother's summer family reunion and Zikora was moved to see that Kwame had ordered a T-shirt for her too, with his mother's family name printed above an image of a multi-branched tree. She wore it with a thrill of belonging as she watched him throw a Frisbee with the teenage boys in a field fringed by cherry trees. They were shouting and teasing one another, and she could see how much they liked and looked up to him, this successful older cousin, a DC lawyer steeped in cool. The women relatives flirted with him and he, generously, harmlessly, paid them compliments. How they loved him, eager to be near him, touch him, talk to him. Zikora was sitting in the shade, eating watermelon with his parents, and from time to time they laughed at Kwame's antics, their body language fluent with pride: he had turned out exactly as they had hoped. When they laughed, his mother nudged Zikora, an invitation to join in their mirth. Zikora felt herself sitting up straighter and eating more delicately, as though she had won a prize she was not sure she deserved and so needed to show her very best side.

THREE

She had always imagined her future in a vivid timeline – first a lucrative and prestigious job, then a splashy Catholic wedding, followed shortly by two children, or maybe three. Minor details changed from time to time – sometimes she saw herself in London, walking briskly to work on foggy mornings, or in Lagos reading briefs in her air-conditioned SUV, or on a different American coast, in California, wearing open-toed shoes to work – but the fundamentals remained unchanged. She did her part, doggedly pursuing the job at Watkins Dunn, and then waited for the heavens to roll out the rest as they should. But the blithe heavens seemed oblivious. She watched the years glide past, and relationships come and go, always thinking: It has to be the next man, it can't not be the next man. Why did it not happen? She had never doubted that marriage would happen, as naturally as day becomes night. A wedding at twenty-seven or twenty-eight was ideal, but twenty-nine was fine too, and by her thirtieth birthday she felt cast out in the wilderness of her mind. Wedding invitations were arriving from friends in Nigeria and here in America, and she was sickened by the envelopes with their subdued sheen, their words written in floral font. The heavens had turned a key and marriages were raining down for everybody else but her. As her thirty-first birthday approached, she felt more sanguine, because she had begun saying novenas, to St Joseph, husband of the Blessed Virgin; to Raphael the Archangel, who had helped a couple in the Book of Tobit; and most often to the Immaculate Heart of Mary. Reciting simple prayers for nine days and then starting again. The repetition brought calm, like a softly moving cloud, the rise and fall of wind, the assurance that hers would come, and come soon. She knew the pope was unwell – he looked frailer by the day, brokenly bent and clutching his staff – but when she woke to the news that he had died, shock spread numbly through her. John Paul II was gone and her certainties were breaking apart and the pieces blinded her. She had been eight when the pope visited Nigeria, and his visit felt even more momentous because her mother said, 'This is his first time travelling since they shot him, and he's coming here', as if it was a sign of how special Nigerians were and how special she and her mother were. The pope's gentle face had smiled from the gilt-edged brooch perched on her mother's collar, and from the framed photo hanging on their dining-room wall, and from church almanacs lying around the house. A face she knew well, but how unprepared she was to see his smile in person, and him, smaller than she expected, vital and vibrant, his skin pinking in the sun, but still no less Christlike. He seemed to come from a blessed spectral place, a generous place, from where he came to bring them only good. That day, in the crowd of people lining the road to the field, she and her mother and aunties were in front, close enough to reach out and touch the pope's jeep, because Father Damian had saved them a space, and the sun briefly fell as the pope raised his hand and waved at her. The pope waved at her and smiled at her, and in that moment when his hand was raised, joy as she had never known before descended from above and rested on her. She was so happy, so unutterably happy. He saw her. She never doubted that he saw her. Her life lay wide open then, her dreams' path secure. Now he was dead and her dreams were no longer nesting where they should. She was almost thirty-one years old and she was unmarried and there was no serious man on the scene. Her breathing quickened while her spirits sank. Her phone was ringing, Chia calling, and she exhaled calmly before she answered, but hardly had Chia said 'Zikor' than Zikora found herself weeping. Her nose was running and she was coughing from choking tears. She had never been so emptied of self-control, crying like that. She should have been married with a child by now; her life was not where it was supposed to be, and she did not know why other people were being given what she too deserved. Her wailing alarmed and confused Chia. 'Zikor, stop crying, please. *Biko I bezina,*' Chia kept saying.

When Chia came down from Philadelphia to see her that weekend, she felt sorry and a little ashamed of the naked desperation she had displayed. Chia urged her, again, to try online dating and she, again, resisted. All she could think of were the TV commercials with unlikely couples looking too blissful, the soft lighting and hopeful music that had a fraudulent tinge, as if designed to lure. Advertising herself on the Internet was out of the question, the final shame. What if one of her classmates saw her picture online? Well, Chia said, if your classmates see your picture, then they are on the dating site, too.

'I would be on the dating sites if my heart wasn't fully taken by Darnell,' Chia said. Darling dreamy Chia, her gauzy expression unchanged since primary school, when she was just 'the twins' little sister', two classes below Zikora. Zikora would go to their house to swim in the pool that was bigger than the Hotel Presidential pool, and there would be Chia, in dresses too pretty for just staying at home, pampered but somehow unspoiled, offering to get her a towel or a bottle of Fanta; courting her, so eager to be liked, and so unaware of her own appeal. 'Not the brightest pea in the pod,' her mother said once about Chia, and Zikora felt the urge to defend Chia, even then, before they were really friends. Not until they both moved to America after secondary school, and found themselves in Philadelphia and then in Maryland, did a real friendship of equals begin.

'Zikor, I'll set up the online dating profile for you. Just try it and see,' Chia said, and Zikora gave in.

In the photograph Chia used, Zikora was sitting at an outdoor café, laughing a carefree laugh in dappled light. Not a bad picture. She signed on and looked warily at potential matches, clicking on each with a reluctant finger, but soon she began to check her always-full mailbox with a sweet rush of anticipation; one of those messages might be from my husband, she would think. She talked to a few on the phone. One of them asked, 'How's your cat?' and she hung up; it was the second conversation and he still mistook her for someone else. Only one she agreed to meet in a bar downtown. On the dating site, he belonged to the subgroup she had favourited from the start, International Black, which she understood to mean non-American Black. A tall Jamaican lawyer, chocolate and thick in his profile photo, responsible-sounding over the phone. His Jamaican accent pleased her ear. She perched expectantly on a barstool, prepared that he might be fatter or shorter, because she knew people used younger photos of themselves, but absurdly, it was a slight, skinny light-skinned man who appeared and said 'Hi, Zikora?' as if all was normal. It was indeed him, the voice and the accent were the same. He made to sit down while she gathered her phone and handbag and left.

She tried another dating site, for Black people living in the DMV, where most of the profiles displayed international travel laurels: pictures of passport pages and the Eiffel Tower, landscapes from descending planes. *I love to travel, do you love to travel?* She thought it a plebeian status symbol, this obsession with international travel that Black Americans had, like people from a bush village boasting about city trips. *Can I come through?* Many Black men asked after a few text messages. *Can I come through now?* How did they know she wouldn't be waiting with a sharpened knife or a poisoned drink?

She tried a Christian dating site but it felt ghostly, with too few men, and even fewer Black men. The only man she matched with looked like the man in the news who had just killed two women and put them in trash bags. She deleted all her accounts. Online dating felt faithless, as if she was doubting the assurance that hers would come.

BY THE TIME she considered freezing her eggs, she was in her mid-thirties. 'I would not advise it at your age. I would advise you start IVF to try and conceive now,' the doctor said, while she nodded sagely to conceal her devastation. Try and conceive now. If she could conceive now, she would not be in his fertility clinic for a consultation about freezing her eggs. Or maybe the doctor meant a sperm donor, which was out of the question, almost blasphemous, to have a baby alone with a father whose provenance was unknown. She left the clinic and drove back to work, and she did not know it then, but she would soon have two relationships with men who were thieves of time, because she stayed waiting for them to propose, waiting while her late thirties slid past, and waiting still. If she wanted a nice necklace, or a holiday, or a condo, she could swipe her credit card and it would be hers, but her truest longing, for marriage, depended on someone else.

Four

The first thief of time had eyes that were never still. He was rabidly ambitious, restless, casting about for what business opportunity to try next, what new peaks to aim for. Seated across from him in restaurants, she always felt like turning back or sideways to see what he was glancing at. He wore too-strong cologne and everything he touched, every room he walked into, smelled of leathery rum. It gave her a mild headache but she never told him. He had a law degree from Enugu, an MBA from somewhere in the Midwest, and a master's in public health from College Park. He was always going to the Baltimore port to ship containers to Lagos, and he liked the word 'dabble'. I dabble in real estate. I dabble in investments. I dabble in pharmaceuticals. The first time she visited him, she was stunned by the state of his house. Cobwebs hung silkily from the ceiling, half-eaten yogurt furred by mould sat on his nightstand, and on the floor by his bed were cups with the dregs of sticky-looking liquid, old beer or maybe juice. The dried pastry crumbs spread over his sofa seemed not just ignored but apparently unseen. How could he appear in public washed and crisply ironed, haircut sharp and shoes shining, and yet insouciantly live in such filth? She felt almost frightened, as if his terrible hygiene held a meaning, a clue not yet deciphered but undoubtedly dark.

'Sorry, it's just that I have not had a woman in this house in ages; you're the first in a long time,' he said, smiling, and waiting for her to look pleased. On her next visit, plates piled with the chewed remnants of chicken bones had been left on his dining table as if he hadn't known she was coming. An oily spoon sat in a dirty bowl near his bed. He said, 'I'll clean it up, sorry', but he sounded unpersuasive, almost breezy, because he expected that she would offer to do it herself. And she did; in her high heels, she wiped his kitchen counters and washed his dishes before they went out to see a movie.

'Do you want children?' he asked, more than a year into her waiting.

'Yes, very much.'

'Have you ever been pregnant before?'

His question was lightly asked but she heard its undertone of ruthless sniffing. It surprised her, and upset her, to think he was the kind of Igbo man who wanted proof of fertility before he proposed. Backward, uneducated men did this ugly hedging, this bartering of baby for marriage; not men like him with many degrees, who donated to the state Democratic Party and played golf with Americans in Turf Valley. His progressive veneer must be thin, selective, maybe even all smoke, and she worried about what else was yet to be revealed. In another time of her life, she would have told him to go to hell with that question.

'No,' she said.

'Your mother had problems having other children?'

'She got pregnant many times, she just had miscarriages,' Zikora said and heard the defensiveness in her own voice. She saw now why he had asked: because she was an only child, she might be infected with the single-child curse at best and infertility at worst.

'We can start trying. What do you think?' He was sitting up in bed looking at her, his expression magnanimous, pleased with himself, as if he was giving her a gift. Was it a proposal? Of course she wanted a proposal without being first asked to get pregnant, and yet her excitement was rising, despite herself.

'I think it's not a bad idea,' she said, and laughed.

'I don't believe in nannies,' he said.

'What?'

'Once it happens, you need to organize your work situation, because I don't believe in nannies.'

Zikora leaned back on the pillow and said nothing. Even the duvet smelled of his cologne.

'I will provide everything for you, my darling,' he said, gently pulling her to him. 'Of course I will; you don't have to worry about that.'

He thought she needed reassurance that he would provide for her. He could not comprehend that she might not want to be unemployed for years, or that she, too, needed to do things in the world, to own things for herself. How baffling, this blindness of his, for someone so ambitious. Or maybe it was the nature of ambition, to be unable to see other instances of itself. She had felt from the beginning that she and the first thief of time saw life's shape in sharply different ways, like those images people sent around asking if you saw grey or if you saw pink, because different people saw different colours even though they were looking at the same thing. Still, she held on because people changed, and she could change him. Let's get married first, she thought, let me get pregnant first. She continued washing the dishes left on his table; at least there was progress as he no longer kept any under his bed.

Once, when she had stopped taking her birth-control pills, he musingly said, 'My father is a pillar of the Anglican church in Mbaise. I don't mind a Catholic wedding, but I don't know if he'll accept it.'

'I'm flexible,' she said, a little too quickly, before her face could show its dismay. Holes cratered in her heart at the thought of a wedding that was not Catholic, an insipid ceremony in a Protestant church; she would not even feel married afterwards, but she didn't want to dwell on it. They could get a Catholic blessing after the wedding, and once they were in earnest planning, she might yet convince him that Protestants didn't care about mixed marriages as Catholics did. What mattered was that they first set sail. Then Chidimma sent her a photo of a wedding invitation. She was in CVS, after work, looking for a supplement she had read about that increased fertility. Later, she would remember this with bitter irony, holding the bottle of pills in its pink and blue packet, while looking at the image on her screen. Chidimma had been a forgettable person in secondary school, but after moving to Houston to marry a man who ended up in prison, she became the bulldog of gossip, sending unwanted updates to everyone about everyone else. At first, Zikora was confused to see his full name in cursive font, before a cold shiver of realization dawned, that he was about to marry a girl in Nigeria. She shook her head, and shook it again. She felt herself suddenly inside a Nollywood film that relied cheaply on caprice and coincidence. She wondered at the nature of deceit. It seemed so unnecessary, that he would bother with this elaborate charade. She was already sleeping with him and he hadn't needed to lie about marriage, if sex was what he was after. Or had he asked different women, planning to bestow the prize of marriage on whoever got pregnant first? She wanted to know, she really did, to quiet her mind, but Chia told her not to confront him, to simply block his number and move on. 'What is he going to tell you that will make sense to you?' Chia asked.

Zikora felt a bifurcation of self, two parts of her existing in parallel. At work she was meticulous, sceptical, reading everything twice and asking questions, but with men she blundered ahead, wanting to believe whatever she was told.

THE OTHER THIEF of time was a man who sulked like a child. Sometimes for no reason at all he would go silent for hours or days, his lower lip jutting out like a toddler who believed himself unfairly deprived. If she tried talking to him before he was ready to talk, he would lapse into humming, tuneless humming. With him, she felt like a medium, intuiting reasons and mending faults whose boundaries were unknown to her. 'I'm very sorry,' she would end up saying, unsure what the apology was for. He liked her apologies best when they were tearful. He rained praises on Ellen Johnson Sirleaf and Angela Merkel; 'I love powerful women,' he declared often; but whenever she disagreed with him, he snapped, 'That's disrespect-ful!' He liked to talk about Nigerian politics and American politics, and he was insightful and funny – 'American politicians are beggars and Nigerian politicians are thieves, but in the end all of them are obsessed with money,' he said once – but of their relationship he said little, and so she was left searching his gestures for meaning. One day he brought her a surprise gift in an elegant paper bag, which was unlike him, to give a present for the sake of it. He was frugal, he considered restaurants a scam; scanning menus, he would say, 'This entrée will pay for one week's groceries.' A square box swaddled in soft cream paper. She felt her stomach knot and unknot, certain it was a ring because there was nothing else it could be. He had never asked what kind of ring she liked, but it didn't matter because she could always buy herself another ring and of course tell everyone that it was from him. She lifted the soft paper sheet by sheet, to savour the moment before she got to the box, and glanced up to see him grin-ning down at her. The box revealed a pink candle, its wick sticking up tall.

'I remember you said you like scented candles,' he said.

She paused before she said thank you. Humiliation swirled richly in that pause. She had never told him she liked scented candles, because she did not like scented candles at all. They were fire hazards for mundane rewards; she didn't see the point when you could get air fresheners instead. She left the scented candle, still in its box, on her dresser. If he gave her a scented candle, it meant the person who liked scented candles was gone from the landscape of his life, or maybe the person who liked scented candles had angrily rejected this candle and was waiting for other forms of atonement from him. She would never ask him about it; silence was her only refuge from the full force of humiliation that would shrink her and make her small. She could have hidden or thrown away the candle, but each time she walked past her dresser she saw a reminder of what she had chosen to endure. And endure she would, because she was acidly aware of time. She was thirty-eight years old and he was a Catholic Igbo man, employed at the CDC, who was good company on his good days. If he proposed soon, she could have her two children, back to back, before turning forty-two. She had read somewhere that the risk of autism increased with the mother's age, as if she didn't have enough to worry about. Somebody on one of her Catholic online groups posted: *All of you waiting on God, remember that Sarah gave birth to Isaac at an advanced age. Remember Elizabeth and John the Baptist. Do not despair.* She did despair, because this was precisely the root of her fear, having a child at an advanced age. She wanted to stop her birth control, but not unless she was sure he planned to propose, and in roundabout ways she tried to ask, but she could not ask directly. Some last scraps of pride had to be preserved.

'What are we doing?' she would ask, and he would say, 'Enjoying each other.' 'What future do you see for us?' and he would say, 'A very bright future.' Marriage self-help guides had always seemed silly to her, their generalizations too sweeping and coarse, but she began reading them because it couldn't hurt just to see. *Be intentional. Show you want to get married without showing you want to get married. He'll run if you're too pushy. It's true about men and food.* Sometimes he met her at the metro stop, and as soon as they got back to her apartment, she would shrug off her work bag and pour him a beer, already heating up rice and stew and sliding salmon portions in the oven. This to show how seamlessly she handled work and home. When he stayed over, she packed his lunch for work, turkey and cheddar sandwiches wrapped in parchment to keep sogginess away. Weekends she cooked batches of stew and okra soup and jollof rice, and took them to his apartment in containers for his freezer. He didn't propose. *Pretend you might be pregnant*, the guide said, but that she couldn't do. She just couldn't, and it was not only because pregnancy still brought a half shadow of pain from the past. One Sunday he was sprawled on his sofa watching an English Premier League match on a sports channel Zikora had never heard of, shouting from time to time, 'Come on, Arsenal! Come on, Arsenal!'

Next to his speaker lay his PlayStation, wires rolled up, like a patient mistress waiting for him. He sat up to open a carton of chicken wings delivered from a pizza place. He glanced sideways at her and asked, 'You want wings, babe?' She shook her head no and he ate two wings and went back to watching his game. She knew in that moment that he was never going to propose. He liked her, the convenience of her, but not enough to disrupt his life before he was ready. And he wasn't ready, he didn't have to be ready, he wasn't agonizing about the age of his eggs. Whenever he was ready, there would be another woman willing to make his sandwiches and slip an apple into his bag for work. Zikora almost envied him this, the luxury of walking at his own pace, free of biology's hysterical constraints.

FIVE

'I really thought he would propose on your birthday, Zikor,' Chia said of that second thief of time. Zikora flinched. She didn't want to bare her distress while eating pancakes in a new brunch spot in Dupont Circle. Especially not with Omelogor sitting beside her. She always felt on edge with Omelogor, as though she needed to be alert and keep watch, but for what she could never really say. Omelogor was always so singularly sure, so confident, her certainties thick with judgement, as if she was saying that everyone else was inadequate.

'*You* should have proposed, Zikora,' Omelogor said. 'If your relationship is solid, it shouldn't matter who proposes.'

Zikora didn't respond, irritation lodged like a tension in her temples. She sipped her latte and scanned news headlines on her phone. She should have declined Chia's invitation, instead of bringing her deflated spirits here, to be further flattened. 'Omelogor is in town, let's do brunch, Zikor, just come, please, just come,' Chia had said,

Chia always wanting everybody to hold hands and go singing into the sunset.

'Men can be shy and weak. Sometimes they need a nudge to do what they want to do anyway,' Omelogor said.

Zikora wished she would shut up, with her half-baked sense of omniscience, laying out opinions she thought were indelible truths. Imagine asking her to propose to an Igbo man – as if Omelogor didn't know the utter draining of dignity that would be. Omelogor's was the kind of idea so removed from real life that you only suggested it to other people and never to yourself. He was gone, anyway, that second thief of time. She had reined in her tending of him, to see if he might worry about losing her, and his response was simply to drift away.

'The problem is men are confused. The world is changing and they hear a lot of don'ts but nobody is telling them the dos.' Omelogor was still blathering. Their table was spread with too much food, bean burritos and truffle eggs, French toast and avocado toast; Omelogor had ordered many dishes just 'to try'. Zikora recognized this profligate strain in Nigerians of means – her father did it too, when he visited America, excessively ordering what he wouldn't eat and didn't need, but for once it repulsed her.

'If he wanted to propose, he would have proposed,' Chia said. Chia was drinking her second or third mimosa; her pale pink nails looked feminine, almost delicate, against the thin stem of her flute.

'Zikora doesn't have time for us today,' Omelogor teased.

Zikora shrugged, not looking up from her phone. 'Just reading about the pope.'

'I didn't know popes could resign,' Chia said.

'Retire,' Zikora said. 'He retired; resign makes it sound bad.'

'Abdicate. He abdicated his throne,' Omelogor said, and chuckled. The waiter came by with a jug of ice water to refill their glasses.

Omelogor had placed her sunglasses case next to her glass, a tall domed case in navy suede that spoke of high style. The waiter said, 'I love that!' and Omelogor said, 'Thank you', and the waiter said, 'As beautiful as the owner', and Omelogor said, 'How would you know?' and the waiter laughed. Did that even make sense? 'How would you know?' How would he know that she was as beautiful as her sunglasses case? But the waiter, with his short dreads and a dragon tattoo on his neck, already looked lovestruck, hovering and smiling at Omelogor. Omelogor asked for a whisky and he asked if she meant a whisky cocktail and she said she meant whisky neat and then she asked him, 'Don't you like your things neat?'

Omelogor was enjoying it, looking him in the eye with her mystery, her bold playful manner which had mockery at its tips, as if she was sending an invitation that said things might be smooth or things might be rocky and she didn't know which. Chia once said Omelogor had turned down two marriage proposals in the space of months. Why were men so drawn to her anyway? She was pretty enough, not stunning like Chia, and she had that kind of thick body men liked, large breasts and a behind entirely out of proportion that looked obscene in tight jeans. But her interactions with men had an uncharitable air. She wasn't nurturing, she didn't take care of men, and in this there was arrogance because she believed she didn't need to. Why did they keep coming after her?

The waiter had drifted from her attention, and she was talking about resigning from work to attend graduate school in America. Next year, or the year after. Zikora knew she was expected to join in the conversation, which felt to her like a gimmick. Who in their right minds decided to return to graduate school to study pornography, for goodness' sake? Omelogor was probably just running away from Nigeria. Everyone knew she would be successful, but the speed of her success was suspect. Ten years ago she could already afford to send her brother to England to do a postgraduate course. Impossible on an honest banker's salary alone. Nigerian banks were cesspits; if you scraped the hands of all the successful bankers, you would get fetid manure. Omelogor had no doubt soiled hers. Maybe she was about to be caught, and graduate school in America was her planned escape.

'The programme director said I don't need to take the GRE, which is good,' Omelogor said. Of course an exception had been made for her. Even before they met in SS3, Zikora had thought of

Omelogor as a person who expected that exceptions would be made for her, because exceptions were always being made for her. Zikora and her friends in the university secondary school in Enugu campus knew the lore of Omelogor in Nsukka campus, the cool girl the boys were chasing who played all the time but always floated on top with the best results. And she was so bright they let her take literature and geography, instead of choosing one. And she got the best junior secondary school result in the history of both campuses of the school. And she was dating older guys already in university.

'Pornography is not a moral issue, it's a social issue. My theory is that it has become a teacher for young people and it's a very bad teacher because it's unrealistic and it demeans women and gives a false sense of what sex is. Young people get the wrong tools that they end up using for the rest of their lives,' Omelogor said.

'That's actually interesting. I hadn't thought of it like that.' Chia was crowing, as always in thrall to her cousin.

'We should be asking who is teaching children about sex,' Omelogor said. 'Where did you learn about sex, Chia?'

'From you, and no wonder I'm single,' Chia said, and they laughed.

'I learned mostly from novels,' Omelogor said. 'Not the best teachers either.'

'Maybe after grad school, you'll just stay, live here, and try and survive without being a Nigerian madam,' Chia said, teasingly.

'Nothing beats living in your own country if you can afford the life you want,' Omelogor said.

'Until you have an accident,' Zikora said, looking up from her phone. 'There isn't one proper hospital trauma unit in the whole of Nigeria.'

'I know, it's scary,' Omelogor said, unfazed, and Zikora felt disappointed to have failed at annoying her.

'So you want to make people stop watching pornography? With an academic thesis?' Zikora asked.

'Oh no, people will always watch porn. I just want to get enough people to laugh at how stupid it is.'

Zikora had hoped for some defensiveness, and now felt at a loss.

'Studying pornography feels too much like sensationalism for its own sake.'

'Pornography is one of the biggest industries in the world, with real social consequences. It is "sensationalism" only if you think it's a moral issue that we should pretend doesn't exist.'

The criticism of Omelogor's words nettled her. 'And what are these real social consequences of pornography? Having sex?'

'Women are dying from what porn teaches men,' Omelogor said. 'I was looking at some statistics the other day, of hospital visits after forced anal, deaths and near deaths after choking.'

'Your waiter loverboy is hovering. Do you want another one?' Chia asked, pointing at Omelogor's glass. And then, as if to soften the air, or cheer Zikora up, or both, she said, 'Zikor, I wonder who the new pope will be.'

'Somebody like Pope John Paul, I hope,' Zikora said.

'Ha!' Omelogor said, a provocative mocking sound.

'Pope John Paul was lovely,' Chia said. Chia was a hazy Catholic who sometimes went to Mass and sometimes didn't, but Zikora knew she still retained the reticence about criticizing the church they had all absorbed while growing up.

'Pope John Paul was too much of a politician and a stage performer,' Omelogor said.

'What are you talking about?' Zikora felt irritation again tightening itself around her.

'Never mind Benedict the Wehrmacht soldier in Nazi Germany,' Omelogor added, and laughed, leaning back, enjoying herself. She pronounced the German word with the V sound. She had the kind of reckless insouciance of the deliberate blasphemers, those Catholics who thought themselves too clever, too full of information about the church. Zikora didn't even know if Omelogor still went to Mass, or if she had joined those Pentecostal churches led by Nigerian pastors with private jets. She was at peace with the agnosticism of others, her faith a sufficient lone plant if it needed to be. Still, these displays irritated her.

'Zikora, where did you learn about sex?' Omelogor asked, and Zikora pretended not to have heard. Suddenly she wanted the solitude of her apartment. She got up and told Chia she had to catch up on some work, but she was leaving to escape the hole of despair that threatened to swallow her whole.

ZIKORA WOULD NEVER admit this to anybody, but Pope Benedict left a sourness in her soul. There was something shifty about his hooded sunken eyes. She knew he had never been a Nazi, just a helpless young man forced to join the German army, but she felt nervous watching him on television, as though some unseemly secrets might suddenly tumble out and bring shame to the church. She didn't expect any pope to match John Paul II, but she at least wanted to feel an uplift of spirit on looking at the pope. That Pope Benedict chose to retire made her hopeful and secretly happy. She read articles on Catholic websites about the upcoming papal conclave, but the analysis felt too ordinary, too secular: how the Italians wanted an Italian, and Latin America was jostling for one of theirs, and nobody knew who the North Americans would back. It brought a dismal terranean quality to an election she believed should be celestial, guided only by the Spirit. So she stopped reading and looked away. Just as she refused to think of the priests back home who were trailed by sordid stories: the priest professor who lured teenage girls into his bedroom and then locked the door, the campus chaplain who slapped Mass servers and had a wife and kids. If she didn't look, then she wouldn't have to think, a habit of evasion steeped in the kind of fear she dared not even call fear, because if she called it fear, then her faith was not strong enough to bear what her thinking might reveal. 'If you start thinking, you never stop, so best not to start,' somebody had said once in a fellowship group in university, and she remembered that quote, not quite agreeing but seeing the usefulness of it. So she looked away. Always she looked away. If she saw news articles about Catholic priests abusing children, she quickly scrolled past, never reading them, because child sex abuse felt to her separate from the church she knew; it was an American thing, a Western thing, a depraved foreign thing. Even though she stopped reading about the papal conclave, she still wondered who the pope might be. What if it turned out to be Cardinal Arinze? Too exciting even to imagine, a Nigerian man, an Igbo man, her mother's distant relative from Eziowelle, as the Vicar of Christ. But even in her determination not to think of it politically, it felt too unlikely that an African would emerge pope.

On the first day of the conclave, her mother called to ask, 'Are you following?'

'Yes,' she said. They spoke so rarely, she and her mother, their silences often weighted with things unsaid. The only unburdened silence she remembered between them was in church, when they would arrive a little early for benediction on slow Sunday evenings and kneel next to each other in the incense-scented stillness, so close that their arms almost touched, until the Mass servers appeared to prepare the altar.

'They will most likely elect Cardinal Scola, the one from Milan, but the Argentinian is the better choice, because it's the intelligence of the Jesuits that will save the church in the next century,' her mother said, and Zikora made a sound to show she agreed, even though she didn't know any details about the cardinals.

Black smoke rose from the Sistine Chapel on the first day of the conclave, and she watched on TV as it turned greyish before it disappeared and she wondered what they burned to make it so, feeling a depth of disappointment that jarred her. A new pope meant a new beginning and she needed desperately to believe that it was not too late for her, almost thirty-nine years old and the future a wasteland scrubbed of eligible men. When white smoke rose like purified clouds from the chimney the next day, her heart leaped. And there was Pope Francis emerging on the balcony of St Peter's Basilica, solemn and majestic and humble. He was unselfconscious, she could see that right away; he did not regard himself, did not seek to admire himself through other people's eyes, and so in this way he was Christlike, and when he spoke, he made a small joke, a joke that brought a smile to thousands of faces. So beautiful to see his humour, his humanity, and by the time he began to lead the crowd in prayer, Zikora was in tears. Holy Mary, Mother of God, pray for us sinners, now and at the hour of our death.

She saw a blessing in this, a sign. Excitement lifted and boosted her spirits. The fate of her prayers was tied to this new pope. Nothing else could explain why she went the next weekend to a vegan cookbook launch she hadn't planned to attend, and minutes after she arrived Kwame was leaning towards her to ask, 'When they say something tastes nutty, do we know which nut they mean?'

Six

On the day they broke up, they went back to her apartment after the gala, and she told Kwame, 'So I'm very late and I'm never late.'

He looked confused.

'I might be pregnant.' She was so certain of his delight that she made her tone playful, almost singsong. But his face, instead of warming and melting in delight, went still, his mouth pursed, and suddenly this most communicative of men retreated into the cryptic.

He said, 'It's a shock.'

She said, 'You know I stopped the pill.'

He said again, 'It's a shock.' He walked to the living room and back to the kitchen where she stood, and he said, 'We're at different places in our lives.'

'What do you mean?' she asked.

He didn't respond.

'Kwame,' she said finally, in a plea and a prayer, looking at him and loving him. Their conversation felt like a poor rehearsal and not the real conversation they were supposed to have. She wanted to reverse their day, just by a few hours, and have them walk into her apartment again, laughing, her saying let's make margaritas and him saying should we order burgers, because I don't know what that tiny Chilean sea bass thing at dinner was about.

'Kwame,' she said again. Then she saw it, the almost imperceptible shrug. He shrugged. His response was a shrug. From the deepest vaults of his being, a shrug, to rid himself of an encumbrance.

'I think I should leave. Is that okay?' he asked, as though he needed her permission to abandon her. But even as he asked he was already heading, in flight, to the door.

THEY HAD OFTEN had sex on her velvet couch, she straddling him. On that same couch she lay blankly reading his past text messages while the hours slid one into another, time spent on remembering and time lost on remembering. She lingered on a message sent when he drove to the Middle Eastern place in Silver Spring to get her hummus. *They ran out of regular, just red pepper, sorry babes.* How well he knew her. It was real hummus or nothing for her; none of those flavours invented to appeal to the American need for variety. She read somewhere that love was about this, the nuggets of knowledge about our beloved that we so easily hold. Each time she called him, she felt newly startled by the burr-burr-burr of unanswered ringing, and she hoped the number had somehow misconnected until she heard that voice, that boyish nice-guy voice, say, 'Kwame here. You know what to do!'

That voice she knew so well. She knew his worries and his jokes, could read the slightest modulations in his mood. She sensed, even before he told her, when he had a challenge at work or a hiccup with a client. And always he told her, always he laid himself open to be known. Or had she seen only what she wanted to see of him? Had she merely cast on him the glow of an answered prayer? But other people had seen his radiance too, and so it could not just be a fantasy built in her head. After Chia met him, she said, 'He's so genuine. The best was saved for last.' They had dinner at Chia's house, and Kwame ate two helpings of Kadiatou's fonio and groundnut sauce, saying he remembered eating groundnut sauce as a child in Ghana. He chatted easily with Kadiatou, asking if ndappa was a kind of polenta, telling her he once did a high-school report on African languages and Pular was one of them. Kadiatou smiled and repeated the word 'Pular', to show him how it was pronounced.

'I wish I knew more of my African side,' he told her, which felt to Zikora an unnecessary confidence, but it moved her to see Kadiatou bloom under his attention and become unusually chatty, telling Kwame about her uncle's farm back home. 'Everything farm,' she said, smiling. 'He grow everything, fonio and groundnut and sweet potatoes.'

The next time Zikora saw Kadiatou, she said, 'Miss Zikora, God bring your husband already', looking delighted, as if the effects of Kwame were yet to wear off. And then, of course, her parents. Kwame travelled with her to Enugu for Christmas and tried kneeling when he met her father, and her father laughed, waving him up, saying, 'No, no, we Igbo don't do that, that's Yoruba', and Kwame said, 'I can't believe I didn't do my research better.' 'Do your research better' became their joke, her father's and Kwame's, in that blustery male manner of men who feel unthreatened by each other. The evening her father took Kwame to his tennis club alone, it was, he joked, to do his research better. Her father had liked Kwame right away, but her mother watched him for a while before she, too, caved. On the phone Zikora heard her mother say to a friend, 'Zikora's fiancé', even though Kwame didn't propose during the three days he spent in Enugu before he had to fly back, without her, for work.

He didn't propose but he asked her father to explain the smallest details of Igbo marriage rites to him. He didn't propose but he told her things like 'You know I can't keep that up when we're in our fifties', or 'We should save that for when we retire.' Once, when he joked about travelling the world after they retired, she said, 'Only if we've put away enough for the kids' college', and a flicker crossed his eyes, before he changed the subject, as if uninterested in talking about children. But he would have told her if he didn't want children. The cruelty required to lead people on was simply not in him.

Kwame was lovely, he truly was. Silence was not his fighting tool; he was a man who talked things through. But day after day he ignored her calls and texts, and then he sent back her apartment key by courier, in a clasp envelope, the lone piece of metal wrapped in plain white paper.

SHE HELD ON TO a deranged hope because he hadn't asked her to return his own key. His apartment doorman looked pitying the third time she turned up, telling her again that Kwame had said he would be away for a while. In the cavernous soullessness of his office reception area, his assistant, Keisha, said, 'I'm sorry, he doesn't wish to see you', and instead of turning around to walk through the sliding door and into the sunlight, Zikora asked, 'Did he say anything else?'

Keisha arched an ironic brow.

'Did he say anything else?' Zikora asked again.

'You mean, apart from he doesn't want to see you?'

Only then did Zikora leave, sunken in the ruins of shame. The insolent paralegal was laughing at her, she could tell; she felt the young woman's eyes on her back. She called Kwame's mother and listened for something in her tone, a clue, a reason, anything. She asked if she could come and visit, and his mother said, after a pause, 'That might not be the best idea.' She imagined herself in their living room, all neutrals and beiges, with pillows perfectly plumped, always prepared to impress whoever came by. She would sit down politely and then, when his parents were seated and unsuspecting, she would leap up and run upstairs to check if Kwame was there.

'He said you had a fight and he seems very upset,' his mother said.

'I can't reach him. I need to talk to him.' Zikora paused, and added, 'Please.'

'My understanding was *you* didn't want to have a conversation,' his mother said, her tone so rich with righteous accusation that Zikora wondered if what had happened had happened, or if she had dreamed it all. She should tell his mother, she should say, 'I'm pregnant', but the words would not form on her tongue. In this antagonistic silence over the phone, her hope was weeding itself out.

'Okay. Thank you,' she said. She hung up and looked out of her tall windows and felt the acute desolation of being alone. God had retreated, and her intercessions to the Blessed Virgin sounded limp, weakening as soon as they were spoken, unable to reach their destination. From outside herself she saw her own dwindling, her drift to depression, and she worried that stress was harming the baby, and her worry only added layers to her stress. She told herself that she could bear the beast of her loneliness alone as she had before in the past, that she must defeat this malaise that lay over her like a mist. She had to do it for the baby, she had to. And as she told herself this, her resolve would rise and swell and then collapse again as her mind deflated itself with the pinpricks of self-doubt. On an impulse, she went to the basilica on Michigan Avenue. Years of living in Washington, DC, and she had never been. It seemed to her a mere tourist attraction, America's biggest Catholic church; even the name felt grandiose, the Basilica of the National Shrine of the Immaculate Conception. As soon as she stepped in, awed goosebumps spread on her skin. The magnificence overwhelmed her, and she looked around as though in a godly wonderland, at the stately marble columns and the mosaics, so alive, with minute details devotedly done: the Jesus in the vaulted ceiling with one angry eye and one loving eye almost blinking. This was faith boldly shouting, 'We are not holding back.' A testament, a rebuke to all doubt. She lit a candle for her baby. She lingered in the chapels on the crypt level, each so different and all so tenderly intimate. In the pale gold light of the Our Lady of Pompei Chapel, her faith soared and steeled itself. This sweeping majestic place built for God, all the people who built it for God, who worshipped and witnessed God here – that God could surely not now forsake her.

'THIS MAKES NO SENSE. Did something else happen?' Chia asked, as if Zikora might be concealing the real reason for Kwame's abandonment. Then Chia collected herself and said, 'Zikor, a baby, a baby! That's all that matters now, what you've always wanted.'

'Not like this.'

Chia talked about hosting a baby shower and Zikora told her she had gone mad, to think of a baby shower while she was still jousting with the monster of shame. She had not told anyone that Kwame had left her, but she was haunted by the sense that everybody knew. The paranoia of the abandoned. Each time a friend called, her heart lurched, thinking they knew and were calling to offer their false sympathy while masking their glee.

'Chia, what will I tell people? I know everybody says don't worry about what people think, but I worry. I care what people will say when they hear that I'm pregnant with no man.'

'They'll talk, and after some time they'll stop and talk about somebody else.'

'When I look in the future everything feels so difficult.'

'It won't be easy but it won't be as hard as you think, Zikor. How you imagine something will be is always worse than how it actually ends up being,' Chia said. The easy wisdom, emollient words so smoothly rolled out, rankled rather than soothed Zikora. She remembered Chia once saying that she would choose to have a baby on her own, with donor sperm, than a baby with a man she did not desperately love. Chia was out there, Chia could not possibly understand.

'Whose surname will the baby have?' Zikora asked, with a short bitter laugh. 'I never imagined giving birth alone.'

'You won't be alone. Your mom will be there. I'll be there.'

Zikora sighed. 'Chia, please don't tell Omelogor, not yet.' Why did it matter about telling Omelogor? She just didn't want Omelogor to know just yet.

'She's not doing too well in grad school,' Chia said.

'What do you mean?'

'I think it's depression, but she doesn't accept that it's depression. Maybe she shouldn't have come to America. It really worries me. The other day she was crying and not talking, just crying.'

Zikora felt cheered by this news, by the sense that misery was now being evenly spread. Omelogor crying? Omelogor could cry? Whatever America had done to her, God bless America.

IN AN UNFINISHED DYING, you feel you must mourn yet you can't begin, because you haven't reached an end that you understand. Kwame was an unfinished dying. She could not accept that it was over; so much lay loose and incomplete. She sifted through her memories for reasons, as though through debris left by a fire to find uncharred fragments. He had always wanted them to make all decisions together, and it amused her sometimes, how seriously he meant this, even for small things like what table to select when making a restaurant reservation online. 'Okay, babes?' he would ask, and wait for her nod.

Was it how she had told him that she was pregnant? He must have heard the lack of doubt in her voice, how settled this news was. It came to him as an already sealed box. But she had said she might be pregnant, not that she was, and if he felt she had already decided without him, couldn't he have tried talking, in that easy open way of his that had shrivelled up so quickly that day? They talked all the time, but just when they most needed to talk, he had walked into a wall and disappeared. He was able do that, just leave unscathed, choose the option of doing nothing, but she would never have that option, because it was her body, and a baby must either be birthed or not. In this way, the decision could never be truly shared. If he was to become a father, of course he should have a say, but how much of a say she did not know, since Nature demanded so much more of the mother. The baby's conception was the one shared decision, perhaps, because they had both participated, knowing what the outcome could be. That ancient story: the woman wants the baby and the man doesn't want the baby and a middle ground does not exist. What would a middle ground be, anyway? They couldn't have half a baby. But she rejected this as their story. She could not accept that he was merely running away from fatherhood, like so many men had cowardly done throughout time. It was too common, and Kwame was not common. She had seen the wonderful father he could be when he went with her to visit her friend Ijemma in Delaware. Ijemma had come to America to have her second child, and brought her toddler and a nanny. It amused Zikora how quickly Kwame displaced the nanny for the length of their visit, and was on his knees, his palm swallowed in a puppet, wiggling his fingers, his voice tuned to a funny high pitch, and the riveted two-year-old so adorably giggling.

'It's frightening when somebody you know just changes, completely changes,' she told Chia. 'It's as if an artery burst inside him and his whole body is now wired differently and he is no longer the person he was. I don't understand how I get off birth control and we have sex for so long and then I get pregnant and he reacts like he never knew it could happen.'

'Zikor, have you considered that maybe he didn't know?'

'What do you mean?'

'Men know very little about women's bodies.'

'Ahn-ahn. Even teenagers who have no business having sex know what the consequences are.'

'You'd be surprised. Omelogor wrote this thing the other day. She's started a website that she's calling For Men Only, where she asks men to send in their problems and she gives them advice.'

Zikora swallowed a groan. The last thing she needed was that smug sureness, but she couldn't help clicking and skimming the link Chia sent her.

Dear men,

Women know more about your bodies than you know about theirs.

Not that there is much to know about yours. Women know your brains are between your legs. Just kidding (not really). Women know you're anxious about getting it up even when you're ninety-eight years old and women know about that gland near your balls that starts to give you problems as you age, makes you pee too often at best, and becomes cancer at worst.

But women's bodies? Phew. Where to start.

What did you learn in sex-education class in school? You were separated from girls and ended up knowing nothing about the inner workings of female bodies.

You rolled a condom over a banana. You don't know where women's pee comes from.

So millions of you in the world who want to learn about sex and women's bodies end up learning from where? Adult films. It's funny that they're called adult films because they are actually very immature. Like a bad cartoon for grown-ups. Even if you enjoy porn, at least be clear that you're watching fantasy, and the whole point of fantasy is that it isn't real life. You watch porn and you think women are always shaved smooth and women never have periods and pregnancy can be wished away. Pornography is actually very disrespectful to you because it starts with the premise that men are stupid, and so it teaches you so much nonsense and gets away with it. The statistics are staggering: more than sixty per cent of you watch porn often. You, reading this, where did YOU learn about women's bodies? Stop being fuzzy and go do your homework.

Remember that I'm on your side, dear men.

The post annoyed Zikora. She read it in Omelogor's voice, resisting the smugness and sureness of it. How absurd to infantilize men like this. But small queries began easing themselves into her mind.

One sleepy weekend morning in Kwame's apartment, after slow sex, and a slower brunch of eggs she made and pancakes he made, he was playing a video game with lots of noise and flash, and she was reading the news online, and she looked up and said, 'Can you believe an elected official in the United States of America is actually asking why women can't hold their periods in?' She laughed, and so did he, but she remembered now his first fleeting reaction, the slightest of hesitations, as though he was holding back from saying, 'You mean women can't?'

Still, even if he did not know about periods, he surely understood birth control. Or did he not? Could it be that Kwame was fuzzy, that when she had said, 'I'm stopping the pill', and he had said, 'Okay, babe', they had not shared the same understanding of what that exchange meant? That night, they had showered together and she was patting cream on her face and examining a purplish discoloured patch that had appeared like a map on her chin. 'It must be my birth-control pills causing this,' she said, and he came closer to look at it. 'Does it hurt?' he asked.

'No, it's a reaction.' And then she said, looking at him, 'I want to stop the pill', and he said, 'Okay, babes.'

Maybe she should have been clearer, maybe they should have talked plainly, as they talked about so much. Why hadn't she been clearer? Did she choose to assume he understood, because she didn't want to give him the chance to say he didn't want a child? Now she was flagellating herself, slipping on the cloak of responsibility, looking for a reason to excuse him. But the alternative was to accept that she did not truly know Kwame, that perhaps we can never truly know another human being.

SHE WORRIED THAT she wasn't eating enough, and in quiet moments of subdued panic, she imagined her baby floating in her womb, sickly and sallow, starved of nutrients. She could hardly keep anything down. She sucked natural ginger sweets, because the pregnancy website said avoid nausea medicine, but always she felt a breath away from vomiting. Nausea became her norm. She no longer remembered when she was free of biliousness. Chia ordered bottles of an organic protein drink from a custom website, and for weeks it was all she could keep down. She craved extra sharp cheddar but the pregnancy website said no soft cheese and she decided not to eat any cheese at all. A sense of desperate guilt dampened everything she did and everything she did not do, because she had already failed her baby with such imperfect circumstances, to be born without a father, without clarity about the future's shape.

'Zikor, you'll be fine,' Chia always said, even before Zikora spoke, as though to give her no room. 'You'll be fine.'

Some days she was fine and some days she was underwater barely breathing. At her twenty-two-week check-up, newly flush with well-being, her nausea receding, she laughed at the grainy-grey image moving on the ultrasound screen, and gaily waved at the front-desk women as she left the doctor's office, but alone in the elevator, she sank to the floor, a stark dissolving all around her. She sent Kwame a text. *I'm 22 weeks today.*

He did not reply. A woman wearing torn jeans had entered the elevator and was looking at her. 'Are you okay? Do you need some help?'

'No,' Zikora said, getting up. 'No, thank you.'

HER JOB TOOK ON a new shimmering significance; it had not betrayed her and she had not failed it, this part of her life that stayed stable, an unconfusing recourse. She began arriving a bit earlier and leaving a bit later, and she volunteered to take on extra tasks. At first, she wore chic loose-fitting dresses that hid her burgeoning middle, and when her belly's gentle swell could no longer be disguised, she stayed late every day, noisily late, and at morning meetings she said with false casualness how traffic thinned so dramatically after nine, so that everyone would know she had been in the office then. She took breaks from meetings to throw up in the toilet, and then walked back in with practised aplomb as though she had just gone to pee and reapply her lipstick. Donna watched her with the eyes of a person willing you to stumble, the two of them the only women vying to make partner. Donna talked often about choosing to be 'child-free', and she always said 'child-free' with relish, as if she knew how much it annoyed Zikora, an expression that made a child sound like a disease. Donna was thin and vegan and did yoga and wore fitted dresses made for flat-chested women, low-cut but still appropriate since they exposed no bulging flesh. Now Donna kept asking about her pregnancy, always loudly so the men would hear, tawny adversarial eyes fixed on her belly.

'Think you can handle that, Zikora?

'You okay? Need some water? Are you feeling lightheaded?

'You look exhausted. Sleeping is tough, right?'

'I don't have a debilitating illness, Donna. I'm only pregnant,' Zikora would say, with a laugh she hoped sounded unstrained. She made jokes about pregnancy. Let's try balancing this file on my belly! She said she still drank once in a while, because her mother had drunk Guinness throughout her pregnancy with her. It was untrue, her mother had not drunk any, nor did she, but she wanted to seem in control, even slightly reckless, as though her pregnancy was a glamorous adventure that would not impede her ascent at Watkins Dunn. Sometimes when she saw Donna's thin form approaching in the hallway, she thought of a demonic bony bird circling to snatch away the last egg in another bird's nest.

'I figured I better have this baby because it might be my last chance. I probably wouldn't want to keep it if it were ten years ago,' she told Donna breezily. 'It's funny how pregnancy is like body hair. We scrub and scrape our armpits and upper lip and legs, because we hate to have hair there. Then we pamper and treat the hair on our heads, because we love hair there. But it's all hair. It's the wanting that makes the difference.'

'I can't believe you're saying a baby is like body hair,' Donna said, deliberately misunderstanding, her lips in a downward curve, the same curve as when she spoke of people who ate meat.

'Oh, come on, I'm not saying a child is like body hair. I'm saying our relationship with body hair is similar to our relationship with pregnancy. It could be the thing we most desperately want and also the thing we most desperately don't want.'

Donna, lips still downward-turned, changed the subject. 'Are you sleeping okay?' she asked.

'I'm great, I'm sleeping really well,' Zikora said brightly, but she barely slept at all, propped on three pillows, tossing this way and that, seeking an elusive comfort, her chest aflame with heartburn and a stubborn throbbing ache in the joints of her fingers. Each morning, she coated concealer over the dark bags under her eyes and wore red lipstick to draw attention to her lips instead. Sometimes she thought her other colleague, Jon, saw through her. He was sensitive, and he made subtle gestures of support, helping her without calling attention to her pregnancy, as if he knew how much energy it took to pretend, how it drained and flattened her, and how much she cried and then upbraided herself for crying because crying meant stress and stress harmed the baby.

SHE WAS LYING IN, on a Saturday morning, falling in and out of unrestful sleep, when the sustained door buzzing startled her.

She had been dreaming that Kwame appeared at her office holding a covered basket, which he placed on a desk and then backed away. In the basket was a dead baby, curled and cold. The dream was so lucid, she saw a mole on the dead baby's cheek, so frightening, and she jumped and stumbled to the door, half-expecting to see Kwame standing there with the basket.

'Miss Zikora, it's me. Kadiatou. I come to braid your hair.'

Zikora stopped, still confused. 'To braid my hair?'

'Yes.'

She opened the door. Kadiatou was holding a big plastic bag. Her short wig looked glossy, and she had the mournful expression of people who went on condolence visits, bearing gifts of alcohol and cash.

'Miss Chia tell me what happen,' she said.

Zikora felt a flash of irritation. Chia needed to keep her mouth shut, nobody else needed to know. She didn't want pity.

But she could have run into Kadiatou on her way to work or back from work, and how then would she hide the rise of her belly, the human being growing inside her body. She let Kadiatou in. Kadiatou smelled faintly of jasmine. Her presence instantly felt soothing; she had an elegant calmness, a lack of abrasiveness, that Zikora thought of as a trait of Francophone Africans. A Nigerian version of Kadiatou would bring a different, more bracing energy and leave the air unsettled, even unpleasant.

'I bring some things to help with your stomach . . .' Kadiatou gestured with her hand, to mimic throwing up.

'Thank you, Kadi.'

'You don't eat. You have food?'

'A little.'

Kadiatou was unpacking her plastic bag, revealing its treasures: fresh grated ginger in a container, leafy herbs, a small bottle of what looked like oil.

'Somebody put curse on Kwame. Like juju in the Nollywood film. Somebody is jealous of you,' Kadiatou said.

Zikora laughed. 'Kadi, you watch too much Nollywood; all those things you watch are not true.' But it comforted her that Kadiatou still believed Kwame to be the person she also wanted him to be, a person too good to abandon her of his own accord, now helpless in the grip of a demonic curse.

'He will come back. He's afraid to be father, so he run. Men run away and after they come back,' Kadiatou said.

A prickle of irritation on Zikora's skin. Kwame was not running away from fatherhood – he couldn't be, she refused to accept it – and Kadiatou had no idea what she was talking about.

'The hair colour two,' Kadiatou said, laying out the long rolls of attachments.

'Kadi, please remember not too tight.'

'Miss Chia always say African braid perfect but break your hair, and African American braid rubbish but your hair don't break. So choose one.'

It was a joke, Chia's joke, and Zikora knew the ending. 'I choose both,' she said.

'Even if Mr Kwame don't come back, always you have your baby,' Kadiatou said quietly, placing a hand to her heart. 'Your baby is your own.'

SEVEN

Zikora pushed out a baby boy. He was wrinkled and silent, scaly-skinned, wet black curls plastered on his head. He came out with poop in his mouth, and the nurse tittered and said, 'Not the best first meal', while somebody swiftly took him away to suction the meconium. Now here he was, wrapped like a tidy sausage roll and placed on her chest. He was warm and small, so very small. She held him stiffly, suspended in a gap between her self and her feelings, and waiting to feel. It was as if every emotion had been rubbed out of her, even the ability to have an emotion. She could not separate this moment from her imagination of this moment – all the films and books about this scene, mother and child, mother meeting child, child in mother's arms. It was not transcendental. She was not flooded by happy hormones. She looked at her baby, knowing it was her baby, but in the space where her joy should be there was nothing. A fog blanketed her, a kind of deadness. She was shaking, her whole body divided in small fragments and each fragment vibrating, and the nurse said it was normal. Somewhere in her consciousness, a mild triumph hovered, because it was over, finally it was over, and she had pushed out the baby. So animalistic and violent – the push and pressure, the blood, the cranking and stretching of flesh and organ and bone. After the final push, she thought that here in this delivery room we are briefly and brutishly reduced to the animals we truly are.

'Beautiful boy, beautiful boy,' her mother said, smiling down at him. To Zikora her mother said, 'Congratulations, *nwa m*', congratulations, my child, and hugged her. Her mother's first touch. Zikora eased the baby into her mother's arms and reached for her phone. There was no response from Kwame. She sent another message: *It's a boy.* He would respond, now that he knew it was no longer about her but about another human being whose genes were partly his, a whole person, a new person who might look like him or laugh like him one day. Or he might appear at the hospital, in the next hour, holding a balloon and flowers, limp flowers from the supermarket because he wouldn't have had time to go to a florist.

'You've had a small tear,' Dr K said, needle in hand. Did it never end? This process had become an exaggeration of itself. Nature must not want humans to reproduce, otherwise birthing would be easy: babies would simply slip out, and mothers would remain unmarked and whole, merely blessed by having bestowed precious life. Why make so tortuous something that needn't be? At the needle's pierce of her tender raw skin, she screamed. 'The epidural stopped working! Dr K! How can the epidural stop working?'

Her mother glanced at her with eloquent eyes. Hold yourself together and stop making noise. Then her mother looked away and asked Dr K a question. 'Will it be possible to have his circumcision today?'

'Not until he has urinated,' Dr K said. 'And I don't do circumcisions. It'll be done by another doctor.'

'When can we expect him to urinate?' her mother asked.

Zikora cried out again at the needle, its unjust, unexpected pain. Tears filled her eyes. Of course Kwame was not coming. She knew he wasn't coming even as she imagined him standing at the hospital-room door wearing jeans and the blue sneaker-like shoes he called his knockabouts. Her mother was asking about circumcision-consent forms. 'Can we get them today?'

'Yes, of course,' Dr K said. 'Almost done, this should heal nicely.'

They were having a mundane conversation while this man slid a needle and thread in and out of her flesh. She didn't matter to them, just as she didn't matter to Kwame; she was a threadbare wrung-out rag, a thing without feeling, easy to ignore and discard.

'I won't circumcise him,' she said.

'Of course you will,' her mother said.

'I said, I won't circumcise him!'

She had never raised her voice to her mother in her life. Even Dr K paused in his movements as if in homage to the import of the moment. But her mother, unaffected, unchanged, coolly asked, 'And why won't you circumcise him?'

'It's barbarism,' Zikora said, surprising herself. She remembered a post on the pregnancy website. *You Americans may circumcise but we don't do barbarism here in Europe. We don't cause our babies unnecessary pain. The only reason it's tolerated at all here is so we don't get accused of being Islamophobic.* She had ignored posts about baby boys because she was sure hers was a girl. Not only did she sense it, but all the mythical girl signs were there: she carried the pregnancy high, she had bad morning sickness and her skin turned greasy. She remembered this post only because she had paused at it, provoked, thinking it was an unfair attack on Americans by a prejudiced person ignorant of all the peoples in the world who circumcised their males. Now it was convenient ammunition.

'Circumcision is barbaric,' she said. 'Why should I cause my child pain?'

'Cause your child pain?' her mother repeated, as if Zikora was making no sense.

Zikora checked her phone: still nothing from Kwame. She sent another text: *Your son.* She felt, for a moment, the intense desire to pass out and escape her life. She sent Kwame another text: *He weighs 6 pounds 13 ounces.* She had already ripped up her dignity and she might as well scatter the shreds, so she called him. His phone rang and went to voicemail, and she called again, and again, and the fourth or fifth time she heard a beep instead of a ringing, and she knew that he had just blocked her number.

'Is that Chiamaka you're calling?' her mother asked.

Zikora paused. 'Yes. She's rushing back.'

'Where did you say she was?'

'South Tyrol.'

'Oh, yes, where the Italians speak German.'

Her mother knew, while Zikora had no idea this place existed until Chia said she was going there. Her mother had been up all night, too, but she didn't look tired, this woman in her late sixties; her resilience, her excellence, began to feel like an affront to Zikora.

'I'll ask the nurse to bring the forms,' her mother said.

'I will not circumcise him!' Zikora said, her voice even louder.

Her mother ignored her and picked up a lactation brochure the nurse had left on the table. Zikora wanted to fight her mother, fling words at her, scratch at that veneer so perfectly in place.

'I knew I was pregnant because I've been pregnant before,' Zikora blurted out.

Her mother looked up, vaguely puzzled, as if she was not sure she had heard correctly, then she turned back to reading the brochure.

'I was so relieved to get an abortion,' Zikora said.

Still her mother said nothing. Zikora wanted a response, crackling anger, hissed recriminations, ugliness to match her inside, but her mother was refusing her the satisfaction of a response, any response. Only moments ago, she would never have believed this scene, telling her mother what she had sworn never to tell anyone, especially her mother. Why had she said it? She didn't know, but she had said it and it was out. She did not feel lighter or better; she felt only that she had let out her secret of many years and her mother had responded with silence.

'Do you want something from the cafeteria?' her mother asked finally, standing up. 'You have to eat more than that apple sauce.'

Zikora closed and opened her eyes. She felt ragged and hopeless. There was a festering red pain between her legs and a sudden ravenous hunger in her gut.

'French fries?' her mother asked.

'Yes,' Zikora said.

EIGHT

Zikora never told the boy who didn't love her, the boy she was trying to make love her when she didn't yet know that you cannot nice your way into being loved. He was her first lover. She had met him in sophomore year in college, her second year in America. A basketball player, near-comical in his self-regard, tall, his head always held high, his gait something of a trot. He often said, 'I don't do commitment', with a rhythm in his voice, as though miming a rap song, but she didn't hear what he said; she heard what she wanted to hear: he hadn't done commitment yet. From the beginning, she was of no real consequence to him. She knew this, because she had to have known, but she was also nineteen, and feeding the reeking insecurities of that age. The first time she knelt naked in front of him, he yanked a fistful of her braids, then pushed at her head so that she gagged. It was a gesture brimming with unkindness, an action whose theme was the word 'bitch'. She said nothing. She made herself boneless and amenable. She spent weekends willing the landline next to her bed to ring. Often it didn't. Then he would call, before midnight, to ask if she was still up, so he could visit and leave before dawn. When her grandmother died, she called him crying and he said sorry and then, in the next breath, 'Has your period ended so I can stop by?' Her period had not ended and so he did not stop by. She believed then that love had to feel like hunger to be true.

'The rubber came off,' he said carelessly that night. He'd been drinking and she had not.

'It's so funny how you say "rubber",' she tittered, wishing he wasn't already distracted and reaching for his clothes, eyes on his car keys. But she thought nothing of it, because the condom slipping off once couldn't possibly matter. Symptoms can mean nothing if a mind is convinced, if a thing just cannot be, and so the sore nipples, the sweeping waves of fatigue, had to have other meanings until they no longer could, and she walked to Rite Aid after class and bought a pregnancy test. How swift the moment is when your life becomes a different life. She had never considered getting pregnant, never imagined it, and for long minutes after the test showed positive, she sat drowning in disbelief. She didn't know what to do because she had never thought she would need to know. She went to the health centre and lied to the nurse practitioner, saying the condom had slipped off the night before. The sad-eyed woman gave her a white morning-after pill, which she swallowed with tepid water from the dispenser in the waiting room. It was too late, of course, she knew, but still she did other desperate nonsensical things: she jumped up and threw herself down on the floor violently, and it left her stunned, too jolted to try it again. She drank cans of lemon soda, dissolved sachets of fizzy liver salts in glasses of water. She disfigured a hanger in her closet and held it steely in her hand, trying to imagine what distraught women did in old films, before she gave up and threw it down. A clutch of emotions paralysed her, bleeding into each other, disgust-horror-panic-fear. Like slender talismans, she lined up different pregnancy tests on her sink, and each one she urinated on she willed to turn negative. They were all positive. Something was growing inside her, alien, uninvited, and it felt like an infestation. There are some kindnesses you do not ever forget; you carry them to your grave, held warmly somewhere, brought up and savoured from time to time. Such was the kindness of the African American woman with short pressed hair at the Planned Parenthood clinic on Walnut Street. She smiled with all of her open face, and she touched Zikora's shoulder as she settled tensely on her back. She held Zikora's hand through the long minutes. 'It's okay, you'll be okay,' she said. Her fingers tightened around Zikora's while cramps stabbed her lower belly. Zikora was utterly alone, and this woman knew it. 'Thank you,' she said, afterwards. 'Thank you.' She felt light from relief, weightless, unburdened. It was done. On the bus home, she cried, looking out of the window at the cars and lights of a city that knew her loneliness. For years after that she avoided going to confession; she could not get herself to say in words what she had done. She would never say it even to herself, and if she locked it up in her mind, then one day it would be as though it had never happened at all. She deserved God's punishment, she knew, but also His mercy, and she continued to receive Communion at Mass, but with more humility than usual, more gratitude. The week before her graduation from Georgetown Law, she spent the weekend with Chia, and on Sunday morning she asked where she could go to Mass, because she didn't want to drive all the way to DC. Chia, vague, trying to be helpful, gave her the wrong time and she arrived at St John the Evangelist in Columbia with Mass already over. But a priest was offering confession and she found herself moving towards the confessional, sinking to her knees in the dim cubicle, the priest behind a screen. He asked her name and she felt the queasy fear of her teenage years when she had disguised her voice at confession, worried that Father Damian would tell her mother what she had confessed. But this priest, this White American man who told her his name was Father Tillman, was not like Father Damian or the other priests back home. There was no doctrinaire drone, no harsh-tongued scolding, no giving out a generic penance of 'five Our Fathers and five Hail Marys' with the bored rote tone of having already said the same thing a hundred times that day. Father Tillman seemed actually to listen to her. Maybe this was because he wasn't overwhelmed with work; everyone went to confession in Nigeria, unlike here, where people seldom did.

'There is no sin that God cannot forgive,' Father Tillman said. 'All God asks of us is true repentance.'

'But what is true repentance?'

'True repentance is what made you come here today.'

WHEN HER MOTHER left for the cafeteria, the nurse came in with the circumcision-consent forms.

'Is it really about causing Baby pain?' she asked gently.

Zikora stared at her, at the eyelashes that made it difficult to take her seriously.

'Baby won't remember the pain. If everyone in your culture does it, you should do it too. Kids hate being different. I used to work in a paediatrician's office and that's one thing I learned. We don't have kids yet – my fiancé is training to be a police officer – but I'm keeping that in mind for when I have my kids.'

The nurse held the forms for a moment before placing them on the table. Something about her manner made rushing sobs gather at Zikora's throat. It was compassion; this nurse thought that whatever Zikora was feeling mattered. Had she missed it before, or had the nurse suddenly changed?

'Thank you,' Zikora said, wanting to reach out to hold her hand, even though she knew it might be a bit too much, but the nurse had turned to leave. She almost collided at the door with Dr K, who had come back to say goodbye.

'Your mother is wonderful. She speaks so well. I like hearing proper English. My relatives in Iran speak like that. She owns a private school in Nigeria?'

'Yes,' Zikora said, and wondered when her mother had told him that.

'It's wonderful that she could come and be with you,' Dr K said.

'Yes,' Zikora said. She never doubted that her mother would come to be with her, but when she first called to tell her mother, 'I'm pregnant and Kwame has disappeared', she felt tense, as she did when she was a teenager and somebody had reported her for doing something bad. She expected sharp recrimination from her mother, wasting no words, for getting pregnant, and for losing Kwame. But her mother said, 'When is your due date, so I can start making arrangements?'

IN THE NURSERY procedure room, her son was placed on a board, restrained, arms and legs strapped down, under a warming light. It felt sacrificial. She wanted to reach out, push the doctor aside, and rip off the straps and free him. Why had she done it? Why had she signed those forms, with her mother looking over her shoulder? She almost believed her earlier empty fighting words, that she was causing her son unnecessary pain. Her son. Those words: her son. He was her son. He was hers. She had given birth to him and she was responsible for him and already he knew her, moving his face blindly at her breasts. Rooting, it was called. How did newborn babies know to do that? He was hers and his tiny translucent arms lay precious against her skin. He was hers. She would die for him. She thought this with a new wonder because she knew it to be true; something that had never been true in her life now suddenly was true. She would die for him. A new lurch in her chest, utterly alien; the intense urge to live, to stay alive, for somebody else besides herself. After they unstrapped him, his tiny mouth was pinkly open and from it came a high-pitched wail. Her baby boy, his skin peeling, his gums bare, and between his legs an angry raw nub. She cradled him and hushed him and pushed her nipple into his mouth. 'I would die for him,' she said into her phone and sent it to Chia, because she needed to speak this miraculous momentous thing that was true. Chia was in Milan, about to board her flight to Dulles, and kept sending text messages with more red heart emojis than words:

Send more pictures!
Zikor, you did this. Odogwu! So proud. I love you!
Is that colour on his skin normal?
Maybe they should check it, Zikor.
Make a video.
Zikor ndo.
He's still crying?

IN THE WEAK HOSPITAL WI-FI, her father's face froze on the screen, mid-smile, and he looked for a moment like a caricature of himself, teeth bared, eyes widened.

'Z-Baby!' he said to her.

Her father told jokes, and laughed, and charmed everyone, and broke things and danced on the shards without even knowing he had broken things.

'Daddy,' she said happily. To see him, in all his good-humoured mischief, was to remember her life as it once was, when she was only a daughter, not a mother.

'Congratulations my princess! My Z-Baby! Where is my grandson?'

Zikora was eight when her mother told her that her father would marry another wife, but nothing would change, they would still live in their house and sometimes Daddy would visit the new wife in her own house.

'Your father will live here. He will always come home to us,' her mother said, with emphasis. She made coming home to them sound like victory.

'But why is he marrying another wife?' Zikora asked. 'I don't want a new mummy.'

'She's not your new mummy. Just your aunty.'

Aunty Nwanneka. Her father took her to Aunty Nwanneka's house soon afterwards, a brief visit, on their way to his tennis club. Aunty Nwanneka was plump, skin glistening as though dipped in oil. She smiled and smiled. She slipped in and out of the parlour, and each time reappeared with a new source of enchantment for Zikora: a tube of Smarties, a small bag of chin-chin, a cup of Ribena. She called her Zikky, not Zikor like everyone else, and Zikora liked that it sounded cooler and older, that Aunty Nwanneka took her seriously. She liked her. Only later did she see how, to survive, Aunty Nwanneka wielded her niceness like a subtle sharp knife. When Zikora came to America for college, she began to call Aunty Nwanneka her father's other wife, because people assumed 'second wife' was the woman her father had married when he was no longer married to her mother. But with Kwame she said 'second wife' because he understood. She and Kwame laughed whenever she mimicked her law-school classmate, an intense American woman, asking her, 'How should we understand the contradiction of your mother?' It was after her presentation on traditional Igbo property laws, and she had used her mother's story to make it come alive: an educated woman from a prominent family marries an educated man from a prominent family, she has one daughter and many miscarriages, after which her husband decides to marry again because he needs to have sons, and the woman agrees because her husband needs to have sons, and it is those sons who will inherit all his property.

'My mother is not a contradiction. She is uncommon but normal,' she had replied to the woman, and then corrected herself: 'Uncommon and normal.'

'Perfect response,' Kwame always said, each time they laughed about that story. He knew of an uncle in Ghana, a government minister, who had married a second wife.

'Can't have been easy for either wife,' he said, and she agreed, loving him for his sensitivity. They told and retold each other stories from their past lives, until they felt as though they had been there. She was flooded by sadness in the hospital room with lights too harshly bright. She could not imagine being with someone else, someone who was not Kwame, who did not know her as Kwame did and did not say the things that Kwame said and did not have Kwame's easy laugh.

'He looks just like me!' her father announced, when her mother placed the phone over her son's face.

'Zikky, congratulations, God has blessed us,' Aunty Nwanneka said, and a slice of her round face appeared above her father's on the screen. 'How are you feeling?'

'Tired,' Zikora said, and sensed her mother's disapproval. Her mother would have wanted her to tell Aunty Nwanneka that she was perfectly fine, thank you.

'Aunty, congratulations,' Aunty Nwanneka said to her mother. She had always called her mother 'Aunty', to show respect.

'Thank you,' her mother said serenely.

'Z-Baby, is anybody else there with you apart from Mummy?' her father asked.

'No, Daddy.'

Is Kwame there? Has Kwame called? Does Kwame know? The questions he wanted to ask but didn't. Her mother hadn't asked either. She sensed her mother's suspicion, as though she had not told the full truth about Kwame, because how could Kwame have left her just because she got pregnant, Kwame who had come to Enugu wanting her father to explain Igbo marriage customs to him?

Her father was asking to see the baby's face again and her mother lowered the phone above the tiny sleeping form.

'Z-Baby, I won't be able to make it after all, but I'll definitely see him before he's one month old,' her father said.

'Okay, Daddy.' Zikora had expected it. When he said he would come from Lagos to be there for the baby's birth, she knew it was just one more of the many promises he made.

'I have a stubborn cold,' he said. 'So it's best not to be around a newborn.'

'Yes,' she agreed, even though she knew the cold was as good a reason as any. It could have been a business meeting or a last-minute issue with a contract. Her mother handed her the phone and walked to the window.

'I've had this cold for almost two weeks now, and it doesn't help that this house is like a freezer,' her father said. 'The air conditioner is so cold, but your aunty still wants to reduce the temperature. I've told her that we have to reach a compromise, because we don't have the same condition!' He was laughing, that mischievous laugh that meant he knew his joke was less than appropriate. But what was the joke? Zikora laughed a little, too, because she always laughed at her father's jokes. Then she realized it was about Aunty Nwanneka always feeling hot when nobody else did, a menopause joke. She looked at her mother, by the window, turned away, separate and apart from the conversation. Her father would never have joked about her menopause. With her mother his jokes were smaller and safer, careful always to show her respect. Respect, a starched deference, a string of ashen rituals. Respect was her mother's reward for acquiescing, for not being difficult about Aunty Nwanneka, for not fighting her father and not sprinkling discord among relatives. Instead, her mother always bought Christmas and birthday presents for Aunty Nwanneka's sons. She was civil, proper, restrained, running her schools, always respectably dressed, a subdued gloss in her gold-framed eyeglasses. Senior wife. It was her mother who sat beside her father at weddings and ceremonies. It was her mother's photo that appeared as wife in the booklet his tennis club published on his sixtieth birthday. It was her mother who was married in the church, while Aunty Nwanneka had only a wine-carrying, under traditional law, and no church wedding. Senior wife. Aunty Amala, her father's sister, said 'senior wife' as if it were a coveted title, a thing that came with a crown. 'You are the senior wife, nothing will change that,' Aunty Amala told her mother a few days after her father had moved out of their house.

Zikora's brother (her half-brother) Ugonna, only in primary school, had been caught cheating in an exam. A teacher saw him sneak a piece of paper from his pocket and shouted at him to hand it over, but instead of giving up the paper, Ugonna threw it in his mouth and swallowed it. Her father decided to move in with Aunty Nwanneka, to set Ugonna right. 'He needs to see me every morning when he wakes up. Boys can so easily go wrong, girls don't go wrong,' he told her mother. It was a Sunday, with the slow lassitude of Sundays, and they were in the living room upstairs, playing Scrabble, as they always did after lunch before her father left to spend the rest of the day at Aunty Nwanneka's and she and her mother left for benediction. Zikora remembered that afternoon in drawn-out, static images: her father blurting out the words, eyes trained on the Scrabble board, words he must have been thinking about how to say for days, and her mother staring at him, her body so rigid, so still. Later, her mother stood at the top of the stairs, in her father's way, as he tried to go downstairs. She reached out and pushed him backwards and he, surprised, tottered. 'This is not what we agreed!' her mother shouted. She was a different person that day, shaken, splintered, and she held on to the railings as though she might fall. Her father left anyway. The next day his workers moved his clothes and his collection of tennis racquets to Aunty Nwanneka's house. For weeks Zikora spoke to her mother only in sullen monosyllables, because she thought her mother could have better handled it. If her mother had not shouted, if her mother had not pushed him, her father might have stayed.

For some months her parents were estranged. Her father did not visit; he sent his driver to pick Zikora up on weekends, and bring her to his tennis club, where they drank Chapman and he told her jokes but said nothing about moving out of their house. Slowly, things thawed, and her mother accepted that he would no longer come home to them, that they were now the family who would merely be visited. Her mother began to hang her newest dresses in his wardrobe, which was almost empty, a few of his unloved shirts hanging there.

Zikora looked now at her mother, standing by the hospital-room window. How had she never really seen her? It was her father who destroyed, and it was her mother she blamed for the ruins left behind. Her parents decided early on that she would go abroad for university, and in the evenings after school, lesson teachers came to their house, to prepare her for the SATs and A levels. Her father wanted her to go to America, because America was the future, and her mother wanted her to go to the UK, because education was more rigorous there. 'I want to go to America,' Zikora said. Had she really wanted America, or did she want what her father wanted, or did she not want what her mother wanted? The way her mother said 'rigorous' had irritated her; her mother's addiction to dignity irritated her, alienated her, but she had always looked away from its cause.

Her son woke up and began to cry. His tiny tongue quivered as he cried his high-pitched, screeching cry. Her mother hurried to his glass-walled crib next to Zikora's bed, picked him up, and began pacing back and forth, holding him until he fell asleep.

NINE

On the birth certificate she entered her own surname, and 'Baby Boy' as first name; she would change it when she had a name.

'I didn't think of any boys' names,' she told her mother. 'I was so sure it was a girl.'

'Your father will choose a name.'

'Are there any names you like?'

'Chidera,' her mother said. 'But let's see what your father chooses.'

And under her breath Zikora repeated the name – Chidera, this is God's decision, God has already decided, this is God's will.

They left the hospital in the early afternoon. Her mother dressed her son in the yellow onesie she had packed, newborn-sized but still big for him, the sleeves flopping around his tiny arms. In the taxi, his car seat lodged between her mother and her, Zikora felt a wind pull through her, emptying her out. An intense urge overcame her, to hide from her mother and her son. Her apartment looked strange to her. She had left it a person different from who she was now, a person without a child, and she was returning to it with new eyes. She walked awkwardly because of the pain between her legs, and when she sat on a pillow to help, it merely felt unsteady and uncomfortable. Everything was uncomfortable. You don't know how bristly sanitary pads are until you have worn post-birth pads in the hospital and switch to sanitary pads at home. She was constipated, and on the toilet she tried not to strain while straining still, tentative, panic in her body, afraid she might tear her stitches. A geyser of anxiety had erupted deep inside her and she was spurting fear. She sat in the warm sitz bath, worried that she hadn't sat for long enough, even though she set her timer for fifteen minutes. What if she got an infection? She would need medication, which would taint her breast milk and affect her son. Her son. Her son could not latch on to her breasts properly; always her nipple slipped out of his little hungry mouth. He wailed and wailed. His cries seared into her head and made her so shaky she wanted to smash things. Her mother called a lactation nurse for a home visit, a tiny platinum-haired woman who coaxed and cooed and tried to get her son's mouth to open and close, but he kept pulling back and wailing. Was it something about being back home? She had breastfed him in the hospital. The lactation nurse gave her a plastic nipple shield, to place between her breast and her son's mouth, and for a brief moment he sucked in silence, and then began again to cry. She pumped her breasts with a machine that vibrated, funnels affixed to her nipples, spurts of thin liquid filling the attached bottles. The pumping was tortuously slow; her breasts recoiled from the machine, reluctantly giving their milk, as if to say she had failed yet again at doing things the way they ought to be done. Her son slept in a bassinet by her bed. At first, her mother slept in the next room, and then her mother pulled her mattress into Zikora's bedroom and set it by the dresser. At night, her mother fed her son a bottle of breast milk with a slim curved nipple.

'Sleep, try and sleep,' her mother said to her, but she couldn't sleep, she hardly slept, and she could hear, in the silence of her luxury apartment, the gurgle of her son's swallowing. Between her legs, her stitched-up tear itched badly. Her appetite grew with a fury, and she ate whole loaves of bread, large portions of salmon. Sunlight slanted through the blinds her mother opened every morning. The tinkly music from her son's crib mobile. The frequent flare of sad longing. She missed Kwame. She looked ahead and saw a future dead with the weight of his absence. She thought of getting a new number and calling him, to tell him they could make it work, that he could do as little as he wanted as a father, just as long as he was there. But she was wearying of his rejection, his ignoring her texts, his blocking her number, and she felt translucent, so fragile that one more rejection would make her come fully undone.

ON SOME EVENINGS, she and her mother prayed one decade of the Rosary together, both kneeling by her bed and fingering their chaplets. If the baby cried, or woke up from a nap, her mother always stopped and went to him, as if nothing else mattered more.

'Why don't I call his parents to inform them? They deserve to know,' her mother said one evening as she fed Baby.

Zikora was startled by the question. 'Who?' she asked foolishly.

Her mother looked at her. 'Kwame.'

'No, no,' she said. 'Not yet.'

'Your father was not the first person I wanted to marry,' her mother said.

Zikora stared, afraid to speak, in case her words made her mother stop talking. Her mother had never said anything like that to her.

'When I was at university in Ibadan, there was someone else. He was a Northerner. Both of our families refused. He told me something. He said, "I will always put you first." That is what he said to me. Religion was a big issue; tribe alone we might have overcome but not religion. The last time I saw him, just before he married, he still told me, "I will always put you first."'

Her mother placed Baby on her shoulder to burp him. 'Very good, my darling, very good boy,' she cooed at him. She looked up at Zikora. 'Men say all kinds of things. It is what they do that matters.'

Zikora said nothing, feeling a little stunned. Her mother was becoming a person before her eyes.

'I'M NOT PRODUCING MILK. I don't understand why I'm not producing milk,' Zikora said, crying, her breasts sore, nipples stinging, stomach aflame with anxiety, terrified that she would yet again fail her son.

'I have to breastfeed exclusively,' she said. 'Studies show exclusive breastfeeding is best for the baby and . . .'

'Zikora, that's enough. I'll go out and buy infant formula and we'll give him formula and he will be fine. In my time we thought of breast milk as a supplement. I gave you formula, and did anything happen to you? Look at you – you have always been so strong, now strong and successful. Look at you.'

Zikora tried to hide her surprise. Her mother thought she was strong? All she remembered were critical words like an open flame against her skin, the feeling of never being enough, always aware of the many holes she had dug in her mother's expectations.

'I could never have managed exclusive breastfeeding when I had you. Your delivery was extremely difficult. I heard that the nurses at the teaching hospital told my story for many years afterwards. I almost died. I would have died if not for my doctor. I was in labour for two days. Which is why I had to have a hysterectomy.'

'You did?' Zikora had never known that.

'Yes.'

'I read about women who had hysterectomies when other things could have been done to save the uterus,' Zikora said, because she was so taken aback she didn't know what else to say.

'No, I had the most brilliant doctor at the teaching hospital, Dr Nkanu Esege. He was the best obstetrician in the east; people used to come from all over to beg to be his patients. That man did everything for me. If Dr Nkanu Esege said there was nothing else to be done, then I was sure there was nothing else to be done.'

Baby began to cry and her mother hurried to him. After she fed him the last bottle of breast milk, she did not continue the story. She called a taxi to take her to the supermarket and Zikora said nothing, too, her heart still tender-skinned from the strange sensation of being close to her mother.

A few days later, her mother said, while mixing a bottle of formula, 'Your father doesn't know that I don't have a womb. I never told him.'

'What?'

'Back then men didn't come into the delivery ward, and he in particular was uninterested in these things. He used to say we would have many sons, three or four, because their family is full of boys. When it was concluded that I had to have the hysterectomy, I felt a lot of panic. To be a wife without a womb was to be useless. I knew how much children meant to him and I knew I had just had a girl.'

Zikora sat up, trying to absorb the words.

'So you didn't tell him?'

'No.'

'Did you think he would leave you?'

'Your father is a good man,' her mother said. 'He's not a bad man,' she added, as if that might be more digestible.

'So . . .' Zikora paused. 'Did your miscarriages happen before me?'

She had known for a long time that her mother had miscarriages after she was born, but now it made no sense, and maybe she had been mistaken when her mother told the story, which she often did on Sundays, with her father present. She told the story with a brave throwaway humour: 'By the time I had the third miscarriage, I think Dr Esege wanted to remove me from his patient list!'

Her mother was shaking the bottle of formula.

'There were no miscarriages,' she said.

Zikora was staring at her. 'What do you mean?'

Her mother sighed. 'There were no miscarriages.'

She was feeding the baby, who was drinking and swallowing in a happy, guzzling rush. Zikora lay back down, overwhelmed by an intensely poignant sweet sadness, because a memory had come to her, of both of them at benediction, kneeling side by side in the sparsely filled church on a rainy Sunday evening, their voices joined in incense-scented Gregorian chant. *Tantum ergo Sacramentum, veneremur cernui.*

CHIA VISITED OFTEN, holding Baby with reverent wonder, asking to feed him, telling Zikora's mother about her travels.

'Zikor, Chuka wants to come with me on Sunday to see Baby, and finally meet you,' Chia said.

And Zikora said, 'No.'

Her mother, seated nearby, said, 'Zikora, let whoever wants to come and see Baby come and see Baby.' Her mother was really saying there was nothing to be ashamed of, nothing to hide. But she wasn't hiding, not any more, or at least not as before her baby was born. She just needed some time to perfect the face she wished to show the world. Already she was training her mind to expect the comments of people, whispering to herself the worst of what might be said, to tame their sting, and mute her own future hurt.

'Okay,' Zikora said. Chia's new boyfriend should be manageable, neutral, and his judgements, if he made them, would not matter so much because he didn't know her as she used to be. He arrived holding a gift bag, behind Chia, his bulk filling the door frame. Big, bald, bearded; he was too male, in an instant his excess of manliness suffocated the living room. As if that wasn't enough, there was his 'good man' lustre, polished and gleaming, the respectful, attentive attitude so obvious in his manner. That vile scam of a man's public goodness. It enraged her. As he came to greet her, Zikora felt uncontrollable hot spurts of hostility. What manner of monsters were hidden in his nice guy skin, and how soon before they emerged to torment Chia? Abruptly, she turned her back to him, and she had never in her life turned her back to a person in that way. After they left, she looked warily at the light blue gift bag speckled with stars. Baby outfits and a pack of teething toys.

'A bit too early for teething,' Zikora said sourly.

'Zikora.' Her mother was watching her, Baby asleep in the crook of an arm. 'Don't ever treat any guest you open your door to like that, ever again.'

'There's something about him I don't trust,' Zikora said, flustered by the sternness of her mother's tone.

'Chuka is not Kwame. No other man is responsible for what Kwame did than Kwame.'

Zikora felt chastised, and annoyed for being chastised. She didn't want to be sensible, she deserved to hold whoever she wanted to hold responsible for her clattering and tumbling earth that no longer spun in orderly orbit.

'Very nice teethers,' her mother said, examining them. 'I remember your father used to give you his chicken bones when you were teething. He thought it was funny to watch you gnaw on them. I never let you have the bones for too long. I was always worried a piece of it might choke you or scratch your tongue.'

How do some memories insist on themselves even when unwanted? Zikora remembered the night of Aunty Nwanneka's birthday party, a big party, with canopies ringed by balloons filling all the space in the compound. Zikora's father asked her to come and her mother asked her not to go. It was shortly after her father had moved out of their house, and the strain between her parents was still ripe and raw.

'Stay and stand by me,' her mother said, and Zikora scoffed silently, saying her father needed her to help organize some servers. She went to the party. When she came home, unsteady from the wine she and some friends had slipped out of the cooler and drunk straight from the bottles, the househelp let her in. Her mother was in the living room reading. She felt tight with apprehension and something else that she now thought might have been shame. 'Mummy, good evening,' she greeted. Her mother said nothing, she looked up from her book, as though to show she had heard her, and then turned away.

HER FATHER CHOSE the name Okechukwukelu, God has given us our portion.

'We'll call him Okey. It's a beautiful name,' her mother said.

It was, but somehow it didn't feel right to Zikora. 'I will call him Chidera,' she said.

Her son began to cry. He was fed, his tiny belly tautly round, and yet he cried. He cried and cried.

'He cries so much. Is it the formula? Maybe it doesn't agree with him,' Zikora said.

'Some babies just cry,' her mother said calmly.

What am I supposed to do with him? Zikora thought. There would be more days and weeks of this, not knowing what to do with a squalling person whose needs she feared she could never know. Only in her mother's arms did his wails taper off, briefly, before they began again. Only while asleep was he fully free of tears. Her mother rocked him to sleep in his bassinet and after a moment said, 'Look at how he's raised his arms!'

Her mother was laughing. Zikora had never seen delight so naked on her mother's face. Her son's tiny arms were raised high up in the air as though in salute to sleep. It made her laugh too. Later, when he woke up, Zikora watched her mother cradle him, lowering her head to inhale him, touching the skin of his face with the skin of hers.

'*Nne*. What blessing can be greater than this?' her mother asked.

The urge she had felt in the past few days to apologize to her mother was only growing. But she did not have the words and did not yet know what she was apologizing for, or perhaps it was that mere apology felt inadequate, a gesture so small and so late that it might be better left undone. She looked at her mother, who was rubbing the sides of her nose where her glasses had left small dents in her skin.

'Mummy, I don't know what I'll do when you leave,' she said.

'My visa is long-stay,' her mother said. 'I'm not going anywhere yet.'

Kadiatou

One

In the morning, in dawn's diluted light, Kadiatou woke up to a sense of loss, knowing Papa was already gone. She tried to wake early, just to see him leave, but she was always too late, waking to a room sour with sleep, hearing the rise and fall of her brothers' and sisters' breaths. Sometimes, at bedtime, she pulled at her fingers and her cheeks, to chase sleep away, but she never succeeded, and would wake up startled to have fallen asleep, knowing he was gone because of the bluish light slanting through the wooden shutters. It always reminded her of loss, that stillness after dawn but before morning was fully revealed. One day she asked him why he left so early, in the dark, and he said the mine was very far away, where he worked peeling gold from the stomach of the earth. She imagined him climbing down a pit, the walls studded with shimmering gold nuggets, more beautiful than the earrings her grandmother, Nembero Joulde, had welded to her ears.

Binta said it wasn't like that at all: Papa and the other men hadn't even found gold, and if they did it wouldn't shine like earrings yet. Binta was right, Binta knew things, but Kadiatou still imagined Papa descending slowly while turning from side to side to behold the radiance of gold. If he left them for long stretches of time, then it had to be because he was toiling at something remarkable, worthy of his exhaustion. He always came home sagging from fatigue, black dirt under his fingernails, grunting as Mama massaged his back. But all he needed was a good night's sleep before his tiredness disappeared. In the morning, he wore his good boubou that was free of frayed hems and went to the mosque and visited friends, and chatted with the neighbours in the yard. He scooped up little boys in his long lean arms and threw them high up in the air and then caught them and swung them around, their laughter ringing in the air. He ate his supper while all the children watched and waited for the storytelling that followed his meal. His folk stories always began with song. The children gathered closer and sat at his feet, the baby crawling up and down and between the legs of his chair. Mama puttered around, shelling groundnuts and telling him one detail was wrong, and it was not men who told stories, anyway, and another detail was wrong, and he would tell her to come and tell the story herself and she would say he might as well continue since he had already started, and they would laugh. In the flickering light of the kerosene lamp, an enclosing lulling warmth surrounded them all. He told stories of cows and hyenas and magic snakes, of vampires that turned into fireflies, and of how the world began with a giant drop of milk. He made faces and changed his voice, gesturing and clapping. Sometimes his words were so drawn out, like a child's early babble, that they all burst into laughter before the story's end. Kadia-tou sat against the wall, looking at his feet in his leather slippers so firmly on the ground. Her small feet looked just like his, flat without an arch. As the last story ended and they began singing a song, sorrow gathered at the edge of her mind, knowing he would leave again before sunrise.

YEARS LATER, Mama told her she always clutched at Papa's legs on the nights before he left, so tightly that they pleaded with her to unclasp her hands. She did not remember this. Binta showed her a picture of a man wearing a boubou and a hat and said Papa's hat had looked like that. But she did not remember Papa's hat; she did not remember him even wearing a hat. The older she got, the more her memories were slippery in her hands. Even his face felt further away, like an image drawn in fading lines. But she remembered the day he didn't come home, the fleeting gust of coolness outside, and the scent of the first rains of the season, of water touching parched soil.

Papa didn't come home because he died, in a rock slide, in the old gold mine. They said he shouted a warning to the other men before the rocks rained down, trying to save others, even in his peril. Kadiatou pressed her ears shut to keep those stories away. It should have been the other men who were left in that mine, trapped and crushed by rocks. It should not have been Papa. She wept herself limp, her body wrung out of tears, until she fell into unrestful sleep. In violent dreams she saw the rocks dislodged in a storming rush, so many rocks crashing down, enormous rocks, and his body a helpless target, mere flesh and bone. By the time he was finally brought out, he did not look like a person. Or so their cousin Bhoye said. None of them saw Papa before he was buried but Bhoye said nothing of Papa was left whole. Nothing of Papa was left whole. Those words tormented her. She imagined Papa's body becoming sand, but it did not feel true, or right, and she wept and wept. Binta said Bhoye was lying; he was too slick, always making up stories, his eyes flashing in that insincere face. Every Eid, when they went to the village and all the children gathered to eat, it was Bhoye's fingers that selfishly snaked through the communal bowl of namma in search of fish, before it was time to share.

'Kadi, he is lying. Papa looked like a person,' Binta said. 'Papa looked like himself.' Kadiatou heard, in the firm spine of Binta's voice, how determined to comfort her Binta was, to comfort them all. When condolence visitors came, Binta suspended her own sobbing to present a face unstained by tears, a testimony that the roof over their lives had indeed collapsed but they would survive still.

Binta. Binta was born dreaming, always talking of other places, other worlds, where girls went to school and clean water gushed from taps. She walked in quick steps, as if holding back an enormous hunger eager to burst free; she did everything fast, she quivered with the restlessness of unhatched dreams. Her eyes and her heart had already travelled the paths of her future. You looked at Binta and wondered what she would become, for become something she must, and it was not a question of if but when. Kadiatou loved her as one loves sunlight. She sat content in Binta's charmed shadow, happy in the backstage of Binta's desires. Girls going to school seemed a waste to Kadiatou, learning books instead of learning how to keep a home, but she said yes when Papa asked, 'And what of you, Kadi? Do you want to go to school, too?' She said yes for Binta, because of Binta, Binta who was always asking Papa to send them to school, while Papa smiled and said they were too precious to him, and girls became spoiled in Western school.

But Papa didn't stop Binta from looking at their neighbour Idris's school books; she would sit on the steps outside, the books on her lap, turning page after page, her eyes lingering on each. Idris told sto-ries of school and Binta listened, enraptured. One day Idris said his teacher beat a student for speaking Maninka, because only French was allowed in school. Idris demonstrated the beating, laughing and chopping at the air with his hand, saying the student had urinated on himself. Binta nodded and laughed along, but Kadiatou was taken aback; she waited until they were alone to say, 'How can we go to school, Binta? We don't speak French.'

'We will learn in school,' Binta said. Kadiatou was unconvinced; how would they learn a language they did not speak, in a place where they could not speak the language they knew? But she said nothing. Later, Binta said that going to school would change their lives. Once they learned French then they could earn money translating letters from French to Pular, and they could live in a better place, not in one room in a crowded yard. They would not have to rush out early to dip their buckets into the well before the water turned brown from being disturbed. They would not have to use a general latrine that was always moist, always dark. Complaining about their life had never occurred to Kadiatou, a life she thought comfortable; the latrine was better than going out in the open field with tsetse flies circling about, the well better than trekking to a stream, but Binta's dreams glim-mered as she dreamed them, and Kadiatou listened, entranced, wish-ing them to come true, for her.

If only those evil rocks had not rained down, Binta said, Papa would have finally agreed to send them to school; he was only wait-ing until the mine yielded gold. Now Bappa Moussa wanted them to move to the village, miles from any Western school, saying they would never go hungry, because nobody ever went hungry in a Fula village, there was always something to eat. At the mention of the village, Binta tightened into a knot of refusal. She said Bappa Moussa just wanted more hands to work on his farm, after all they were not starving here in the township, and hadn't Mama managed for years to feed them from her yogurt trade?

'You know we have to obey Bappa Moussa,' Kadiatou said.

Of Papa's seventeen brothers, Bappa Moussa was the eldest. He spoke in a muffled mumble, as if pools of water were stored in his mouth. When Kadiatou looked into his eyes, she saw the world reflected back at her, as a frightening place that frightened him. For no reason, he would often mutter, 'They will send people to kill you and nobody will talk.' Binta said the government had killed some Fula people and closed their businesses, including the transport company where Bappa Moussa had worked.

'But it happened a long time ago and he should have found another job by now,' Binta said, and Kadiatou said nothing, afraid of speaking ill of an elder, their new family head. So resistant was Binta to village life that a wild idea sprouted in her mind: she would go to Conakry and live with Mama's sister Tantie Fanta. Kadiatou's mouth fell open. Conakry! The centre of it all, the faraway other world where stories were made. Going to live there at a young age felt too big and brazen a plan, even for Binta.

IN URGENT WHISPERS, Binta told Mama she could go to school there and after school she could work as a trader's assistant, and soon she would be able to send money home. Mama said Binta had to be patient, stay in the village for a while, appease Bappa Moussa, but Binta asked and asked, pushing and needling, until Mama said she should not mention Tantie Fanta or Conakry again. For all the years they lived in the village, Binta's spirit circled above, never landing, waiting until her real life could begin with Tantie Fanta in Conakry. When Tantie Fanta came to the village, her visits turned days into ceremonies. Magical Tantie Fanta, slender and small, her skin like sheer gauze, letting light in. She brought them sardines and packaged cheese and fresh loaves of bread. The car always stopped at the village square because the path to their house was too narrow, and Kadiatou and Binta ran to Tantie Fanta and struggled for who would slip her handbag off her shoulder and hold it as they walked up to the house. Kadiatou never really struggled; she let Binta hold it. Tantie Fanta's presence was enough, her arms around their shoulders, talking to them, asking them questions. She smelled of the city, of perfume and metal, an intoxicating, intimidating scent. Binta said that it was the smell of beautiful avenues lined with trees where if you strained hard as you walked past you heard pampered children playing the piano. Not that Tantie Fanta lived in such a place, that Kadiatou knew, because Tantie Fanta was a secretary in the government ministry. Kadiatou watched how Tantie Fanta's long fingers grasped food, her relaxed hair, shiny and thin-stranded, the glitter of her gold necklace, her dress belted slimly at the waist, her red fingernails. Binta watched too, but differently, not admiring but absorbing, to mimic what she knew she could become. She would become even more, Kadiatou thought, and it made her happy, imagining Binta in the future, her nails red and her hair straight, coming back to see her, bringing sardines and bread for her children.

BINTA DID NOT demand it of her, but Kadiatou wished that she, too, disliked the village, as an act of solidarity. But she liked its unhurried, untroubled air, and the evening gatherings in the square, children playing with an abandon so foreign in town. The loud frogs at night during the rains, the long humid days, the tall termite hills like giant mushrooms along the path, the whisper of the waterfalls not far away. She liked to shoo the chickens in at dusk, to gather with her siblings and cousins around the communal bowl, chattering and eating fonde and namma, licking tiny stray grains of fonio from their lips. Their grandmother, Nembero Joulde, watched them from her small wooden bed, with her prayer beads and bag of kola nuts, blinking as she chewed. Her wizened beautiful face alert to every child, every movement, every wandering goat and chicken. Kadiatou thought kola nuts were sweet until one day their grandmother went to the mosque and Binta took one kola nut from the bag and bit into it. 'Very bitter,' she said and spit it out. Binta's word was enough, Kadiatou did not taste it.

'Binta, next time you want to eat kola nut, tell me,' Nembero Joulde said when she came back.

Binta laughed. 'How did you know?'

Nembero Joulde shook her head as if children were out of control these days. But there was a twinkle in her eyes, a light only Binta's mischief could bring. It was there, too, in Mama's eyes, the day Binta and Kadiatou climbed a tree.

On the way back from an errand to their aunt Yaaye's house, Binta said to Kadiatou, 'Let's climb this tree.'

'But girls don't climb trees. What if someone reports us?'

'Nobody will.'

'We'll fall,' Kadiatou said.

'And we'll get up,' Binta said. It was a hardy acacia, branches spread like welcoming limbs. The day was dazed by sunlight, and Kadiatou hitched up her skirt and climbed behind Binta, her heart beating fast, scared to be stepping outside of her own careful lines. She stopped at a forked branch while Binta climbed higher. She could see the sloped roofs of the village spread below, and further in the distance, the majestic valley bathed in the moody vapours of mist. She had actually climbed a tree, she was on top of a tree, she was aloft above the earth. How exhilarating, to discover that she could overcome the boundaries she had set for herself. Later, as she made her way down, she was pleased to have climbed but knew she would never do so again. They were not sure who told Bappa Moussa. He scolded them, and said they would bring shame to the family, behaving like uncouth girls. Kadiatou said she was sorry, while Binta looked at him, glum and silent. And so Kadiatou said sorry again and again, to make up for Binta's silence. It reminded her of when the village chief passed them by, Kadiatou greeted him with respectful lowered eyes while Binta gazed directly at him, making Kadiatou bow even deeper, as if in compensation. Kadiatou knew how to shrink herself in the presence of her betters, but Binta didn't even know she had natural betters. Later, Binta said to Mama, 'I can even climb higher than Bhoye', and Mama, spreading out hibiscus petals on a mat, laughed with twinkly eyes and said, 'Binta!' Kadiatou knew Mama loved her, for being dutiful and dependable, but sometimes, secretly, she wished Mama loved her as she loved Binta, for being free.

THE FIRST TIME Kadiatou cooked ndappa and folere for the family, Mama tasted it, surprised, and said she was so young and already her sauce was perfect, just the right amount of wateriness for the tang of the hibiscus.

'Your father loved folere,' Mama said. 'Do you remember?'

'Yes,' Kadiatou said, unsure she remembered. They had not lived in the village with Papa, there was nothing here, no chair or tree or smell, to prod a memory alive. Yet she felt him close, his presence and essence, because he had grown up here, long before she existed, and he, too, had pulled grain stalks from the damp soil and walked past huts with calabashes nailed to their doors. She was living the life he once lived. She saw him in the young boys splashing around at the shallow end as she washed clothes in the river. He had worked in his Nembero Joulde's vegetable garden; now she weeded and watered it, fed the soil with kitchen scraps and manure from the animal pen. His spectre hung even over her cooking. Sifting dry fonio comforted her in an unusual, almost spiritual, way, her fingers sunk in the tiny grains, a warming feeling, disappearing and emerging again. She sliced okra and plucked sour leaves and pounded cassava, instinctively knowing that she would not love it so much if she had not started cooking here, with her mother, close to where his own mother had cooked.

'Kadi cooks so well, she will make a good wife, and she has not yet been cut,' Yaaye said to Mama.

'It is not too late,' Mama said defensively. They were outside shelling groundnuts and Mama threw down a shell in a quick, irritated movement.

'Their age-mates here have all been cut,' Yaaye said.

Later, Binta asked Mama, 'What really happens when you are cut?'

'Stop asking,' Mama said.

On the day they were cut, Kadiatou thought, They are going to cut us today, but they did not tell us that they are going to cut us today. It happened in the rainy season, in their grandmother's hut. The air smelled of damp, of mildew sprouting in the outhouse. Mama woke her and Binta, shaking them gently, shadowy figures moving about. Mama and the aunties were talking in whispers. Blue-black early, no roosters crowing, and smoke from the stove in the corner. Mama held Kadiatou down, pressed firm on the mat, while her aunt Nenan Mawdo bent between her legs. In Nenan Mawdo's hand, the razor blade was warm from boiling water. It must have been sharpened over and over to quickly slice through human flesh. Kadiatou felt the metal's warm touch and then the pressure against her skin before the exploding pain. She was shocked that she had been cut, so shocked she made no sound. Such painful pain. Her head felt like a whole waterfall trapped in a shell. Binta was screaming while the aunties told her to be quiet, to be brave, to be a woman. 'Mama, you are wicked!' Binta shouted. 'Mama, you are cursed! How can you do this to us?' Mama was hushing, comforting, padding a rag soaked in herb juices between their legs. The rag stung, like a hundred insect bites all at once. Kadiatou was floating up above the ground, her weight gone, all substance drained out of her. Mama's face morphed into the gleaming face of a magic snake, and Kadiatou stared, too flattened even to scream, until the features softened and became Mama's face again. A throne appeared, hanging still in the air. Hot peppers were spread on its seat, and the throne began to shake from side to side, and then to spin, red peppers flying in the air.

'Kadi, Kadi,' Mama said. 'You want some water?'

Kadiatou tried to say no but her tongue had dissolved in her mouth.

An aunty said, 'Leave them to rest. In a few days they will not even remember it.'

Another aunty said, 'I remember mine. Pus was coming out. I smelled so bad.'

It was days before Kadiatou could look fearfully down at herself, her lower body felt detached, a thing apart, no longer hers. Every day, Mama cleaned them, singing softly and caressing their legs. Always, Binta squirmed away from Mama. 'You did not tell us,' she said, her tone accusing. 'You did not tell us what was going to happen to us.'

But alone with Kadiatou, Binta said, 'They had to cut us because if they don't, then we can't marry.'

'Yes,' Kadiatou said. Mama and the aunties had said so, too, but from Binta's mouth, the words brought calm, Kadiatou's shock slowly fading.

'We have to get our periods first,' Binta said.

Kadiatou did not know the details of periods, but she knew old women went to the mosque because they no longer had their periods, and young women could not go if they had their periods, and you needed a period to have your children and girls could get married as soon as their periods came. Kadiatou dreamed of marrying her cousin Tamsir, and having seven children, and selling yogurt, so she looked forward to her period. Binta's came not long after they were cut, heavy dark blood full of clots like pieces of raw liver, and for a few days Binta lay writhing from pain. Binta pulled up her skirt to show Kadiatou the menstrual cloth folded in her underwear, and Kadiatou reared back, slightly repulsed. Her own period confused her when it came, utterly painless, a simple announcement of blood, and she wished for pain, because hers felt wrong, like an imitation, while Binta's was real.

Two

Years later, submerged in savage sadness, Kadiatou thought she should have known something was wrong, Mama should have known, Tantie Fanta should have known. But what could they have done, even if they had known? If it is already destined, can we change what is written for us? And Binta, how could she know so much and yet not know that something was wrong? Binta, who taught herself to read and speak French. Kadiatou knew Binta looked at Idris's schoolbooks, but she didn't know how much Binta had learned until that day at the clinic. Kadiatou had a fever, again; her fevers came too often, and Mama said it was because mosquitoes loved children born in the rainy season. Binta rubbed Kadiatou's joints, saying, 'I want to take your pain from you', rubbing a little too hard, as though the force might dislodge Kadiatou's pain. The government clinic gave free medicine, but it was in the next village and the wait there was always too long and Mama couldn't spend a whole day without selling any yogurt or they would have nothing to eat at supper. So Mama plucked herbs and made infusions that Kadiatou inhaled. Binta said the infusions didn't help. They were hardly old enough to go that far on their own but Binta insisted. 'I will take her, Mama, I can go to the clinic with Kadi. I know the way. We can manage.'

At the clinic, the corridors were crowded, people waiting, babies crying, and Binta spoke to the woman giving out cards, she spoke in loud rapid French, and Kadiatou gaped, dumbstruck, because Binta was suddenly a new being, a winged angel made of sun rays, and not the sister with whom she had walked side by side for more than an hour in the humid heat.

'You can speak French!' Kadiatou said.

'But, Kadi, I listen to the radio,' Binta said, as if Kadiatou did not listen to the same radio, too, as if everybody who listened to the radio could open their mouths for French words to come sailing out. When Bappa Moussa finally allowed Binta to go to Conakry, years later, she came back to visit, speaking to everyone, even their grandmother, in Pular crammed with French words. She said 'share' in French when she gave a packet of biscuits to the younger children. She seemed, again, transformed by French, but in a different way, as a darkened angel, her eyes lined in very black kohl. Binta was bursting to tell Kadiatou about a young Malinke man named Fodé, Fodé this and Fodé that, Fodé thought and Fodé liked, Fodé taught her this and Fodé bought her that; she was so much under his spell that she was unaware of the spell itself. Vague uneasiness settled over

Kadiatou like a cloud. Binta unfolded the long jeans skirt she had bought for Kadiatou, with money Fodé gave her. 'Kadi, try it on. All the girls in Conakry wear this,' she said, and when Kadiatou seemed slow at changing, Binta picked up and unzipped the skirt. Kadiatou barely liked the skirt, it was tight at the hips, but she feigned pleasure as they both looked in the cracked mirror leaning against the wall. Something new in Binta, she sensed, would not tolerate a lukewarm response. It was either the highest notes or total silence. From underneath the pile of clothes in her bag, Binta pulled out a cassette tape of Sékou Touré's speeches and showed it to Kadiatou.

Transgression sat in the air. Kadiatou glanced at the door as if Bappa Moussa might walk in. She did not know how the first leader of Guinea had harmed Fula people, but she had recognized from childhood the intensity of feeling he aroused, the bitterness of uncles and aunts. Some Fula people wouldn't even mention his name in their homes. And here was Binta brandishing his words.

'Guinea prefers poverty in freedom to riches in slavery!' she intoned, laughing. At least those French words Kadiatou had heard before. Binta said Tantie Fanta had hissed when she saw the tape, asking Binta to throw it away, to think of what that man had done to Fula people, and Binta said he hadn't harmed all Fula people, only his political opponents who did him wrong.

'Do you want to listen to the tape?' Binta asked. 'It teaches you so much. We can play it in Bhoye's player.'

'No, I won't even understand it,' Kadiatou said, her unease ripening to worry. Binta was shedding her old skins too quickly, her flame burned uncleanly, garishly, as if the world might recoil from its glare. Kadiatou's skin prickled at Fodé, this stranger inserted into Binta's life. If Binta could no longer clearly see herself, if her dreams became shielded in Fodé's fog, then she would never reach her destined greatness. Kadiatou wanted to see Fodé. She asked Mama if she could go back with Binta, for a week or two; after all, Tantie Fanta had been asking her to visit, to come and see Conakry. Binta bristled when Mama asked for a few more days, to get enough money for Kadiatou's transport fare. I am missing my lessons, Binta said, irritated, and Kadiatou thought, sadly, that it was not about her lessons. In

Conakry, Binta showed Kadiatou the secretarial centre where she was learning typing and shorthand, and the market stall where she worked as an assistant, and the part of the city where tree-cooled avenues flowed one into the other. But she did not show her Fodé. He was on a training course, Binta said, and Kadiatou nodded, even though she did not know what a training course was. All she knew was that a person so close to Binta should have made time to come and greet Binta's sister. She cooked latchiri and kossan for Tantie Fanta, sieving the cornmeal smooth in the tiny kitchen of the self-contained flat. At night, they watched TV, English films with French subtitles crawling across the screen, and they slept on the bed along the wall, their bodies blurring, Tantie Fanta's, Binta's and hers. A kind of happiness warmed Kadiatou, a long-ago feeling from childhood, when they lived in the township with Papa, all in one room. On the day before she left Conakry, Binta gave her some cash and said it was from Fodé. They were standing by the table where Tantie Fanta's hand mirror was placed face down, her creams and perfumes arranged in tidy lines as if for sale in a shop. 'He said it's for you to buy something for the people at home,' Binta said.

Kadiatou hid her hesitation. If he was away then how had he sent money? 'How can I thank him?' she asked Binta and Binta evaded her eyes and said, 'Next time you come.' Kadiatou felt the urge to cry and plead with Binta, to say please, please, please, but for what she was not sure. Please let us be as we used to be. Please don't avoid my eyes. A memory came to her then in vivid light, of herself sitting on the floor as Papa ate his supper of ndappa, alert, watching him, eager to refill his enamel cup of water, but just as he took the last sip, Binta sprang up and took the cup.

On the way back to the village, squashed in a rickety Peugeot, Kadiatou felt almost relieved. It was good to see Conakry, but she couldn't live in this place that was never at rest, breathing in the exhaled breaths of too many people. Smaller, quieter things appealed to her; she did not see the point of reaching to touch or feel what might bring discord.

———

WHO WOULD HAVE THOUGHT that she, Kadiatou, would have a boyfriend before Binta did, and sit with him under the tree by the abandoned house on top of the hill. It was the year before Binta left for Conakry. They called the abandoned house Mariama's Kitchen, and at village gatherings at dusk the teenagers would wander away and sit there talking, the girls a little apart from the boys. Some of the boys took sticks and poked in the eaves for the large black termites that hid there. A woman called Mariama had lived in the abandoned house until some years ago, when her husband beat her until her eye was swollen shut, because she served him bad kossan, the yogurt not properly soured. He often threatened to take a second wife, and she often begged him not to, but this time she cradled her eye and told him, 'Please divorce me.' She had had enough. Even when the elders and imams intervened, Mariama still said she had had enough. Binta liked to perch on the verandah of the small shabby house, the roof already caving in, and the rustle of mice in the single bedroom. 'Maybe Mariama is in the city, maybe she is working in Conakry,' Binta would say dreamily.

'Maybe she is a beggar on the streets,' Amadou would say, and then he and Binta would argue, Amadou saying other women got beaten but didn't desert their marriages, and Binta saying imagine all the years of beatings since Mariama married at fifteen.

They were good friends, Amadou and Binta, and similar; both of them were born dreaming. There was a bone that birthed courage and Kadiatou believed she lacked that bone, or if she had it then it was feeble, soft and chewable like biscuit-bone. Binta and Amadou's courage bones were strong, hardy, they might bend but never break. Kadiatou was astonished when Binta told her, 'Amadou wants you.' She was so unlike them; she was quiet and shy and she didn't know the things they knew. How could Amadou want her? Amadou, popular, swaggering Amadou, hands perched on jeans pockets, a township boy visiting the village. He cracked jokes and was full of big talk of the businesses he would start as soon as he completed his apprenticeship in his uncle's leather goods shop. He pointed at a truck rumbling past, stacked with bags of grain, and said he would own twenty of those, transporting fonio and fabrics and pottery, and he would own twenty station wagons, carrying people on all the main roads across Guinea. He smoked a cigarette openly, in the grove of trees. The other boys gathered around him and listened, wanting to be like him, wanting to be him. In the blaze of his attention, Kadiatou melted, and she never stopped being astonished that he had chosen her. They stood hand in hand behind Mariama's Kitchen and looked in the distance at the valley, dreamy with mist. He kissed her, her life's first kiss, his tongue like a warm slippery fish in her mouth. It was not pleasant but also not unpleasant, because nothing with Amadou could be unpleasant. She always brought her face willingly to his. He shaved sticks of sugarcane for her and slowly she ate them, and sticky juice ran down her fingers like liquid silver. 'You will be my wife,' he said. Kadiatou wanted a harmonious home, and if you wanted a harmonious home, you married a close relative, to keep the lineage clean. Like Papa and Mama, who were first cousins. So she had dreamed of marrying her cousin Tamsir. He had patient eyes like Papa and he was doing well, trading in Senegal with relatives, and Mama and his mother made comments about how they were a good match and as good as engaged. The few times she saw Tamsir, in the village at Eid, she glanced shyly at him, both of them aware, in their rich, bashful silence, of a future already sealed. Suddenly she no longer wanted Tamsir. She had chosen without knowledge, had accepted Tamsir, unaware that boundless joy could be spun just from talking to a boy. She wanted to be Amadou's wife, she wanted nothing more, but Bappa Moussa would reject Amadou: he wasn't related to them, he wasn't wealthy, he was too young, close to her age. Amadou talked of their future like a blind person, oblivious of the boulders in their path. 'I'll make money and buy a white Peugeot and come and carry you away to Conakry,' he said often.

Other times he said, 'There's something called a visa lottery, and I will get it and go to America and then send for you.'

Which would happen first, she gently teased him, the big white car to take her away to the city, or sending for her in America? And he replied, 'Whichever God brings first.' The last time she saw Amadou, she did not know it was the last time she would see him, until his cousin brought her a message, saying he had left for America in a hurry, his paperwork had suddenly come through, and he could not wait. His cousin pressed an envelope into her hand. Inside was his baby picture, in black and white, slightly faded. Even as a baby he had that exuberant smile. 'Amadou said you should keep it and bring it when you come to America to join him,' his cousin said.

She took the photo and said, 'Okay.' Paris was a fable you could touch, she knew of the Champs-Élysées and the Eiffel Tower, but America was too removed from the spherical shape of her imagination; she could not see herself living there. If she thought at all of America, she thought only of films.

KADIATOU KEPT THE PHOTO at the bottom of her small metal trunk, protected by camphor balls. Months passed in silence from him, and then it was almost two years with no letter, no message, no word. A sign if she needed one, that it simply wasn't meant to be. Not that she ever truly believed she would marry Amadou or go to America; her future was fire-dried, too firm to change without chaos, and she dreaded chaos. It was unbearable to think of being without her family's approval, cast out alone and shivering. Yet there she was, as all that time passed, still imagining her marriage to Amadou, the imams gathered in prayer amid her aunts' joyful songs, and then the children they would have, four boys and three girls. One day, in a rare reckless moment, while Mama was bent over a wood fire and Kadiatou was peeling cassava, Kadiatou told Mama about Amadou, that he had gone to America and would send for her as soon as he could. Mama straightened up and said, 'Kadi, you must keep the lineage clean and marry close to home.'

'Yes,' Kadiatou said. What had she expected, opening her mouth like that? Of course Mama would say exactly that, as any good mother would. Mama said Tamsir's father would send word soon, very soon. 'Tamsir is your husband, Kadi,' Mama said, and Kadiatou said, 'Yes', and resolved to starve her mind of longing. When word did come, it was Yaaye and another aunty shuffling in one evening, their faces downcast, but their eyes alight with the excitement of a scandal.

They said Tamsir had married a Susu girl in Senegal, and she was already pregnant, and his parents were drowning in shame. Kadiatou listened, not fully comprehending.

'Is the girl Senegalese?' Mama asked, a strange question, as if in her shock she could think of nothing better to say.

'No, Guinean. But she lives in Senegal like him,' Yaaye said.

'A Susu girl,' Mama said and snorted in disbelief. 'The blood of that faithless tribe will now poison the lineage.'

Mama glanced at Kadiatou and Kadiatou averted her eyes. The lineage would have been kept clean if *she* birthed Tamsir's children. She felt ashamed, even guilty, as if by longing for Amadou she had triggered the scandal of Tamsir's reneging. A photo was passed around, of a svelte dark girl, about Kadiatou's age. The person Tamsir had chosen. The inheritor of Kadiatou's future. From the photo alone, she was beyond reproach: a pretty face, pious-looking, a sweet-natured smile. More aunties and cousins had gathered, their contempt, like peppery fumes, directed at the Susu girl, and their voices no longer hushed, saying she had entrapped Tamsir, she was diabolic, how else could Tamsir, so level-headed and responsible, end up in this shameful mess? In the midst of her disorientation, Kadiatou felt a strained relief, a small sprinkling of hope. Amadou could come and make his intention known now, while Tamsir's disappointment was still a fresh open wound. Bappa Moussa would accept him, if only to cover their shame, because Susu girl or not, Tamsir had rejected her. Cast her aside. But the scale and surprise of his betrayal was almost redeeming and for this she felt a dark gratitude – it so occupied everyone that her own humiliation sank unseen. Had Tamsir left her for another Fula girl, the rejection would have more deeply stained her.

IN THE FOLLOWING MONTHS, Kadiatou drifted. No longer waiting to marry Tamsir and have children. A feeling of being empty-handed, which was different from being empty. All thoughts of Amadou were banished, finally, she told herself, no more fanciful imagining of a man who had forgotten her. In place of those thoughts was a dull void. Mama told her Tamsir was not God's wish for her, and a better husband would come, but shame glowed in Mama, in the false defiance of her words. Only Binta was untroubled, even pleased.

'I told you Tamsir was never your husband,' Binta said. 'Amadou will come back. Even his own family has not heard from him since. It is not easy abroad. He must be trying to get himself settled before sending for you.'

Kadiatou shook her head to shake off Binta's words, afraid they would bring back her hope. Binta had come back because Bappa Moussa asked her to, and he told her she must marry first, as the elder daughter, as if to push attention away from Kadiatou's failure. Only their cousin, Thierno, could handle Binta, Bappa Moussa said. He had finished secondary school and was trading in Ivory Coast, he was wealthy and forward-looking, he condemned men who took second wives and had assured Bappa Moussa that Binta could work as a secretary if she wished.

A perfect match, Kadiatou thought: a successful, impressive groom, a beautiful ceremony, fragrant bandages for Mama's broken pride.

'Kadi, I don't like him,' Binta said.

'You've seen him three times. You'll come to like him,' Kadiatou said.

'He doesn't talk much,' Binta said.

'Because he knows you will talk for both of you,' Kadiatou teased.

'That necklace he sent me is so cheap,' Binta said.

'He will start buying nicer things after he brings your taignai,' Kadiatou said.

Binta scoffed. Then she said, 'Malinke men are not tightfisted like Fula men.'

Kadiatou kept silent.

'They take good care of their wives. Tantie Fanta said they only want Fula women for our beauty but that is not true,' Binta said.

Still Kadiatou said nothing, her chest tight. She was never outraged by Binta, but now she felt something close; Binta could have all the Malinke friends she wanted but, for marriage, of course she had to show good sense. To marry her Fodé, or any man who was not Fula, was a blasphemy too dire even to entertain.

'Kadi, you're not saying anything.'

'There is nothing to say.'

'Tamsir married a Susu girl and yes, nobody is happy, but when he brings his child, they will welcome the child and soon they will welcome the Susu girl,' Binta said.

'It's different for men.'

'In Conakry, I see Fula women married to Malinke men,' Binta said.

'They must not come from good families. We come from a good family.'

'True,' Binta said and sighed, resigned. Kadiatou exhaled. Binta hadn't meant any of that, couldn't have meant it, she was just playing, hovering a teasing foot over murky water.

Later, Kadiatou wondered: What if Binta had insisted on her Malinke man, might things have been different? Or was it Binta's destiny, written into her life, bound to happen no matter who she married? She often wondered about people who sought to know their futures. Why would they want to know of tragedies hurtling down towards them that they could not step aside to avoid? It was Binta who wanted to have the surgery before her djamougal ceremony with Thierno. Tantie Fanta agreed that she should, but it was Binta who wanted it. A doctor in Conakry had told her the heavy bleeding would stop, the days spent hunched over in pain would end. She did not tell Thierno because she said it frightened men to think their wives might not easily birth babies. Only Kadiatou and Mama and Bappa Moussa and Tantie Fanta knew. Even Bappa Moussa Binta had not wanted to tell, but Mama said they should, to give him respect. Maybe they should have listened to Bappa Moussa. He was resistant, afraid of any kind of surgery, asking, 'Why must she have an operation instead of enduring it like other women?' Things were growing inside Binta's womb, Tantie Fanta explained, and the surgery would remove those things, which would stop her heavy monthly bleeding. Still, Bappa Moussa was unconvinced. Only when Tantie Fanta said

Binta would not be able to get pregnant without this surgery did Bappa Moussa agree.

KADIATOU'S FIRST THOUGHT WAS — why has Tantie Fanta come, she was supposed to send word, and why has she come with all these relatives?

Already in Kadiatou's head, darkness was gathering. Tantie Fanta opened her mouth and said five words and her voice cracked to pieces. She said, 'Binta did not wake up.'

Kadiatou did not understand. 'What do you mean by she did not wake up?' Mama asked, which was exactly what Kadiatou wanted to ask.

'They did the operation, and after the operation, Binta did not wake up,' Tantie Fanta said.

'When will she wake up?' Mama shouted. 'Fanta, when will she wake up?'

A sudden furious blur of motion. Mama was flat on the ground, jerking violently, and the ground was brimming with dust, and somebody was trying to hold Mama but her body refused to be subdued. From deep in her throat came a guttural keening as ancient as unformed earth, the ugliest, most spine-chilling sound Kadiatou had ever heard. It shattered the shock-strangled air. In that moment Kadiatou understood that her sister was dead. She felt an implosion in her heart, the beginning of a deathless sorrow, the moment that love forever turned to loss. For years to come, she would bolt awake from a dream about Binta, so achingly clear that she always looked around, searching the room as if Binta might be there. In the dream, Binta was startled by her own death, and she was standing in the government hospital, which looked strangely like Mariama's Kitchen, wearing a floor-length caftan, saying, 'Kadi, you said you would stop the bleeding. Kadi, why did you say you would stop the bleeding?'

THE HOUSE SWELLED and filled with Binta's shadow, Binta's scent, Binta's voice. Sometimes, in the sway of the palm trees and the quickening of a breeze near the abandoned house, Kadiatou felt Binta, a small shiver, a cascading of goosebumps. Binta was every-where. A cruel offering of false hope. Kadiatou watched Mama and her siblings cry, and she felt no urge to comfort them. They were in the same room but they were so distant and far away. Mama, with her white scarf, a widow's scarf, draped over her head. Would she get another scarf? But there was no scarf for mourning a child, because a mother was not supposed to lose a child.

Mama said to visitors who came with small gifts to pay their con-dolences, 'I have other children, God gave me other children.' But it was a lie and Kadiatou felt angry to hear Mama say that, as if Binta could be replaced. Binta was her sunlight child and Mama's heart had died with her. 'You are my first daughter now, Kadi,' her mother told her, and Kadiatou did not respond, feeling again the anger spread through her. I am not your first daughter, she wanted to say, nobody but Binta can be your first daughter. When she overheard her mother tell a close friend, 'Binta would have become somebody. She would have brought me glory', it made her angry too, but the anger was cleansing because it was a response, finally, to truth. Binta would have brought Mama glory. It was true, Binta was the child blessed with the kind of graces that brought glory, and Mama should not pre-tend that Binta could ever be replaced. Kadiatou began then to feel angry with Binta for dying, because by dying Binta had malformed all their lives, and their future, and left her with a burden she did not know how to lift. To bring glory to Mama, to become somebody.

THREE

It was an evil year, the year that took Binta. The har-mattan was harsh, the crops were shrivelled, and rams lay dead on parched farmlands like rumpled cloth. Kadiatou cooked namma with too much water to make it go round, small okra pieces floating to the top of the sad soup. Clinics no longer gave free vaccines, or free malaria medicine. Tantie Fanta said America and France had forced the government to stop free primary education and free medicine;

it was the only way to become friends with America and France again, by not behaving like communists. Yaaye's grandson Lamin died of malaria. When Mama and Kadiatou visited to pay condolences, Yaaye stared blankly at them and kept scratching at the dirt on her floor. Death was everywhere, life vanishing at every turn, and when Bappa Moussa first mentioned their relative Saidou, Kadiatou thought he, too, had died. She knew Saidou, vaguely, from before he left the village to work in a mine somewhere in the northwest. 'He is your husband,' Bappa Moussa told Kadiatou. 'You see how difficult things are. He will help us.'

'I do not want to disobey you, Bappa Moussa, but I will not marry a man who works in a mine.'

'His mining work is different. He does not work in the small artisanal mines but a big one run by Whites,' Bappa Moussa said.

Kadiatou started saying again, 'I do not want to disobey you—' but Bappa Moussa cut in and said, 'My brother would have approved.'

Bringing up Papa upset Kadiatou. Bappa Moussa knew that mentioning Papa would confuse her emotions. Would Papa have approved of Saidou? Her memories were even more faded, like photos rinsed out in water, and Papa's image was frozen in her childhood; she could imagine him singing the songs of folktales but not talking to her about a husband. Would he have approved of a husband who worked in a mine? But what did she even have to lose? If she married Saidou and he died in a rock slide, then so be it. Binta was dead. Amadou was in America, as good as lost. She might as well marry Saidou, who was much older than her, with thick veins running over his forehead. He came wearing a watch with a big shiny face. His uncle came with him, an elderly man who worked in Conakry, and he and Tantie Fanta talked about the situation in the country while Bappa Moussa listened, as if he understood what was being said. Binta would have understood; Kadiatou didn't understand, nor did she care to.

We produce bauxite that countries all over the world use for aluminium, but look at our suffering. Austerity programme this, austerity programme that. Why should we sacrifice education and health to pay debts that we know nothing about? Those French and Russian companies stealing our bauxite should be expelled immediately.

Tantie Fanta said that a Guinean Fula man had been killed in America. An immigrant in America. He was pulling out his wallet when policemen shot him forty times, leaving many bullets in his body, too many bullets for one body. Terrible, Saidou said. Tantie Fanta joked darkly that he was a Fula man, tightfisted, and was only trying to make sure they didn't take his money. Neither Saidou nor his uncle looked amused by the joke. Saidou said he had heard that many American journalists were coming to Conakry to write about the case.

'None of them knew Guinea existed as a country until they killed this Amadou,' Saidou's uncle said.

Amadou? The dead man's name was Amadou. A chill spread through Kadiatou, her stomach heaved, about to come up to her throat.

'I hear he comes from the lineage of the famous Diallo traders,' Tantie Fanta said.

And Kadiatou reeled, dizzy with relief. It wasn't Amadou, her Amadou.

'In America the police shoot people for no reason,' Saidou said.

'At least they make noise about it. Everybody in America is talking about it,' Saidou's uncle said.

'Here they kill you and everyone stays quiet,' Bappa Moussa said, eagerly, finally able to join in.

Kadiatou could see that Tantie Fanta approved of Saidou, she smiled along as Saidou boasted of his nice two-bedroom flat in a compound of mine workers, and said the mine had a clinic for the workers and their families, with real doctors mending broken bones and not just treating malaria. Bappa Moussa was nodding and trying not to look as impressed as he was. His small eyes glittered with unexpected pleasure, as if he had managed to sell old goods at new prices. He did not say how many cows Saidou's family brought as taignai, mumbling only that it was good, very good. He praised even the kola nuts they brought for the djamougal, saying they looked expensive, unscarred and fresh-skinned. An aunty put one of those kola nuts in Kadiatou's mouth before they spun her around seven times, checking after each turn to see if she had spit it out. She hadn't, of course, but she wondered what would happen if she had. Would they start all over again, with her in her sparkling veil, her embroidered dress, the imams' prayers, the crush of singing aunties, urgent words of marriage advice, everybody entangled and happy for her, the dance and noise, and all the purifying rituals for her husband's home? Finally, at the end, she drank the ceremonial sour milk, suddenly aware of an echo around her of absence. Mournful absence as tactile as a presence. In the perfumed embrace of her aunties, she began to cry, tears that most believed were of joy.

THE MINING TOWN was noise and dust. Kadiatou woke to the unending rumble of machinery hacking and digging and extract-ing at the mine, trucks driving away and returning and driving away again. The dust astounded her, dust everywhere, dust on scavenging chickens, dust coating the hair of playing children. Her body com-plained only a day in, thousands of tiny bumps erupting on her skin, on her face, across her torso and legs. She coughed and sneezed all day, and she was so itchy she longed to reach in and scratch at the centre of her soul. Tears trailed from her reddened eyes and on her tongue a constant grittiness accrued. Saidou took her on a motorcycle ride, to show her around, and they rode out of the staff compound, past the mine and into the town. They passed fields of sick-looking grain, young stalks already shrivelling to straw. The stream had become a muddy pudding on whose surface a few dead fish floated round-eyed. Kadiatou stared in disbelief, turning from side to side. She felt as if she had been dropped inside a world shorn of its feathers. The air was soiled, the soil arid. To look at the mine itself on their way back was to shudder at a vast harsh expanse of disembowelled earth, gap-ing helplessly, stark and stripped of life. An urge seized her, to run to the motor park and return to her village where the grass still grew as grass should.

'Has this place always been so bad?' she asked Saidou, who stared, surprised, at her.

'You'll get used to it. It's just a little dust,' he said.

'The small children are always coughing.'

'You want the Whites to shut this place down and we lose our jobs?'

'The streams are dried up, the people here have no water.'

'Enough!' Saidou's expression was like Bappa Moussa's used to be when he scolded Binta for speaking: anger, but also amazement that she had actually said what she said. Kadiatou felt a sudden rush of pride, to have evoked the kind of response Binta did. To be like Binta. Maybe Binta's spirit was there, guiding her to bravery.

Saidou changed the subject, and said his mother was asking if she was pregnant.

'But we have only just married,' she said.

'She is asking,' Saidou said, and shrugged.

'It will happen by God's grace,' she said, and already her earlier bounce was deflating.

She missed the slow languor of home, her siblings and aunties, the majestic silhouettes of tall anthills on moonlit nights. To weaken her homesickness, she folded fully into her duty, cooking, washing, sweeping, kneeling to serve Saidou's food. None of it was disagreeable, nor was Saidou, not always. He praised her food and sometimes he praised her skin, which she kept supple with shea butter, her rashes gone, her itchiness reduced, her body attuned to breathing air burdened by the mine's debris. Saidou began teaching her French. Nobody spoke Pular in that part of Guinea, and how would she talk to traders in the market where she shopped for food? A thin note of criticism ran through his words, that she could not speak even a little French like most people could. He was right, she should have learned some words, she could have followed Binta's lead. She was determined now to acquire the new shift of tongue and lip that French demanded of her. Saidou said they would speak no Pular during weekends and she agreed, fumbling and struggling her way through to comprehension. Why everything, chairs and trees and even the earth itself, had to be male or female in this language, she did not understand. Nor why a single person and a group of people needed different words for doing the same act. Saidou asked her to repeat phrases from the radio and as she cleaned and cooked, she whispered French words to herself. She understood them more and more, but they came out of her mouth sounding nothing like the radio. Saidou said she must practise by speaking to the neighbours, but she saw the mockery in their pursed lips, as if they were struggling to hold back their laughter at the rural lilt of her broken French. Once, she heard someone call her 'Saidou's village wife'.

The dust defeated her; she wiped the floor on her knees, reaching under the table, wringing out the wet rag, and moments later a new layer of dust settled – on floor, armchairs, television, everything, as if they had never been wiped at all. She cleaned again, and again, scrubbing as tears fell, and she scolded herself for crying. What was she crying for anyway? Imagine the foolishness of crying just because the room was dusty. She thought of Amadou in America driving a big white car and she saw a glimpse of her own future, cleaning dust day after day, her knees scabbed from kneeling, her loneliness aching in her bones.

One day, Saidou came home and she could smell him even before he was inside the room.

'You drink alcohol!' she said, horrified, backing away from him.

He lurched past her, then turned to pull her into his cursed breath. She knew she should surrender because she was his wife. She never refused him. Mama's words of marriage advice, 'Never refuse him, never refuse him', always rang in her ears. But she felt violated by the alcohol; that smell was the smell of pure evil. How could Saidou drink? How could he risk bringing a curse down on the family? Everyone knew the story of their relative Mammadou and his many businesses, so successful he built a mosque in the village, receiving baraka, God's special blessings, for he who builds a mosque builds a house in heaven for himself. Then he began to drink alcohol and his businesses crashed, one by one, they failed and he went bankrupt. How could Saidou drink?

Kadiatou held her breath so that the smell of alcohol would not suffuse her body. 'Please bathe first, Saidou,' she said. Later, after he had bathed, smelling still of alcohol, but faintly now, she told him, 'You will bring a curse down on us.'

———

SHE DIDN'T KNOW she was pregnant until she had a miscarriage. There were the two missed periods, yes, but she was always irregular. One afternoon, while scrubbing the windows, she felt a gluey wetness between her legs, pain stabbing and spreading from her belly to her back, and she leaned against the wall, feeling helpless, faithless; there was nothing else she could do. She held her breath, not moving for fear things would worsen, and maybe if she stayed as still as possible she could delay it, stop it even. But delay what? Already she could feel more that was gluey, gelatinous, sliding down her inner thigh. Her body was destroying what was precious to it. She thought of Binta, bleeding, not waking up at the government hospital, and wondered if hers was the same kind of blood as Binta's. But it couldn't be, of course. Binta's bleeding was from vengeful growths invading her womb, while hers was from a rejection happening in her body without her permission. She lowered herself to the floor, gingerly, very gingerly, faint from pain, and waited for her body to complete its betrayal of her.

SAIDOU TOLD HER the miscarriage was her fault because she had washed his clothes bent over the bucket instead of standing upright. She said nothing. His drinking had caused the miscarriage. He knew it. He had brought a curse upon them, and to defend himself, he was saying such nonsensical things as washing clothes with her back bent. 'You'll get pregnant again,' he told her. 'But you have to be careful.'

She did get pregnant again, only weeks later, and even though she did not believe Saidou, she was still careful not to wash clothes bending down, until she gave birth to her son, in the mining hospital, in a white airy room so restful she did not want to go home afterwards. Her son looked like Papa, the lean face and the forehead, and she felt acutely aware of how close and how large life's mysteries were. She wrapped him in a soft blanket Saidou brought to the hospital and held him to her breast, caressing the bald patch on his face where his brows were yet to grow. His tiny body brought a delight she had never before known, trembling, overwhelming and yet so sublime.

She wanted to stay here, just her and her baby, in this air-conditioned hospital on top of a hill, away from the relentless, marauding dust. But they went home, they had to go home, in a taxi with Saidou holding her bag. That evening her baby had diarrhoea, his belly gurgling through the night, and by morning he was dead, already stiffening on the mattress next to her. A ghoulish blank-eyed doll lay next to her, and all she wanted was her son. Saidou wept loudly like a woman. As his colleagues carried away the small stiff body, she sat like a statue, rigidly asking for her son. A cold wind had torn through her chest at night, and she knew now that it was not from breastfeeding; it was a spirit foretelling this horror, but why warn her of something she could not change? She felt such coldness in her heart, such freezing, numbing coldness, and her coldness chafed into a furious resentment of Saidou. Sometimes, the resentment tipped over into hatred. She looked at the back of his head as he watched television and she imagined raising a pan and smashing it down hard on his head. The violence of her own thoughts felt normal to her. Once she saw him sitting outside looking at some playing children with tears in his eyes. 'We didn't even take a picture of him,' he said of the baby. His slump of sadness enraged her. That he dared to feel a right to sorrow. He knew what drinking alcohol would cause and yet he drank and now her son was gone, the image of her father, the baby sent by God to comfort her, the one true companion she might have had. Saidou's evil act had taken him away. And Saidou smelled of alcohol, still, even after his curse had destroyed their lives. She barely spoke to him, cooking and serving his food in silence. When he tried to touch her at night, Kadiatou flinched, resisting at first, and then later she lay there and imagined herself dead too, or dying.

After two missed periods, she felt ravaged by fear. Fear breathing through her. She must shelter this delicate growing life from the claws of a curse, but how? She did not know. She would wait until her belly began to push out and then tell Saidou she hadn't known she was pregnant. Men, of course, never knew these things.

She would avoid Saidou, avoid his touch, avoid eating any food he had also eaten; maybe the curse would remain solely on him. It was Saidou who should have been taken instead of an innocent gift from

God. It was Saidou who had spit at the laws of God. She prayed and prayed in those early weeks, and she was wiping the table while praying when a woman called Salamata, the only other Fula person in the compound, came to her door with some workers from the mine. When they come to your door with Salamata because she speaks Pular, the closest to a relative, you know it is to break not bad but terrible news. Salamata said, 'Something happened, Kadiatou, you have to come to the clinic', and Kadiatou, in her housedress and rubber slippers, mutely went with them to find Saidou's body lying still, covered from head to toe with a flowered bedsheet, on a bed with the mattress now bare.

She staggered. Shock rolled over her like heavy slaps. She had been praying when Salamata knocked on her door but had she been praying for harm to come to Saidou? She had wished him ill, yes, but not this, not a hastening of his death. Or had she prayed for this without knowing it? Her entreaties were to defang the curse, to guard the life growing in her body. She did not mean that Saidou should die. Saidou's siblings had come to the hospital. Some workers were telling them that Saidou touched something, or stepped on something. Kadiatou wasn't sure, the meanings of French words suddenly ungraspable in her brain. She did not ask, she dared not ask, sitting exceedingly still, consumed by guilt. Her hatred must have caused this. It could not be Saidou's fate to die like this.

'I did not mean that he should die,' Kadiatou said.

'What?' his brother asked. 'What are you saying?'

'You poisoned him? You poisoned him?' his sister screamed.

Salamata spoke to Saidou's siblings, calming them, saying Kadiatou was a widow in shock, and did they not know that grief was a brief madness? Did they not know of madness that erupted from the mouths of the bereaved? What did Kadiatou gain from killing the husband who clothed and fed her? Saidou's sister seemed mollified but one of the brothers kept glaring at Kadiatou. They wrapped Saidou's body in white cloth. They took away his motorcycle, the television and the stove. And then his sister searched Kadiatou's bag and drawers, to make sure she had not stolen and hidden Saidou's money. 'If only Kadiatou was pregnant, we would still have something of him,'

Saidou's sister said, watching her after the funeral, and Kadiatou hurriedly moved away from the shrewd eyes of a woman who herself had many children. If Saidou's people knew, they would keep her, and she couldn't survive living with his mother, bearing the burden of her guilt, and her fear of a curse.

TEN FINGERS AND TEN TOES. Her baby had ten fingers and ten toes. She counted most mornings and nights, sometimes she woke up just to count, and it comforted her to know that there were ten fingers and ten toes. A complete baby, and hers, all hers. After she was freed from the mournful landscape of that mining town, her solace had been Conakry with Tantie Fanta, living quietly and watching her belly grow.

She laid her baby girl on the bed and slept on the floor, for fear of rolling over her in sleep, and woke through the night to gently touch the tiny chest and feel for her baby's breath; so great was the terror at the centre of her love. She called her Binta. She tied Binta on her back as she worked; sometimes she felt the spreading warmth of Binta's fresh pee. Tantie Fanta had helped her find this job, housekeeper for a rich family in Conakry, cleaning and cooking in the coolness of the marble mansion. When she was free, she laid Binta by the tall water fountain in the front yard, the sound of the water restful, like eternity. She sent a message to Saidou's family, saying she would bring the baby soon, but not saying how soon. Their anger was raw in the messages they sent back. How dare she send a message about a baby when they knew nothing of her pregnancy? Relatives intervened, asking to see Binta, to take Binta to her father's people. Kadiatou never raised her voice, or her eyes, in disrespect. Quietly she said she would bring Binta but just not yet. She wanted Binta to get a little older, to be sure the curse no longer lingered, but she wouldn't tell Saidou's family about the curse. She had already hastened his death without meaning to, and she would not further dishonour him by exposing his sin. The village was swirling with rumours, and Mama believed Saidou's people started it all; the baby was not Saidou's, they said, or she would have since been brought to them. 'I will not let them soil my daughter's name,' Mama said and so she told the village gossip Aminatou that the baby was Saidou's but there was the issue of a curse. A curse had first to be drained of its power. 'What curse?' Aminatou asked and Mama answered in a whisper, knowing the scandal of Saidou's drinking would spread throughout the village before dusk. It did, and his parents stopped speaking to Mama. Sometimes Kadiatou wished Saidou would appear in her dream, so that she could beg his forgiveness, but he never appeared. Nothing of him endured. She did not miss him, or think of him, she blamed him with bitterness for losing her son, but she felt, too, that she had not done right by him. Death was too final; she had wished for him a punishment with an ending.

FOUR

The Monsieur said he liked how quiet she was, doing her work and keeping out of his way. He asked often for her fonde and namma, and he loved latchiri and kossan, like a proper Fula man, for he *was* Fula, after all, even if his ways were foreign and his Pular marred by French. He had guests in the evenings, wealthy men like him, sometimes government men, who came in government cars, and she took plates of food out to their drivers and uniformed guards. The Madame lived in Paris, the children were in school there, and they visited once while on holiday, walking with the donkey-like gait of people born abroad, sneering at the fonio Kadiatou served. When the Madame brought a sophisticated Senegalese man, a restaurant chef, to teach her how to cook, Kadiatou concealed how offended she was.

'You yawn so loudly' was the first thing the Senegalese chef said to her. 'Why do you make that sound when you yawn and why are you yawning?'

She had yawned only once. Binta was unwell, feverish, her little body shuddering with coughs, and so she had held Binta through the night, and she was tired, but she had yawned only once. 'Excuse me, sorry,' she said politely. This Senegalese man merely wanted to belittle her; he was similar to Madame in pomposity. She listened and watched as he simmered chicken in an onion sauce, mixed rice in a tomato sauce, mashed potatoes. Poulet yassa and riz gras – and whatever else uninspired meal he was making. He asked Kadiatou to set the table and said, 'I will come and inspect it', and Kadiatou bristled silently. Monsieur, just home from work, was stretched out on a sofa in the living room.

'I brought the head chef from Chez Simone to teach her,' Madame said to Monsieur, as Kadiatou began setting the table.

'Oh, but Kadiatou is very good. She doesn't need teaching. She should own a restaurant of her own in the future,' Monsieur said. Kadiatou kept calmly placing the cutlery down while her heart danced. She could not resist glancing at Madame, who was looking at Monsieur with eyes full of arrows. Monsieur ate the Senegalese chef's food, but later, after Madame left with the children, he told Kadiatou, 'Now you can start giving me good food again.'

Kadiatou lived in the servant's quarters in the back, a large room with a fan and a nice linoleum floor. She asked Monsieur if she could take some of the old children's things piled in the store, and he said yes, with a vague wave of his hand. She sent clothes and toys and two small bicycles to Mama, and then she began to take things without telling Monsieur, because she knew he would never notice and Madame, on her brief visits, never even looked in any of the rooms downstairs. Mama had no idea what to do with the sewing machine she sent her, and Kadiatou said they could sell it. Another time she sent old pairs of Monsieur's shoes, and Mama said she would sell those, too, and did not show them to Bappa Moussa.

Each time Monsieur travelled to Paris, he asked her to stay and look after the house, but asked any visiting relatives to leave, saying he trusted her more than his own blood. She felt content, grateful; maybe she was finally being allowed a measure of peace and for this she prayed in thanksgiving. Monsieur was in Paris the morning soldiers barged into the compound. It was as if Kadiatou blinked and there appeared a herd of soldiers, red berets on their heads, long black guns looking dull in the bright light. It was like a film, men going to war, men whose legs stomped strong with the purpose to kill. They had come to kill Monsieur. Somebody in the government sent them to kill Monsieur, and since he was not here, what would they do to her? She clutched her baby, her legs trembling so much she feared she might fall. One soldier opened the fridge and took a can of orange juice. The others dispersed inside the house as if they had known it before. They were in the living room, yanking cabinets open and leaving them open, ransacking Monsieur's bedroom. They pulled his mattress off his bed and shook the mattress. They were insulting Monsieur, calling him a dog. Binta was crying her high, screeching cry. Their leader said, 'Let's go', and one of them said to her, 'Follow us!' But the leader snorted and said, 'She's just a maid. What are you questioning her for? Let her go.'

Kadiatou packed her things as swiftly as she could and loaded a taxi to take her and Binta to Tantie Fanta's.

MEN LIT UP when they heard she was a widow. They would have lit up even if she had a revolting face. She was a widow and a widow walked trailing behind her the scent of defenceless availability. She served at the beachside restaurant, enduring their leers, knowing they saw her as an opportunity, because men were men. She began covering her hair, and she kept her expression pleasant with her eyes and not her lips; there was no smile that a man might misread. She did not expect the owner, François, a busy, important man, to protect her, but he barked at the men who did more than leer: one who brushed her hip, and another who grasped her arm as she placed down a plate. She was grateful that he deigned to protect her. He owned other restaurants, and she would impress him with her work and then ask if she could work as a cook, not a waitress. She had mentioned her cooking when she first got the job, but François said he already had two cooks. The other day she heard him shouting at one of the cooks, about too much salt in the chips. She would ask him to at least let her help the cooks. She would say a Senegalese chef had trained her in cooking, which was not quite a lie but felt like a lie. As she served and cleaned she imagined owning a restaurant, Monsieur's words forever fresh in her mind. Her dream lifted her spirits. She would serve Guinean food, not the chicken and chips everyone ate at restaurants, and she would make it beautiful, as that Senegalese chef had done with his food, cupping the rice into an elegant small hill, designing syrup over dessert like an artist. If François agreed to let her work as a cook, she would learn how restaurants preserved their food, how much they bought when they shopped. She was shy about asking François but she would; he already saw how hard she worked serving food, and he protected her from those men; maybe he would say yes. François was light-skinned, his eyes light like marbles, his hair curly from his Lebanese mother; he was so handsome, like someone on television. He would never notice her, of course, not like that. She wished it but she did not dream it, because she dreamed only of achievable things. François came by one evening as she was closing up the storage room where crates of soft drinks were stacked. He stood at the door and said, 'Well done, Kadiatou,' and she flushed with excitement, to be praised by François, to be here with François. He came into the room. He smelled of ginger. He was always sucking something, a ginger sweet maybe, his mouth puckered to a kind of insolence. She thought perhaps she should ask him now, but it didn't feel right, it was late, they were closing, the room was stuffy and he had only stopped by briefly. Maybe next week. She thought he would leave after glancing at the crates but he didn't leave. She was done but stood there, respectfully, waiting for him to leave first. He walked towards her. The room was too small for the crates of drinks and her and him. Usually when the other waitress came in here, Kadiatou waited outside until she was done. François was now inches away from her and Kadiatou felt awkward, wanting to apologize, ask if there was something she could help him do. He pushed her against the table, saying, 'Just a little, just a little, be nice to me.' Surprised, she looked at him. Then came the stark startling clarity that he intended to hurt her.

'No sir, no sir,' she said. Not like this, she wanted to add. Not like this. The shock of his heavy alien weight. He was so heavy, like a giant bag of cassava pressing and deflating the breath from her. Why did he not ask her, why treat her as though she was not worth asking? It could have been different, he could have asked her, she could have gently touched that soft foreign hair. When he was done, in a minute or two, he looked at her in the face and she thought for an incredulous moment that he would say he cared for her. But his lips curled in disgust and he said, 'Cover yourself.' He was telling her to cover herself, but it was he who had yanked up her dress and pulled down her underwear. He stood hulking over her, his disgust so palpable it turned the air rancid. She heard the hatred in his voice. He did not know her but he hated her, and he did not need to know her to hate her. 'Cover yourself,' he said again, a threat in his tone. Would he harm her again? He wanted her to cover her body and cover his crime, to look as she had before he walked into the store. As if nothing had happened. Shame, shame like hot water scalded through her. And shock. Shame and shock. She pulled down her dress and wrapped her arms around herself. Her legs were trembling but she stared at him, right in the eye, to make him know that she saw him, she saw that he was a monster and not a man. He did not deserve to be a human being. His heart was full of dead leaves. He evaded her gaze and turned and left. She stayed for a while to steady her breathing, staring at the crates of soft drinks stacked against the wall, the nest of cobwebs above. Finally, as she opened the door, she tripped and nearly fell, catching herself, stumbling. The room had spit her out. She was now so worthless as to repel even a storage room. She felt hemmed in by shame, a shame forced upon the innocent, glowing in unfairness. She had done nothing wrong, it was she who had been harmed, and yet she felt shame as an acute rupture of her internal order. She resolved then to reach the end of her life with this shame buried away. Nobody would ever know. She would tell Tantie Fanta and Mama that François fired her because she asked to be a cook and not a waitress.

AMADOU APPEARED SMILING at Tantie Fanta's door, just like that, after all those years. 'How are you, my Kadi?' he asked. Her joke-cracking, light-footed, big-dreaming love. He was still the old Amadou and yet also fresh with the dew of newness, fuller and fleshier; he walked with a foreign bounce in his step. He begged her to forgive him for his silence, saying he was sorry, he was so sorry, he had problems, his papers were incomplete, he was hustling. He said 'hustling' many times, and the English word filled Kadiatou with the enchantment of the unknown. He hugged Binta so tightly her toddler body squirmed to free itself. 'She looks like Binta,' he said, his face crumpling, his eyes growing glassy with tears. 'You are crying,' Binta said, watching him curiously, and he said, 'No, no, there is sand in my eye, can you help me blow it out?' Eagerly, Binta blew at his eye, her small cheeks inflating and collapsing, before Amadou said his eyes were perfect now and asked if she could close her own eyes and open her hand. A small pack of colourful gummy sweets appeared. For Kadiatou, a bottle of perfume. Amadou pulled out the stopper, and with his finger, dotted some behind her ears. 'Now you smell like jasmine,' he said. She heard her own laughter as it faded away, and realized she had last laughed like that when her sister was alive. She felt the surge of memory, the return of fugitive emotions: love, trust, the willingness to be happy and the faith that she could be.

Amadou visited old friends and places, and he played football on the same pitch as he had before he left. The clamour of his presence was unchanged, drawing people. He exchanged some dollars for a large bag of Guinean francs, and he divided the cash into small piles on the bed, listing the names of many relatives, trying to make sure that each got some money, no matter how small. There was a decency to him, a goodness gifted at birth. He told everyone that he had come to take Kadiatou and Binta back with him, and she shushed him, saying he should not speak of what was uncertain. It pleased her deeply, how casually he said 'and Binta'; how easily his heart had opened; he understood that she no longer existed as a single being.

'Uncertain? Who says it's uncertain? Kadi. I am taking you both back with me,' Amadou said.

He knew somebody, a man called Dee, who used to work at the American embassy.

'Dee says the only option we have is to apply for asylum,' he told her, as if she knew what other options there were.

As he talked of his big plans for them, she smiled, sated, warm in his arms in the small room in his cousin's house. So many people got rejected at the embassy, educated people, people who spoke English well, and she didn't see why she wouldn't be rejected as well. She didn't mind Amadou living in America. She knew of a couple, Tantie Fanta's friends; the man lived in America and the woman here, and he visited twice a year. She and Amadou could get married and she could try to have a baby right away. As long as Amadou sent money and visited whenever he could, she would be content. 'No, no, no,' Amadou said, when she told him. 'We will be together.'

He said they would buy a house in America, you could easily buy a house and pay little by little every month, a house with a play-room. Imagine a room for Binta to play in, he said, a whole room just for playing. Kadiatou thought it wasteful and lonely, a single child playing in one room. Then Amadou talked of schools and Kadiatou began tasting the dream on her tongue. 'Binta will go to a very good school, for free, and she will learn science and music and she can even travel to other countries with her classmates and she can be anything she wants to be, anything,' he said. Kadiatou thought of her sister and knew that Amadou was thinking of her, too. Suddenly she saw herself in America, where buying a house was as ordinary as a seashell on a beach, and she saw Binta, in full exuberant bloom.

'So how we do get this asylum?' she asked.

'Dee says you must talk about FGM for the asylum,' Amadou said.

'FGM?'

'Cutting,' Amadou said.

'Cutting?' Kadiatou asked, puzzled. 'Why?'

'It is what the Americans like to hear. If you tell them the truth that you want a better life, they will refuse you. You'll say they cut off everything and sewed you up and now you can't pee well.' He was laughing and his laughter rumbled warm and deep and she felt that sweetly strange shiver that comes with the body's remembering.

'You'll say you're running away to protect Binta from suffering the same fate as you, even though we know you won't cut her,' he said.

Kadiatou looked quizzically at him. 'But I will.'

'You will take Binta to be cut?'

Was that disappointment in his expression?

'Yes, of course.'

'Kadi, Kadi, no, you do not have to agree to that barbaric action.'

'But how will she become marriageable?'

'Kadi, many women don't do that any more and they marry.'

Kadiatou bit her lip. America had seeped into his skin. In some ways good but in others, like this, not so good, labelling the ways of their people as barbaric.

'Okay,' she said, 'I will tell them of my cutting.'

He was rich with plans, calling people, running around, and soon she had a passport, and a visa interview date at the American embassy. Just days before her interview, he said, 'Dee is saying he has a bad feeling about this, he says FGM is not enough because too many people are using it. We will need more than that. So now we'll say you were raped. That many men raped you.'

Kadiatou flinched, an instant headache splintering in her head.

'He gave me a tape for you to practise with,' Amadou said.

'What is it?'

'A story about the rape.' He slid the tape into a cassette player. It was a woman's voice, in the manner of a radio play. *They said I disobeyed the curfew. They came into the restaurant already drunk . . . one of them said he would do his turn with his gun.*

Kadiatou was in distress, chest so tight she feared the air was being squeezed out of her.

'I do not want to tell these lies, Amadou,' she said.

Amadou came to her, tenderly kissing her.

'It's just a story, my love. We need a good story that will get you to America. You're not lying. It's just a story. Dee said they have been rejecting more and more asylum seekers and so we have to make our story better, to stand out. He says you should first talk about your cutting, and how you want to protect Binta from being cut, before you tell them this rape story in the tape.'

They came into the restaurant already drunk . . . one of them said he would do his turn with his gun . . . I was bleeding from everywhere . . .

She practised and memorized the words, but only on the surface, her inner self she kept apart, far away from it. The last time she practised for Amadou, she began to cry, because her barricades came crashing down and she saw herself in the storage room after François told her to cover up.

'My love, what is it? What is it?' Amadou asked, holding her. 'Don't cry. It's just a story.'

'But it happened to somebody,' Kadiatou said. 'I heard what soldiers did during the curfew period.'

Amadou stayed silent, holding her.

FIVE

An ambulance noisily racing through crowded streets to save a single life. Just one life. What a country. If something happened to her, an ambulance would come racing to save her, too, and nobody would ask her to pay in advance. For this reason alone, if for nothing else, she wanted to stay forever in America. A heady miracle, to think that this was Binta's inheritance, this land of ease. The asylum process was too easy, and she felt a lingering discomfort still, a sense of the unfinished, at how easy it had been. The visa interviewer at the embassy, pleasant and patient as Kadiatou spoke, then nodding at the translator's words, as if she cared about the wedding Kadiatou said she was attending in New York. The person at the airport, another pleasant White woman, wincing when Kadiatou said her aunt had cut her with a razor blade, offering Binta a lollipop, telling Kadiatou 'Good luck.' Kadiatou had paused. The story of her cutting was easy to tell, words rolling out, the memory so far away as to have happened to someone else. But she had paused, before starting the other story. To gather herself, to rouse the spirits she needed, because to echo the voice on that tape was to poke at her own bound and banished ghosts. She was telling another woman's story, a woman she did not know, but of a pain she did. And so she had paused. With a heave to her shoulders, she began. She was about to say 'there were four soldiers' when the pleasant White woman said 'Good luck' and pushed a piece of paper across to her. She looked at the woman and then at the translator. It's finished, the translator said in French. You're approved. Kadiatou breathed deeply to shield her astonishment. Was this a ruse? How could it be over already? Amadou said it would be very difficult, he said she should talk first about her cutting only as an opening before repeating the story of the voice on the tape. He said the story on the tape would sway them, make her case stronger. But the pleasant White woman was smiling an encouraging smile, the slight movement of her head saying 'You can go.' It really was over and she had not told her practised story. She had not wanted to tell it and yet she felt deflated, now that she would not tell it after all. All that memorizing, staining herself with words, coming to nothing. Was there another part of this process? Maybe they would call her again to ask her questions. But Amadou said there was no other process. 'See, you didn't lie! You didn't want to lie and God helped you and you didn't lie! You are in America, my love! All we have to do now is wait for your papers to come in the mail!'

She spent her early months in a language haze, floating in and out of comprehension. American English was spoken at a higher pitch than normal, and she wondered if she would ever perfect that pitch, even if she managed to get the words right. She felt unsteady on her feet, walking the crowded streets of Queens, as if the secret of truly belonging here was yet to be revealed to her. She was disoriented by the closeness of strangers, the graffiti scrawled on buildings, the long lurching buses. The subway scared her, at first, to be descending deep into the earth, but when they climbed up the stairs and emerged again into the light, a giddiness overcame her, as if she had reached an unexpected peak.

'I want you and Binta to stay with my uncle, I don't want to dishonour your family,' Amadou said.

'Amadou, as far as I am concerned, I am your wife.'

'Give me time, my love. To do things properly. You can be with me all day but I want you to sleep at my uncle's house, until we're properly married.'

'And when will that be?' She wanted to ask but did not. In Conakry he said he would send kola nuts back home as soon as they arrived in America, so they could begin as a married couple, but now he was asking for time. She moved with Binta into his uncle's house, in a basement room that was dark even in the afternoon. His uncle,

Elhadji Ibrahima, was warm and wise, and her spirit felt at peace with him. He told her often how he had been one of the workers on the Monument du 22 Novembre 1970, alongside Chinese and other foreigners, all of them proud that Guinea had quashed that terrible Portuguese coup. Kadiatou didn't understand what he was talking about, but she understood his nostalgia, his need to talk about home with a person recently from home. He stayed in the kitchen while she cooked, asking how he could help, while she tried to hide her awkwardness from having a man in the kitchen.

'They say we Fula can't rule and we should stick to trading. We produced a man like Diallo Telli and they say we cannot rule? They killed him in Camp Boiro and chased so many of us out of Guinea, to Senegal and Sierra Leone and Ivory Coast. Okay, now what has happened? The country is even more divided today. But I still believe we can be united. This government must acknowledge the injustice done to us Fula, and we, too, have to identify first as Guinean before Fula, otherwise they will be right to call us outsiders. They say we are not citizens like them, because they are the true inheritors of the Manding empire, but that is not what citizenship is about. Sékou Touré was a great liberator but also a great dictator and we can teach a history that tells the full story.'

'Yes,' Kadiatou said. When she was with knowledgeable people like him, she always thought, with a stab of wistfulness, that Binta would have known what to say. Most evenings Elhadji talked and talked, and she felt slightly appalled by his emotional manner, so lacking in the stoic reserve of a proper Fula man. But he was kind, endlessly kind, explaining America to her, taking her to the public school to enrol Binta, teaching her to drive, showing her which TV shows to watch, to learn English.

AMADOU BOUGHT HER a pair of denim shorts and asked her to wear them to a summer barbecue and she baulked; it felt like being naked. She couldn't wear them out, she was horrified by women on the streets who bared so much skin in shorts and tiny tops. But she wore them for him, in his apartment, and he asked her to walk around so he could look at her and she did, shyly, laughing girlishly, and then flopping down on the sofa next to him. She was unused to looking at her own body and her exposed thighs felt unfamiliar, the skin much lighter, a thin crisscross of veins underneath. When his friends came by, she ran into his bedroom to hide, so they wouldn't see her so uncovered, and Amadou laughed. 'You have to loosen up a little, Kadi. Just a little,' he said. She didn't wear the shorts to the summer barbecue in the park, but she ate some of the food in large pans covered in foil, because she knew he wanted her to, as her newly loosening-up self. Potato salad, pasta salad, macaroni cheese, all of them as tasteless as chalk. Binta was running around, shrieking happily, while Amadou chased after her. He had painted her face blue and red, and a blob of vanilla ice cream, fallen from her cone, had left a patch on the front of her dress. Kadiatou watched them with a tug in her chest of pure joy. She hoped to always remember this moment, the sky a boundless clear blue, their life beginning in Binta's new world.

BUT AMADOU WAS DIFFERENT in America, not as light on his feet, nor in his spirit, as he had been back home. He wasn't answering her questions fully, his eyes always darting to distractions. 'I want to take Binta to Coney Island,' he said. 'I want to take her to the Bronx Zoo; it's the biggest in the world.' Anxiety spread over his face whenever his phone rang, and he would glance at the screen, and then turn back to her with a fake forced cheer. Sometimes he sat despondent on the edge of the bed, looking into the distance, and he would say a business deal fell through, something to do with a supplier from China. She sensed he wasn't yet where he wanted to be, and his unfulfilled dreams, his failures, ground him. With her here now, he could no longer hide.

'Amadou, tell me how things really are, please,' she said.

'My love, it's okay. No problem,' he said.

'I want to get a job. We will do it together.'

She decided she would no longer wait until she could speak English well before looking for work. She started at a braiding salon owned by a querulous Ivorian woman, and got a cash commission at the end of each day, a few folded dollar notes. The salon was alive with chatter, French spoken in Ivorian and Guinean and Malian accents, and from the women she learned useful nuggets of information, the best Greek yogurt for kossan, the African store where she could buy sour leaves and even, occasionally, fresh garden eggs. But the salon pay was poor, and Elhadji Ibrahima said she could do much better; after all she had her papers, while many of the other braiders didn't. He found a home health aide job, caring for an elderly American man, but after she spoke to somebody on the phone, they turned her down, saying they couldn't understand her English. He told her there was an opening for a good hotel job, as a housekeeper, but it was in Washington, DC. Kadiatou didn't want to leave New York without Amadou. The weather was cooling, summer becoming fall. Amadou was often away. Sometimes he told her he would be gone a few days; he was 'hustling,' he said, and it was all to give her and Binta the best life. He took her to the bank to open an account, and then said he needed to keep some money aside, in her account, explaining something about taxes that she didn't understand and didn't need to understand. She wanted only to have their plans made molten, blending each in the other.

HIS GUINEAN FRIENDS were Fula and Malinke and Susu, and even some Christians from the forest region. They were moths drawn to Amadou's flame of rebellious charm. In his apartment, they lounged barefoot, English and French mashed up in fierce arguments about Guinean politics, about football, about random useless things. Amadou always started the intensity, then he ended in play and laughter. One day, Kadiatou overheard them joking about pork, his friend Joseph was stuttering, and she did not fully get the joke. She hoped she had not heard what she heard. They were all excitable that day, checking their phones, following the protest in the stadium in Conakry. 'I would have been in front!' Amadou said. And one of the friends said, 'The government cannot ignore this, this is big!'

She called him into the bedroom to whisper, unable to wait until his friends left.

'Did you eat pork in Joseph's house?' Even the question from her own mouth horrified her, to think that Amadou might have pushed open the door to another curse, now that she and Binta seemed finally free.

'Did Joseph say you ate pork in his house?' she asked again, wanting him to be offended that she would even ask. His eyebrows furrowed, and she saw his mental shift from Conakry protest to pork. 'What? Oh, don't mind Joseph.'

'Did you?' Kadiatou asked.

'Did I what, my love?'

'Eat pork.'

'What if pork was the only food left in the world?' From his tone he was laughing at her without laughing at her. One of his friends called out from the living room to say there was trouble in Conakry, and she watched him go back to become reabsorbed by them.

She could not imagine Tantie Fanta joining a mass protest, but still she went out to buy a phone card to call and check on her. Later, she told Amadou, 'Tantie Fanta said soldiers killed Fula people in the protest.'

'It was not just Fula people. We have to stop playing victim all the time. Those soldiers shot at all the protesters.'

'Bhoye told her. He said he had to lie down next to dead bodies and pretend to be dead.'

'Bhoye is always lying!' Amadou said.

Kadiatou was taken aback, his dislike of Bhoye more blistering than she knew, his voice sharper than it needed to be. It felt as if he found her wanting or had chosen something else over her. She went silent and moved away from him.

'Sorry, my love,' he said. 'All I am saying is that we are all Guinean and this thing that happened in Conakry is terrible.'

The sanctimony shining from his face upset her.

'Did you eat pork in your friend's house, Amadou?' she asked quietly.

'What is all this, Kadi?'

'If you did, you have brought a curse down on us,' she said.

He laughed, he actually now laughed, a short and brutish laugh. With all his knowledge, he lacked the wisdom of knowing that curses were real.

'No, Kadi, I did not eat pork in anybody's house,' he said.

She had thought that he did eat pork, that she heard Joseph say so, but Amadou would never lie to her. Her relief lifted the dark clouds.

ON WEEKENDS WHEN Amadou wasn't there, she went over and cleaned his apartment while Binta watched television. One day she found two photos in Amadou's drawer of a child, maybe two years old, smiling in a stroller in a woollen hat. He was Amadou's son, you only had to look at his face. That exuberant smile. A face so like that black-and-white baby picture of Amadou that she now carried in her purse.

She screamed and shouted at Amadou. It was unusual for her because she existed best in a low key, but she shouted to show him the roaring nature of her hurt. Amadou said it was a fling, long over, and the child was in Texas with the mother, a woman from Mali who cashed the cheques he sent but refused to let him see his son. Even the Malian woman knew about Kadiatou, he said, knew she was his only love, his destined wife. As he spoke, there was, in Kadiatou's mind, the loud creaking of doubt.

'A child. A whole precious child, and you did not tell me,' she said.

'I was going to tell you at the right time.'

'I thought you told me everything,' she said. She felt betrayed, not because he had a child but because he hadn't told her. If she was indeed his true love, he should have told her. She felt the ground shifting beneath her, suddenly certain there were other things she should know but did not. That evening she told Elhadji Ibrahima that, yes, she would go to Washington, DC, for the hotel job, if it was still open. Elhadji Ibrahima looked surprised. 'You have discussed with Amadou?'

'Yes.'

'Good. They pay well. I know a Fula woman you can stay with until you get your own place.'

'Thank you,' Kadiatou said. She tried not to show how much her own decision frightened her. The galloping heartbeat flooding through her. Find her own place on her own. Alone with Binta.

'Washington, DC, is not too far away,' Elhadji said, kindly, as though to soothe her.

'Yes,' Kadiatou said. She looked into the future and saw herself empty without Amadou and Binta crying for Amadou and the painful gash of distance between them. But she saw, too, slowly unfolding, the first slender shoots of her own autonomy.

Six

Kadiatou knocked on the door, calling out, 'Housekeeping!' The family in the suite asked her to come in and clean, they were just leaving, the mother gathering her shopping bags. They were Nigerians, Kadiatou could tell, from their glaze of self-assurance, and the mother's expensive wig, the kind she saw only on Nigerian women, just silky enough to look like the real hair of foreigners. Africans who could afford to stay in this hotel made her proud, and they were nearly always Nigerians. This family was probably Igbo; the mother and daughter had the same yellowish skin tone as the Igbo traders she knew in Conakry. They were so beautiful, they could have been Fula women, with their finely boned faces.

'What's your name?' the daughter asked, smiling, surprising Kadiatou; she must have lived a long time in America, rich Africans never asked the names of servants.

'I'm Kadiatou Bah,' she said.

'Oh, you're African!' the daughter said. 'I wasn't sure. I thought you might be from Haiti. Are you Senegalese?'

'I come from Guinea Conakry.'

'Long live Sékou Touré!' the father said, and smiled.

His daughter shared his smile, open, warm, a smile that invited you in.

The mother was too preoccupied with herself to smile. She said, 'Oh, Francophone', sounding disappointed, her attention on her shopping bags.

'Your hair is so neat, where did you braid it?' the daughter asked, as if to make up for her mother's hauteur. Kadiatou said she braided it herself, and then followed more admiration from the daughter, and numbers exchanged. The daughter's name was Chiamaka and she said her parents were staying in the suite because she had started remodelling the kitchen in their house and hadn't finished. It seemed to Kadiatou too much information, but Americans did that all the time, they gave details that nobody had asked them for, and Chiamaka must have lived a long time in America. Chiamaka said she had just been in Senegal, and actually she had a book in her bag that she'd bought there, which Kadiatou might like. Kadiatou had never felt so flattered, to be thought of as a person who could read.

LATER, THEY WOULD JOKE about this. 'You gave the best present I never use,' Kadiatou would say, and Chia would cover her face in her hands. From braiding Chia's hair, she began cleaning Chia's house. Chia paid her well and marvelled at ordinary things she did. *How did you manage to remove that carpet stain, Kadi? You changed the window screen already?* Rich people, the good ones, could be so impressed by the normal things they never did, and it made them overpay for those things. When the hotel closed for refurbishing and the manager said he wasn't sure she would be rehired, Chia said Zikora knew somebody who could help, and soon Kadiatou was hired at George Plaza, a better job, with better pay. Beautiful Chia, always trying to make people happy, co-signing for Kadiatou's apartment, teaching Binta to play the piano. The first time they stayed the night at Chia's house it was because Chia said Binta needed to practise the piano, and it became the first of many nights, until Kadiatou was the caretaker, with her own key, coming and going, even when

Chia was away. Chia's cousin, Omelogor, was visiting then, on that first night, and she sat at the dining table while Chia and Binta were at the piano. She was watching them; her watching made Kadiatou uncomfortable. Omelogor was strange, difficult to read; she looked at you stonily, only to say something nice, and then she smiled before she called you a fool. Was she thinking that Chia was wasting time teaching the servant's child how to play an instrument she would never own? But all Omelogor said was 'Chia, stop hovering, let Binta trust herself.' Kadiatou always felt a sense of precaution flood through her body whenever Omelogor was there. To be careful, but for what exactly she was not sure. Omelogor lived in Nigeria and she didn't affect a blindness to life's pecking order; she sent Kadiatou on errands without apology. *Kadi, can you boil some water for tea. Kadi, can you clean these shoes for me.* Chia would never ask her like that, nor would Zikora. America had infiltrated them both and taught them to sprinkle life's realities with the seeds of apology, as if to say, 'I am sorry I have to ask you but I will ask you still.' *Sorry, Kadi, please wash this,* Chia would say. It was the same with some White people who looked with pity at her as she arrived to clean their rooms, thanking her too profusely, and they made her feel sorry for being the cause of their pity, a pity that was not in any way useful to her. Her co-workers, Chinese, Caribbeans, other Africans, joked with one another about this, sharing snacks, trading stories. Lin had the best stories; she was the most animated, tiny Lin, a Chinese woman. It was Lin whom Kadiatou had shadowed when she was training, and she was startled at how strong Lin was, how quickly she moved furniture, flipped a mattress, vacuumed long hallways.

Lin said the manager always escorted guests to her floor – the twenty-eighth floor, the special floor, the floor with suites – as if they could not go up in an elevator on their own. One night a guest on Lin's floor trashed his room, ripping up the sheets, smashing the mirrors, puncturing the walls. It was like a war zone, Lin said. Kadiatou was mystified. Why would a guest just destroy a hotel room? 'White people are strange,' Lin said. 'The Black rich ones don't do it, the Asian rich ones don't do it, the Hispanic rich ones don't do it; only the White rich ones. They're bored, so they destroy.'

Lin's favourite story was about a guest who called Lin into the room to say that the complimentary flowers were not fresh.

'And she shows me one stem of the flower! One stem! They are crazy,' Lin would say, laughing. Kadiatou laughed, too, a slight laugh; she was uncomfortable mocking guests, and always cast a surreptitious glance around, to see if any managers were nearby, worried that her laughter might somehow jeopardize her job. When the others asked if any guest in her room had done a crazy thing, she demurred, saying no, nothing. Which was true. But she could not see herself telling stories about crazy guests. 'You never complain,' the manager told her once, his tone admiring, but his words did not please her. He made her behaviour seem like a repudiation of her co-workers. Lin whispered to her, weeks in advance, that she would win Best Employee at the Christmas party, and Kadiatou did not believe it until her floor manager, Shaquana, called her into the manager's office to tell her, and they gave her the certificate. Each time she looked at the gleaming seal below 'George Plaza', she felt like an educated person with a certificate, her name written in gold.

HER PHONE RANG, and a voice asked if she was willing to take the call and accept the charges from Arizona. Yes, she was. Arizona made her think of a desert because it was what Elhadji Ibrahima said when he first told her where Amadou was being sent to prison. *I hoped it would be somewhere close but they're taking him to Arizona and that place is a desert.* It stuck in her mind – *that place is a desert* – and each time they talked she imagined Amadou thirsty in an unforgiving landscape, until his voice and his laughter dispelled the image. His upbeat tone, laughing off his stories of life inside, how they were made to wear pink underwear and how his lunch packet always had a rotten apple. He spoke of the other inmates as if he just harmlessly happened to be living alongside them: they were good guys and he had made many new friends. The food was terrible, he said, one hot meal a day, a slop whose ingredients were impossible to tell.

'I dream of your fouti and latchiri every day, Kadi. No, I dream of you but also of fouti and latchiri!' he said. After he got privileges for being consistently disciplined, she paid credits into his prison account and he told her what he bought at the commissary, chicken tenders cooked in bad oil, Philly cheesesteaks in overbaked buns. 'They should give you the contract to supply prison food, my love. Nobody will want to be released!' When he wasn't laughing, he was apologizing, saying he hadn't told her about selling marijuana because he wanted to keep her clean. He slid the English word 'clean' into his Pular, as if its meaning were different from the Pular word.

She said it was okay, because it was. She had come to understand that dishonesty had its shades, its layers, its twists and knots. Sometimes we lie because we love, and sometimes we lie to serve or save those we love. She could not shake off her guilt, the ever-present drip of blame, because as soon as she left New York, he seemed to fall apart, first losing his apartment and then being arrested. If she had stayed, she might have kept him whole. And he had stolen nothing; he had merely sold something that was given to him. There was no true dishonour there. She began saving for a plane ticket just weeks into his confinement, but it was more than a year before she flew to Arizona. She felt fluttery, like a bride allowed to choose her own husband, as Chia did the paperwork, filling out forms and ordering a background check, and Binta read the visitation guidelines on the prison website. She was not to wear anything that was see-through or above the knee, no cleavage, no spandex, no camouflage, no orange-coloured clothes. She thought it strange, all the specific details of this rule, as if people visiting their loved ones in prison would be so preoccupied by clothes.

Chia paid for a motel room, not far from the prison, and for a rented car, a small sedan with clean shiny wheels. Kadiatou drove carefully, unused to the landscape; even the sun was different, sparkling off the windscreen. As she approached the sprawl of prison buildings, she felt the ebbing of her excitement and the first pulse of shame. It was not shame for what Amadou had done, but a more intimate shame that crawled under her skin as she stood in line, a metal detector grazing her caftan, a brisk guard patting her down. Two brown dogs came sniffing at her and disgust welled up in her throat. Dogs, unclean dogs. She came from an upright and honest people, even if they had little. They were not thieves. And Amadou had stolen nothing. Yet here she was being sniffed by dogs, unclean creatures judging how clean she was. A woman in the next line, wearing a long red dress, began to shout at the guards, 'What the fuck do you mean by inappropriate?' while her two little girls, their braids clinking with bright beads, asked, 'So we don't get to see Dad? So we don't get to see Dad?'

The stone-faced guards were telling the woman she should have read the visitation dress code. Kadiatou watched them, stunned. These people really enforced their clothing rule; they were controlling not only the men locked inside but the women left outside, too. What harm could a dress do inside a prison? The red material sat on the woman's skin, clinging all over, to her belly, her breasts, her behind, the kind of dress Americans wore all the time. The woman turned to leave, and called to the children, who hesitated before following her, glancing back as they did. Those innocent children, denied of their father because of a skintight dress. But why did the mother wear it anyway? Kadiatou's cup of shame was full, now spilling over, to include this woman she did not know, and her two little girls.

She sat in a cubicle, feeling trapped by the plexiglass walls around her. The black two-way phone in front of her looked ancient and clunky, a thin grimy line of dirt below the mouthpiece. A forlorn roll of toilet paper sat on the ledge, perhaps for visitors who might need to wipe their tears. Amadou was brought in by a guard, confident, bouncing Amadou, wearing what looked like an orange sack. He flashed the guard a meek smile before he sat down. Even though he had lost no weight, he looked reduced to her. The hollow at his collarbone had deepened. She understood then the true debasement of prison, that you no longer owned yourself. Suddenly she didn't want to be there, didn't want to see this Amadou, who was beaming at her through the plexiglass and talking fast into the phone. Kadiatou held her receiver limply to her ear.

He said, 'You look beautiful, my love.'

He said, 'Seeing you is like daybreak.'

In the face of her silence, he finally asked, 'Kadi, what is it?'

'I want to go,' Kadiatou said. And then she dropped the phone and stood up and Amadou looked dumbfounded. If he called out to her, she didn't hear it, because by putting the phone back on its cradle, she had given up her desire to hear him. She should not have come here just to look at him, like an animal in a cage. Seated separated from him by hard glass, so far from him that he could not even smell her jasmine scent.

When she returned from Arizona, Chia said, 'Oh, Kadi. I love your love,' wistfully, like a child longing for a make-believe sweet. Chia loved the idea of love, so eagerly, so unwisely. 'I love that you're waiting for Amadou. They better release him early so he can hurry up and bring kola nuts already!' Chia said. They were in the kitchen with Omelogor, and Kadiatou did not want to talk about Amadou at all. She was making fouti; Omelogor had just arrived from Nigeria, and had brought her mother with her, for a medical check-up, and Chia thought her aunt would like the sauce. The vegetables were boiling in a small pot. Now Chia was brightly telling Omelogor about Amadou, details of Kadiatou's life revealed, as though unclothing her: he was her childhood love, he brought her to America, he was now in prison for marijuana possession.

'The judge that sentenced him probably went home and had a joint to relax,' Omelogor said.

Kadiatou did not understand and she wanted to understand. She poured the vegetables into a colander, aubergines and okra and peppers, all soft from boiling. But she delayed blending them, to better hear Omelogor.

'He shouldn't be in prison this long, just for selling marijuana,' Omelogor said. 'I was reading about incarceration the other day. Black and White Americans use marijuana at the same rates but Black Americans are four times more likely to be arrested for it.'

'I didn't know that!' Chia said. 'I mean, I know about how they treat crack and cocaine differently.'

'It's pure madness. America has the most people in prison in the world. Many of them have no business being there.'

Kadiatou paused, to digest the words, before turning the blender on. She should not have left Amadou like that; suddenly she felt weak and disloyal, and ashamed for succumbing to her shame. He didn't truly deserve to be there, he hadn't stolen and he hadn't killed, and she should not have felt any shame. A new resolve grew inside her, to do better by Amadou, to rinse herself clean of emotions that did not benefit them. She would save up for a ticket and go back to Arizona and this time they would smile and smile at each other through the plexiglass wall.

'Kadi, Amadou doesn't even deserve all the years he got. You have to hold on to him, it won't be easy but hold on to your love,' Chia said, as if reading her mind. For the first time, Kadiatou appreciated Chia's dreamy grasp of love. She had sensed a welling up of dissatisfaction in Chia for a while, about her boyfriend, Mr Luuk, the tall White man who seemed unable to sit still. Chia would leave him soon, she had not found what she was looking for, and she didn't know she never would, because it simply did not exist. Kadiatou wished Chia would descend from her cloud and get married; a baby would ground her, calm her restlessness. Kadiatou wondered whether to tell Chia that it would be a mistake to leave Mr Luuk, but she never volunteered her opinion, she waited always to be asked. The weekend he visited from Mexico, he kept coming into the kitchen to talk to Kadiatou while she wished he would let her cook in peace. But she liked him because he loved Chia; he was nothing like that professor, Darnell. Darnell, who made the effort, took the time, to rudely ignore her greeting – she, Kadiatou, a mere housekeeper. Such unnecessary contempt she had never seen before. She had prayed so much for Chia then, for Chia's blindness to come to an end.

Kadiatou turned off the blender, pleased with the mix; its watery texture was just right. She felt Omelogor's intense eyes, as she spread the fouti over some rice, and drizzled warm palm oil on top.

'Jesus Christ, that is disgusting,' Omelogor said.

'Omelogor!' Chia said, but Chia was laughing and Kadiatou could not help but smile. It amused her, how sure Nigerians were that their narrow-minded food was superior. Just like Madame, Chia's imperial and imperious mother.

'Kola nuts for marriage ceremonies,' Omelogor said suddenly. 'We're all related, we Black Africans, we really are, the fundamental cultural ideas are the same. It's beautiful, it's just so beautiful.' Her eyes were flashing with passion, a passion out of proportion, too large for its cause. And the conversation had long moved on from kola nuts anyway. There was a hint of instability in Omelogor, as if she might think herself to madness one day.

KADIATOU LOVED the brisk walk to the hotel after she exited the metro, then going down in the back elevator to the staff area to change into her uniform. She was accustomed to wearing stockings now; they had been itchy at first, clinging to her legs, and she would pinch and lift and tug at them, unused to something so close to her skin. Her uniform made her feel like a professional: a smart button-down dress, and an apron tied over it. In it, she became a person with a purpose, ready to go. Sometimes she hummed as she worked, hanging the cleaning sign, stripping the bed, restoring a lost order to the world. The loud buzz-hum of the vacuum soothed her. Once a White businessman came in to collect his bag while she was in the room. 'Thanks for cleaning,' he said, and he pushed his hand into his pockets and offered her a crush of dollar bills.

Guests rarely tipped, and when they did, she felt the stirrings first of embarrassment, before gratitude. Wasn't it gluttony to be tipped when she got twenty-five dollars an hour plus health insurance for her and Binta? Recently she had gotten even more benefits, sick days fully paid, and it felt like a miracle, to have a union that battled for the rights of workers. She always wished God's special blessing on them.

She paused often, while cooking for Chia, or cleaning a hotel room, or talking to Binta, to think this was her life, it really was her life, a life of stable things, trimmed with small pleasures. She sent money to her mother and paid school fees for her siblings now in Conakry. She paid rent on her two-bedroom apartment. She had a car. Binta was taking AP classes – her American accent faultless, and Binta herself sometimes bewildering in her mix of familiarity and foreignness. Her childish superiority had emerged; she now refused to eat bread and mayonnaise. 'Mayonnaise is a condiment in a sandwich; it's butter you should eat on bread,' she said. Each time Binta slipped more English into her Pular, Kadiatou mourned a small loss, and yet she wanted nothing more for Binta than this ability to own two worlds. In the mornings Kadiatou prayed, the airing of worries that she hoped to numb. Relax, she told herself, but always something lingered. Clouds gathering, or already gathered. The cruel promise of loss always there.

Seven

The years passed as waiting. Sometimes she wondered, but always fleetingly, if her future with Amadou could bear the weight of their past, the waiting in their past. The forced embrace of loneliness. The lack of touch, a relationship only of voice. There was a year of unstoppable sadness, when she welcomed a man named Mamady into her life, because she was seized by a sudden wish to fill in the holes with a man's presence, a father figure for Binta. The desire mellowed and passed; she eased Mamady out of her life. When she told Binta she wished there were a father figure for her, Binta looked surprised. 'Why, Mom?' Sometimes she felt unworthy to have birthed Binta, a child so easy to satisfy. Binta was waiting for Amadou, too. She sent him photos and letters, saying she didn't want him to be the inmate who never got any mail, and Amadou would tell Kadiatou, 'Binta writes French and English so well!' his tone gloating, like a proud father. She thought often of his son, that smaller copy of Amadou, a discovered secret, living with his Malian mother in Texas. Amadou always skimmed over talk of his son, wary of offending her, but she knew the Malian woman now refused to send even a photo of the child. She did not blame the Malian woman, Amadou must have left her nursing wounds, but if Amadou had not earned knowing his son, at least his son deserved to know him. She was willing to lend her voice to Amadou's, to plead with the Malian woman, when he was finally out.

As Amadou's release neared, they talked only of the future, and Kadiatou felt excited and expectant each day, a feeling like peeling sweet fruit. Their calls felt more urgent with a heightened sense of time, even though for years they had talked with the same fifteen-minute limit, always aware that a stranger was listening in and recording their words.

'I will take you to Florida,' he said, or 'We will go on a nice honeymoon', and it felt to her like their very early years back home in Mariama's Kitchen, when he had spoken of carrying her off in a big white car. So many plans, each exquisitely wrapped in shiny paper, unwrapped to savour, and then saved again. She was planning her djamougol, she wanted to have it in New York, closer to their people, especially Elhadji Ibrahima. Amadou often told her, in his laughing voice, that he would present all the cows and all the land in Fouta Djallon for her taignai.

ONE DAY Omelogor asked her, 'Kadi, where did you learn about sex?'

It was when Omelogor was staying with Chia, after she abandoned her studies, saying she had to recover, even though Kadiatou did not understand how a person recovered from studies they did not even finish. Omelogor spent her days unwashed and barely eating; she would type in quick bursts on her laptop and then fall asleep on the couch throughout the day. Each time Kadiatou saw her awake, Omelogor seemed to be pouring whisky into a glass, or drinking whisky from a glass. Kadiatou gagged at the alcohol smell in the living room, glasses with the last few drops of hazel liquid left scattered around. Kadiatou knew how worried Chia was. But she thought it an indulgent weakness, turning to alcohol in the midst of distress, and felt disappointment rather than worry, until she one day found Omelogor's phone inside the washing machine. She had opened it to load some bedsheets, and there was a silver iPhone lying in an empty washing machine. She retrieved it and gave it to Omelogor.

'My phone?' Omelogor asked, looking befuddled.

The washing machine had not been used in a few days, so Omelogor had opened it and put her phone in there. The strangeness frightened Kadiatou. This was not mere self-indulgence, Omelogor was in the grip of something outside of herself. She came by every day after work, to check on Omelogor, offering her food, making her bed, and she could not help herself, she opened and peered into the washing machine each day. Omelogor always shook her head, saying she didn't want any food; she ate cashew nuts and drank her whisky. Finally, Chia convinced her to eat something Kadiatou cooked. 'It's like Nigerian swallow, just not as heavy as garri,' Chia said.

'What is it?' Omelogor asked, looking down at the plate placed in front of her.

'Fonio,' Kadiatou said.

'Ah. So this is fonio. Someone said it's the latest American superfood.'

'Superfood,' Kadiatou shook her head. 'My people eat fonio for long time and now they say superfood.'

Omelogor cackled with laughter. She laughed and laughed, clapping her hands. Kadiatou was bewildered because it was not that funny. Later, Chia whispered, 'I'm so happy you made her laugh, Kadi.' Chia said the laughter, or the fonio, or both, energized Omelogor like a tonic, and the next day she showered, her face marginally brighter, the same day that she asked, 'Kadi, where did you learn about sex?'

Kadiatou had come in to turn on the security lights, and Omelogor looked up from her laptop and asked, 'Kadi, where did you learn about sex?'

Kadiatou kept her face free of expression. 'My sister, Binta. She tell me what husband and wife is about.'

'Where is Binta?'

'She died.'

'Oh, sorry. I am so sorry, Kadiatou.'

'Thank you,' Kadiatou said. She saw something of Binta's spirit in Omelogor, in how unshackled by fear she was. And they had the same way of looking at you, an unnerving stare, as if in search of something you would not willingly tell. Kadiatou never spoke of Binta to anyone else but her daughter, Binta, but now she surprised herself, her jaws unlocked and she said, 'My sister, Binta. She's not afraid, like you.'

Omelogor was silent.

'Like you, too,' Omelogor finally said.

'Me?'

'Yes, you.' Omelogor said and turned back to her laptop. Kadiatou felt a sudden flush of pleasure, the small, surprising awareness that Omelogor respected her.

Another time, Omelogor asked, 'Kadi, what is your dream?'

'My dream?' She was not sure she understood.

'Yes, what do you want to do with your life if you could choose anything?'

Kadiatou thought this question the kind of thing only idle people could conceive. She shrugged. 'I love my job. I'm so happy to come to this country, so Binta can have this country.'

'Don't be so grateful!' Omelogor snapped, with a vehemence that startled Kadiatou. 'America is not that wonderful. And you are not here for free; you're working and you're part of what makes America America.'

Kadiatou said, 'Yes', just to calm Omelogor down.

'I was reading about your country. You know about Opération Persil?'

'Persil for cooking?'

'Oh, of course it's parsley in French. That's interesting, the parallels of parsley. The Parsley Massacre was when the Dominicans murdered Haitians in the 1930s. They asked every Black person they saw to say the word "parsle", and if they said it in a French Haitian accent instead of a Spanish accent they were killed.'

Kadiatou said nothing. It was not the first time Omelogor had said something whose head or tail she didn't know, and it would not be the last. She was making fonio for Omelogor, and it pleased her that Omelogor liked it so much. Whatever had bedevilled Omelogor when she first abandoned her studies had slackened its grip, only one glass of whisky lay around all day, and she had laundry in the basket, which meant she now changed her clothes.

'Opération Persil was a terrible thing France did to destabilize your country. Your country was the only one in Francophone Africa to say no to de Gaulle's constitution, and so de Gaulle ordered that everything the French had in Guinea should be destroyed, like a petty child breaking a toy just so that somebody else won't use it. And then they did Opération Persil, where they printed fake Guinean currency and flooded the country with it and the economy collapsed.'

'Okay,' Kadiatou said.

Omelogor laughed. 'Okay indeed. Can you make me tea? English breakfast.'

'Okay.'

When Kadiatou came back with the tea, Omelogor held her gaze and said, 'Kadi, you must dream of something. What about when you retire? Your Guinea Fula people are like us Igbo people, good at trade and commerce, so do you dream of trading?'

Kadiatou paused. It was true, she did dream.

'When I finish my job, I will open restaurant. When Binta finish college. Now I have to keep my job for money to come steady. I braid sometimes. For extra money. Maybe one day I sell hair attachment.'

'You can do that now.'

'I save first.'

'Give me your account details. There's a special fund that my bank has for small businesses owned by women. It's a grant, not a loan. The money just arrives in your account and that's it. But you must use it for your business.'

Kadiatou stared at her. Omelogor was unstable and it was too good to be true, nothing in life was ever free, but she saw in Omelogor's face that it was true. 'Thank you,' she said. 'God bless you.'

EIGHT

The day that changed her life began in an ordinary way, as most extraordinary days do. There was no cold wind in her chest, no sense of impending doom. She woke up thinking of the movie they were going to see, happy that Binta still enjoyed going to the movies with her. She and Binta would sit next to each other in the dark cinema with large popcorns, fingers greasy with melted butter. The popcorn always disturbed her stomach, but the pleasure was in sitting next to her daughter, the warmth of her daughter, so known and yet so new. To think they now talked of the weather like Americans.

'It's actually not going to be too cold today, Mom,' Binta said.

'Yes,' she said. December's chill had lifted slightly.

She wore a new soft brown sweater, bought from Ross last month, nice enough for the cinema; she would go from work to the cinema and meet Binta there. Her jeans felt a bit tight, she was putting on more weight than she wanted. Amadou loved her wide hips – he called her body 'stop work', because it distracted him – but maybe she should watch it. She didn't want him to return from prison thinking she had gone beyond the bigness he liked.

She bought a coffee from the food truck, her usual, with milk and sugar.

It was owned by a Hispanic man with a carefully tended beard. She didn't know his name, but after she once bought Binta a hot chocolate, he began to ask her, every day, 'How's your daughter?' and she said, 'Fine, thank you.'

Lin was taking a sick day and so she had the twenty-eighth floor. She hoped the guests didn't have late checkouts, so she could leave early enough, maybe even wander around with Binta in the shop near the cinema.

Almost every room on the floor had the DO NOT DISTURB sign on the doors. She walked by each one, deflated, thinking of how much time it would now take her. Near the linen closet, Jeff from Room Service was wheeling away a trolley.

'Nobody in 2806,' he said. 'All yours.'

'Oh great,' she said. The kind of thing she said to sound American. *Oh great. Oh my God.* Words that felt foreign in her mouth, more foreign than other English words. She knew that 2806 was the largest suite on the floor, but if she started it now, she might still make it out on time – if none of the other suites had late checkouts. She knocked loudly, just in case, calling out, 'Hello? Housekeeping! Housekeeping! Hello?'

She unlocked the door and walked into the room. Room, indeed, this soft-toned space bigger than her apartment. Each time she entered a suite, she thought it was such a waste of space, with beds wide as fields and whole sections of the suite often left untouched by guests. Guests liked it, but she thought they liked having stayed there, more than they liked the suites themselves. How do our tranquil musings become stabbed by shock? She registered swift movement before she saw the naked White man. He had silver hair, he was not tall, he was pudgy, his belly was thick, and he was coming towards her. Before she averted her eyes, his erection registered as an aggressive pinkish blur. 'I'm sorry! I'm sorry!' she said. Her hands flew to her face, to cover her eyes, backing away, mortified, thinking of how she would explain invading a VIP's privacy to Shaquana. *Jeff said the room was empty and nobody answered when I knocked and next time I will wait another minute . . .*

But the man was still moving, now next to her, not trying to cover himself at all. He reached out and slammed shut the door she had left half-open.

'Don't be sorry,' he said, and he enclosed her breasts in his hands. Both his hands on both her breasts as if they were his, as if her body was his, as if she knew him and he knew her. Surrealness was descending around her like fog.

'Please sir, no. Please, stop, please sir.'

He pushed her towards the bed and down to sit on the bed. He was strong, which surprised her, as he was not a young man. His pushing was a propulsion, a separate unheeding energy of its own. She felt shocked, dazed, wondering if it was happening even though she knew it was happening.

'Sir, please. Stop. My supervisor is outside,' she said.

'Nobody is there,' he said.

It happened quickly, the speed dizzied her. He yanked up her dress, and as she tried to pull it down again, he wrenched down her stockings, and slid his fingers furiously between her legs. She pushed him away, but she did not push too hard – he was a VIP, she could not lose this job – and she ran for the hallway, but he was relentless, alarmingly swift, upon her again, animalistic, possessed, a brute animal. He was pushing her down to her knees, her back against the wall, roughly shoving her shoulders, to get her down, to keep her as he wanted her, and her shoulder shifted and cracked in dissent. He was forcing his penis into her mouth. She clamped her lips together, shaking her head. His hand, in a swift sharp squeeze, forced open her jaws. She knew in that moment that he did not think of her as a person alive and breathing like him. She was a thing, a thing to own and invade and discard, and this frightened her. His penis was in her mouth and with both hands he shoved her face against his groin. He was thrusting quickly and grunting and she left her mouth open, because even in her shock she was afraid to hurt him, this VIP, this naked White man. A final violent thrust, and he withdrew. Her mouth was full of worms. She ran out of the room, spitting the vile sourness from her mouth. Her throat itched and her stomach turned, and the overwhelming sense was of her body, her spirit, her soul in rebellion. She was spitting and spitting. She was spitting on the opulent floor that it was her job to clean, but she could not help herself. Near the elevator she stopped, clutching her belly to restrain the vomit.

Then he appeared, wearing a jacket and shiny shoes, pulling a black carry-on. It shocked her, how quickly he had dressed, how unaffected he was by what he had just done. He saw her standing there and he looked blankly at her, through her, and then walked into the elevator. Goosebumps prickled her skin. It really felt as if he was an evil djinn, not human, part ghost and part animal. She did not know what to do. She went into room 2820, which was unoccupied, and stared confused at the perfectly made bed, then walked out of the room again. Her stomach was heaving. Had what happened really happened? She had walked into a room and, like evil made incarnate, a naked White VIP had come rushing at her. She heard footsteps and jumped, panicky.

It was Shaquana. 'Everything okay, Kadi?'

Kadiatou wanted to nod and say everything was fine, but she was overcome by the liquid sensation of losing control. English was difficult enough; now the words refused to come.

'What will happen if a guest . . .' She stopped, feeling the cold wind in her chest, a gathering fear that things would fall apart.

'What happened, Kadi? What happened?'

'The guest push me and force me. In my mouth, he put . . . I spit it out.' She gestured.

Shaquana's eyes widened. 'Oh my God. In room 2806?'

Kadiatou nodded.

'He's a VIP, but I don't care,' Shaquana said, already reaching for her phone.

HER LEFT SHOULDER ACHES, as if something inside has been moved from where it should be. She feels the urge to hold that shoulder, to try and keep it whole, or stop a further splintering, but she doesn't want to call attention to it. Between her legs, where he grasped with animal force, she feels not pain but dull violation, a faded throb. Outwardly she holds herself rigid, standing beside Shaquana, but her whole body teeters, unsteady, disoriented. All the parts of her previously at peace no longer are. Mike, the head of security, is talking to her. She sees him sometimes in the hallways, and he always says, 'Hi, how are you?' He is tall and walks with authority, his back straight. He is talking to her in a kind voice, saying, 'We'll go downstairs now, we'll go downstairs to the manager's office', speaking slowly, as if he thinks something has happened to make her unable to understand. When the elevator doors slide open, he stands back to let her go in first. Shaquana is hovering, a blur of black uniform, saying, 'You'll be okay, Kadi, it will be okay.' In the elevator, nobody speaks. Her mouth is sour. Disgust fills her at the thought of what is left in her mouth, the remnants of worms, the lingering slithering slimy worms that she did not fully spit out, and now her throat is rising in resistance, her stomach churning, and the heave of the elevator makes her want to bite down on her lips to keep herself still, but biting down will only make the worms sink deeper into her mouth, her saliva, and sully her, stain her in a way that she can never undo.

'I want to wash my mouth,' she says.

'You can't rinse your mouth, Kadi,' Shaquana says. 'Not yet.'

Shaquana reaches out to rub Kadiatou's shoulder, to show support, but it is the left shoulder, the one in distress, and Kadiatou tries not to flinch. The manager is standing by his office door, looking restless and agitated, clutching an unusually large mobile phone. Shaquana tells the manager the guest's name, and the manager says, 'Oh my God!' and glances up at the ceiling as if suddenly overwhelmed, calling on his God.

'Tell me what happened, Kadiatou,' he says.

'I want to wash my mouth,' Kadiatou says again.

'No, you can't. You have to go to the hospital so they can check you out and collect evidence,' the manager says. 'And we'll call the police.'

Mike says to the manager, 'You go ahead and call. I'll get in touch with the detective.'

'No, no,' Kadiatou says. 'I don't want hospital. I don't want police. Please.'

Everything is happening too fast, swelling and ballooning. She is causing too much trouble, with this talk of hospital and police. All she needs to do is rinse her mouth and take Tylenol and she will be fine, she will soldier on. She cannot lose her job.

She looks at the manager, fearing that he will fire her for making a fuss, causing him to be so nervous, a man who always seemed so confidently in charge.

'Tell me what happened,' the manager says.

Shaquana gently rubs her shoulder again.

'Jeff tell me the guest has check out, but I knock, knock, knock. I say, "Housekeeping!" I say two times. I go in and I check the study, nothing, so I want to start. Just fast-fast I see a naked man, he's coming from the other side, the bathroom. I say, "I'm sorry I'm sorry!" And I start moving back. I'm very surprise because when I come in, there is no noise, I don't know that somebody is there. He just come fast to me, very fast, he say no need to be sorry. He go fast to door and close it, he push it hard. He . . . just touch my breasts. I say please sir, no, please. I say my supervisor is outside, because I want him to stop. I say I don't want to lose my job. He say you're not gonna lose your job. Everything is so fast. I'm so scared. This happening my second week in the VIP floor. I don't see something like this before in this work, never. He take up my dress, but I hold it and I say no, no. So he pull down this, my stockings, and he push his hand in . . . my private part. Then he push me. He strong, very very strong. He use force. I'm surprise because he's not young man. He push me. Just push me very hard.'

'Pushed you where?'

Kadiatou points at her shoulder. 'Here. So I am down. He push his . . . thing inside my mouth. And then he hold my head and . . . he finish and I run and spit.'

The manager stares at her, saying nothing.

Mike says, 'I'm so sorry, Kadiatou.'

'I don't want police. Is okay,' Kadiatou says.

'Kadiatou, we have to call the police. This is a crime. We have to do the right thing,' Mike says.

'No, please, is okay,' Kadiatou says.

The manager is already on the phone to the police. He sounds hesitant, unsure. He says, 'One of our room attendants was assaulted by one of the big guests.'

Shaquana asks her to sit down. Mike says they have to be quick, the detective in charge of special victims is on the way. Kadiatou hears 'special victims' and thinks of a TV show Binta likes. The air is hot, she wants to rinse her mouth and wash her face and scrub her body. She feels dirty, so dirty. 'Your stockings are torn,' Shaquana says, and Kadiatou looks down to see the jagged hole in the stockings that runs down her legs, and her exposed skin, in contrast, looks like a wound. She reaches out to touch it as if to hide it.

'We're going to the hospital now, Kadi,' Shaquana says. 'Go bring your stuff, your bag with your clothes.'

'My bag?' She wants to come back and finish cleaning her rooms. If they want her to take her things now, then maybe they want to fire her.

'They'll have to keep your uniform as evidence,' Shaquana says.

Kadiatou walks to the staff area, hoping no one will be there to see her take her things. The new maid from Haiti is there. 'What's happening?' she asks, and Kadiatou says, 'Nothing, nothing', and hurries to get her bag. She feels dirty, and dirtied, and she holds her bag low, hoping it shields her ripped stockings.

In the car to the hospital, she shrinks into the seat corner to keep herself away from tainting Shaquana, clutching her bag to her chest. Her brown monogrammed bag with a sturdy single zipper. It is one of the best fakes, Amadou said when he gave it to her. It has been some years and it has lasted. She can feel, through the faux leather, the lump of her jeans and sweater, the firmness of her wallet. The manager's words ring in her ears. *One of our room attendants was assaulted by one of the big guests.* Stalled in traffic, she looks at the people walking in their coats, holding a coffee, pulling along a furry dog, their lives normal and unchanged, their day going just as they expected it to when they first woke up. Tears gather in her eyes, but she will not cry, she will not. There is already somebody waiting for them in the hospital lobby. A brisk nurse in blue scrubs. She leads them upstairs and tells Kadiatou that the nurse who will examine her is on her way. 'She'll be here any minute,' she says.

As Kadiatou walks, a wave of anger seizes her, to think that she was doing her job, just doing her job, and a guest turned into a wild animal, and now she is in this hospital, with sick people being wheeled by, but she does not belong here, she is not sick. A nurse glances quizzically at her, as if wondering what she is doing there, wearing her hotel maid uniform, white apron tied neatly in a bow at her back. They go up to the third floor, and someone is talking to Shaquana, and then someone else, and there is such bustling all around her, such urgency and movement. Kadiatou thinks: All this for me. And she feels grateful, but also upset, because it should have been for something good, something beneficial to her. Maybe if Binta was seriously ill, or she was ill, all this trouble would make sense. Shaquana is saying she can have an advocate in the examination room but she can decline if she doesn't want one, and she stares, not sure what 'advocate' means. Someone who will protect her, like security, but why she needs that here she cannot say.

'Do you understand?' the nurse asks Kadiatou, and she turns to Shaquana. 'Does she speak French? Maybe I could use Google Translate.'

'I understand,' Kadiatou says.

A policeman in uniform appears, a camera stuck to his chest, a walkie-talkie on his sleeve. He asks her to tell him what happened, exactly what happened. He asks as if she has done something wrong, the camera on his chest blinking a red light. She tells him that checkout time had passed and Jeff said the room was empty, and she shouted 'Housekeeping' two times, there was no answer, and she went in, and a naked White man ran out to her. She says this loudly, so that Shaquana can hear too, so that Shaquana does not forget that she knocked, she said, 'Housekeeping.' She followed the rules, she didn't just walk into a room.

'And then what happened?' he asks her.

'Then he just . . . grab me . . . force me.'

'Grab you? Grab you where, Ms Bah?'

She looks down, embarrassed to be saying this to a man she does not know. From him she senses that it would be better if she did not report at all, if she kept silent about all this. His uniform looks tight; their unforms always seem tight, uncomfortable, with all the weapons stuck at their waists. She wonders whether they might not run more easily in less tight clothing. But they don't run, American police, they shoot more than they run. They shot Amadou Diallo.

'Ms Bah!' he says, a little sharply, as if to get her to focus. 'I need you to tell me exactly what happened, Ms Bah, with as much detail as possible.'

The nurse who will examine her has arrived. Even though she is young, she has a motherly aura, an authority with a smile. Between the nurse and the policeman, a strained tension descends.

'My name is Krystal. I'm a sexual assault nurse examiner. I'm trained in helping people who have gone through what you've gone through,' the nurse tells Kadiatou. Her yellowish hair is tied back in a ponytail, but in the photo on her ID card, clipped on her sleeve, her hair is much darker, almost black. She curtly tells the policeman, 'I'd appreciate if this questioning happens after my examination is done.' She leads Kadiatou into a room and shuts the door firmly, draws the curtain closed, and Kadiatou is glad of the cocoon, this space in which she might forget what happened. Krystal asks if anything hurts and Kadiatou says no, even though her shoulder is on fire now, a brittle burning pain.

'Are you sure? It's okay to tell me if anything hurts.'

And so Kadiatou says, 'Here, but small.'

Krystal gently presses down on the shoulder, then gently moves her arm, and a small sound escapes Kadiatou's mouth, the pain surprising her, and she is ashamed of herself, for not bearing it. 'You'll need an X-ray,' Krystal says. 'But we'll do the examination first, okay?'

Kadiatou nods.

'I'd like you to tell me what happened. Tell me what you can. Tell me what you remember. Nothing you say is wrong, and you've done nothing wrong, and I am so sorry this happened to you,' Krystal says, as if she knows, or somehow overheard, how the policeman spoke to her. Kadiatou is so grateful for this small kindness that her tightness loosens, her heart calms, and it is easier telling Krystal. Krystal listens, taking notes, nodding from time to time, to encourage, and sometimes to sympathize. She never looks shocked or surprised, and Kadiatou knows it is because she has heard this story many times, in different forms, from all kinds of women, but in the end the same story.

'You have a bruise on your neck, right here,' Krystal says. 'Does it hurt?'

'No.'

'Bruise on neck, pantyhose ripped,' Krystal says into her phone, and then looks at the screen, head tilted back to make sure her phone has written what she said.

'We'll have to keep your clothes, for evidence. Do you have something to change into? If you don't, it's fine, I'll bring you something.'

'No, yes, I have,' Kadiatou says. They will actually take her uniform? She has two sets but already this feels like a loss, a failure. Krystal says she will step out so Kadiatou can take off her clothes, and put them in a big plastic bag, and lie under the disposable blanket. Alone in the room, Kadiatou takes off her uniform and folds the apron, the dress, and places them on the table. She shivers. The room is cold. Her bra and underwear she puts in her bag, under her jeans for privacy, until she can put them back on. She lies naked, thin paper blankets spread over her, wanting to hug herself for warmth, but she doesn't, it feels inappropriate in some way, as if Krystal might be offended by such a posture, and so she lets her arms lie limply by her sides like a corpse. She does not want to offend anyone; she has caused too much trouble as it is. Krystal knocks before she comes in.

'I'm going to do a head-to-toe exam, okay? I'll be taking pictures of everything. You can let me know if you want to take a break at any time, or if you have any questions, any questions at all,' Krystal says.

As Krystal slips on her gloves, Kadiatou watches tensely, unsure what this examination will mean.

'I'm going to take swabs of parts of your body, okay?'

Kadiatou opens her mouth; she doesn't want to feel so scalded by shame but she is. Krystal puts a cotton-edged stick in her mouth, then another, then another.

'I want to raise this blanket and look at your chest, is that okay?'

Krystal is careful to cover every part of Kadiatou's body that she is not looking at, as if to give back as much honour to her body as she can. A moist swab on her face, her lips, her neck, her leg.

'I'm going to take a picture of your leg, okay? You have a bruise on your knee.'

She has got to the legs, Kadiatou thinks, so it has to be almost over. Kadiatou is telling herself to relax when Krystal says gently, 'Now, Kadiatou, I have to examine your private parts.'

She pushes out the stirrups, asks Kadiatou to put her feet in them, and to shift herself downward.

'Does that feel okay?' Krystal asks.

It does not feel okay, it cannot feel okay, but Kadiatou says, 'Yes.' Lying with her legs apart, feet held up higher than her body, she is reminded of birthing her son, in that hospital, in that mining town full of dust. The thin blanket, bunched up at her waist, feels useless. She is exposed. To be exposed for birthing a child or for a test to benefit her health, yes, but this, this is an affront.

'You have some swelling and redness in the vaginal area,' Krystal says. 'Do you feel any pain?'

'No.'

This time she says no because it is not pain, it is a desecration, and it cannot be healed. Another wave of anger courses through her. Her period just ended, but what if she had been in her period today? What if this wild-animal guest desecrated her body while in her period? What if she had to spread herself like this while also bleeding?

'I'm going to take some photographs, okay?' Krystal says.

Kadiatou springs up and the paper blanket covering her chest slips off and falls to the ground. She makes to pick it up. Krystal gives it to her.

'Picture of there?' Kadiatou asks, horrified.

'It's okay, Kadiatou. I know it feels like an invasion of your privacy. I'm so sorry. We have to document everything. We have to make sure we don't miss anything that can help with the prosecution of your case. I know it's hard, but we need to make sure you get justice.'

Kadiatou closes her eyes; it is unbearable to watch somebody take pictures of her like this. Krystal asks her to get on her knees so that she can take more pictures. Her knees?

'Yes, I'm sorry. I know it's hard.'

Kadiatou feels like a condemned dog, a useless, hated thing. She is on all fours, the blanket hanging on her back like a cruel joke, emphasizing her humiliation, covering nothing. She woke up in the morning to come to work and now a stranger is photographing her most private parts. Where will the photographs go? Who will see them?

'We have to do everything that can help your case,' Krystal says, in soothing tones. The words 'your case' fill Kadiatou with sudden dread. What wouldn't she give now to make this all go away, to return to cleaning an empty room, and then go afterwards with Binta to the cinema to see *The Maid's Brides*?

'Do you need the bathroom or anything?' Krystal asks.

'I want to wash my mouth,' Kadiatou says.

At the sink, she fills her mouth with water and gargles, and spits, fills her mouth with water again. She gargles and gargles, she washes her hands and, with her finger, she scrapes her tongue. She fills her mouth with water, over and over again.

'Are you okay?' Krystal asks, from outside the tiny toilet.

Kadiatou peers at her face in the mirror, surprised that she looks the same; after all that has happened, she still looks the same. She returns to the room, still wrapped in the blankets. Krystal gives her a bottle of pills for her shoulder pain and tells her how to take them.

'I have some questions for you, but you don't have to answer them all,' Krystal says.

Kadiatou does not understand this; why ask her a question and then tell her she doesn't have to answer it? Krystal asks how long she has worked at the George Plaza, if she worked before, where she lives, how long she has lived there.

'These are some demographic questions,' Krystal says, and Kadiatou's stomach clenches, pressure rising, fearing questions about her asylum application. But Krystal merely asks where in Africa she is from, if it is okay to check her race as Black, and Kadiatou wonders what else her race could be.

'You've done very well, Kadiatou,' Krystal says.

Krystal gives her a packet of new cotton underwear, saying, 'I think these should be your size.'

There are three in the packet, one pink and two white. Kadiatou takes it, turns it over in her hand, looks at the photo of a White woman, her body beautiful and full-figured, wearing a pink one, pulled up to her navel.

'Even my underwear?'

'Yes, the police will need everything you wore when the assault happened.'

Krystal gives her a small bag, and Kadiatou hesitates to look inside, as if wary of yet more underwear. Inside is a toothbrush, toothpaste, soap, deodorant, hand cream, and pamphlets with pictures of women looking downcast. Kadiatou touches the deodorant, feeling embarrassed, again, as if she is being rewarded for her own violation.

Krystal leaves, to let her get dressed, and Kadiatou retrieves her own underwear and bra. Both black, the bra her favourite, firm and comfortable, fraying at the back from all the times she has hooked and unhooked it. She looks at her underwear. There is a stray string dangling at the front and she wants to pull it out, but she stops. If she had known she would have to give them her underwear, she would have worn the newer bra; at least it wasn't so worn. She sighs. There is nothing wrong with her underwear, but it is not what she wants anyone to see. She puts them in the plastic bag on the table, where they join her uniform. She rearranges things so that her uniform shields her underwear, and then looks at the bag, touches the plastic, sad that she is leaving her things behind, as if abandoning them. The new underwear feels wrong, slides in between her buttocks as soon as she puts it on. She slips on her jeans. How strange, to wear her sweater without a bra. She won't ask Krystal for a bra, she does not want to be presumptuous, but the loose feeling of being braless is disconcerting; she has never been out in public without a bra.

Krystal knocks to ask if she's okay, if she wants some water or coffee before she goes for her X-ray. 'No, thank you,' Kadiatou says. The thought of anything in her mouth nauseates her.

Krystal takes her into another room to have her blood drawn. A man looks at her as if he is sorry for her, and when he ties a thin cable tightly on her arm, she reaches on impulse to pull it off; she is skittish, jumpy, at the thought of any kind of restraint. As the sharp needle approaches her skin, she looks away. Krystal takes her to another room and, again, she takes off her sweater, stands with her bare back pressed against very cold metal. The man tells her to be very still, very very still, don't move, and she wishes she could remain that way, unmoving, silent, sinking into the metal of forgetfulness. Krystal hugs her gently, saying goodbye, and in a smaller voice, she says, 'Take care.' Kadiatou thanks her and then feels a flare of panic; she does not want Krystal to leave. Relief washes over her when she sees Shaquana waiting for her near the elevator. She is grateful not to be alone, and sorry that Shaquana is here because of her, in a hospital, instead of walking the hallways of the hotel, overseeing the maids. Shaquana tells her the detective is waiting downstairs for them and will drive them back to the hotel. Kadiatou's spirits fall. The detective waiting means yet another beginning, while she longs for an end. The detective is not wearing a uniform and Kadiatou is confused for a moment, unsure if he is actually a policeman. She does not want to tell this story again, and not to a man. But she has no choice. 'How are you?' he asks her. His eyes are warm, patient, like an uncle keen to protect. He wants her to show him exactly where everything happened, and he says he knows it's hard but it's necessary. She walks with him into the hotel, eyes downcast, hoping the manager will not be there. She does not want to see the manager's face, to witness that strange disorientation that she has caused. They go in the staff elevator to the room. She almost doesn't want to walk in. Shaquana opens the door and the detective goes in first.

Somebody is taking photographs with a big camera held to their face. There are four or five other men. The detective asks her to show him exactly where – where she was standing when she saw the naked guest, where he pulled her, where he pushed her down to her knees. As soon as she points at where she spit, one of the men bends down and begins cutting out the carpet there with a small buzzing knife. She is horrified. No, she wants to say, no please don't destroy it. She will lose her job, they have destroyed the room carpet because of her. She feels a sudden smothering inside her, a heaviness in her chest. If this guest had not been so fast, so much like a crazed animal, so lacking in control, she would not have been as shaken and she would have had time to collect herself, and not report this, and all would be normal now. The weight is growing on her chest. She knows, in that moment, that she has lost her job, she will never come back here again, to clean rooms, to put worlds in order. How will she find another job? The relief agency she works with will say she has been long enough with the George Plaza to get a recommendation letter, but she does not know if the manager will write one for her, after she has reported something that left him so shaky.

'You okay, Kadiatou?' the detective asks. He is talking on his phone but moves it away from his mouth to talk to her.

'Yes.' She wants to go home. She had wanted to finish cleaning her rooms, but she really wants to go home, to sit on her bed and think of how to keep her job, to hug Binta.

'You want to sit down? We'll be done here soon,' the detective says, and gestures to the armchair in the suite living room. Kadiatou shrinks. No, no. Of course she cannot sit on that chair; imagine sitting on a chair in this VIP suite. When she cleans the rooms, she doesn't sit on anything, always careful not to jeopardize her job. The detective says she will identify the guest when they get to the police station, as if she already knows she is going to the police station after this.

'Can I call my daughter?' she asks.

'Yes, of course,' the detective says.

She whispers in Pular to Binta, tells her there has been an accident at work and she will tell her details later. Sorry we can't go to the movie, she tells Binta.

'Mom, why are you whispering?' Binta asks. 'Are you hurt? What kind of accident?'

She says it's not serious and she will explain when she comes home. She ends the call feeling ashamed. She will have to tell her daughter that a strange man forced himself into her mouth. It is not a conversation she wants to have with her daughter. Maybe she can tell her something else, make up a story. But if she loses her job, she will have to explain why. No, she will tell Binta the full story. Binta is mature, a high-school junior wiser than her age. The detective asks if she wants something to eat and she shakes her head before he is even done asking, unable even to think of food.

At the police station, she looks down as they walk, wishing she had a scarf in which to hide her face. The station is noisier than she expected, many voices talking, many people, and she imagines them looking at her. The underwear keeps slipping into her buttocks. She is too embarrassed to pull it out, and so she walks awkwardly, and her gait adds to her embarrassment. In a small room with a table and a few chairs, the detective asks again if she wants something to eat or drink. She shakes her head. He tells her he knows it's difficult but he needs every single detail she can remember, but first she has to identify her attacker. He says 'attacker' quietly. She starts to shake her head, scared about confronting the guest, because he behaved like an animal and because he is a VIP.

'He won't see you, Kadiatou. He'll be in a different room and you look at him through a one-way thing where you see him but he doesn't see you. Okay?'

The detective talks to her as if she is somebody. This is the best kind of American, a simple, wise, and hardworking man; she can tell that he sees people as people. In her heart, she wishes blessings upon him and his family.

The room is dim and she looks into the next room, at the men standing there. Without a pause she points at him, the fifth in line. The guest. Him, yes, that is him. She will recognize him anywhere. 'Number five,' she says. The men file out of the room and another group of men file in, and there he is, the guest, the third one, and the shortest. She points again and says, 'Number three.'

The guest looks irritated, his face twisted, as if they are bothering him.

The detective asks her to tell the story again, and as she talks, she feels as if the guest is forcing himself into her mouth again, and disgust rises in her throat. Finally, the detective and his partner drive her home. She rolls a ball of tissue in her hand, and as they drive she spits inside the tissue, quietly, discreetly, raising the tissue to her mouth. She cannot wait to shower.

Binta opens the door before she can unlock it. She has been standing by the door, listening for her.

'Mom, what happened?' she asks.

Kadiatou hugs her, holds her close, inhales the scent of her. Something fruity she buys in the mall.

Then she pulls back, worried that Binta has noticed that she is not wearing a bra.

In the merciful quiet of her apartment, her body is suddenly confused. She looks away, avoiding Binta's eyes.

'Let me shower and brush my teeth first,' she tells Binta.

'Should I make ndappa for you?' Binta asks. *She* always makes food for Binta, and it warms her to hear her daughter offer to make her food.

'No, no, I'm not hungry. Thank you, my sweet child.'

'Who were those men?'

Kadiatou pauses. 'The police.'

'The police?'

'Don't worry, it's nothing serious. I'll just shower.'

Her room feels like an embrace. She looks down at her bed, up at the water stains on her ceiling, and she looks at her leppi cloth folded on top of her dresser, the leppi she wore to a cousin's child's birthday two weeks ago, and she looks at her TV where she watched a Nollywood film that Binta put on for her, and halfway in, she took a picture of an actress in the film, wearing a wig she liked. She peels off her clothes and wishes she could rush to the laundromat now and throw them into a machine. In the shower she scrubs herself, everywhere, once, and then again. She is so grateful for hot water; she has never been so grateful for hot water rushing out of her shower, a cleansing wondrous American miracle. She dries herself, sits on her bed. She wants to send Shaquana a voice note to ask about her job, or maybe she will just go to work tomorrow. If they see her tomorrow, ready to work, they may not fire her. She will call Lin and ask her what to do, maybe how to talk to the union representative. She feels overwhelmed, the weight in her chest is back. She turns on the TV, gets up to call Binta, still thinking of how to tell her, how much to tell her. At first the picture on the screen does not register. She has almost walked past the TV before she stops, shocked, and stares. The guest. His face fills the screen. A shout escapes her mouth. On the screen she sees words she cannot read and then she sees 'maid', which she can read. There is a clip of him speaking French. He is French! Binta is in the room asking, 'Mom, what is it? What is it?' Binta looks, puzzled, at the TV screen, and then back to Kadiatou. Kadiatou is shouting, still, in disbelief.

IN HER DREAM, Amadou was knocking loudly on her grandmother's door in the village, and she woke up to the sound of knocking, thinking it was still the dream. Knocking, knocking, and then banging on her door. This door, the door to her apartment in America, the door a short distance from her room. Her heart was beating fast. She flew up, confused, calling for Binta. The apartment was empty. Binta had gone to school.

Whoever was at the door must have heard her. Now they were shouting.

'Kadiatou, open, please! Kadiatou, we want to get your story! Kadiatou, this is how you can get justice!'

She stood trembling from fear. Who were they? How did they find her apartment? She walked very slowly, as silently as she could, to the peephole. She could see four people, two holding cameras. A sudden banging on the door made her jump.

'Kadiatou! We just want to talk to you!'

When did they come? Had Binta run into them? She remembered now the two pills Binta had brought her last night, with a glass of water on a tray. 'It's for cold but it will help you sleep, Mom,' she had said. Kadiatou's head felt stuffed with cotton wool. She checked her phone. There was a voice note from Binta saying she was fine, in school, and would see her later. 'Mom, please eat,' Binta said at the end of the message.

Banging and banging at the door. It sounded as if more people had come. She was trembling. How could this happen in America? Strangers banging on her door, demanding to be let in. She did not trust them at all. Some of them might indeed be journalists, but what if the guest had sent someone to kill her? Powerful people could do anything. What if they shot a gun through her door? She had heard of somebody shot through the door. She got on her hands and knees and crawled to her bedroom. The banging started up again. 'Kadiatou! Open the door! Just a few questions!'

Her phone was ringing, a number she didn't know. More calls came in, all numbers she didn't know. She sent Binta a voice note, saying Binta should go to her friend Yaa's house after school. 'There are people banging on the door. I don't know what to do,' Kadiatou said. Then she wished she had not said that, she didn't want to worry Binta. She crawled back to the living room and pushed her couch, in tiny moves, as quietly as possible, until it was against the door. She was shaking. Back in her bedroom, she locked the door. Her apartment was so small, she heard the banging as clearly as if she were still at the peephole in the living room. There were new voices. 'Kadiatou!'

She was trembling. The guest would send people for her. A man as important as him, there was no way he would not send people to kill her. She thought of Bappa Moussa and his frightened eyes, saying powerful men could kill you and nobody would talk. She was trembling more. Had they also found Binta's school? She called Binta a few times. Binta's phone would be in her locker, it was class hours now, but still Kadiatou called. Her hands shook. She could not think clearly. Calls were coming into her phone, back to back, clogging up her phone line so that she could not make her own calls. She switched her phone off. She switched it back on, and quickly called Chia.

'Kadi,' Chia said.

The buzz of call-waiting marred the line.

'Miss Chia, he will send people to kill me! He will send people to kill me!' She felt herself losing control, breaking into the smallest pieces of fear.

'Kadi, what is going on? Where are you? Why are you talking like that?'

'Yesterday, in the hotel, a guest, he force me . . .'

Chia shouted, 'No! I just saw it on TV! I was going to ask you about it! It's you? Oh God. Kadi, are you okay?'

Chia's shock was calming, it allowed Kadiatou to collect herself, to think more clearly. She told Chia that there were strangers at the door, that she was scared they would harm her. Chia asked her to call the detective, and to ask for help leaving the apartment, and to come to her house right away. Kadiatou called the detective, and he said he was sorry, they were just talking of moving her into protective custody before her name leaked to the press. Kadiatou did not fully understand. He asked her not to open the door, and said he was sending people to her. She packed a small bag, feeling disoriented. She put her jeans in the bag and then brought it out. Two uniformed policemen were at her door. She heard them saying 'Police!' and asking the hum of people to please give way, to please move. The detective, on the phone, asked her to unlock her front door and then go into her bedroom, so the policemen could let themselves in. He didn't want anybody taking pictures of her. Even the policemen scared her, large White men with weapons stuck on their waists, taking up all the space in her small apartment. They had a white cloth, like a blanket. They asked if she was ready to leave, and then draped the cloth over her head, and led her out, past the strangers gathered at her door, to their car parked outside. The white cloth, like what was used back home to wrap dead bodies in before they were buried. In late morning's unforgiving chill, the car smelled of stale coffee, and the policeman driving seemed irritated. 'Heat okay?' he snapped at her, and she wanted to say, 'Sorry', thinking she had done something, before she realized he was asking about the heat. As they drove, Kadiatou stared at a tear in the back seat while her legs kept trembling. She thought of how she had barely seen through the white cloth, the firm policeman's hand guiding her, and how she had wanted to stay like that, an unseeing moving white cloud. They said they would take her to the police station first, keep her at the station for a while, in case some journalists had followed them, and then another car would take her to Chia's. 'Thank you,' she said. 'Thank you.'

SHE TOLD CHIA what happened, just as she had told the detective, the nurse, the manager, the investigator, but as she told Chia she allowed herself to relive it, moment by moment, the naked White man, his swift rush to her, his force. His force was careless, so careless, as though he was handling an inanimate thing that could not break. A thing. He had done this before, many times, she was sure of this, because his force was so casual, so natural and unthinking. There was no hesitation to his carelessness, no tugging of conscience. But she was not a thing. She was a woman and she was breakable. He was a powerful man, he could have all the women he wanted, and yet he did this to her. Her old life was over, the careful life she had built for herself and Binta, the future with Amadou; the certainties she held, all were gone. Her fear was souring and sinking, and now rage grew in her, circling and rising until all she could feel in herself was rage.

Nobody understood. She felt nakedly alone. Chia and Miss Zikora were complaining that she was being called a 'maid' in the press and she didn't understand that. So what if she was called a maid? She was a maid, after all, and she loved her job, and she wanted nothing more than to rewind time and go back to being a maid with a perfect daughter and a man finally about to come home. After she first told Amadou on the phone, slow-crawling seconds of silence gave way to the hiccupping sound of sobs. He was crying. 'I'm not there to protect you, I did something stupid and they locked me up and I'm not there to protect you,' he said. His tears repulsed her. He was supposed to be stoic, like a proper Fula man. Later, he comforted her, telling her everything would be okay, and shouting about that bastard old White man, that waste of a human being, but by then his crying had already left a residue of resentment. Amadou said the guest was a rich man, and he must pay, he must pay her millions, the bastard dog. Amadou's excited tone, the rise as he said 'millions' in English, upset her, as if it was all just a game at which they would win. She shouted at him; didn't he know the guest could send people to harm her and Binta, and why did he keep talking about money, money, money? Wasn't she doing well with her job? Weren't her younger ones in school back home, wasn't her mother well taken care of? She hung up on him and firmly said, 'No', when the operator asked if she would accept a collect call from Arizona. Her phone rang non-stop, relatives calling over and over. One waspish cousin asked, 'Is that really what happened? Have you told us everything?' Another cousin said, 'Kadi, you never had this kind of ambition', as if it was ambitious to be assaulted by an important White man. Tantie Fanta said, 'He is the head of the Multilateral Nations, he is the overall head, a powerful man in the world', as if that was what mattered the most, and Kadiatou silently hung up, pretending the line had cut off. She didn't want to talk to Tantie Fanta, or to anybody else, even her mother. Mama had placed a curse on the guest and his children and their children, her voice stronger than usual, as if she had suspended her recent ailing health. And she kept asking Kadiatou what would happen next, what would happen to her job, and Kadiatou kept saying she did not know, she just did not know. Each time her phone rang, Kadiatou stared at it, until Binta reached across and took her phone and said, 'Mom, I'll switch this off now. You need to rest.'

But, of course, she didn't rest, she couldn't rest. The detective said she and Binta would have to leave Chia's house and be in protective custody for some time – a week or two or three, he couldn't tell her.

They would live in a hotel, without their mobile phones, and Binta could not go to school. Why? Kadiatou did not know, she did not understand. Her longing for her apartment was a subterranean ache, that small square of the world that was hers alone. The solace of her kitchen. She thought of the day, not long ago, when she was in her kitchen, on her day off, and felt contentment wash over her, calming, refreshing waves of contentment, as she stood by the sink, sieving cornmeal, breaking apart dried fish, and pausing to watch a whole pepper float in her pot, yielding its spice and heat.

ZIKORA SAID AN AMERICAN LAWYER, an expert on assault cases, wanted to represent Kadiatou for free. But Elhadji Ibrahima had already found a lawyer, an African American man he said had helped many Guineans get their papers. Kadiatou trusted Elhadji Ibrahima to know what was best, with his steadfast avuncular love supporting her all these years. She had been reluctant to tell him in detail what had happened in the hotel room, ashamed that her story would disgust him, a disgust he would feel towards her, too. But the unflinching condemnation in his voice freed her. The guest's status did not intimidate him or dim his blazing outrage. He never whispered. He said he had long heard stories from hotel workers, about the bad behaviour of powerful men.

'He was naked and waiting for a maid. It could have been any maid, any woman. What a godless specimen of a human being,' he said. 'This is America, that man will pay for his crimes no matter who he is. He dishonoured you, Kadi, but God has a plan for you. I predict that generations will honour your name, because this case will stop all those wild animals who call themselves men from abusing hotel maids. Our lawyer is good, and this is a straightforward case to win. You will see, many will bless you in the future.'

And as he spoke, she wept, her tears, for once, lighter and less troubled.

Now Zikora was asking Chia for the lawyer's name.

'I'll look him up, I've never heard of him,' Zikora said crisply.

As Zikora got up to leave, Kadiatou followed her to the porch.

'Miss Zikora, thank you,' she said. She didn't want Zikora to feel slighted. If she didn't already have a lawyer then of course she would go with whomever Zikora brought. But she could never reject anything that came from Elhadji Ibrahima.

'No problem, Kadi,' Zikora said.

Zikora was different from Chia, closed where Chia was open; she wanted you to know of herself only what she wanted you to, and nothing more. From the beginning, Kadiatou felt a kinship; she, too, understood the desire to pour yourself inward, back inside yourself. She recognized Zikora's new brittleness after somebody placed a curse on Kwame, the paranoia and helplessness, the confusion, of being under a curse, unable to save yourself. But the evil potency of curses leaked away over time, and Kwame would come back to Zikora, and to fatherhood. Kadiatou no longer told Zikora this, and more time had passed than she first predicted, but she was sure Kwame would come back. One day he would be untied. Little Chidera would yet have a father.

'Thank you, Miss Zikora,' Kadiatou said again.

Kadiatou didn't want to meet even the lawyer from Elhadji Ibrahima. But Chia said she had to. 'Kadi, I know you don't like talking. But you'll have to talk for us to get justice. I'll stay with you. Omelogor and Zikora can call in, too.'

Chia wanted to drive her to the lawyer's office but the lawyer said he would come to them; he didn't want to risk someone recognizing and following her. Zikora was busy at work and couldn't call but Omelogor did, Chia's laptop screen filled with her face. Kadiatou felt tense. The lawyer's name was Mr Junius. He came wearing a crisp suit and a blue tie that intimidated her; to think he drove from DC dressed up like that just to meet her. It felt to her like a waste of an outfit. He had an easy, amiable air, which seemed at odds with the sharpness of his suit. He sat at the tip of the sofa in Chia's living room, as if to better focus, for fear he might not if he sank in more comfortably.

He asked Kadiatou where she was from, and said he knew Guinea well, he had travelled all over, Kankan, Kindia, Koundara. And Conakry, of course.

'How come?' Omelogor asked.

'Sorry?' He turned to the laptop, slightly to his side.

'How come Guinea? It's not very well known. When I was in grad school somebody actually still called it French Guinea.'

He laughed, an unexpected sound, and Omelogor laughed, and instantly a team was formed, he and Omelogor on one side, the people who did not know Guinea on the other.

'Well, Stokely Carmichael for one. I grew up in a very conscious family. My father wouldn't even tolerate my calling him Stokely right now! But I was also fascinated by the country and its ties with the civil rights movement. John Lewis talks about visiting Sékou Touré. Nobody in Georgia gave him dignity and everyone in Guinea did.'

'Fannie Lou Hamer went to Guinea, too,' Omelogor said.

'Oh yes, yes. Many others—'

Chia cut in, 'Kadiatou is anxious about all this, as you can imagine.'

Mr Junius seemed reluctant to move his eyes away from Omelogor's face on the laptop screen. He told Kadiatou that he would guide her through it all, it would be okay, and they would win the case. He said 'it will be okay' so often that Kadiatou knew it would not be. If cross-examination was so easy, then he would not have said it so many times, prep you for cross-examination, cross-examination, cross-examination.

NINE

Every day Kadiatou watched the time displayed on the microwave, the numbers changing minute by minute, thinking she would have been vacuuming a room now, straightening a bedsheet, chatting with Lin while on break.

Lin called often to check on her. The guest, it turned out, the naked man who came bulldozing at her, had over the years asked hotel staff to come to his room for champagne. Shaquana said he asked her a few times. The maid from Haiti said he asked not long ago.

'So nobody went up there to drink his champagne?' Lin said. 'Only the ones that said no are talking about it. Maybe he doesn't like little Chinese ladies, because he never asked me.'

Lin was trying to be funny, but Kadiatou could not muster the energy to smile.

'Instead of asking you to have champagne, he attacks you and forces you. Terrible man. He must pay you big money, Kadi, and you can retire.'

Kadiatou shifted, and Lin, sensing her discomfort, said, 'In America, justice is money. You don't see how they celebrate big money judgments? This man attacked you, so you deserve American justice, money.'

Kadiatou said nothing.

'It'll be okay, Kadi,' Lin said. 'So many people support you. Do you know how many letters have been arriving for you, even some by courier from other countries.'

Kadiatou hadn't known. She asked if Lin would open and read them to her. The first one Lin read was from France, sent by DHL, and the unusual envelope crackled over the phone as Lin opened it. *You will die. You have destroyed a great man. He is innocent. You will die.* Lin stopped, held up the card so Kadiatou could see it, as if she could not believe what she was reading. Somebody somewhere in France went looking for the hotel address, and sat down and wrote in a card, *You will die,* a pink-and-blue card, a field of flowers painted on its front. Lin said she would not read any others. 'Maybe later. You rest, Kadi, you rest.' The next day, Lin sent her a bottle of Chinese sleeping aids, whorls of dried bark slices that looked unappealing, which Lin's friend dropped off outside the front door of Chia's house.

THE MAN WAS ASKING her to tell him, again, and again, what happened in the room. He kept shifting in his chair, his body fluid with the language of irritated impatience. She sensed that he wanted her story to change, but she did not understand why. His icy blue eyes rarely blinked, trained on her, focused on her, a hostile stare rich in contempt. Tom Bone, even his name sounded cold, this pale-haired, pale-faced White man with a flat expression that vowed to remain flat. He was the prosecutor's investigator. Chia said the prosecutor was on her side, fighting for her, but she knew as soon as she arrived that she was not among friends. He wasted no time on courtesy, or her comfort; he started asking questions right away, before she was fully settled. The room was overheated, the tepid water in a paper cup tasted of bleach. There was a woman already seated at the table. She looked African, her rough ghana-weaving held up in a ponytail. 'I am Mariama,' she said. 'I am Fula like you and I will be your translator. They have asked me to tell you that you must tell the full truth and answer all the questions and they are recording everything.' Kadiatou found the woman difficult to understand, as if each word was smudged before being spoken. This was Fula but it was not Guinean Fula, Pular; it was a Senegalese Fula, spoken in an accent with strains of Wolof. There were words the dialects did not share, meanings Kadiatou had to deduce. 'Did you have any knowledge, any knowledge at all, of the guest before you knocked on that door?' Bone asked.

Kadiatou understood but still, to be sure, she waited for the translator to echo the question.

'No,' she said.

'No?' Bone asked.

'No.'

'No? Are you sure?'

She nodded then shook her head, confused, thinking back on the question, in search of lost meanings, because why did he keep asking if she was sure, when she had told him a few times already that she did not know.

'What happened when you opened the door?' Bone asked. 'Think about it carefully and tell me exactly what happened.'

But she had already told him, three times. She began again. It was easier, in Pular, to describe the guest's surprising strength, how astounded she was to see him rushing naked towards her, a ghoulish spectre forever imprinted in her mind. The translator asked her to repeat herself a few times, perhaps to intuit the meanings of some words.

After the translator's stream of English, Bone said, 'You went back and cleaned the room after the assault? That can't be possible!'

'No, no,' Kadiatou said, without waiting for the translator. The woman, Mariama, wasn't quite saying what felt accurate, but Kadiatou didn't have the sufficient depth of English to reach in and correct her. Maybe she should speak English, slowly, so Bone would understand her.

'I say I go to the room near elevator. I enter and come out, after . . .' She paused, searching for a name to give this desecration. They said 'assault', the Americans. She had not known that word until Shaquana told the manager. He assaulted her. 'After he assault me,' she said.

Bone's eyes narrowed. 'Why do you need a translator?'

Kadiatou was sure she had misunderstood. 'Is he asking why I need a translator?' she asked Mariama in Pular. Mariama, ruffled, said yes.

'Your English sounds good to me. You didn't need to have a translator,' Bone said. In a different time and place, she would have been pleased to hear an American saying her English was good. This man seemed certain of her guilt in a crime unknown to her. But having a translator was surely not a crime. Her lawyer said she could request one and speak in Pular, if she preferred, and of course she was relieved: no searching her brain for correct English words that were often never found.

'Did you ask for a translator so you'd have time to decide how to respond to my questions?' Bone asked.

'No,' Kadiatou said. She did not know what he meant, only that he was suggesting a dark intention from which she had to defend herself.

'You have to be honest here, completely honest,' he said.

She nodded, feeling overwhelmed by her bewilderment.

'I'm going to ask you some questions about your asylum application to the United States,' Bone said, and her heart leaped. What did her asylum have to do with this? Amadou always said immigrants never asked other immigrants how they came to America, each person's story was a private mystery, what mattered was that they were in America. She had never spoken to anyone of her asylum case.

'Were all the details you gave in your asylum application true?' he asked.

'Yes.'

'Are you sure about that? You have to be completely honest.'

Why was he asking if she was sure? She could not think of what he meant, but she felt as if she was stumbling towards a trap. 'No. Yes,' she said.

'No? Yes? Which is it, yes or no?'

'Yes.'

He rolled his eyes and threw back his head, awash in exasperation. She feared he had an uncomplimentary expectation of her that she had just fulfilled.

'What was the basis of your asylum request?' he asked. 'Why did you request asylum?'

'I don't know,' she said.

'You don't know why you requested asylum in the United States?'

She reached for the cup of tepid water and drank. She did not understand why he was asking about her asylum, with the manner of a person who already knew a terrible secret of hers. Sweat pooled under her breasts. He must be looking for a reason to send her and Binta back to Guinea, so that all the fuss about the guest would end. Bone was working for the guest. Or maybe he was just angry with her for reporting a VIP, a small insignificant maid like her, disrupting so much.

'You haven't answered my question,' Bone said.

'I tell you what happen in the room,' she said.

'We actually still don't know what happened in that room,' he said.

She stared at him, astonished. He didn't believe her. He thought what she said happened had not happened at all. She went into a room to do her job and a guest turned into a wild animal and ran towards her. She had told him this many times, in the same sequence, with the same words, and all the while he thought she was lying. It wasn't that she had dared report a VIP. It was that he disbelieved the content of that report. Why would she lie? She wanted none of this. She wanted to go back to work, talk to Amadou on the phone, go with Binta to the movies, cook attieke on weekends, look after Chia's house, watch her Nollywood films. Her life was good. Why would she lie about something she did not in any way want?

'I tell you what happen in the room,' she said again. 'Why will I lie?'

'Why would you lie, indeed,' he said.

There was an ugly spikiness in the air, true positions being unveiled, the gap widening of mutual unreachability. She did not look at him. Through the window she saw forlorn snow flurries floating by.

'This case depends entirely on your credibility. Do you understand that?' Bone's voice was slightly raised. His narrow face, his white beard, his white hair, his glassy stare. He scared her.

Now he was asking her about the money Amadou put in her account, and she almost gasped from panic. Liquid rushed loudly in her ears. How did he know about that, from years ago? If he was asking about Amadou, maybe he knew of that tape Amadou gave her, the voice of a woman talking about soldiers, words still undimmed in her mind. Maybe he knew how easy it had been, how the kind woman at the asylum interview said congratulations too soon. But what did that have to do with this case? Something happened in a hotel room and Bone was asking her about her asylum?

Mariama was tapping her pen on the cover of her notebook and the noiseless movement of that pen made Kadiatou dizzy. Nothing felt right. She had come to talk of the desecration the hotel guest had done to her, to a person said to be on her side, but instead she was sitting here tense and heavy-tongued.

'Any lie told on your asylum application needs to come out now,' Bone said.

But she hadn't lied. Why did he keep suggesting she had? Everything she said during that interview either was true – the razor blade her aunty cut her with – or had become true – that she did not want Binta to be cut. From the moment, years ago, when Amadou put in her mind the idea that a girl could marry without being cut, she had thought of it, and grew certain with time that Binta would not be cut.

'If there is any discrepancy in your asylum application, any at all, I need to know it now,' Bone said.

A rising headache, from thinking so much, the convoluted confusions of it. He wanted something from her and she did not know what.

'No,' she said.

'No? What is it you're hiding?' Bone asked. 'What are you hiding? What are you not telling me?'

Suddenly the words from that tape were rising to the surface of her mind and were rolling out of her mouth.

'It was four soldiers. They said I disobeyed the curfew. They came into the restaurant already drunk. One of them said he would do his turn with his gun. I was bleeding . . .' She stopped abruptly, with a frightening sinking feeling at the bottom of her stomach.

'You were raped in your home country?' Bone asked.

'No, no.'

'You just told me you were raped.'

'No, I make mistake. It is just the cassette tape.'

'You made a mistake and said you were raped?' And he laughed a barking laugh. The translator leaned back, as if to move away from Kadiatou.

'It is a cassette tape,' Kadiatou said. 'But I don't use the tape.'

'What cassette tape?' Bone asked.

What had she done? She wished lightning would strike, somebody would burst through the door, anything to interrupt this. Maybe if she fell to the floor she might distract him. And so she pushed back her chair and fell writhing to the floor, forcing tears from her eyes.

'I think we need to take a break,' somebody said.

Kadiatou allowed herself to be helped up. Her forced tears had become tears, and she cried, her nose running. How could all this have happened to her, and where would it end?

As she walked out of the room, she heard Bone say, 'She's a con artist.'

Later, she asked Binta, 'Con artist, what does it mean?'

'Like someone that is a very good liar, someone that deceives people.'

'Oh.' Kadiatou's breath caught in her chest.

'Why? Mom, did somebody call you a con artist?'

'No, no,' Kadiatou said.

ZIKORA CAME TO CHIA'S with bottles of zobo for Kadiatou. Kadiatou didn't like the Nigerian version of hibiscus juice, but she said, 'Thank you', and sipped from one bottle. The kitchen sticky with the swell and rise of expectation. Omelogor was on a video call, iPad propped up on the kitchen island. Chia perched on a counter stool, next to Kadiatou, and Kadiatou felt the urge to get up and walk away, like leaving a distressing ceremony she had been forced to attend.

Zikora stood near the window and began reading out the charges from her phone.

> *Forcible touching*
> *Sexual abuse in the first and third degree*
> *Unlawful imprisonment*
> *Attempted rape*
> *Criminal sexual act in the first degree*

'What's the major one?' Omelogor asked.

'Criminal sexual act in the first degree. He can get twenty-five years for that,' Zikora said.

'Good,' Chia said.

'Well. Only five per cent of rape cases get a conviction,' Zikora said.

'Five per cent?' Chia asked, eyes round.

'That's just monstrous,' Omelogor said. 'Honestly. Why do men rape?'

'You're probably going to explain it all to us and it will have something to do with pornography and with your website,' Zikora said.

'Pornography is part of it, actually. All the violence in contemporary pornography can make men think rape isn't so bad.'

'Is pornography also why men steal and kill and lie?' Zikora said.

'Zikora, seriously,' Omelogor said coldly.

Chia looked drained and tired. 'What is their defence going to be, Zik?'

'They say it was consensual.'

'He doesn't give her money. He isn't good-looking. It was too quick to be a seduction. So why would she fuck him?'

'Omelogor! Don't use that word! It's assault we're talking about!' Zikora said.

'I'm responding to their defence, that it was consensual. If it isn't what Kadiatou says happened, then how did the consensual version happen? In eleven minutes, she is either overwhelmed with attraction for him and quickly agrees to sex, or in eleven minutes she quickly concludes a transaction that somehow doesn't involve any money?'

'The only way their own story makes sense is if you think of the woman involved as a complete idiot,' Chia said.

Kadiatou shrank away from their words, her stomach churning, imagining words like these flung about, but in a larger space, an alien courtroom, Americans speaking fast, her name on strangers' lips, chopping her story into bits with a knife, as if anybody but her could discern what truly happened to her. This image of the court bulked forbiddingly in her mind. They would hack at her with a machete and invite vultures while she lay, still alive, her open wounds exposed.

ON TELEVISION, she saw hotel workers gathered in front of the court, wearing their uniforms, like her own uniform, and she thought of her uniforms, one now lying forlorn in her staff locker in the hotel, the other in a plastic bag in the police station. Some of the women were being interviewed by journalists. 'It happens often,' one said. 'Powerful guests assault us. It has happened to me twice, but I didn't speak about it.'

Kadiatou felt sorry, for being the cause of all this, for disrupting their day; she hoped they would be paid for the hours they were out there, protesting, and supporting her. The world was spinning and would not slow down, her phone always ringing and beeping, Chia hovering, Binta watching her. A photo appeared on her phone, from one of her cousins. She looked at it, uncomprehending, confused, because it was a photo of two White people, but it made no sense because they were in Mama's compound, in her village. In the background were trees she knew, near the vegetable garden where she plucked sour leaves. She knew that grey-brown patterned terrazzo floor, she had sent Mama money for it; she knew the buckets and metal trays stacked in the corner. 'Journalists are in the village questioning everybody,' the cousin said in a voice message. 'Bhoye is saying he will give them a picture of you if they pay him well.'

They had banged on her door, chased her away from her apartment, lay in wait outside Binta's school, and now they had gone all the way to Africa, to Guinea, to her village in Fouta Djallon. Her days had taken on the texture of a dream from which she longed to wake. So much was wearing out or already worn out.

When she saw Binta's face, she knew something was unsaid.

'What is it?' she asked.

Binta said, 'I saw it yesterday', and then reluctantly turned her phone towards her. It was a newspaper headline, in large print, above a photo of her. PROSTITUTE. She knew that word, but it could not be.

'Is it what I think it is?' she asked Binta.

Binta nodded. 'Mom, they don't know you,' Binta said quietly.

Kadiatou stared at it in disbelief. How? How could they call her a prostitute? Thank God her father died, thank God he was long dead, to save him the shame of this, seeing her called a prostitute in front of the whole world. She began to cry. All the crying she had not done, all the tears held back, erupted in ferocious wails and she found herself on the floor, and all around her a terrible scattering of despair. This would never end; she could not see how this could ever end. She would never wash off this stain. Her life would never be the same. How could she rebuild, what would she rebuild from, how would she ever get a job when she was now a prostitute in the eyes of the world? She had never wished others ill. What had she done to deserve this?

Chia had come into the room, she didn't know when, but Chia was beside her on the floor, a feathery touch on her arm, saying, 'Kadi, you're not alone, Kadi, you're not alone.' But she was alone, she felt alone, never as alone in her life as then.

Omelogor

Early morning in early January, with the air so crisp and dry as if it might crack. I am in my front balcony, looking at the new day. A sheen of ochre dust has descended on the world, all hazy light, and the hills in the distance are now blurry spectral shapes. Harmattan brings its nuisances – cracked lips and hacking coughs, itchy eyes and lethargy – but something of this season has always appealed to me, with life dried down to a spartan state that seems purer, truer, stripped of excess, as if the earth is telling us that there is so much we do not need. Wind is astir. Soon dust-whirls will sweep across and leave on the trees and cars and signboards an even thicker glaze. My windows stay closed in January, because to seek fresh air now is to find fresh dust. The loud blare of a truck's horn sounds at the gate and Mohammed hurries out of the gatehouse, sliding his feet into his slippers. You can tell if he's in by the blue rubber slippers that lie outside by his door. From above he looks like a thin column of white cloth blowing in the wind.

He glances up and waves and calls out, 'Good morning, Madam.'

'Well done, Mohammed!' I say.

He opens the gate and the diesel-supply truck edges in, old and noisy, whirring and burping. Exhaust fumes blended with dust probably destroys the lungs, but I inhale in gulps because it is a scent I like. Mohammed shouts to the truck driver, to stop and then steer to the left, to avoid Madam's flowers. My long-limbed harmattan lilies are in their orangish bloom. I love their hopeful probing shape, and how they survive year after year, and how they dare to flower without the rain. Mohammed must think it a silly indulgence, my extreme fussing over plants. Not that he shows it, with his lean face always free of expression in that stoic reassuring way. He should have seen my mother's fevered guarding of the flowers in our campus compound when I was growing up. He motions for the truck to stop, away from my plants but close enough to the diesel tank. The tank is almost empty: I can see through the white plastic, mounted aloft above the generator. The truck driver jumps down and begins to unfurl the hose. Aunty Jane's words are swirling in my head. *Don't pretend that you like the life you are living.* She called this morning – the phone buzzing woke me up – to say there was something important she wanted to discuss. Everybody is talking about the virus in China, but this is her concern, calling me at dawn to say I should adopt a child.

'Omelogor, I wanted to talk to you in the village but you said you had to return to Abuja for an important meeting.'

You said. As if I didn't have an important meeting.

'Yes, Aunty, I had a meeting.'

'You are doing so well and we thank God, but all that work has chased men away and left you childless at the age of forty-six. It is unfortunate that your time has passed, and the only option now is to adopt a baby. I have prayed over this and I have made enquiries at a very good motherless babies home in Awka.'

I should not have been so surprised. Nosy, nattering Aunty Jane, who draws dark rectangles on her forehead in the name of eyebrows and talks non-stop about the most inconsequential things. How she and my father came from the same parents I will never know. At our Christmas reunions, her words always float over our heads and dis-solve into the forgotten like background music. For many years she kept asking me if there were no men in the places where I worked, then about two years ago she stopped asking, perhaps defeated by the reality of my age. And now from nowhere she calls, with the urgency of a secret revelation, to say I should adopt a child.

'Aunty, *mba*, thank you, I don't want to adopt,' I said, with that mellow tone best used on the unhinged.

'In fact, it's better to adopt two and raise them as twins, so they can play with each other.'

How did she go so quickly from adopting a baby to adopting two?

'Aunty, I don't want to adopt.'

'It is the only option left to make sure your life does not remain so empty,' she said, as if we had previously agreed on the emptiness of my life. 'Just because a husband did not come for you, it doesn't mean you must live an empty life. Even in the olden days single women could adopt. You perform some ceremonies and if the child is a boy, he will become a full member of the lineage and inherit property like any other male in the family.'

'Aunty, I don't want to adopt a child.'

'Omelogor,' she said, sighing. 'Don't pretend that you like the life you are living.'

Those words pierced and sank in and cut. *Don't pretend that you like the life you are living.*

My driver, Paul, walks into the compound, fastidious as ever in his fitted jeans and buttoned-up shirt. He's a little late. With those watchful sneaky eyes, I know he has seen me up in the balcony, but he acts as if he hasn't. He never gives me change from errands run unless I ask, and lately keeps sending long-winded texts begging for money. I suspect he is drowning in sports betting, the way he is always furtively glued to his phone. Just before Christmas, one of the cleaners at work came to me, crying like an actor, to say he had lost everything on Nigerbet. 'Madam, I will drink Sniper if I don't find help for my children's school fees. I have Sniper in my house and I swear I will drink it.'

'Then go quickly and drink the rat poison!' I said, to match drama for drama, but later I called him and transferred some money into his account, telling him it was the first and last time I would. I must speak to Paul before he gets to that stage of a cunning fool who expects somebody else to pay his debts.

The diesel truck is backing out of the compound and Paul begins waving and shouting at the driver.

'Wait! Let me move the car before you climb Madam's flowers.'

A performance for me. If I wasn't up here watching, he would leave the car exactly where it is, hoping the diesel truck's manoeuvring would crush my plants, so he can hurry in to tell me with relish what a useless man the truck driver is. I lean forward, looking down, and touch the railings covered in finely powdered dust, and when I take my hands away, the metal bears the soft imprint of my fingers. My ixora plants are dry and shorn of their flowers, but in a few weeks they will burst out in a thousand clusters of the brightest red, almost too beautiful to bear. The bougainvillea has finally crept and spread itself in full, every inch of my compound walls wreathed in leaves, and each time I come home I feel the ethereal enchantment of an intimate secret garden. White stars are printed all over the green tarpaulin awning of the carport, and the high hunched backs of my two SUVs stick out from beneath.

The diesel truck is gone, a misty silence falls, and I am moved to be standing out in my balcony on a new morning in this new year. I am mistress of all I survey. Actually, Aunty Jane, I do like my life. I flail for meaning sometimes, maybe too often, but it is a full life, and a life I own. I have learned this of myself, that I cannot do without people and I cannot do without stretches of sustained isolation. To be alone is not always to be lonely. Sometimes I withdraw for weeks merely to be with myself, and I sink into reading, my life's great pleasure, and I think, and I enjoy the silence of my own musing. Sometimes I revel in long spells of satisfying sexlessness, unburdened by the body's needs. Sometimes my house lights blaze brightly with dinner parties and game nights, and I bring together my different friend groups who otherwise might never meet. People I grew up with in Nsukka meet friends from university in Enugu, and people I met in the many permutations of my job here meet other Abuja people I know from outside work. Many of my friends are dependable and trusted and close. Jide is the oldest and closest, and of course Hauwa. In the past few years, Hauwa. It makes me happy to think of the high peal of her laughter and the focus of her brows as she deep-inhales her Loud. These days I have fewer nights out, but I still enjoy my whisky neat, and dancing in lounges till dawn, and returning home with my eye make-up smeared, tired and happy and high. I should have said to Aunty Jane, 'There is always another way to live, Aunty, there are other ways to live.'

PHILIPPE KNOCKS AND HOVERS at my bedroom door in his shuffling manner that feels insincere, asking if he can dismantle the Christmas tree today. I tell him he can and ask what he plans to cook. Some friends are coming at eight, a smaller group than usual, as not everyone is back from holiday travel and some are stuck, with local flights being cancelled because of the harmattan haze. Kano is so bad that people are driving in the afternoon with their headlights on. Or so Hauwa said, even though she didn't go to her hometown this season; she went with the children to Dubai, and the husband joined them for a few days. She will be here early for dinner because she has to leave early too; she never stays past ten thirty when her husband is in town. She will arrive wearing that oriental vanilla scent, as if she is my co-host, my planning partner, and we can have a leisurely gossip by ourselves before the others arrive.

'I should bring Madam breakfast?' Philippe asks.

'Yes. Downstairs.'

On my phone a text appears from my father, that beloved man who often now asks 'Has anyone seen my glasses?' even when he's wearing them. He and Mummy want to know if my cough is better. I reply yes, chewing bitter-kola helped, I will call them later, and end with a heart emoji. Emojis, of course, never feature in his meticulous messages, which never have missing full stops or commas. I text my mother a heart emoji as well, knowing she might not see it for days, inept as she is at using her phone for anything other than calls.

I scan the news headlines before I search out coverage of Kadiatou's case, as I have been doing every day, as if in vigil, as if by reading these articles I might somehow shield her. One headline asks, 'Kadiatou Bah, angel or demon?' Another speculates about whether she is part of a set-up by the political opponents of the man who raped her. I snort reading that, Kadiatou as part of a dark political plot indeed. I will call her in a few hours, when she's awake, to see how she is. She never says much when I call, not that she ever said much before. I often think of her expression that day in December when the police brought her to Chia's house, how she looked as one might look at the precise moment of being struck by lightning.

Philippe serves my breakfast on a lacquered tray that Chia bought for me in Seoul, its edges decorated with images of long-necked birds in flight. He folds the paper napkin into a miniature tent. Breakfast is always moi-moi and fruit, a meal I approach day after day with my pleasure undimmed. Philippe has learned to make moi-moi exactly as I like: no crayfish and no eggs, just pureed beans and tomatoes steam-cooked in fresh leaves that unwrap layer by layer like an exquisite gift. I would happily have pineapple every day, but Philippe some-times makes ambitious fruit salads, with cubed mango and bananas, and the bananas I always quickly eat first because bananas exposed for too long feel to me like a health risk. Philippe is from Cotonou; every chef in Nigeria seems to be from Benin Republic, but I cannot imagine any with more Francophile pretensions. For years he has tried to convince me to eat what he calls 'cuisine', as if that word might apply only to food made by the French.

'Madam eats only moi-moi, garri and soup, jollof rice, yam and stew. Every time the same thing.'

As he lists the foods I eat, he touches the tips of his fingers, to show the appalling paucity of so few options.

'I can make soufflé for Madam,' he says from time to time.

'I know you can, Philippe, but you won't.'

'What of bouillabaisse for Madam. Madam will like it.'

'No, Philippe. I prefer fisherman soup from Cross River.'

Only when I have dinner parties do I let him do as he likes, but jollof rice must always be made. Years ago, when Philippe had only just started working for me, my mother visited and brought me okpa, not just any okpa but Ninth Mile okpa. No better okpa exists than from those agile women hawking at Ninth Mile with basins balanced on their heads. I was so excited I told Philippe I would have it right away, for breakfast, and in response Philippe mumbled, '*Sauvage.*'

Standing in the middle of my large kitchen, the ceiling fan spinning above, trim in his short-sleeved white uniform, he said, '*Sauvage.*' A swift scattering in my head followed and I heard myself screaming at Philippe as I have never screamed before. 'Idiot! Ignorant fool! Go and pack your bags and leave now! You are sacked! Get out!'

Philippe stood with his eyes and mouth rounded from shock. Or maybe confusion. More confusion than shock. My mother had just gone up to take a bath. My cleaner, Mary, came running; my young relative, who was in Abuja to take a job aptitude test and was staying at the time, came running. Atasi was away in boarding school then.

'Madam, what happened?' Mary asked.

'Aunty, what happened?' the relative asked.

Already they were looking at Philippe with eyes narrowed in condemnation, because it had to be that he had stolen something from me. I told them he had said I was a savage for wanting okpa for breakfast, and they looked baffled and soon shuffled away. The story became that Philippe insulted Madam and she nearly sacked him. But it wasn't the true story. Later I told Philippe I had nearly sacked him because I will not have African self-hate in my house.

'Do you know that okpa is much more nutritious than your crêpes?' I asked. He meekly said yes, but only because he was still in shock at having almost been sacked. He didn't believe me and he still doesn't, but he's canny enough now to express his Francophilia without showing his contempt for African food. Jide has told this story many times to friends at my dinner parties and it always makes them laugh.

The poor man must have thought his madam had gone mad!

Omelogor, you have come again!

This is the problem with reading too many books, Omelogor; after all, is okpa not bush?

I laugh along too, not because I agree but because I see why they are amused. Only once did my reaction pale, when Jamila said to me, 'It looks like you get very angry about small things.'

'They are small things only to small minds,' I replied, and made a face to show I was only playing with her, even though I really wasn't.

She had the calibrated charm of a person who can turn fully nasty in a heartbeat. I tolerated her, but barely, because she was Hauwa's childhood friend.

'Ouch!' Ehigie said.

'Jamila, they said your mind is like groundnut,' Chinelo said.

'Your own mind is like coconut,' Jamila said, too brightly, to show how unaffected she was. It was the first time Hauwa had heard the story and she laughed along, but later she looked at me with tender wonder and said, 'You're so passionate. You really believe in what you believe.'

It is still one of the loveliest things I have ever been told.

Two

I wake up thinking of Aunty Jane. Days have passed and still her words chafe. My drawn-out disquiet must mean something, but what? That she struck close to truth, or else I would not now train this searching light on my own life? How easy it is to manufacture a problem; I had never thought of liking my life, never mind proving I did, until Aunty Jane said I didn't. I should send her a link to read For Men Only, but even if she gets it, and she won't, how does that show I like my life? You can write popular posts on a website, you can have a surfeit of things, and still have an empty life, so there really is no way to prove to someone else the fullness of your own life. Your true experience is the only proof.

In the evening, in the warm gathering of friends, I stand outside of myself and watch myself, as if to assess one of my life's passing scenes. I pour red wine and choose song playlists on my phone and tease Belema about her chunky chain anklet: 'Are you sure you can walk with that thing?' Laughter floats above oldies music turned low. Nine people who without me might not be friends are eating and sharing their small sorrows and triumphs. Ehigie says his New Year's resolution is to give up smoking Loud, and Jide says that is unnecessary self-punishment, and Belema asks if he has any left at home so she can come by and take it. Hauwa says nothing, raising her glass of water to her lips, and I admire the henna patterns that circle her wrist in ornate whorls and run gracefully down her finger. She's very careful, even cagey, and while everyone knows she doesn't drink, not everyone knows she smokes. At the centre of the table, Philippe has floated some leaves in a vase filled with water and they look striking and give off a herby scent.

'Please, does Philippe want us to eat that thing too?' Chinelo asks, peering at it. Chinelo is the cheery one, a bright pitcher brimming with jokes. We met during Youth Service Corps and I enjoy her relentless joyfulness, even though I do not believe that anybody can be that happy all the time. Ahemen is saying Christmas holidays depress her. Eval and his wife Edu look at each other and start laughing, because they were just saying the same thing on their drive here.

'Next Christmas we are not going away and not doing anything,' Edu says.

'It's January broke blues. You're depressed because you're regretting all the money you spent,' Chinelo says, and scoops one more piece of peppered turkey onto her plate.

'My own problem is that everybody in Abuja is taking pictures wearing pyjamas on Instagram. Just looking at them makes me tired,' Adaora says.

Belema says her family's cross-over prayer on New Year's Eve was all about her reconciling with her husband. 'He's still jobless! They should pray for him to get a job. I was the one feeding him and he was beating me. At least if you want to continue beating me, then you should be employed.'

Everyone has some jollof rice on their plates, and I am satisfied to see that the peppered turkey and stewed goat meat are more popular than Philippe's French chicken that smells too strongly of mustard. Jide forks a piece in his mouth and says, 'This virus in China is very bad', and for a moment I think he is talking about the food.

'Very bad how?' Hauwa asks.

'They're not telling us everything,' Jide says. 'My cousin lives in China. He came back for Christmas but he has decided he's not going back. He lives in Guangzhou, which is where many Nigerians are, and even though it's not close to the town where this virus thing is happening, he says the hospitals are full of infected people and that it's spreading like mad.' Jide stands to reach for another can of beer from the drinks on the sideboard. He always manages to look dishevelled, as if something about his clothes needs straightening out, and I cannot count all the times that I have taken one glance at him and gone on to tug at his collar, or flatten his trousers bunched up at the belt loops. He was sweetly round-cheeked when we were children and now he's sweetly plump.

'What if it comes to Nigeria? We'll be finished,' Jide says.

'But isn't it from something they ate in the market in that town?' Edu asks.

'There is nothing they don't eat in China, even frogs,' Chinelo says.

'Whatever they ate, they have already eaten and this thing has started. If it comes to Nigeria, we are finished,' Jide says. He is drinking too fast, can after can of beer, as he always does in the aftermath of a phone call with his parents. I want to calm him down. My tongue tingles from peppered turkey, and a bit too much pepper in the jollof rice too.

'Jide, it's not coming to Nigeria. I read the WHO statement. There's no human-to-human transmission,' I say.

'Omelogor has spoken. Jide, leave it,' Ehigie says.

'My cousin said it is much worse than Ebola,' Jide says, almost defiantly.

'God forbid,' Chinelo says.

Ahemen, as if to change the subject, tells us yet again the story of her former househelps who twice stole her jewellery. You might be discussing rockets going to space and Ahemen will find a way to bring in the wicked housegirls who stole all her gold. She now has Filipino househelps and often tells me, with the vague air of a threat, that my staff will show me their true colours one day.

'With foreigners, you pay them and it ends there. They don't steal from you and they don't tell you about their mother's leg pain and their sister's kidney failure,' she says, in ending her much-told story. She can't accept that I actually like the Africanness of unclear boundaries with staff. If I didn't, I would not pay Paul's children's school fees or Mohammed's mother's hospital bills or rent for the tailoring shop where Mary spends the rest of each day after her cleaning is done.

Philippe appears and begins to clear away the empty platters.

'The au gratin was very nice,' Eval says.

'Is that what they call that tasteless potato full of cheese?' Chinelo asks. 'This is the problem with going to school abroad, you start giving complicated names to tasteless food.'

'My sister!' Ahemen says in agreement.

For dessert, with a self-important flourish, Philippe presents a pineapple upside-down cake.

'People: Monsieur Philippe!' I say, and we all clap and hoot, our usual routine, and I remember Chinelo once telling me, 'You know why everyone likes coming here? A big house, no husband that we have to tiptoe around, and you are a seriously generous host. Many of these rich people, you go to their house and they don't even give you food.'

Glazed slices of pineapple gleam on the cake. Philippe says sorry and dashes back to the kitchen to get a knife. Affection is softly rising in me, and softly spreading out first to my friends seated around my table bathed in light and then to the whole phosphorescent world. I do like my life. Hauwa leans over the table to sniff Philippe's vase of herbs. 'Oh, lovely,' she says. Diamond earrings in the shape of intertwined Os sparkle on her ears. She often wears them to work. I noticed them right away when we first met, diamonds too big and flashy for the office, just what you would expect from the woman Amanze said was the spoiled Northern wife of a very rich man. Amanze the gossip queen, dishing with bile about everybody in Abuja. She said Hauwa was like all the other Northerners, a know-nothing employed in a government agency only because of who she knew. 'Empty vessel' was the expression Amanze used. 'That Hauwa is just an empty vessel, and they made her a unit head even though she doesn't know anything.'

So when Hauwa brought me some accounting documents, which were orderly and transparently done, I asked, 'Who prepared these? I have a few questions.'

She laughed a high laugh with an inappropriate edge. She had a darting, playful air that felt unsuited for formal work.

'They told you all the Northerners here are Big Men's children and don't know anything,' she said.

'Yes,' I said bluntly. I was newly back from America and I must have had some lingering disagreeableness from my sour saga there. I wanted only to do the project well, to convince myself that I had made the right decision by leaving the bank to do my own consulting.

'I prepared the documents,' she said. 'I have a master's degree.'

I hadn't looked properly at her until then. So many Northern women were pretty in an expected way, their features even and their skin light, and Hauwa was like that but also not. She had large enquiring eyes, a pronounced cupid's bow on a small childlike mouth. She seemed like a person who asked questions of life. She said 'I have a master's degree' with all traces of laughter gone from her voice, and I felt sorry for the brusqueness of my earlier 'Yes.' How often she must deal with the poison of assumptions, and how easily she let out that laughter to shield herself from it. I understood something of this, the pressures of proving oneself.

'I can see they were wrong about what they told me,' I said, thinking that I should just say sorry for earlier and yet not knowing how to just say sorry for earlier.

'They weren't wrong,' she said. 'All the other Northerners here are thick. Don't ask the women on the second floor for anything, because all they do is gossip and plan what outfit to wear for this nikah and that nikah.'

Her face was expressionless in the halo of her pink silk scarf. I looked at her and thought: Here is a person who enjoys unsettling people. She sounded rehearsed. She had said this before many times to many people, and this thought annoyed me because suddenly I wanted her to tell me only what she had told no one else.

'How would you know?' I asked, quite coldly.

'What?' She seemed disappointed by my response. I was supposed to laugh at her surprising outrageousness. I was supposed to admire the courage it took to joke like that about her own people.

'How would you know that all they do is gossip?' I asked. At least I did not add, 'If you don't gossip with them too.'

'It was a joke,' she said.

I turned back to the documents and said, 'Thank you.'

She made to leave but she didn't leave. We laughed about it later, because she said if she had walked out of that office, she would have hated me for the rest of her life, rude, arrogant Igbo woman that I was.

THREE

It's midnight by the time everyone leaves, except for Jide, who is spread out on a sofa with the thousandth can of beer balanced on his chest.

'My mother has found another girl,' he says. 'And listen to this, she went to a *polytechnic*. A polytechnic. Remember the days of "Jide you should marry a medical doctor"? See how desperate my mother has become? She even started crying and doing that self-pity thing: why is her own different, all her friends have grandchildren, this and that. She never asks me "how are you" before she starts. Then my father came on to say I need to do a borehole for our compound in the village.'

The nasal ring of Jide's complaining voice irritates me and I feel guilty for my irritation. He is the only son, and he is burdened enough with expectations even without this pressure to marry. The other day his parents said he has to start building a house in their village, as if anybody with a telecoms job like his can afford to build a house.

'Omelogor,' Jide says. 'Can we get married?'

I look at him, surprised. 'What?'

'And stay married for a few years, so they can stop harassing me.'

'The incestuous energy will be out of this world, Jide. Even your parents won't believe it,' I say. Still, I imagine marrying Jide. What a way to stick it to Aunty Jane. *Look, Aunty, I have a husband! So much for my empty life!*

'They just want me to marry and marry a woman that I will marry,' Jide slurs.

He has lost command of his tongue; until his chin drops to his chest in sleep, his words emerge mangled and torn. His loud snoring rises and vibrates and ends on a mournful note. I spread a throw over him. His body fills the couch's entire width. I remember years ago when Jide told me, 'Just stay on the couch', while he wiped my mattress with a soapy cloth. I was so sick, I had thrown up violently everywhere, my bed, the walls, the floor. As Jide cleaned some dribble on the floor, he looked up at me and said, '*Ndo*, sorry, just stay on the couch', as if to protect me from my own effluences. He has never brought it up and when I did, not long ago, he brushed it aside. My eyes are filling with tears looking at Jide sleeping and thinking of that day.

Atasi comes into the parlour and right away I know she wants to ask me for something; she asks only when she knows I've been drinking, and I don't know if her scheming is forgivable teenage behaviour or something worth worrying about.

'You're still awake?' I ask her. I hope she hasn't noticed my tears and doesn't think it's drunken crying. A sweet-faced kitten is printed on her blue nightshirt. She's so skinny she swims inside the shirt. She tells me she needs a personal trainer to work on her problem.

'What problem?' I ask.

'I have hip dips,' she says.

'And what is that?' I ask.

She explains and explains but I don't understand until she pulls her nightshirt tight across her hips. According to Instagram, her hips do not flare outwards as they should, and the inward dints she has instead constitute a gross abnormality which, luckily for us, some guided exercises might correct. I think again of Aunty Jane, and how easy it is to invent a problem where previously there was none.

'When did you know?' I ask.

'Know what?'

'Did you know you had hip dips before you saw the video on Instagram?'

She sighs and glances up at the ceiling in lieu of an eyeroll.

'Atasi, somebody woke up and had a cup of coffee and decided to call a perfectly normal body part a "hip dip" and make it a problem, because they want to create content or sell something or just make themselves feel important or better. Your body is normal and normal is fine,' I say, and teasingly I add, 'If you eat a little more, you'll go from normal to perfect.'

But she doesn't smile. She sulks away without another word. She's always pouting and photographing herself with her phone fixed on a tripod, or with Philippe or Mary as her photographer, while she stands by the flowers in some contorted pose, midriff bare, crop top glued to her bony frame. Modelling-school flyers magically appear almost every day, on the dining table or sometimes in my study, of photoshopped girls with vacant expressions and impossible skin. But my no is no; no modelling classes. *Increase Your Confidence*, one of the flyers said, and I told Atasi the contrary was true. 'Modelling will give you low self-esteem,' I said, and she looked at me with, of all things, pity, but not for long enough to be considered disrespectful.

She had been the one hundred metres sprint star in school, until she stopped abruptly in SS1 because she feared she would grow muscles and look like a man.

'People with muscles live longer and healthier lives,' I remember saying to her, and now I think I should have said something else. I should have reassured her that she won't, of course, ever look like a man, and that exercise will benefit her health. With Atasi, I say things and then later I wish disappearance on them.

JIDE WAKES UP sober and sombre, saying he should go home and, yes, he knows our getting married won't work. He looks like a giant rumpled pillow, lying there, his discontent so gravely etched in the shadows of his face. For years he has wanted to move to Lagos, to escape the slow waste that his love life here has been. He says Abuja is like a prefabricated stage, with older government men looking for transactions and younger men primed only to take, while what he longs for is the simple wonder of talk, of touch, and time. Lately, he keeps asking if I don't feel the menace in the city's air. His unhappiness is so ripe and yet it doesn't push him to act, as if all his unhappiness really needs is to be witnessed by someone else. 'Go to Canada, Jide. Nigerians are colonizing Canada now. I'll pay for everything until you're settled,' I tell him often, and each time he says okay, he'll look into it, but he never brings it up again until I do. He's a gesturer, Jide, not a finisher; he starts things or makes to start things and then he stops. It frustrates me that nothing is too intolerable for him to bear, and that he bears it all, so plaintive and passive. You don't stop at longing; you use the force of your longing to bring into being the life that you want, or you try to, at least. I told him something like that once, I don't remember my exact words, and his reply left me stunned with a glimpse of a resentment I didn't know existed at all: 'We are not all fearless like the great Omelogor.'

He is slowly raising himself from the couch. I would marry him if marrying him would help, but anyone who knows us even in passing will easily discern the glaring farce. We met in kindergarten in university primary school but we became best friends in grade 2G, seated next to each other in Mr Ngwu's class. He would come to my house to play after school and I marvelled that he was allowed to walk all the way up campus by himself. We liked chasing the butterflies that forever flitted over my mother's plants. Once Jide farted loudly and I shouted in gleeful accusation, 'You polluted!' and he promptly replied, 'I didn't pollute, it was the butterflies!' I remember what he was wearing that day: a blue He-Man and the Masters of the Universe T-shirt, with a haloed He-Man holding a sword. It's been more than thirty years and we still joke about farting butterflies.

WE WERE NEOPHYTES together in Abuja, Jide and I, in the early days after we first got our jobs here. We didn't know the roads; we would set out driving to the market and end up on tree-lined residential streets. We didn't know of the rich Northern boys racing expensive cars on the highways, or how abusive the sun's heat could be. We didn't know of the Friday somnolence of offices as so many went off to mosque, or that some hair salons don't allow men to step inside their doors. One Saturday I searched online for a natural hair salon and I asked Jide to meet me there so we could go right after my braids were done to look at the mini-flat he wanted to rent. He was still living with his uncle then. The salon did not smell like most salons, no burnt notes of singed hair, no sickly-sweet perfume of harsh chemicals. It was fragrant with the scent of coconuts and shea butter and essential oils of lavender and mint. Freshly mixed hair puddings sat in bowls on the counters, as appetizing as something you could eat. The women there were all Northerners, their headscarves draped across their chairs. They had such beautiful hair, bouncy and coily, their edges lush and full, and it seemed a great loss to me that their hair so lovingly done would then be closed off again to the world.

One of them said, 'My cook made me a large yogurt before I left home.'

So strange and exotic, these Northerners, eating a large yogurt at home. I had no picture in my mind of what a 'large' homemade yogurt could be, because yogurt to me was something you bought in little cups in the cold section of the supermarket. They were people whose ancestors herded cows and I was a person with forest-dwelling forebears, and this ancient distinction made them interesting to me, more than that they were Muslim and I was Christian. They spoke Hausa, with some English sprinkled in. Even then, my Hausa was good, learned in the few months between interviewing for and getting my job.

'I do all my groceries in London. I take British Airways overnight and spend the day and then come back,' the one who had eaten a large yogurt said. She looked slyly from side to side, as if to ensure that everyone had heard her, her hair flowing to her neck like lustrous black wool. When Jide appeared at the salon door, the receptionist shrieked loudly and these imperial women, utterly aghast, began reaching for scarves and towels to cover their hair, and all the while they were casting about to expose the usurper who had brought in a man. I understood right away and I should have said, 'Please sorry, I didn't know men can't come in.' I should have owned up and faced their livid eyes. I didn't. Jide had hurriedly backed out, and I stayed silent and didn't answer his calls in case that gave me away.

I wanted to be one of the people who knew what everybody else knew. There was so much I didn't know in those early days, and because I was used to knowing things, it disoriented me. I knew Igboland well and Lagos fairly well, but the North had a texture so unrelated to them, not that Abuja is even truly North, stuck in the centre of the Nigerian map. Capital territory, seat of government, city of parks with leafy trees. I had always imagined a life in Lagos, but the job I got here was too good to refuse, levels above what new graduates got. Already I was plotting to scramble up higher, and if it meant living in a staid city of no imagination, then so be it. Abuja was too dull, too caged in the formality of its own existence, a city built for a precise reason, like a Lego house. Or so I thought, until one day in a phone shop in Ceddi Plaza somebody called out my teenage nickname, 'Logos!' A very fair-skinned woman wearing a boubou and flat designer slides, the casual uniform of the socially chosen. I looked, head tilted, at her. Maybe she knew someone who knew me.

'Logos! It's Nodebem,' she said, her manner all sweet warmth. 'From university secondary school.'

She looked nothing like Chinodebem, the girl who was so dark people called her 'Black Maria' in secondary school and boys said she had a bad body odour and teeth discoloured from infrequent brushing. Now she smiled to show teeth so white they distracted me, as though she had pasted printer paper in her mouth. I would never have recognized her with that new yellow face, a blasé face, the face of a rich Igbo man's idle wife, flat from layers of foundation applied with scant regard for the rise and fall of a human face.

'I go by Nodie now,' she said, and moved her metal-studded designer bag from hand to hand in case I might miss it. We exchanged numbers knowing I would never call her, but as she walked away, I admired her for daring to remake herself and for the audacity it took to affably say, 'It's Nodebem from secondary school', as if her dramatic skin bleaching was nothing at all. She rattled my view and shook me to see that Abuja's margins were fluid. There was room at its edges for reinvention, and I began to think it might not be just a job stopover and maybe I would stay. And so began the shadows and surprises of a city I would yet know. At my first finance training course, a routine course in risk analysis, we were asked to take drug tests. The coordinator gave us lanyards and folders and plastic vials for our urine samples. I was baffled but all the others looked unsurprised, so I tried to look like them. We drifted to the women's toilet, odorous with Izal, where a stout woman wearing a CLEANER badge was standing by the sinks with a solicitous and slightly shifty air.

'Please pee for me,' a woman called Hadassah said to the cleaner. Hadassah wore a showily bejewelled watch and a blue scarf draped around her head. She handed her vial to the cleaner, who promptly hurried into a stall. Another cleaner came in, a mild matronly woman, her eyes flitting from person to person in silent offering of her pee. She did this often; she had probably hurried to be here before the training course started, as there was clearly money to be made. A woman named Chikamso wearing a silk shirt under her skirt suit gave the second toilet cleaner her container and said, 'I'll transfer to your account, I don't have cash.'

I went into a stall. I heard somebody say the cleaner needed to drink water to make her pee more and somebody else said, 'I have Eva water here.' It startled me that these women were all worried about what their urine might reveal. Had they done drugs at the weekend, or did they snort something as they primly dressed for work? In the end, every woman who walked into the toilet to get a sample of her urine left with a sample of a cleaner's urine, except for me. Chikamso and I became good friends, and sometimes in the middle of our conversations I would blurt out, 'Please pee for me!'

FOUR

More days have passed and still I think of pretending, and of why Aunty Jane would think I am. *Don't pretend that you like the life you are living.* It feels so unbeneficial to pretend to like your life. Would you pretend to yourself or just to the world, and if you pretended to yourself too, then does the pretending become in some way real? And what, anyway, is real? The opinions of people unimportant to me have always slid easily off my mind, so why am I now held bound by the words of a dotty aunt? Maybe my superstitious spine is signalling a new year off on an inauspicious start. I lie in bed long after I have woken up, feeling my spirit grow tart, my body strangely weighted, as though needing to cast off parts of itself. I should probably walk on my treadmill, although I hate to exercise. Walking outside is the only tolerable thing, but the sun is already scorching, and so I'll have to wait for the cooling of dusk. I tell Philippe I don't want any breakfast and he asks, 'What of small pineapple for Madam?'

'Okay, just pineapple.'

I eat fresh pineapple slices while browsing the news. The WHO now says the virus is transmitted human to human, which means they don't know what they are talking about and probably never did. But how can they know? A novel coronavirus is novel because nobody has seen it before. There are hundreds of new articles about Kadiatou's case, and everywhere that unflattering photo of her where her eyes are puffy with a meretricious gleam. An op-ed calls her 'an unlikely choice'. An unlikely choice for assault. It starts with the words 'The hotel maid does not look as one would have expected', then goes on to say she must have agreed to sex in exchange for money. Who writes this and then goes home and sleeps well at night? It is in the *Post*, but who sat at their keyboard and typed words to say Kadiatou is good enough to be paid for sex but not good enough to be raped? There are a few articles about him, the man who raped her. They all have a mournful tone as they list his accomplishments and the dreams he will now forfeit. Last month, when I watched his arraignment on television, I tried to read his face each time the camera closed in on him. He was unshaven, his thin lips unsparingly straight, and from time to time he looked at the court and seemed to restrain himself from shaking his head at the absurdity of dealing with this preposterous case of great ignorance. That he was exasperated, actually exasperated, showed how he thought of himself as the one who was wronged. A small dark purplish bruise lay on his chin, and I thought perhaps his wife had slapped his face and left the mark for the world to see. The attractive rich wife whose photo is splashed about with every news update. She has rented a house in Georgetown, a gilded cage with seven rooms, where they will stay until the trial starts. Chia says Luuk once met her in France and says she is very lovely. Of course she is lovely. They always have lovely wives.

ON FOR MEN ONLY, I heard from a man who raised money for himself and his mother and his sister to cross over to Lampedusa on a wooden fishing boat and then watched his mother and sister drown when the boat capsized. He is in Lomé and his wife wants to leave him because he cries all the time and spends what little they have on local gin. Nobody should expect him ever to be whole again but everyone does. His relatives are telling him to be a man, now that his life is better with a job and a house from his father-in-law. He has to play hero of the tale, because he's a man, but what if he doesn't want to or isn't suited for it? I want to write a post to say you don't have to be a hero, but maybe you can find other ways to be broken – a little less gin, a little more trying to see what is present, your wife and your baby – or maybe you can think of what your mother would want. But the words don't come. The words don't come and so I shut down my laptop. From my window I look out to see Mohammed praying in the corner by the compound walls. The grace of his kneeling, forehead to earth, and rising again; the humility of his bowing and kneeling again. His movements are heartfelt and fluid, almost joyful if joyful were restrained; it is not mere habit or duty, he is a true believer. I've always felt that it's why he is so honest, his tongue unable to form a single lie. I trust him completely. Is he one of those people born with the good fortune of a purity of spirit, or did being raised in faith create his? Maybe both. So many people raised in faith are nothing like him, after all. The men who murdered Uncle Hezekiah were raised in faith. I feel the sensation that thoughts of Uncle Hezekiah always bring: an internal churning, a rushing of fluids in my head. If I don't sit down, my body wavers and threatens to fall. Uncle Hezekiah, my father's only brother, a man I loved, but I did not cry when he died. Which might have been explained by distance, since I saw him a few times each year, but why did I fall apart soon after when another man was murdered, a man who was a complete stranger to me? I wept and moped, shrouded for weeks in lassitude and drifting in its hold. I sought out books on grief and learned that grief is unpredictable, that our bodies know how best to grieve, and that sometimes we cry long after what we are crying about. So crying for that stranger was crying for my uncle. I often tell myself this but I am not convinced. The stain of betrayal and shame remains. He was a gentle, kind man, a deserving man, and I cannot understand what is so deficient in myself that I could not simply cry for him. How demeaning, how diminishing, to have cried for him by crying for someone else.

IT IS A DROWSY SUNDAY and Hauwa stops by after dropping her children off on a playdate. She brings me a bag of plantain chips, the fancy kind she orders in small packs tied with gold string.

'Thank you,' I say, and only after I say 'thank you' do I hear the listlessness of my voice.

'Omelogor, is something wrong? You've been different. Did something happen in the village?' Her face is soft with concern. I'm not sure why I haven't told her what Aunty Jane said, but I haven't. Maybe she hopes that something bad did happen in the village, since she begged me not to go, to come to Dubai instead, and I said no. I know it's unfair, and almost certainly untrue, but I think it all the same. I remember her asking flippantly, 'Why do you Igbo people always go to your village anyway? What is in the village?'

In response, I showed her photos of Chia's father's castle, no word better describes that house than 'castle', and she swiped through the images and said, 'I can see nobody uses the tennis courts', with that tinkling laugh of hers. It was true, weeds were pushing through the concrete at the edges of those courts, but still it felt like something said just to nettle me. I shouldn't have shown her those pictures anyway. It was impulsive and silly, as if the tone in her question called for a marshalling of defences, and in predictable ways, by brandishing big houses. To say the village is not as you imagine it to be. Of course Chia's father's house has nothing to do with my attachment to Abba, and of course it's a unicorn and much of the village is just as villagey as Hauwa imagines. If I spend Christmas and New Year's anywhere else, I feel as if I have been served a meal of cold leftovers about to go off. I love the scent of the village, an ancient smell, of centuries of rainwater and wood fires and earth worship, and I love to watch the bats flying about at sundown as if suddenly freed from jail. I think of a time when women let their wraps fall at the spring, in worship, bringing to the goddess their sacrifices and despair. I love the cadence of rural Igbo, the blunt and brash conversations that suffer no fools. And the striving, the striving, everybody wanting to start a small business, everybody with big trading dreams. I always eat too much: fresh ukwa my mother makes with dried fish; abacha Aunty Nneka brings from Agulu; onugbu soup that old Nne Matefi, my grandmother's sister, cooks in her smoke-filled mud kitchen that she has refused to have torn down. Our relatives tease Chia and call her a foreigner because she hates ukwa and won't touch onugbu soup from the sooty pot. This Christmas she said to our great-aunt, 'Okay, I'll eat', and I eyed her a warning to stop trying to please, but she went ahead and swallowed the pounded yam and soup, then said in a tight voice, 'Omelogor, I'm going to vomit', and I said, 'Chia, please not on me.'

As soon as I arrived, days before Christmas, a wiry slip of a woman named Nwando came to our gate demanding to see me, to show me her new keke rickshaw taxi. I scolded her and said she should not have come, since she knows the only way to thank me is to help another woman. But secretly my heart swelled with pride. Two years ago, when I gave her a Robyn Hood grant, she was selling small red peppers on a rusting tray. Of all the women I have given Robyn Hood grants in my village, only one, a tailor, has failed at her business. Hauwa will not understand how I come back from all of this feeling sacramental and sated.

'Did something happen in the village?' Hauwa asks again. 'What's wrong? You just look down. Or you don't want to spend time with me?'

How quickly Hauwa can change from playful to petulant; she knows it has nothing to do with spending time with her. The next thing she'll say is, 'Okay, I'm going', which is a prompt for me to say, 'No, don't go.'

As if on cue, she says, 'If I'm disturbing you, if you want me to go, just tell me to go.'

She has an expression on her face that I think of as shrewish, and I think this guiltily because I dislike words like 'shrew' and 'termagant', for not having male equivalents.

'Hauwa, you know you're not disturbing me,' I say. 'Nothing happened. Just the normal thing in the village, everybody praying for me to find a husband.'

'Are you serious? *Wallahi.* Didn't you say they had stopped?'

'I thought they had.'

'You really don't want to marry,' she says, watching me as if in revelation. 'You really didn't dream of a wedding dress and all that?'

'No,' I say. I did sometimes dream of a child, a little boy, holding his hand as we crossed the street, but in those half-lit dreams there was never a husband.

'Me, I like being a married woman. Marry and then you are free to do what you want. Don't marry and they will always be on your case. Or at least marry and then divorce,' Hauwa says.

She almost never speaks of her marriage. I know only that her husband is related to her mother, and travels on business all the time. He appears in her conversation as a reason more than a person. *Rabiu is in town so I can't stay late.*

'I see we're being cynical today,' I say.

'It's just the truth. You know I will always tell you the truth,' she says, with emphasis on 'you', as if to others she will tell lies. 'It's kind of funny, and I don't mean to add to the stress from the village, but they will stop talking about you in Abuja if you get married.'

'What do you mean?'

'Hadassah's brother is going around saying you're dating the vice president, and that he will swear on it, that you are the one who spoiled his contract bid.'

Her gossipy tone surprises me and makes my irritation flare. The stories about me are the same stories that trail all the single young or youngish women with money in Abuja. They say I was a runs girl in university and started sleeping with governors then, and I got my promotions from sleeping with CEO and I got contracts from ministers I slept with and my consulting company is a shell for laundering an ex-governor's spoils. That last part, of course, is partly true, although I laundered the money when I still worked at the bank. They tell these stories because it is men who built the secret caves where fortunes are made, and a woman seen inside them must somehow be explained. Once, at dinner, Jamila brought up some rumour about me, with a malicious smile, and Hauwa flicked her hand in a swift, dismissive way. 'All the people that talk about Omelogor want to be where she is,' she said, and then looked around the table and spoke of other things. I felt pride like a sugar rush in my blood, pride and pleasure at how she shut Jamila down. Now she has this gossipy tone, making the stories matter.

'Hadassah's brother must be very important for you to suddenly have time for idle gossip,' I say.

'I just felt you should know.' Her tone is wounded; she feels herself unfairly reprimanded. We're in my room and she gets up from the vanity table and walks to the door that leads to the balcony. She's wearing jeans and a button-up tunic and her hair is in one of those turbans dotted with stones.

'You're going to smoke?' I ask.

'I shouldn't smoke?'

'I thought you were picking up the kids.'

'So? You think they can tell when I'm high? Just say you don't want me to smoke. You always act funny when I smoke.'

'Hauwa, that's not true.'

Smoking Loud makes me itchy and then foggy-brained, but sometimes she decides to forget this and offers me a spliff, and when I turn away she says it is a moral judgement on her.

'Okay, I won't smoke, sorry,' she says, in a way that reminds me of how much younger than me she is. Eight years. I am relieved when my phone vibrates and it's my mother, and even though I know it's just one of those desultory calls to ask how I am, I make a sign to Hauwa to say my mother and I have to have a serious talk. I want Hauwa to leave. I have never wanted Hauwa to leave before but now

I want her to leave. I feel an internal agitation whose boundaries I cannot map. She doesn't wave, not properly; she merely lifts her palm as she picks up the handbag lying on my bed.

The next morning, I send her three *How are you?* messages that she ignores. Finally, I text, *We were not in equilibrium yesterday,* and she calls almost immediately, and asks, 'What does that even mean?'

'I thought sending something stupid like that might make you react,' I say.

She is silent for a while. 'Omelogor, sometimes you can be cold. Very cold. Like a man.'

To be called cold is not new to me, but it jars to be called cold by her. 'I'm sorry,' I say.

'Something is going on that you don't want to tell me.'

'It's nothing. Being in the village just made me think.'

'You're always thinking but this is different.'

'Hauwa, it's not, honestly.' I pause. 'You heard that somebody has died of the virus in China?'

'Yes, I saw that. And confirmed cases in Japan and Thailand. We have to make sure nobody tells Jide that this thing is spreading.'

I laugh and so does she.

'Why do I want your approval so much?' she asks, and her asking makes me suddenly happy.

'Just as I want yours. Isn't that what friendship is, to want each other's approval?' I say this feeling faintly false. Friendship should have prefixes, suffixes, gradations. To capture specifically the contentment that descends from having Hauwa near me.

'Is it?' she asks. 'I have many friends but I've never met anybody like you.'

I RETURNED FROM AMERICA with a jaundiced spirit and a mood like midnight. Without Hauwa I might not have lifted myself so quickly. Hauwa was all little gifts and little discoveries: where to get the best kulikuli heated up with ginger and pepper, bath oils that I said would be too messy in my bath and she said just try it, and when she asked me how it was I said sheepishly that it was soothing.

I loved her laughter, especially after she smoked and it took on near-hysterical heights. 'I don't like salad because it makes my poop come out in pellets, like a goat's,' she said, with her hysterical laugh.

We argued once, about a group of Shia Muslims murdered by the Nigerian army after they crowded onto a road, blocking the path of cars.

'They shouldn't have blocked the road,' she said, looking at nail-polish colours.

'You're just saying that because they are Shia. If they were Sunni, you would care more.'

'Of course I would care more. Do you care equally about your mother and a random woman in the street?'

I paused and could not think of what to say in response. The blithe open simplicity of her positions was refreshing, the way she was instinctive, almost impulsive, the lightness she brought. She wasn't interested in my time in America, like my old friends were, and it freed me to put my wounded self away.

I HAD KNOWN HAUWA a few months before I first went to her house. She opened the enormous wooden front door herself and let me in. Glazed urns stood in a line and the perfectly round faux boxwood that sat in each one made her anteroom look familiar, like a big generic hotel's entranceway. Her children were upstairs with their nannies. Her husband was away. She wanted to show me her books in a small square room whose walls were covered entirely by shelves.

'I told you I had books,' she said, with her high laugh. 'See, I told you my father gave me some old Shakespeare volumes.'

'I didn't doubt you.'

'Yes, you did. You thought people like me don't read books.'

She was wearing a purple satin boubou which sheathed her body in a regal sheen, and as she walked, the fringes on her sleeves swayed.

'Is there any painting in your house that isn't of galloping horses?' I asked.

'You're judging me.'

'As I should. These paintings are terrible.'

'Not all of us have highbrow taste and know about art, Madam Omelogor,' she said, and she mispronounced my name in that Northern accent I loved.

'Honestly, Hauwa. You can buy some decent paintings.'

'I would rather buy a new handbag or jewellery. How can I be wasting money on paintings?'

'Bags are such poor investments,' I said.

'If it gives you pleasure, then it's a good investment. Me, I buy diamonds. Everyone likes gold, but I don't like gold.'

We were in her living room, or one of the many living rooms. She crossed her legs, and her boubou rode up to show a thin shimmering anklet encircling her leg. A photo of her and her husband was hanging on the wall. He was older than I imagined, late fifties maybe, portly, good-looking in an accomplished sort of way.

'So, Omelogor, there's something I want to tell you. There's a party on Friday, my friend's party. I don't know if you would like to go,' she said.

'You could ask with a bit more animation,' I said.

'Well, it's not . . . it's a bit alternative. Okay, look, she's going to have strippers, and some guys doing tantric massage. I'm not sure if you'll be interested, I mean . . .'

'Are you serious?'

'How can I be joking?'

'Of course I'm interested.'

She was laughing now as if relieved. 'I was worried about how you would react.'

'Why?'

'You know you're not normal.'

I was by then used to the unexpected curves of life in Abuja, but still it surprised me that Hauwa was inviting me to a party with strippers in a rented flat.

'What's your friend celebrating?' I asked.

'Life,' she said. 'It's all women, and all of us are married. You're the only single one.'

———

AT THE PARTY I had a rare attack of trembling shyness. Short-stay apartments depress me, with their aura of impermanence, as if many people have trooped in and out, all feeling unfulfilled. I rang the doorbell and somebody shouted, 'It's open!' The music was turned down low and smooth and the speakers must have been in the walls of each room. A chef in white was in the kitchen making small chops. I could smell the frying puff-puff, while a man in a blue uniform was setting up shisha in the living room. I peered in. Two women were on the couch looking at something on a phone and laughing. I wandered inside, looking for Hauwa. In the first bedroom, a naked woman was on the wide bed and a man without an ounce of fat on him was massaging her back. The room was dark, and for a moment I thought it was Hauwa, until I saw, in the light from the bathroom, the woman's weave falling over her shoulders. Not Hauwa. The woman's moans sounded theatrical and I stood at the door watching, feeling faintly theatrical myself and thinking that the man's muscles looked theatrical too, glistening in the low light like an oiled bodybuilder.

'Do you want happy ending?' he asked her, and she moaned again before she said, 'No, I have some stripper girls coming. Let me save myself.' Then she laughed. The man turned to me and asked, 'Do you want me to massage you?'

I didn't like his forwardness and I didn't realize he had known I was standing there, and there was no greater turn-off than his bush accent. 'No,' I said coldly. A feeling came over me, of self-disgust, to be in this tawdry place watching this scene and to be spoken to by this man whose voice was edged with mocking disrespect. But Hauwa appeared and the feeling disappeared. It was the first time I had seen her without her scarf, her hair in cornrows snaking down to her neck, and she looked younger and smaller and jauntier, like a very pretty popular prefect in secondary school.

'I went downstairs to look for you!' she said. 'Come. I made sure they have good whisky.'

When the two strippers arrived, slender and shapely and not more than twenty-five, I watched them dance naked, touching and licking and shimmying. One of them playfully pretended to push her nipple into my mouth, and I smiled and moved my mouth away, and asked, 'How long have you been doing this work?'

'Omelogor! Let the girl do her thing! Everything is not an intellectual study!' Hauwa said, laughing.

'This one is so beautiful,' one of the women said, placing her hand on the stripper's unusually narrow waist.

'She's not bad, but I have a girl who comes to my house to service me whenever my husband travels. You should see that one,' another woman said.

One stripper was trailing her tongue down Jamila's body.

Hauwa turned to me. 'You want her to do it to you?'

'No,' I said. 'Not my thing.'

Hauwa stood up and pulled her long boubou over her head and flung it on the couch. A short black spaghetti-strapped slip was underneath, and for a moment I thought she was going to take that off too, and beckon to the stripper. But she kept it on and got up and said she was going to call her dealer, because she didn't like the Loud here. 'It's too mild, it's not catching me!'

Jamila took Hauwa's spliff and inhaled. 'How can you say it's not catching you? Nothing is catching you today.'

I went with Hauwa to the balcony. In the slip, her bare shoulders looked exquisitely smooth. Soon Chi-Chi and Jamila joined us.

'Do you have food?' Hauwa asked the dealer on the phone. 'One quarter ounce. Hurry up, please.'

'Ask him to roll it!' Chi-Chi said, and Hauwa shook her head, ending the call.

'You know I won't smoke anything that I don't roll myself. I have my Raw here,' Hauwa said.

'Hauwa is an expert crush-and-roll babe,' Jamila said.

The dealer delivered quickly. The greenish-greyish clusters Hauwa unwrapped reminded me of the herbs my mother dried and put in her breakfast eggs. I told Hauwa that I had never smoked in my life, because I had never been interested in smoking.

'Omelogor, people will see you looking so fine and they won't know that you're such a square.'

She was laughing at me, and I liked that she was laughing at me. I understood then that this evening was an act of trust, and she wanted me to see the fullness of her, this secret part of her life.

'Let's make the square a little rounded. Roll one for me,' I said, and she did.

I inhaled and coughed, and the itching started after I inhaled again. But I didn't mind. I was learning to inhale with Hauwa sitting beside me, our faces so close they almost touched. Hauwa inhaling with her brows furrowed as if in thought. Hauwa exhaling and throwing her head back in a kind of ecstasy. Hauwa who could hold flames like flowers and flowers as if they were flames. Hauwa.

Somebody wearing only a bra leaned over us and asked me, 'Can I have a drag?'

'No,' I said.

That tinkling laugh came from Hauwa. 'Omelogor, everybody shares.'

'Not me. I don't want anybody's germs,' I said firmly.

The woman in the bra left and Hauwa asked me, 'What about my germs?'

And then came the attack of shyness. Suddenly I could not look at Hauwa's face, so I got up and went into the kitchen, saying I wanted small chops that I didn't want at all. I came back to see that someone was passing around tiny white tablets on a plate. When it came to me, I simply passed it on. How do people actually swallow something whose provenance is unknown? Inhale, yes, but swallow? Swallowing felt more intimate and the consequences more dire. The woman in the bra, it was a sparkly bra with rhinestones and crystals, was playing with a balloon, blowing it up and then letting it deflate.

Hauwa said, 'I don't like the balloons, the high is too short. They fill it with gas and you inhale from the balloon.'

'Oh,' I said, because I didn't even know what the balloon was.

Hauwa's eyes were glazed now and she was talking and talking, saying cocaine was overrated, a Lebanese man in Kano supplied her but it made her nose bleed and the high wasn't even smooth. 'It's Loud for me any day!' Hauwa said in the tone of an announcement.

Chi-Chi came to us and began to dance a slow drawn-out dance. She was chubby and glitzy, everything about her in high decibels.

'Omelogor, you don't want to bless us by letting us see your body,' Chi-Chi said. I was the only one who had not taken any clothes off, in my flowy palazzo pants and a low-cut satin top.

'You haven't earned the blessing,' I said.

Chi-Chi laughed the kind of laugh she would not laugh if she were not high. 'Okay, but watch out for the rich old women in this town!'

'Why are you telling me?' I asked, amused.

'They like fine babes like you, with front and back, and they're always looking for babes that are new to Abuja.'

'Omelogor is not new to Abuja,' Hauwa said sharply. 'She just went to America to do her postgraduate and then came back. She can handle all those old aunties.'

After Chi-Chi left, Hauwa said to me, 'Why were you laughing with her?'

If Hauwa were a man, I would have known how to handle her possessiveness, swatted it away or coddled it, but I shrugged, silent, and still in thrall to the final tremors of that trembling shyness.

Five

    I wake up in a fog of melancholy that I cannot dispel, and I blame the weather, because I need something to blame. After all, harmattan can feed a nihilistic strain, when you watch the world afloat with dust, lit up in dust, blurred by dust, and start to wonder – what is the point of water, what is the point of life? On an impulse, I open my laptop and search for motherless babies homes in Awka, wondering which one Aunty Jane contacted. Maybe I *should* adopt a child. A ridiculous idea. Still, I am curious about how it is done. Do you walk into a room and pick out the baby you want? How do you know which baby you want, and how can your heart not break leaving behind a room full of motherless babies with hopeful eyes? I scan the news headlines about confirmed cases of coronavirus in France and Germany and Italy. It sounds like a ghoulish stalker, this virus, appearing unannounced and unwanted everywhere you turn. I text

Chia to say maybe she shouldn't go to Bilbao just yet; let's wait and see how this virus goes. Chia replies to say she's already postponed Spain, and have I seen that the media has discovered Kadiatou's man Amadou? She's lying sleepless in bed at home in Maryland, worried about Kadiatou's case, and she wants us to have a group call with Zikora, to put our heads together. Put our heads together indeed. Why Zikora and I need to put our heads together I do not know. In Chia's mind we are a united trio, as though her separate intimacy with each has somehow tightly knitted all, a delusion I do not understand. How blind she is to Zikora's venom, my darling Chia.

Read the article, she texts.

The article about Amadou is already growing tentacles online, being republished on different sites, sometimes with slight changes and sometimes not. One headline reads, 'The convicted drug-dealer boyfriend of the hotel maid'. They make him sound like a big mafia-style crook, rather than a man who sells fake bags that everyone knows are fake, and who from time to time once also sold small quantities of weed. I remember Kadiatou once shyly showing Chia a fake designer bag from him, a tote in faux leather with cheap metal hardware.

Chia texts the time for our group video call and even though I don't feel up to it, I cannot say no in the face of her worry. On the call, Zikora is wearing make-up, her complexion evened out, her lashes long and sooty. It is early Saturday morning her time, and if I wasn't on the call, I know she would be in pyjamas, face unwashed and night scarf wrapped around her head.

Chia looks puffy-eyed, clearly in need of sleep. 'How can they publish all these lies about Kadi? People are reading and believing! I just saw one that claims she is a drug dealer because of the money in her account! I don't know how to help her. Zikor, can we get somebody, like a media adviser?'

'There's only so much a media adviser can do,' Zikora says.

'What is her lawyer Junius saying?' I ask.

'You know, he's actually a civil rights lawyer,' Zikora says.

'What, you don't think he's right for her?' I ask.

'It concerns me, but let's see,' Zikora says.

That American word 'concerns', another slimy slippery word, easy to shift and shape into meanings to free yourself, like 'exploring' difficult topics in graduate school. *It concerns me.* I don't know if she is saying the lawyer is incompetent or not, and I don't know why this concern is only now being known.

'Should she leave him?' I ask.

'The lawyer came to Kadi through Amadou's uncle, who she respects,' Chia says. 'She won't leave him.'

'Let me talk to him first,' Zikora says. 'Meanwhile the useless Amadou is in prison and Kadi is sending him care packages. Men. Honestly. You know he has a child that he didn't tell her about for years? I can bet he will want to profit from this situation.'

'I don't think so. He has his faults, but he cares about Kadi,' Chia says.

Zikora snorts. 'Yes, he cares so much about her that he secretly used her bank account to move drug money. She has to stop discussing the case with him.'

Chia makes as if to speak but doesn't. My melancholy heaves. I wish I had not agreed to this doleful downer of a call. After the father of her son abandoned her, a part of Zikora decayed into a bitterness which she imagines is wisdom. Imagine asking Kadiatou to stop discussing the destruction of her life with Amadou. What if Amadou is Kadiatou's only real solace? What if he is the one person to understand her silences?

'A man with Amadou's history will see this only as an opportunity to make money. And he'll lie about it. They're all the same. They will lie about everything. Sometimes it doesn't even make sense, the kinds of things they lie about. Chia, just like your Englishman forgetting to tell you he was married.'

'What's the point of bringing that up, Zikora?' I ask. Chia's Englishman, for goodness' sake. From ten years ago.

'My point, which seems self-evident enough, is that every woman has a story like this, where a man has lied to her or betrayed her and left her with consequences. Look at Kadi now facing reputation damage simply because she trusted Amadou.'

'True,' Chia says, and I think she merely wants to appease Zikora; this call cannot possibly be going as she planned.

'Every woman,' Zikora repeats.

'Except Omelogor, of course,' Chia quips. She probably shouldn't have, but she says it playfully to thin the heaviness of the call.

Zikora's pause is expectant, even encouraging; she wants me to say that Chia is wrong. A story of how I discovered on Facebook that a boyfriend was engaged, or of how a boyfriend took my money for a fake business deal, or suddenly stopped calling me after proposing marriage, and she will lower her venom's volume.

'I guess I've been lucky to be with mostly good men,' I say.

'Who all hate porn, I'm sure,' Zikora says, her expression dark, as if confronting a traitor. She relates with women only through the pain caused them by men. That I do not trade in stories of my love-inflicted wounds is my unforgivable failing. After we end the call, Chia calls me back, laughing, and I am happy to hear her laugh. 'Mostly good men? Please, which of them were you with for long enough to know if he was mostly good?'

CHIA COINED THE LETTERS SPA for 'short passion attack'. I'll tell her I met someone and she'll croon, 'New SPA alert!' Jide says 'thirst-quench', for both person and process, often shortened to 'quench'. 'Are you seeing your quench today?' he'll ask, or he'll say, 'This poor quench is falling in love and he doesn't know the quench is already coming to an end.' I call it emotion. 'Emotion happened' is how I put it. I met someone and emotion happened. Sometimes I think emotion will happen with a self-aware or cerebral or very dark man, my usual draws, but it doesn't. Other times, with the most unlikely man there's that crackle in the air and our shared and seeking eyes and a shiver down my neck. I enter an exalted state of being, with everything exaggerated; his glance becomes a beam and my thoughts come in torrents. Emotion happens, a rush and crush of emotion. Always it brings happiness in reckless gusts. It doesn't grow; it strikes fully formed, electric and intense, my mind suffused by him, and I want it all right away, today, now. It lasts a few months, at most. Usually, I start it and always I end it. I have never had regrets, except for with the Big Man with the big head, just before I left for America, my strangest and shortest case so far. The first perfume he sent me was supposed to be a neutral gift, a thank-you for how well we advised Adic-Petroleum on raising money to buy their facility. Then followed calls and texts and more perfumes that I gave away to friends. He was not my Big Man type; my Big Man type was self-effacing, but he was puffed up like boiling beans. When we first started the project, he questioned my competence, asking, 'She is the team leader?' with an arrogant raised brow. I thought him boring and bush, an accidentally wealthy, ill-educated man; he said, 'The individual communicated that he purchased the vehicle for the tertiary institution', because he believed it was too simple and therefore unimpressive to say, 'The man said he bought the car for the university.' I did not reply to his texts or return his calls until he appeared at my office door one morning, asking, 'What do you want me to do so that you pick my call?' He was smiling, and as he smiled, emotion happened and the air crackled, or so I thought. I invited him to my house and he looked delighted but said he had to be security-conscious and preferred to host people in his guest house. 'Well, I'm not people,' I said, and he chuckled. He came to my house wearing a baseball hat perched atop his head, as though too small and unable to curve around his skull. A certain kind of older Nigerian man thinks that to look youthful is to wear sneakers and a baseball hat. He removed the enormous ring on his middle finger and he removed his watch, placing both on my nightstand with ceremonial care. I knew there was some girth, his suits always seemed strained, but I was taken aback by the force of the full belly unleashed. 'Am I hurting you?' he asked, over and over, while I thought: Hurting me with what? I barely felt a thing, never mind navigating that belly. I saw behind him a trail of faking women; it was the only reason he could ask, 'Am I hurting you?'

He walked to the bathroom and back, walked to the window to draw the curtains, with no inhibitions at all, this bulky naked man who so loved his own inadequate bits. I felt he should have had the grace to be even if only fleetingly abashed.

'I will do for you what no other man has done for you,' he said, and his lascivious smile repulsed me. As did his post-sex sprawl, legs spread out on my bed as if it were his. Why had I invited this man? Waves of disgust made my skin feel clammy. He tried to hold me again and I slid away to check the time on my phone.

'Please, you have to leave. I want to pray,' I said.

'Eh?' he asked.

'I pray at a particular time every night,' I said, and his surprise changed to approval, or admiration, or both. He gathered his clothes, saying, 'Okay. Text me when you wake up.'

I had never used that one before – *I pray at a particular time at night* – but I guessed it would work, as invoking religion invariably does. Just the mention of prayer shuts down all thought. And there is the superstitious flavour, too, because not only would my praying at a particular time at night lend me a moral star in his eyes, but he would not dare question it lest something bad happen to him. I changed my sheets and scrubbed myself as if to slough off my self-disgust. From men I steadily hear, 'You're so different. I've never met a woman like you.' Most are compliments and some are not. With Big Head, it wasn't, because he could not comprehend my cutting him off. *What kind of woman are you?* was one of the many unanswered texts that flooded my phone before I blocked his number. He lodged a complaint with CEO, claiming I had made a major error with the funding documents; his pettiness shouldn't have shocked me but it did.

CEO laughed it off. 'Some men can be very childish. I know he's chasing you and didn't get what he wants.'

But didn't he? When I came back from America, I lost two consulting projects with two petroleum-servicing companies in quick succession. Later it turned out that Big Head told the companies that I was incompetent and that CEO had recommended me only as reward for warming his bed. Two whole years had passed and I was shocked by how long his wounded ego had bled and how far the blood had spooled. I saw him recently at the wedding of a senator's daughter, in Lagos, a senator I helped buy a house in Dubai with laundered money. I had that intuition of being looked at and I turned to see him staring, his eyes beady with anticipation, keen to know what my reaction would be. If I had imagined seeing him, I might have imagined I would feel enraged. But he was simply one of the many Big Men who for some reason refused to have their tailors cut their caftans more generously, and so paraded themselves with their large bellies straining against cotton, groaning to be freed.

If I felt anything it was towards myself and not him: bewilderment, in a frame of self-loathing. How could I have opened my door to this man who I did not want at all and could not possibly have wanted? I told Chia about him, how he had an object of insufficient size, further encumbered by a significant belly, and yet had the nerve, as he was huffing and puffing, to keep asking 'Am I hurting you?'

Chia laughed as she always did about my stories of men, but I knew she sensed my self-disgust, how different this was beyond the details. If I needed further proof that this was no emotion happening, it was the painful hailstorm of cascading regret that hit me each time I remembered him. None of the others led to regret and all had better endings. The ending with Arinze, who I briefly wondered if I loved because he lasted the longest at eleven months, was not as painless as the others but still brought no regrets. I can tell the ending is near when I start talking to my curtains, saying words meant for the man while looking at the bronze-toned curtains drawn across my windows.

There was a man with long elegant fingers. A charming secretive man, his mind full of dark alleyways. I suspected he did credit-card fraud but he claimed he imported cars. We laughed so much together. We talked all night and into the morning about things we soon forgot, sometimes until I had to get up and get dressed for work feeling groggy and giddy.

'I haven't suddenly lost the ability to drive in daytime,' he told me, towards the end.

'What?'

'Just in case you think the sun is too bright for me to drive. Because you've stopped inviting me during the day, only at night now, and very late.'

We ended with laughter, and even now are good friends. There was a man who said 'I love you' over and over in bed, like an incantatory chant for raising the dead, which distracted and disrupted my desire.

'Stop saying that, please,' I told him.

He looked warily at me. He went to a Pentecostal church and I could only imagine his thoughts. What else but a demon would cause a woman to say I don't want to hear you say I love you? He had proposed not long after we met, saying the Spirit revealed to him that I was his wife. I planted little heart stickers all over his things, his shoes, his laptop bag, and each time he discovered one he laughed and asked whose child's pencil case I was raiding.

There was a lovely man who stared at me at a conference in Lagos until I went over and asked for his number. He liked grilled croaker, and so I would order grilled croaker and have it delivered to him at random hours. At the end he asked me, 'Have I done anything wrong? Tell me what and I will correct it.' His saying 'correct' and being so welcoming of blame filled me with wistful sorrow.

'No, no, it's me. I'm sorry. I just switch off. I can't do the kind of commitment you want,' I said.

THERE WAS A MAN I wish I could have loved, a man I wanted to love. Chijioke. It always felt comfortable being with him. I heard Chijioke's voice before I saw his face. 'Private equity is a terrible cancer, it always wins in the end,' he was saying on a call, walking ahead of me in the hallway of the bank. He was my type, erudite and self-possessed, and not crushingly handsome; nothing bores me more than the self-regard of men who have their whole lives been praised for their looks. But when finally we met I didn't feel that rising force, that burst of raw excitement. CEO recruited him from England, and he spoke like a person who had lived there since he was six. In meetings his rounded British voice was jolting, something off that did not belong. While the directors talked casually of a loan that had to disappear, he stood nodding like an eager new apprentice. Amanze said the directors called him London Goat. In CEO's office I heard him complaining about someone on his team. 'She just lied, but the evidence is there. She just lied to my face.' He sounded stunned. CEO was mild and vague, murmuring that the person would be queried, while more interested in manoeuvring a compliance issue.

There was no rush of emotion, and yet I felt a need to protect him, or preserve him.

As we left CEO's office, I asked him to lunch. I felt hard and sophisticated and knowing. I wanted to teach him to survive here.

'Look, you have to understand that lying and deceiving are not moral issues in everyday life here, they are just tools, survival tools. Compunction is not even an option, because you would need to think of these issues first as moral. And many of our people just don't. When Nigerians talk of moral issues they really mean sex, and some of the more high-minded mean corruption. But there's a kind of amorality in everyday hypocrisies and pretences, because they are just survival tools. So don't be so shocked about her lying, you should expect it and deal with it but don't show them how shocked you are.'

He looked weary, eyes trained on his small bottled water.

'I know life is difficult for people,' he said finally. 'This is a poor country, after all.'

'There are poorer countries that do not have this kind of madness.'

He looked at me as if to say, 'What exactly is your point, then?' His lunch was untouched on his plate, stewed chicken garnished with two slices of green pepper.

'It's not that Nigeria is poor, it's that it's virulently materialistic,' I said. 'Money is at the heart of everything, absolutely everything. We don't admire principle or purpose. Even people who can afford to take ideas and ideals seriously don't. We don't live with grandeur.'

His eyes widened slightly and even I wondered where that had come from. I intended to toughen him up about life here, the son newly returned to a country both alien and his, and here I was rambling about grandeur.

But he was smiling a tender smile and later he said he fell in love at grandeur.

'Do you?' he asked.

'Do I what?'

'Admire principle and purpose.'

I wanted to say yes, but it felt like absolving myself too easily, so I made a facial shrug. Not long after, he left the bank to start a boutique investment firm and kept asking me to come join him. 'I'm too tainted, Chijioke,' I always replied. 'You deserve better.'

WHEN JIDE IS HAPPY-DRUNK at my dinner parties he boasts about how quickly men fall in love with me, while I glancingly dip in and out. They laugh and call me iron lady lover and teasingly wonder about the man who will finally make me fall. Jamila, with her sly slanting manner, listened to Jide's story the first time she heard it, then turned to me to ask, 'Do you think you would try harder with men if you didn't have money?'

'Omelogor has always been like this,' Jide said, but Jamila was unconvinced.

'Wallahi. It's because Omelogor has money,' she said.

I didn't have money when I was sixteen and told the popular boy, Obinna, who I liked, that I didn't want to be his girlfriend because I wanted to be free. But Jamila is really saying that money is an armour and she is right. Money is an armour but it is a porous armour. No, money is an armour *and* it is a porous amour. It shields you, feeds you the potent drug of independence, grants you time and choices. Because of money I can go where I want and when I want, and this is still heady, and still intoxicates. When I first began to make more than I imagined I would, I would cajole myself to spend, whispering to myself, 'I can actually afford this now, I can afford this now.' Then the implosion of money, almost overnight, when PGT went public and the shares made millionaires of us – us being a tight, tiny circle, the men in the secret cave and me. I stared at the figures in my personal account, telling myself it really was mine and not a client's, thrilled and dizzy, thinking of what I could now do for the people I loved, how I could reach out and touch dreams that just yesterday were too impossible to be dreamed. Yet money deceives in how much it cannot prevent, and in what it cannot protect you from.

SIX

I wake up unrested, shaken by a dream. I should not have read the book about German terrorist cells before I fell asleep. It must be why I dreamed of Uncle Hezekiah. In the dream a man in a dirty white jellabiya was tightening a blindfold around Uncle Hezekiah's eyes, and at first I was running away from them and then I was running towards them, Uncle Hezekiah on his knees while the man in the jellabiya taunted me, saying he would spare Uncle Hezekiah if I ran fast enough, and I kept running and then I stumbled and woke up to the man's gleeful laughter and the glint of a raised knife. I feel jittery. I rarely have vivid dreams and each time I do, I wonder why, because it cannot be random that some dreams are in colour and others are not. If it is a disturbing dream, then it hovers darkly, each event of the day freighted with foreboding, because I think of dreams as glimpses of the afterlife, that we die when we become the self that dreams. I usually brush my teeth before I read the news each morning but I read the news first, impatiently, as if to find a clue to my dream, or a reason for this sense of impending doom. More people have succumbed to the coronavirus in China. It is now officially 'a public health emergency of international concern'. The Chinese doctor who warned about how bad it can get has died from the virus. His photo on the screen, his open trusting face, makes me feel for the first time a frightening portent about this virus. What if it does come to Nigeria? Jide's voice rings in my head, saying, 'We are finished, we are finished.' If only there were possible precautions to take, if only it wasn't as limp as wash your hands, wash your hands and don't touch your face.

My mother calls to say that Aunty Jane asked her to convince me to start the adoption process now, just in case the Chinese virus comes to Nigeria.

'Did Aunty Jane say an angel appeared to her?' I ask. 'What is this obsession with my adopting a child?'

My mother sighs and says, 'Your father's people and their strangeness.'

'Yes,' I say, knowing that if her own sibling did the same thing, she would not call it strange.

'Jane means well,' my mother adds, almost reluctantly. 'She feels for you.'

Sometimes I sense that I disappoint my mother by not being ravaged by my own childlessness. 'Don't worry, not everyone is meant to have children,' she will tell me sometimes, seeking sorrow from me. I have never mourned not having children, but Aunty Jane's words brought the cold drip of melancholy at facing the reality that I now almost certainly cannot, at forty-six. It's possibility I want, doors kept open. Shut a door that I never even wanted to walk through and I grieve something lost.

'How is Daddy?' I ask.

'Today is the anniversary, your Uncle Hezekiah. You know how it is.'

'Today is the anniversary?' I almost shout. A shiver spreads goosebumps on my skin. What does it mean, that I dreamed about my uncle on the anniversary of his death that I do not even remember?

'Yes. Why?'

'No, nothing. I just didn't remember.'

To tell my mother is to open the door to a catalogue of worrying and more and more talking. As she gets older her superstitions have multiplied, and she attributes supernatural causes to coincidences and illnesses. On New Year's Day, a poor confused bird slammed itself against the glass of her bedroom window and my mother launched into prayers about unknown spiritual forces and weapons fashioned against us.

I text Chia to tell her I dreamed about Uncle Hezekiah on the anniversary of his death that I did not even remember, and end my message with a confused emoji. *It's kind of beautiful that you dreamed of him today, you remembered in your unconscious,* she replies. She says she wishes she had remembered and that she has just texted Aunty Nneka, Uncle Hezekiah's wife. I text Aunty Nneka, too, to say, *May Uncle's gentle soul continue to rest in peace.*

When I first got the bank job somebody told me, 'Speaking Hausa in Abuja opens doors.' I called Aunty Nneka right away, and over a few weeks she taught me enough Hausa to have basic conversations. It was an elegant language, mellifluous and easy to learn, but I learned so quickly I thought maybe my tongue still wore faded memories of the simple Hausa Uncle Hezekiah had taught me as a child. He would visit from Kano and bring us stalks of sugarcane in a sisal bag, and when he first taught me to say one to ten in Hausa, he made it a song. One-*daya*, two-*bui*, three-*ukwu*, four-*hudu* . . . and on saying the last words, ten-*gwoma*, he would clap for me as if I had made a great accomplishment. He was gentle, like my father, and they would sit for hours in the half-lit living room talking in quiet tones. For years I thought his was an Igbo name, Izikaya, until I saw my father write it on a Christmas card, and it amused me, and the next time I saw him I called him Uncle HEZEKIAH with teenage pomposity and he smiled and said don't pronounce it like that in the village because nobody will know who you are talking about. I was in university when he was murdered. Something in my father went to sleep. Often, apropos of nothing, my father took to saying, musingly, 'We once were four.' Each time he said it, I would count, actually count: my father and Chia's mother and Uncle Hezekiah and Aunty Jane. They once were four.

On my last birthday, I sent photos of my small party to my parents and my mother asked who everyone was, and what they did and where they were from, and when she asked about Hauwa – 'This beautiful Northerner, in the scarf, where is she from?' – I didn't want to say Kano because Kano meant Uncle Hezekiah, and Kano meant the man whose head was impaled and carried on a pole that had once held a signboard, and so I said, 'She's from Kaduna.' It was close enough to Kano without having the wound of Kano.

MY VIVID DREAM leaves an aftertaste of fear, a diffuse circling fear. Throughout the day I feel afraid and I cannot say what I am frightened of. Maybe it is an inherited African strain, to view unusual occurrences not with curiosity but with fear. At Uncle Hezekiah's funeral, my great-aunt Nne Matefi gave me a small plastic bag of bitter kola. 'We must be careful,' she said solemnly, and told me the

Okonkwo children came back for their grandmother's funeral and by the time they left the village a few days later, they were very sick, their bodies covered in pus-leaking boils. They had been careless; they had not taken precautions, like always having a piece of bitter kola lodged in their mouth. Villagers were so full of envy, they lay in wait for the successful to return for funerals and then they made ogwu to kill you or make you sick or make your business fail. I didn't reply in my usual mocking way, to say, 'Why can't people make ogwu to bring constant electricity, or fix the bad roads?'

Instead, for the three days of Uncle Hezekiah's funeral, I went everywhere with a slight swell to my cheek from the piece of bitter kola left unswallowed in my mouth. And from time to time, I would slip my hand in the pocket of my dress and rub between my fingers the bald smoothness of the nuts and find it oddly calming. Chia had just had an appendectomy in America and could not come for the funeral and she laughed, asking if the bitter kola didn't make my mouth feel disgusting. A bit dry but not disgusting at all. I had never tasted bitter kola before. I thought it would be unrewardingly bitter, like a kola nut, but it had the aura of a medicinal herb. Now I eat a bitter kola at the first sign of a cold and the bracing bitterness cleanses me, and always shortens the cold. I don't believe those small nuts kept me safe from evil spiritual forces at Uncle Hezekiah's funeral, but after the funeral I began to think that I can respect what I do not believe. Belief in ogwu made no sense, this large unwieldy concoction with no logic at its core. But so much else lacks logic. What is the logic of sacrificing to an omniscient God, the point of Jesus dying first before God could save us? Maybe logic is not the point of faith; maybe succour is.

It amuses Chia when I say these things. The Christmas before she graduated from college, Chia came back with her Black American friend LaShawn. We spent a day wandering around the village, LaShawn wanting to photograph everything. A woman in a shop selling hair attachments asked her in Igbo why she was taking pictures of dirty shops and suddenly LaShawn was crying. 'She thinks I belong here, she thinks I'm Igbo,' LaShawn said. I felt myself tumbling into history, watching LaShawn. She might indeed be from here; her ancestor could have been taken from here two hundred years ago. It moved me and made me like her, and when we returned to Chia's house, I gave her a book about the history of our village, shoddily printed, opened to the page about my grandfather's brother who was stolen away as a boy. That evening, the big news on television was of the man arrested in Lagos with a bag of fresh human parts, two breasts, a head, a kidney and two hands.

He was shown sitting on the floor of a police station cell in a dirty singlet and underwear, gaunt as if his crimes had sucked away at his body and left him looking starved.

'I wouldn't trust *him* for a new kidney,' LaShawn said.

Chia burst out laughing and told LaShawn that the body parts weren't for organ transfers, that people used them for rituals to get rich. Chia was laughing as if to say 'the whole thing is so dumb' and LaShawn began laughing too and I felt uncomfortable, and then annoyed with Chia. Later I said to her, 'Don't laugh at us; you'll make LaShawn not proud of her African heritage', and she looked incredulously at me. 'How are rituals with body parts *us*?' She had that resigned Omelogor-is-being-Omelogor expression, as if she could not help her cousin who sometimes said crazy things.

'I don't mean ritual murder, I mean jazz in general; it's about a belief system and a worldview. There's good jazz and bad jazz, and this man is obviously doing the bad, but when you laugh like that you make it all look bad,' I said, and Chia laughingly replied, 'Our Husband Has Gone Mad Again.'

I learned in university to call it jazz instead of ogwu, a younger generation's hipper name, and pan-Nigerian since it was English, and so we could speak of Yoruba jazz and Hausa jazz and Igbo jazz. In final year a girl I hardly talked to whose room was on my hostel floor said another girl in my department had said the only reason boys kept chasing me was because I used jazz. I imagined myself bending low to enter the spooky home of a dibia, with its tortoises and dead chicks and whatever else, and then emerging with potions in small dirty bottles, or maybe a string around my waist which, as I walked past men, would make them follow me. To make the gossip-bringer feel satisfied of my hurt and expectant of my confrontation with the other girl, I raised my voice and said, 'What rubbish! How can she say that about me!' The gossip-bringer left looking pleased; there are people who find satisfaction in setting up the stage for other people's battles. I never confronted the girl in my department, of course, but each time I saw, I looked at her with fascination, thinking: She believes this, she really believes this.

THE DREAM OF UNCLE HEZEKIAH, the coronavirus spreading, the news coverage of Kadiatou. It's all too much and I absently study the rice and stew on my plate, my appetite gone. Philippe says nothing as he clears away the food and shuts the kitchen door more gently than he normally would. I walk slowly and I feel an internal liquid softening, as if with a little exertion my insides might begin to melt. Suddenly all I want is to sit with Atasi. When she was a small child she would sit in my lap while I read to her, or while I ate, slipping her a piece of fish or meat from time to time. Only a year or two ago, I could still coax her out of her isolation to watch game shows on TV, or sometimes to go for a walk. Now it seems we talk only when she is asking me for things. I find her in her room, lying in her bed, fashion magazines scattered around. She looks at me with puzzled eyes, as if there must be a reason why I've come into her room but she can't remember it now.

'What are you doing?' I ask.

She shrugs, then extends her phone to show me a photo of a girl wearing a bikini.

'This is ab goals,' she says.

'Poor soul didn't eat for the twenty hours before this photo was taken and she is sucking in her belly,' I say.

Atasi looks at the ceiling to show she expected me to disappoint her as usual, and I wish I had said something different.

'Did you hear about the women who died in Lagos after Brazilian butt surgery?' I ask, gesturing to my own phone as if it is now my turn to offer it to her. The women were twenty-two and twenty-three.

They couldn't afford the American-trained doctor everyone went to, and when his nurse offered them the surgery for less, they accepted. On social media there are photos of the nurse in what she called her operating room, and photos of the girls with the letters *RIP* splashed across their bodies, pretty girls with arched eyebrows and glittery highlighter on their cheeks.

'It's so bad what that nurse did,' Atasi says.

'Yes, terrible,' I say. I hope she will say something else but she doesn't.

I ask if she's decided what to wear to the party tomorrow, her friend's sixteenth.

'Not yet,' she says, and looks at me expectantly, waiting for me to leave.

'It's in Maitama?'

'Yes.'

'Paul will take you.'

'Can Chiso and Cynthia come and get ready here in our house?'

'Yes,' I say, and I like the sound of her saying 'our house'.

MY MOTHER WAS UNHAPPY when I bought this house. She walked reluctantly from room to room, as if afraid that showing excitement would give the house an approval it did not deserve.

'Is this marble floor a little slippery?' she asked, standing in the middle of my vast living room.

'No,' I said.

'You're too young to have this kind of house. Men get intimidated. Why not a flat, a very big flat, bigger than your last one?' she asked.

'There were no big flats on the market,' I said brightly.

At the door of the bedroom next to mine, she stopped, not entering. 'Ahn-ahn, there are things here.'

'This is Atasi's room,' I said.

My mother sighed. 'Why does she have a room? A man that wants to marry you might not like this arrangement.'

'What if I find a man who likes it?'

She was in Abuja because I was taking her the following week to America for a check-up. She did not feel unwell but said she wanted a check-up in America. Among her friends, the latest boast was your child organizing a check-up abroad. India was popular, the care was as good and cheaper than England, but America carried the heaviest boasting weight. On the phone I heard her say to a friend, 'Omelogor is taking me to America for a check-up. You know these children, I told her everything is fine and that I don't need it, but she is insisting.'

I held back from laughing. My mother's expertise at fake modesty often astonished me. I was looking forward to the trip just to see Chia. My darling Chia. My mother once said, 'You really have time for Chia', as if she wished I didn't.

'She's my cousin.'

'You have other cousins.'

My mother throughout childhood kept pushing me to be close to her brother's child, Chinyere, but we never had much to say to each other; Chinyere had a faded personality, as if she might have been vibrant in a different life. Then Chinyere died in childbirth and for weeks I shied away from thinking of her, because it left me overwhelmed with an irrational guilt, the sense that if I had been nicer to her and replied to her tedious text messages, then she might not have died.

Yes, I have time for Chia. Chia is easy to love, but had she not been, I would have loved her still. Sometimes two humans have spirits fully at rest with each other and lucky for us we are also related. My mother likes to say, 'Chia is just roaming around not doing anything serious. If you leave it to her, by the next generation all their money will have been frittered away.'

Bless my darling mother, but she drinks a glass of entitlement every morning, in a strong Igbo flavour, the kind that leaves distant relatives calmly convinced that all you have toiled for is also somehow theirs.

'There is only so much Italian gold one person can wear,' my mother would often say about Aunty Adaeze, in my teenage years when her resentment was at its peak.

'Mummy, Aunty Adaeze owes us nothing.' Then I would list what

Aunty Adaeze had done: she bought my father a car, she sent money when academics were striking and the government stopped paying salaries.

'They could do more and not even notice. They could have sent you abroad to university; they know how bright you are.' My mother would then mumble about my father being so vague and uninterested in these things, otherwise he could have pressured his sister to do more. I didn't want Aunty Adaeze to do more for us because I did not want to drown in the lake of thank-you. I wanted to be able to do more for us – myself and my parents and my little brother Ifeatu – and therefore leave my skin unmarked by the stigmata of eternal gratitude. At fourteen, I already planned to study finance in Enugu campus, because I had read a story of a young man who as a banker became exceedingly rich. After our junior secondary exam results came out, my favourite teacher, Mrs Orjiani, began lovingly crafting my future. 'Omelogor is our best student, of course she will study medicine,' she said in the staffroom and I smiled agreeably, knowing she was wrong.

WITH MONEY FROM my PGT shares, I could fund my father's research and send my brother to the UK and appease my mother's ancient entitlements. Ifeatu went to do a master's in engineering, and in all these years he has not been back home; he lives in Wales, a recluse who never calls. 'I don't know, maybe Ifeatu should have stayed in Nigeria,' my mother has taken to saying, in a voice strained with the faintest reproach. Yet it was she who pushed and pushed for me to pay for the master's and for his rent until he found a job. She pushed for the new house in the village, the house outside campus in Nsukka, the car, the gold jewellery she apologetically said was 'so expensive' while still asking for it. I felt she no longer deserved the luxury of resenting Aunty Adaeze and Chia, but it had been a part of her for so long that she could not stop her sniping, her calculating and measuring.

She was visiting me when a Malaysia Airlines plane went missing, and on television people were asking how a whole plane could just disappear.

'Better check that your cousin is not on the plane that disappeared since she is always flying up and down,' my mother said. It was the first time her cracks at Chia deeply upset me. It felt mean-spirited, an unacceptable joke.

'So if Chia is really travelling, this is how you'll say it?' I asked.

'Of course I know she is not in Malaysia.'

'How do you know?'

She looked at me then, her face still with hesitant doubt. 'She's not, is she?' she asked in a small voice.

I knew Chia was in Germany with her new man, the Swede with long hippie hair, but still I stupidly called her just to be sure. 'Yes, I'm in Berlin,' Chia said, sounding downcast, her voice mumbling over the phone.

'Kedu? Are you okay?' I asked, more concerned than usual because my mother's comments had left me on edge.

'Yes. We just got back from a dinner at this German woman's house. I'll tell you later,' she said.

'But no problems?' I asked.

'No,' she said.

The Swedish man sounded like the kind of unserious White person who was happy without a real job. Chia already had the unserious gene and she needed somebody with his feet firmly on the ground, and if it must be a White man, then somebody like Luuk. When I first met Luuk, in New York, we went out to dinner and he looked at the menu and made a sound to show the absurd. 'What is this, squid ink? It sounds bad, no? If they must serve a dish with squid ink, then give it a different name; who wants to eat ink? And the ink of a squid?'

I liked him right away. (When we went swimming, I watched him float, long and lean, and his paleness made me think guiltily of uncooked chicken. I watched Chia swim over to him and tenderly touch the side of his face, and thought to myself: Amazing how we like what we like.)

Luuk at least had a sense of humour, unlike Darnell, that love of Chia's life, who didn't feel any emotion but could talk about the semiotics of emotion. I remember how Chia kept scratching at hard unyielding dirt, looking for reasons everywhere but at him. She says the Englishman was her great love, but it is Darnell who left her serrated with scars. My darling Chia, so sophisticated and travelled and yet so innocent and new.

There's a helplessly feminine quality about her, with that beautiful face and small slim body: her breakability, her dreaminess.

SEVEN

I feel weak and congested, as if on the cusp of a cold, about to be served another helping of harmattan's malaise. A news article appears on my phone screen, about how the coronavirus could become a pandemic, a plague like the Black Death. I cannot bear this speculative gloom. To distract myself, I search for motherless babies homes, first only in Anambra and then I widen my search to all of Nigeria, and look at the sparse details online. Some now call themselves orphanage homes or children's homes. On their Facebook pages, there are pictures of famous people posing beside bags of rice and cartons of Indomie noodles, children playing outside, children at a birthday party crowded around a tired-looking cake. In that picture there is a little boy at the edge wearing a torn T-shirt that is down to his knees, too big for his slight frame. I feel sorrow swell up in me, thinking of children growing up in a place called a home that is not at all a home. A Facebook commenter asks why it costs two hundred thousand naira more to adopt a baby boy and the reply posted below reads, *Due to scarcity and demand.* What am I doing, looking at this? What is this sense of internal splintering I feel? I should read messages on For Men Only instead, and write a few posts that I will spread out this week. In the years of writing these posts, I have learned that there are so many spaces in the world where love should be but isn't. And that it is too easy, on the Internet, to pretend to expertise. The lack of love makes us believe in expertise when we have no reason to, because the lack of love burrows painful holes in us which we fill with whatever we think will soothe. I have so many subscribers who need to believe that I know what I'm talking about because there's so much pain floating around in the world. Some days I think I have helped people and other days I think I have not. Today, I have not.

Dear men,

I understand that you don't like abortion, but the best way to reduce abortion is to watch where your male bodily fluids go. Keep your fluids to yourself and do not leave them in undeserving places.

Remember, I'm on your side, dear men.

Dear men,

I'm sure you were raised to be emotionally strong, tough, and when you're overwhelmed you feel that you can't show it because your role is to be stoic. And so you carry all this alone and quietly. Some men can do stoic and some men can't. My suggestion is if you can't do stoic then don't. Lots of women out there want stoic and lots of them want men who can show when they feel overwhelmed. Never mind all the fearmongering telling you there's only one way to be a man. There are many ways and there's enough to go round.

Remember, I'm on your side, dear men.

Dear men,

I have potential sympathy for your situation, and understand what you mean when you say that women never apologize or take responsibility these days. Silly creatures. However, some men (not all men! not all men! not all men!) become irrationally furious when women speak and when women rise and when women shine. Please ensure that this is not the case here, before we continue.

Remember, I'm on your side, dear men.

Dear men,

You splash around pictures of watches and jewellery and cars on Instagram and you say women are gold-diggers because all they want is money? May I gently suggest an experiment? Post pictures of you building a bridge with your bare hands or volunteering at a soup kitchen. And let me know what happens. You attract what you advertise.

Remember, I'm on your side, dear men.

Dear men,

Your gamer girlfriend isn't exaggerating. Women who love playing video games online don't like to play with their own voices, because once they do, men start threatening them with rape. Good guys like you need to call this out. If you are one of those that hear a woman's voice and starts threatening rape, you're just advertising what a loser you are, and the thing about being a loser is you shouldn't advertise it. Keep your loser genes under wraps.

Remember, I'm on your side, dear men.

Dear men,

Look, I get it. All the stuff they told you was what a boy should do when you were a kid and suddenly they're saying that's not what a guy should do. But nobody is clear about what the deal is now, even they don't seem to know. They say you're sexist when you mean well. You're strong but now they're saying strong is bad. So you get angry, and because you're angry, you drink and you beat people smaller than you. But here's the thing – abusing women and abusing alcohol actually just means you're weak, not that you're strong and angry. Men, you ARE strong. Anyone who says men are not strong is lying. So step up and show it. Being strong means having self-control. Talk to other men. Make them sit up.

Remember, I'm on your side, dear men.

Jide calls to say he's only been at work for an hour and can't wait for the work day to end. I imagine him at his desk, computer blinking in front of him, his tie askew, his trousers not quite straightened. His colleague just got an American visa and is scrambling to leave Nigeria immediately because he's afraid. America is now banning travellers from China, and next thing you know they'll be banning travellers from everywhere else. I can tell this colleague's leaving has left Jide depressed.

'I shouldn't be here in this town, there's nothing for me here,' he says.

'What if you try America? Try for a visa,' I say.

'America that you hated.'

'Yes, but I'm in the minority. You might not hate it.'

'It's the UK I sometimes see myself in. The American scene is too racist. Nnaemeka said he doesn't use a profile picture and doesn't select an ethnicity on dating apps, just his interests, and he gets all these people contacting him and they get into really animated chats and they ask him for his picture and as soon as he sends it, they block him. He said it has happened to him six times, six times, and he's not even fat like me. He's always in the gym.'

I feel the irritation of having a conversation I have had many times, each time as static and unmoving as the last. Jide thinks of his hopes as thwarted even before he hopes.

'You never know,' I say, and I try not to sound as if I am thinking that he doesn't try and doesn't follow through, even though I am thinking exactly that. It hurt the last time when he said, 'We are not all fearless like the great Omelogor', although I didn't tell him I was hurt. He did try once to leave, when he sent his CV to the graphic design agency in Lagos that was his dream job. He got a nice no. On a whim I asked him to shorten his first name and use his middle name as his last, and so he went from 'Jideofor Thomas Okeke' to 'Jide Thomas' – from an obvious Igbo name to a Yoruba-sounding name. He applied again and was shocked to be offered the job.

'How can I work there knowing they don't want Igbo people?'

'Jide, this is your dream job.' I wanted him to go because if he moved to Lagos he would oil his wings and free himself, and he could find another job, or find that not everyone at the agency was like the person who did their hiring.

'I can't,' he said, and so he didn't.

The incident with the gateman at his new flat filled me with fury, and I hoped it would finally push him to act, but it didn't. His old flat in Gwarinpa had no running water and the gate was too narrow for a water tanker to come through, so he always paid those Hausa water boys to bring him water in plastic containers, many trips made until his drums were filled. Then he found the new flat, just perfect for him, airy and clean, with a borehole in the compound and enough space inside to park cars. The gateman seemed harmless enough, until one day he knocked on Jide's door and said, 'I saw that man last weekend. He is not your brother and he slept in your bed.'

Jide said it took a moment before the words formed in his mind as the threat they were intended to be. He went inside and came out with some money, and after he wordlessly gave it to the gateman, the gateman said, 'Oga, this is small', and so Jide asked for his account number and the gateman waited with his arms folded for the transfer to be done, as though for payment due to him for his honest labour.

I knew, listening to Jide, that my photograph with the president would finally come to good use. CEO took me to a luncheon with the president and a member of the European Parliament; it was easier to see the president when he travelled abroad. An elegant old dining room in a hotel in Brussels with tables covered in white cloth. The president fumbled about, looking in his pockets for something he did not seem to find. He considered the salad of mesclun and cheese and first picked up a spoon and then a fork. At some point he put his cutlery down and, with his thin fingers, massaged his slightly swollen wrists. 'They said it's arthritis,' he said to the MEP seated next to him, extending his arm as if the European might give him some superior insight into the condition of his wrists. Throughout the meal, he leaned often towards the MEP in a manner that embarrassed me, an ancient, unconscious deference. His demeanour made me think of the men of his generation as eager boys in colonial schools with exacting English headmasters who they revered.

'Nigeria is extremely corrupt,' the president said, and the MEP nodded quickly, trying to hide how startled he was. The president sipped some water and left a smear of chewed food on the rim of his glass. How was it that I came from a country ruled by this thoroughly unremarkable man? To be up close with him was to feel contempt growing like a bulb and bursting free.

Later, as we took pictures, CEO eager and excited, I smelled the president's cologne, a scent from another time, a long-ago world.

'Tell the PR people to make sure the pictures circulate,' CEO said.

'Yes, sir,' I said.

I was vaguely embarrassed by the photograph with the president. But with Jide's gateman, it was the perfect weapon. I drove to Jide's and stopped at the gate and gestured to the gateman to come. He stood at my window and said Mr Jideofor was not in and I said I know he's not in, you are the one I'm looking for. I showed him the photo in my phone, of me standing next to the president, and his mouth went slack with awe. 'I have the president's number in this phone,' I said, tapping the phone screen for dramatic appeal. 'I have his number right here. Jideofor is my brother. If he has a problem with anybody, I also have a problem with that person. If you ever try that nonsense with him again, you and your whole family will go missing. Do you understand me?'

I hoped the gateman could not see my uncertainty in this act, this flourishing flamboyant melodrama that is Nigerian life. He was waving both hands in the air, and saying sorry, sorry, then in keeping true to the script he sank to his knees still saying sorry, sorry, it will never happen again.

'I PREDICT COUNTRIES will start closing their borders,' Jide says.

'We don't want your prediction,' I say.

I look out of the window at my tranquil dust-lit front yard. Paul walks across carrying a bucket of water from the tap in the back and disappears under the carport to wash the cars. He is taking Atasi this afternoon to her parents' place; Atasi often jokes that I share custody with her parents. Her mother wants her to spend more of her time with me, but I wonder if Atasi might be more resilient if she had been with her parents more. A horn sounds at the gate and Mohammed opens to let in a black SUV with dark tinted windows. Atasi's friend Chiso leaps out, wearing an aggressive pair of shorts, a slice of her lower bottom exposed like a dare. She will spend some time here until Atasi is about to go to her parents' place and Chiso will leave. Atasi's other life, with her parents, is like a private but not secret club, closed off to her boarding-school friends. I go to the parlour downstairs and find them sitting side by side on a sofa, their faces bent to their phones, AirPods stuck in their ears. Chiso pulls off one AirPod and nudges Atasi. 'She called him her boyfriend and he didn't say anything, so I guess they're in a relationship now.'

There's a lurch in my chest, but I pretend I haven't heard. Is this how relationships begin now for them, with girls scheming and then assuming? It is supposed to be better for their generation; the daughters should be better off than the mothers.

'Good morning, Aunty Omelogor,' Chiso says when she sees me.

Atasi looks up at me and I smile and she looks back unsmiling at her screen. I feel an inevitable distance between us that I do not want to dwell on, because to do so would be to consider that it might never be bridged. Maybe I shouldn't have sent her to boarding school. But it was what her parents wanted, and I imagine them saying with pride to their relatives, 'She is in private boarding school.' Lately Atasi has been skipping more meals, asking Philippe to make her bone broth, her arms thin as a bird's legs. I keep watching for sadness in her and I keep finding it, a submerged sadness, its full contours unknown even to her. She is obsessed with modelling, that sea of glimmering sadness, a profession in which joylessness is prized. How edited the pleasures seem, with nothing sensual or real. Every time she shows me yet another photo of models on a runway, I think of how little they must eat. Those bony square-shouldered sylphs, clavicles jutting out like knuckles, and always morose, blandly morose, the same kind of morose for all of them, because even personality has become unfashionable.

'Get the fat from her belly and that's an automatic tummy tuck,' Atasi says, and Chiso replies, 'And thighs too, they need to put more fat in because you know some of the fat cells die after a while.'

They are talking about the Brazilian butt surgery deaths in Lagos. They do not question the longing for big buttocks that makes you agree to go under anaesthesia in a darkish room with peeling paint. They know irony and hyperbole and sass, but self-love is strange to them. I think of myself at sixteen. It was a slower-paced time and our troubles were different, of course, but we weren't so willing to believe the worst of ourselves. If our daughters do not know how beautiful they are, just as they are, then surely we have failed.

I CALL CHIA just to call Chia, and she says, 'Today is not a good day for you, I can tell.'

I say I'm worried about Atasi and I feel I have failed at giving her something she needs. It is easy to be sad; sadness is a low-hanging fruit. Hope and happiness you have to reach higher for and I didn't teach her how.

'She doesn't eat, she's just bone wrapped in skin,' I say.

'Do you think she's angry?' Chia asks, and it sounds to me like a uniquely American question. Even her tone is American and she says 'angry' like an American, the first syllable twisted and bent.

'Angry?' I repeat, even though I understand.

'About you. Being her benefactor, her family's benefactor.'

In the midst of my worry a sapling of annoyance has sprung, as it often does when something happens to push America back in my face. This is the reason girls like her are sad. America tells them this kind of nonsense. Be angry with the person helping you and your family, be angry with the person who pays your school fees and your parents' rent.

'Chia, I don't have energy for this Americanism now.'

'Okay, it's an Americanism, but do you think she's angry?'

I feel deflated and exhausted. 'She probably is,' I say.

————

ATASI WAS NOT an easy child to love. I knew from that first day when fate pushed her to the point in the road that I was driving towards. I wasn't driving fast so much as I was driving distracted. It was in the beginning, when we were so new to Abuja, and Abuja so foreign to us. Jide was sunk in the front seat reading up on pap smears online. We were on a road whose name I did not yet know, a wide scarred stretch of road, with people darting between cars and a medley of every imaginable shop, vegetables and secondhand clothes, car tyres and bread. I was going to the clinic to repeat my smear test. The doctor had called and said my result was irregular, and it could mean nothing but she wanted to be sure. I was in my first Abuja home, a tiny self-contained flat in Wuse, and I held the phone pressed close and silent as she spoke, thinking: She didn't finish the sentence, which was that my result could be nothing or it could be cancer. At my first check-up, she had seen my surname and asked if my father was the great professor and afterwards took her time attending to me, pressing down on my belly more firmly than I liked. She told me to be careful in Abuja, that everyone was on tramadol or Benylin with codeine. 'Everybody in this city is on something. The poorest of the poor are sniffing pit latrines to get high,' she said, and I wondered why she thought I needed that warning, or if it was something she told anyone new to the city.

It could be nothing or it could be cancer and so I was distracted as I drove. My very first car, the hatchback with bad shock pads, bought so shortly after I started working that of course there was whispering about a man buying it for me. Usually I drove with care, wary of those unwise Abuja intersections where nobody gave way, everyone tearing in at the same time. Usually I was alert to people standing by the sides of the road, especially on roads like this where the press of people was so close to the cars. Jide said something before I hit the little girl. I didn't hear what he said but I heard the panic in his tone, and it was his tone that unconsciously moved my foot to the brake. The little girl, a swish of movement, a red scarf on her head. Jide shouted, 'Jesus! Jesus!' I stopped and was already flying out of the car and Jide was trying to pull me back, to keep me in the car. The little girl lay on her side. She was still and unmoving like a doll made of wood. There were voices, people, horns, and dust.

LIFE CAN CHANGE because of what could have happened. The little girl did not die. She stared at me with an expressionless round face and I feared something had happened in her brain. Then she stared down at the blood from her thigh that had stained her dress a darkish shade of red. Her mother was sitting under a small umbrella selling sun-faded packets of biscuits and sweets and didn't realize her daughter was hurt until somebody shouted for her. As I drove frantically to the hospital, her mother sat in the back crying, saying, 'I tell her don't play near the road, don't play near the road.' She made to hold the child but the child pushed her away. The child sat by herself, unheld and uncomforted. She was so young. I thought: Why was she allowed anywhere near the road?

Her name was Atasi. She spoke Hausa but they were Gbagyi, the indigenous people of Abuja, the owners of the land which the government took and went off to build a capital. Her father was a cleaner in a ministry and her mother called him on her mobile phone, speaking urgently in their language, and repeating the hospital's name. I had never been in a hospital children's ward and the dank sadness of this one startled me. Children on narrow beds crying or blank from medication, children in pain, and tired mothers stretched out on mats next to their beds. A greasy enamel plate was next to one of the women lying on a mat. The nurses lounged about as if nothing was urgent. Atasi was put on a bed without a bedsheet. I scanned the nurses and decided on one with thinly pencilled eyebrows, and I called her aside. I slipped her some money and asked where the closest ATM was, and in this way I bought Atasi an advocate. The teenage boy next to Atasi had a broken leg, which was not yet in a cast. The nurse told me, 'Do you know this boy's mother brings food here and then she sits on his bed and eats all the food herself.'

'Why?'

'To teach him a lesson. He broke his leg when he went to steal cement at a building site.'

'So what does he eat?'

'Our hospital food,' she said. 'Even us, we don't eat it.'

I saw the boy's mother later in the day, and when she said her son's name, Olisa, I spoke Igbo to her. 'Oh, my sister, good evening,' she said. She sat down and began to eat a piece of agidi which she had unrolled from its wrapping of leaves. She said only, 'Olisa, did the doctor come?' to her son and then nothing else. She looked at me and at Atasi and at Atasi's mother, who was sitting at the top end of the bed near Atasi's head.

'People like you don't come to this kind of hospital,' she said to me in Igbo.

'We had an accident. This was the nearest one.'

'I saw your husband talking to the nurse,' she said.

'He's my friend,' I said.

She gave me a sidelong glance. 'Your mates are marrying and you are still doing "friend".'

She amused me. I asked if she thought her son wasn't hungry, and she said he didn't need food; what he needed was a big slap to reset him. She had spent so much on transport to come here, she said, after a day of running up and down, trying to get the papers she needed so that the task-force people wouldn't demolish her shop again.

'What of Papa Olisa?' I asked.

'Oh, that jobless one ran back to the village a long time ago because he could not cope. I am the person raising the children.'

She suddenly looked at me, eyes narrowed with a measure of calculation. Where did I work? Could I help with the problem of her renewing the papers for her provisions shop? Just then, Jide came to say we could leave now that Atasi was stable, and had I called the woman at my clinic? I hadn't. I told Jide I wanted to stay. I looked at Atasi, thinking: What if this child had died?

Atasi stared and said nothing, a brooding lonesome child. When I tried to hug her, she shrank back, her face still expressionless. Later, Jide said he tried to keep me in the car because he heard that crowds in the rough parts of Abuja would gather and beat the driver after an accident, so the best thing was to drive to the nearest police station. I don't know where he heard this tale, but we were so new to Abuja and Abuja so foreign to us.

WITH ATASI GONE the house is shrilly quiet. I know newspapers lie but I am astounded to read about Kadiatou's life in details invented from pure air. She was part of a hotel workers prostitution ring, a brothel madam, trafficked as a child, also traffics children, she planned to steal his phone, she stole his phone, she was paid by the French government, she sent him a message asking for ten million dollars, and above all else it was a set-up. She's working with his political enemies and was paid to set him up. Chia texts to ask for another unnecessary group call to put our heads together.

'Her lawyer wants her to do a television interview, to tell her own side of the story. He thinks it's the only way to counter the press stories,' Chia says.

'Before the trial? Isn't that unusual?' I ask.

'She has nothing to lose,' Zikora says. 'I talked to Junius and his view is that an interview will let people see her as a human being and maybe force the media to cover the case more fairly. Right now almost all the coverage makes it look like it's The People vs. Kadiatou, instead of The People vs. this Very Important Frenchman.'

'Apparently, so are the prosecutors,' Chia says. 'You know Kadi is not talking much. But she said something yesterday about the prosecutors. She said, "They are questioning me as if I am the one that did something bad."'

'Zikora, will it be in English?' I ask.

'What?'

'Will the interview be in English?'

'I would imagine so,' Zikora says, with the pained patience of having to deal with a stupid question.

'Can't she have a Pular interpreter?' I ask.

'Kadi speaks English,' Zikora says.

'It will be easy to disbelieve her if she's not speaking the language she knows best,' I say.

'Kadi speaks English,' Zikora repeats. I don't know if it's merely to disagree with me or if she has that American trait of lying about people who are not privileged in life. Kadiatou's English is not very good and pretending that it is won't be of use to her. In the recovery weeks I spent with Chia, after America had battered me, Kadiatou's Africanness felt like a balm, the way she hunched over her plate when she ate, the way she said, 'Miss Omelogor, I'm going', and still stood there, in that radiant pause of mutuality that said I have given you the courtesy and you have acknowledged it.

'When will the interview be?' I ask.

'They're still talking to the networks,' Zikora says.

EIGHT

The coronavirus is here. An Italian man who works in Lagos went home to Milan for Christmas and has come back and tested positive and is now in quarantine in Yaba. I stare at the news for a while.

Jide calls in a panic. 'I told you, Omelogor, I told you!'

'It's just one person.'

'We can never control this thing. We're finished.'

'Jide, calm down. Remember, Ebola came to Nigeria. Did we all die?'

'We don't even have tests for this coronavirus.'

'Lagos State said they do.'

'We are finished. I heard that there are no ventilators at National Hospital and only one oxygen tank.'

'It can't be that bad.'

'All the politicians in this country had better go and bring back the stolen money in Swiss banks, because we'll need it to fight this thing.'

I laugh. 'Jide, from where to where?'

'I'm serious. The other day they said there is no money in the Central Bank. We're going to need money.'

'Most of the stolen money is not in Swiss banks, not any more.

The money is right here in Nigeria. There is more money in dollar domiciliary accounts here than there is in the Central Bank.'

I WOULD KNOW. I gave CEO the idea. We liked the Zurich banks because they asked few questions, and transactions were always discreet and quick, as though they feared you might change your mind. Until the American government began probing and poking around, in search of tax evaders and whatever else, and the Swiss banks turned skittish and careful, and CEO said we could no longer move dollars to Switzerland, we had to look elsewhere. 'But why do we have to, sir?' I asked, and to the question in his eyes I replied, 'Why don't we strengthen our own domiciliary accounts so they can keep the money here?'

He nodded, his whole head slowly bobbing up and down, and I knew he would call a meeting and tell everyone the idea was his. I didn't need recognition. I wanted only to be his star right hand, whispering in his ear, and wielding the soft and secure power of it. I wanted this from my first day at work, when I had barely settled in my cubicle before they said CEO was asking for me. His office was all marble and glass, awash with light from the wide windows, their stately blinds fully drawn. He sat wearing a suit, a small man almost swallowed by the gilt-edged girth of his desk.

'Good morning, sir,' I said.

He looked surprised. His eyes travelled down from my face and then up again.

'You got the best score in our entrance test?' he asked, as if expecting me to say no.

'Yes, sir,' I said.

Mr David rose from where he was seated in the corner reading documents, and came appraising towards me.

'Ah, this is the person? God blessed you with brains and also blessed you front and back like this?'

'More back than front, sir,' I said.

For a moment they were taken aback and then, disarmed, they began to laugh.

'I like this girl!' Mr David said.

But only a year later and he did not like me at all, because I had too much power too soon. Each time we met in CEO's office, he sized me up with distrustful probing eyes, as if to gauge the details of my latest dark intentions. If I were him, the director closest to CEO, I would resent my young and nimble hunger, my eagerness, the bright scarlet letter of my stark ambition. I had studied the company and learned its innards, and I saw the empty apathy at its core. How perfunctory most staff were. They chose the smallest effort and the easiest way out; they overlooked details and paid scant attention, as if everyone had agreed to a second-rate will, a mass failure of seeing. Almost all the books I checked in internal audit had wrong analysis of loans going bad. It emboldened me. I brought new ideas to CEO, and I always said, 'We have to do this before they do, sir', *they* being the other bank owner in Lagos, who in public was CEO's friend. In private, CEO said his name as if spitting out something foul on his tongue. Their hatred was mutual and blistering, from a series of business betrayals when they were first starting out. I kept telling CEO about his legacy – your legacy must be bigger than theirs, sir, consider your legacy, sir – until he absorbed the word and began to say my legacy this, my legacy that. The male ego is a phenomenon easy to predict. He walked in a short trot suited to his short height, head held high and eyes afloat, as if too busy for minor people and minor issues, and as he passed by the halls, staff melted into corners. In the head office in Lagos, nobody came out into the halls at all until he had walked into his office.

I first impressed CEO when I told him I had a spy high up in his enemy-friend's bank, which was a lie, but I did not become his right hand until we were investigated for the US Treasury bonds case. Those long tense weeks, everyone hushed and rushed, CEO screaming like a toddler and throwing things at us – his desk diary, his mobile phone, even his suave expensive pen. A grown man behaving this way, the sort of thing you saw in films. The directors cowered in the face of his frustrated rage, all jittery, all stammering, and Mr David went on sick leave, claiming he had a mini-stroke, and then came back to work at the end looking healthier than before. The transactions happened before I was employed, but CEO hurled insults at me, saying my position in internal audit was a waste of space, calling me a stupid idiot, a prostitute, a fool. I always cast my eyes down until the tantrum passed and then continued reading documents to show that all was well. I stayed in the office late, I repeated platitudes, I exuded self-possession and showed more hope than I felt. *They do not have the capacity to check every bank transaction, sir. They cannot prove collusion, sir, because there was no collusion. Sir, we need to make it clear that we import everything and so we must have foreign exchange.* I didn't stutter or say 'yes sir, yes sir, yes sir' before he was done talking like other staff did. I disagreed with his suggestions. I revived documents he preferred to forget. I memorized tiny details and recited them to him, and when something was overlooked, I pointed it out. But in my boldness, I never failed to perform respect. A delicate balance with powerful men like him, whose shockingly thin skins I came to know well. One of the directors screamed at me when I said there was a mistake in his team's analysis. 'Are you insulting me? Am I your mate?' He sounded like a shrill market woman ever ready to pull off her wrapper and jump into a fight. It took so little for these men, these men who held so much power in the palm of their hands, to dissolve like a cube of sugar in tea, unable to take any criticism at all. CEO was better than most, to be fair, and even found it in himself to apologize to me after the bank was cleared in the US Treasury case.

'Omelogor, I'm sorry about the way I spoke, I was under stress,' he said.

'It would happen to anybody, sir,' I said.

He was watching me. His glasses overwhelmed his face, which was much thinner from the many weeks of strain.

'I've noticed something about you. You don't cry,' he said.

'I did not come to work to cry, sir.'

He chuckled and shook his head, and I thought to myself: I'm reaching my goal of becoming indispensable to him. I laughed at his bawdy jokes and I shrugged aside the lewdness of his friends. The more they talked of my braininess, the less they mentioned my body or asked for my number or joked about taking me home. In front of my bathroom mirror, I practised and practised until I perfected my neutral face, features free of all expression, blank but open, my strategy face. I wore it each day like a pair of work shoes. At the mention of a shady deal, I talked of how best to document and what strategy to take. CEO would call me and I would sail past his executive assistant and into his office.

There, I saw the putrid centre of Nigerian finance and its oozing pus. I already knew of the small deceits of the banking world, the tiny side profits made in foreign exchange deals, the unqualified client cleared for a small loan in exchange for a cut of the loan, but with CEO, I saw massive non-performing loans piled high and magic money that disappeared with a signature scrawled in ink. I was astonished to discover that the wealthiest men borrowed with the clear and calm intention of never paying back, and when they defaulted, the bank swallowed the loan; by writing it in the profit and loss statement, the loan just disappeared. It was a kind of theft – or theft really, not a kind. These same men paraded wealth that they knew to be mere hull and all hollowness beneath. If I stole so much, I would not flaunt cars and private planes, but brazen theft has never been the act of subtle people. Foreigners go on and on about the challenges of emerging markets, not knowing that the biggest is the hubris of irresponsible men.

Once, one of the wealthy men fell out with CEO. He gave an interview in a newspaper saying CEO's bank was local and he preferred to bank abroad, even though his loan was one of the largest, and so CEO sent the bad-loans division to his office. The wealthy man screamed at them and threatened CEO and said he would invade the bank with the military and throw CEO out.

'He's threatening me because he doesn't want to pay what he owes? Madness. How can he now claim I am targeting him because he is a Yoruba man? If I was Yoruba like him, he would not dare disrespect me.'

Each time CEO joked about being from a tiny ethnic group in northern Cross River that nobody had ever heard about, I saw the bulging shape of the chip on his shoulder, under his crisply cut suits.

'Sir, you have to push back, for your self-respect and legacy. It's good to make some of these people a little uncertain, without scaring them off,' I said.

And CEO nodded in that slow dramatic way. He called in the loan and the wealthy man's hotels in Abuja were sealed off, and his buildings in Lagos were about to be sealed off when the wealthy man caved and called CEO to say, 'My brother, let us discuss, we are not quarrelling', and CEO, chortling with self-satisfaction, let the loan go.

So much of the banking world was about whose ego would bend, whose will would break, who would kneel down before whom. It was at about the time CEO made me treasury officer. 'I know you will take carefully the subject of who should get our surplus money in loans,' he solemnly told me, as if we were in a beginning class on banking, but soon I discovered that CEO himself was borrowing from the bank and not paying back, and I knew right away this was a test. He wanted to know what I would do. I walked into his office with papers prepared and said, 'Sir, I know a better way to disguise all this.'

GRUMBLING ABOUT MY rapid promotions rose and spread from all parts and branches of the bank, nebulous as clouds, and they were right to complain, but nobody did so directly. CEO was lord of all.

'Your mentor', people began to call him, their sneers concealed under smiles, asking me for favours, to get through to him. *Your mentor*. And he was my mentor, in a way, if your mentor can be a person you do not respect. He made me assistant general manager too quickly and said he would have made me an executive director, only it needed to first go to the board. 'And we don't want too much attention, so we can continue the work we are doing,' he said. The work we were doing was helping his politician friends. 'His Excellency needs our help' was all CEO needed to tell me. Pearls of sweat clustered on the forehead of the man from the governor's office who heaved in large bags filled with freshly minted cash. Always in the late evening, when our building had emptied out. At a corner of CEO's sweeping office sat a swollen red leather chair. The bags of cash were deposited near it and counting machines brought in. Governors have medieval powers, and their daft and breathless acquisition was something to behold.

I moved millions into new accounts and changed them to dollars and sent them back to the governor in suitcases whose zippers I clasped with silver locks. I was proud of the suitcases; layers of cash in a suitcase was tidier and classier than stuffing money in those squashy chequered ghana-must-go bags. Usually the private secretary picked up the suitcases. Sometimes it was just his personal driver and an orderly wearing a long gun slung on one arm. It wasn't always cash; it wasn't even mostly cash. We issued advance payment guarantees for contracts inflated by three or four hundred per cent, and I moved the surplus from the contractor's account to accounts owned by the governor but which were not, of course, in his name. One was in his cook's name. Other signatories were friends, siblings with different surnames, companies registered in the Caribbean. For the beneficial owners of his foreign houses, he used the name of his friends, knowing how badly it could go if their loyalty were ever overcome by their greed. The fragile security of stolen wealth. He was always surrounded by many people but he trusted so few, because his power had robbed him of the ability to trust. CEO liked to tell the story of a politician who made his driver the sole signatory of an account, which the driver then emptied of millions of dollars, dollars not naira, before running off to Canada. The politician did nothing, because what can you do when a person has stolen what you stole? The moral of the story, CEO said, was 'Use trustworthy staff that you've known for years.'

CEO talked often of governors losing their immunity once their term is over, and his words brought to our actions a flavour of ritual caution.

'A sensitive transaction that can't be traced after handover,' CEO would tell me, and sometimes I would say 'sensitive' even before he did. We said 'sensitive' like a mantra, a special code that bound us in a giddy sense of secrecy. The stories leaked anyway, because there are too many people involved in the project of grand theft and they tell someone they trust, or love, or want to impress. The commissioner for works, the person who organizes the fake contract bid, the typist who types it up, the drivers, the orderlies, the guards at the door. I moved hundreds of millions through Thailand and the US, or some iteration of that, and it came back looking clean. Liechtenstein was easy, with its lax reporting. We deposited money there and to the question 'Source of earning?' we said, 'Consulting.' Consulting meant whatever you wanted it to mean; consulting wore the blessed aura of concealment. In just a few years, I had learned to paint fraud in pretty colours. I knew what to write in the books to hide bad transactions and how to make fictitious transactions look real, and I wrote elegant memos approving loans for companies that didn't exist, and for collateral I accepted fake land titles and worthless deeds and dismal documents signifying nothing. CEO was generous; I got bonuses and two company cars, and he always approved my training courses abroad. But I wanted and wanted. I eavesdropped on discussions and read every document, even of transactions in which I was not involved. I peeked into the caves where Nigerian fortunes are spun, caves filled with men, some of them bright and some of them not, but all talking and sharing and colluding. Then, in the week that I heard them buying and buzzing about PGT shares, I took money from dormant accounts of forgotten customers and bought shares for myself.

THAT THE GOVERNOR was coming himself and not just sending his people as usual had CEO in a tizzy. He kept pushing his glasses up his nose even though they were not sliding down. The advance team arrived first, three men in dark plastic sunglasses and ill-fitting cheap suits. They marched about CEO's office with comical importance to make sure it was secure, before the governor himself appeared. He looked better on television, an average, ordinary-looking man with an easily distracted air. It was said he was once imprisoned in London for fraud. In the bright light of CEO's office he had the pallor of a person with some kind of illness, something to do with the kidneys maybe. I looked more closely and thought it wasn't his kidneys: the unnatural paleness and the discoloured smudges were from bleaching creams. How strange vanities can be. He made me think of an intern I once had who was bleaching her skin with cheap creams that turned her face into a peeling lemon, because she had applied for an usher job at a corporate event years before and was told she was too dark. You would think this governor with his medieval powers would at least use better-quality creams, the kind Michael Jackson must have used.

The governor went around and sat on CEO's chair and swivelled from side to side. 'So this is the seat of true power, where you sit and control so much money! So much money!' he said.

'Your Excellency, this is not power compared to you,' CEO said, with the fawning tone he used for all politicians, until they left office, and then he stopped taking their calls.

The governor had brought his own brandy. His assistant unveiled the bottle from a long suede box, asked for a glass, and then went into CEO's bathroom to rinse it, as if we might have poisoned it. The governor drank the brandy in a gulp and began talking about the best part of Dubai to buy another house; he had one in Green Community but was buying another in Emirates Hills. Then he turned suddenly to the television at the other end of the office and pointed at a newscaster on the screen. 'I want that lady. Get me her number.'

CEO looked slightly confused but quickly recovered himself, mumbling, 'Yes, yes, yes.' We were helping the governor move millions of dollars and he barely looked at the papers I presented to him. He was so casual, so throwaway, slouched on the swivel chair with legs stretched out. If something went wrong, there was always more money to steal. I looked at the figures on my screen: so many zeroes, a parade of zeroes, lined up one after another, dizzying and daring. How many lives all that money could change. What dreams it could make. I thought of Mama Olisa, who was always sending me checking-in texts. *How are you, Sister Omelogor? Happy New Month, Sister Omelogor. I said let me greet you, Sister Omelogor.*

What she was really saying was remember me and help me when you can. Her patience was a strategy and I admired it. Imagine what Mama Olisa could do with a tiny fraction of this money. Imagine if she had a fraction of this. Well, what if she did have a fraction of it?

I had never thought of this before, but in that moment a clear map formed in my mind as though it was long fated to be. We often registered new companies to move money around, and so I called the lawyer to say could he check if the name Robyn Hood was already taken, Robyn with a Y. When he said it wasn't, I felt like laughing a mad and happy laugh. I didn't even feel afraid when I slipped out the first packets of cash from a bag hauled into CEO's office that evening. The loss could have occurred with the people in the governor's office, the driver who put it in the trunk, the man who carried it up to CEO's office. Not that the governor would check. What difference did a few hundred thousand naira make? The next time we had a bag of dollars, I slid two packets into my laptop case. A moment later I slid in two more. Packets of dollars were much slimmer and easier to handle than naira. Later I brought wide handbags to work, then I began to slip out the cash at the end, in the stillness of time after the counting was done but before the money was taken to the vaults. Jide said it was a crazy idea, going around giving money to women with small businesses.

'Free money just like that? They'll spend it. They'll never use it for business,' he said.

'You don't know women,' I said.

'There are two types of gay men, the ones who love women and the ones who hate women. Lucky for you, guess which one I am,' Jide said. It was one of his favourite things to say when he was happy-drunk.

'Loving women doesn't mean knowing women,' I said.

IN SECONDARY SCHOOL, I read in my father's newspapers about General Abacha's failed banks tribunal, the Big Men he threw into decaying prisons in Lagos for running failed banks. Failed banks, they were called, as if the banks just happened to stumble and fail, as if the banks wrote the wrong answers in an exam and failed. I never forgot a story about a woman and her eyes. She was a teacher, going blind, saving a little each month for eye surgery. When she finally had enough, she went to the bank to withdraw her money, only for a tense-faced teller to say, 'Sorry, madam, the money is gone.'

'Gone to where?' she asked. To where? In the newspaper photo, she looked dazed, her eyes milky behind thick glasses. She never recovered her money, none of the ordinary people ever recovered their money. What became of her, a woman who was going blind? What became of her when she went blind? I thought of her on my first Robyn Hood trip, when I went to my village to give out ten grants. I saw a woman who was losing her sight but still weaving cloth at an ancient loom, and I gave her twice the amount I gave to others, as if to mollify that teacher from years ago.

But before the women in my village, I gave Mama Olisa a grant. I went to her shop in the late evening, when buyers had petered out, and sellers were closing up and packing up to walk to the bus stop. Mama Olisa screamed and danced and hugged me and said her pastor had told her she would see a sign, that her helper would come that week. 'I knew from day one that God brought you to my life for a reason.'

She asked if I kept in touch with that small girl who had been in the accident years ago, and when I said Atasi lived part-time with me, she said, 'Just because of one small accident. You paid her hospital bills. Did you also have to take her to live with you? Who does that?'

'Mama Olisa, stop talking nonsense,' I said.

'I have seven children, if you are looking for another one to pay school fees for,' she said, and then began to laugh and to hug me again and to say she was praying for me and asking God to bring me a husband before the year ended.

THE FIRST WOMEN I gave grants to, I marginally knew. They were from my own village, Abba, and from nearby villages – Abagana, my great-aunt's ancestral home, Umunnachi, where my maternal grandmother was born, and Nimo, where my grandfather once lived. I stopped at their shops and greeted them, and they greeted me, pleased that I stopped by: Omelogor, professor's daughter, the one doing well in Abuja.

'I want to support your business. Use this for your business, keep it between us, and the only way you will thank me is to help another woman when you can.'

Shocked delight and prayers and dance and song, the cash unbelievably in their hands.

'Don't waste it,' I said, but I knew they wouldn't waste it because they were bursting with dreams. These village-raised women who barely finished primary school, querulous and wise and sharp-tongued; they guarded their money and spent with good sense, and never missed a thing. I sat with them and listened as they stared at the cash in their hands. *I want to go to Anam and buy plantains. I have been pricing another dryer for my salon. I will buy hand grinder so that I can now do my beans myself. I will buy electric sewing machine.*

I FLEW TO ASABA and took a taxi to a town I didn't know. There was a woman frying akara by the roadside, an ambitious operation with three large pans, a few helpers, a small crowd of buyers. I waited for her to be done selling before I extended my hand with the envelope of cash. It was late morning and a stray chicken was pecking in the mud. She wiped her brow with the edge of her wrapper and looked suspiciously at me. Was this some kind of fraud, was the cash fake, was it some way to entrap her in a ritual? Why just give her cash, and so much cash? She shook her head and waved her hands in the air. 'No, no, keep your money, please. I don't want it.'

Back in the taxi, the driver said, 'Aunty, you did not mention God.'

'What?'

'You said you want to help her business but you did not mention God. Business and God go together.'

I stared at the small keloid on the back of his neck. What was he even doing listening to my conversation?

'What's your name?' I asked.

'Eze.'

I hired Eze to scout the villages for women with small businesses. He was unsparing and spare, with a long neck and truthful bluntness that was perfect for the job. He gave me reports and suggestions, and I flew to Asaba, Owerri, or Enugu airports and drove with him to whatever village he had found to push cash into a woman's hand and show her my bank ID card and say, 'God blessed me and I want to bless my fellow women. Use this for your business. Don't ever come looking for me to thank me. *I mekatakwana bia I kene m.* Just pray for me. The only way you will thank me is by helping another woman when you can.'

NINE

I playfully back away from hugging my cousin Afam. 'Are you safe? You Lagos people have the virus.'

The Italian man with the virus may be in quarantine, but now there is talk that the people on his flight won't come to be tested, or the people in his company's health clinic in Lagos. Doctors don't have the protective equipment they need. Some doctors have tested positive but refuse to quarantine.

'I'm safe. I haven't been close to any Italians,' Afam says.

Our hug is warm and lasting. I tell him he is growing the symbol of successful Nigerian men: a paunch. When he smiles, I see Chia's father in the kind crinkle of his eyes and in his teeth, the front two slightly large. Whenever he is in Abuja on business, he comes by to see me, and we enjoy our time together. He has a warm, genial air, unlike his twin, Bunachi, that gaseous trial of a man. Chia always says Bunachi and I should never be left alone in a room because it will result in a corpse and another near-dead form. Afam has brought me whisky and he places the bottle on a side table and says, 'For one of the boys.' I went with him to a wedding in Lagos and this man he knew came lapping around me, asking for my number, asking what I would drink. I said a whisky neat and he replied with displeasure, 'That is not a feminine drink, it's a drink for one of the boys.' Afam laughed and laughed. 'Don't mind the bush man,' he told me, but since then he has taken to sending me texts saying, *Just checking in on one of the boys.*

'This coronavirus thing is scary,' I tell Afam.

'I don't think it will affect us much. You know Nigeria has a way of being outside of the centre of things, for good and bad,' Afam says, and something in his voice, reasonable and sane, makes me feel better.

'I know.'

'So how is the solo consulting going?'

'Not bad. You should see my client list.'

'Did the guy from Vestex Investments call you?'

'Yes. Thank you, Afam, darling cousin of life.'

'I haven't told you what percentage of your fees I want as project finder.'

We laugh. 'I haven't resumed this year. I decided to take some time and stay home doing nothing.'

'Don't get complacent,' Afam says.

'You know me. I won't.'

'It's not as glamorous, being on your own,' Afam says, and I think of how through the years I enjoyed seeing my photos in the newspapers, beside the great and the rich, at our bank events and at every major corporate do. I don't miss it. Those years were filling and I no longer wanted more servings.

'Do you ever regret leaving?' Afam asks, and I don't think about it before I say, firmly, 'No.'

I MUST HAVE THOUGHT of leaving, from time to time, over the years, musingly, fleetingly, but my decision was made when my mother told me Mr Nduka had died. It was a day before my birthday and my hairdresser had come to install a kinky-straight wig. I gestured for her to stop the fitting and tugging so that I could focus on the call. Mr Nduka had not been paid his pension in eleven months and the government kept delaying and dallying and organizing endless pension-verification exercises, claiming dead people were still collecting pensions. Mr Nduka was there early at seven to prove he wasn't dead, and he stayed waiting in the sun for hours and he wasn't feeling too well and he collapsed and died, and from the pension-verification centre he was taken in the boot of a car to the mortuary. Mr Nduka was my father's old friend, a civil servant of the old breed, and my image of him was in a crisp short-sleeved shirt and a tie, eternally proper and straight. I had just laundered money for the governor of his state. A minuscule fraction could have paid the pension of thousands of workers like him.

When I graduated first class he brought me a gift, a grey rooster with a floppy red comb that we kept for weeks before finally having it for Sunday lunch. The night he died, I dreamed of him, and even though in real life he was stocky, in the dream he was gangly and thin. Then he collapsed and turned instantly into dry bones. A heap of dried bones, whitish in tone.

The government did not pay pensions because they said family members were claiming pensions on behalf of dead people, but I had hoarded billions of state money in a short-term high-interest account and called it after some months and deposited the interest in the governor's private accounts and then put the money back in another high-interest account. Cycling public money to make private money. While Mr Nduka was slumping slowly to his death, his pension was earning interest for the governor of his state, all impeachably done by me. My self-contempt came in waves that made me nauseous. From circling the mediocre, I had embraced it, and now I had become it.

My mother must have felt my expression was a little too pained for a man I had not known that well. '*Nne*, anything wrong?'

'No, no, I just feel bad,' I said.

'It is sad, but it has nothing to do with you.'

She had no idea what I did, what I really did; my parents were naïve to so many deceptions of Nigerian life. They trustingly waited each month for the university to deposit their salaries in their bank accounts, and they had only one account and did not understand what investing was about. They believed I was doing honest, brilliant work. On my birthday, my father began his birthday message with 'Our pride and joy'. My domestic staff surprised me with a small cake and a handmade card in which each of them wrote messages in blue ink. I was surprised that Mohammed could write English; his message, the shortest, read, *Madam you are good.* It felt like a taunt, or a rebuke or a final chance at redemption. Why hadn't they written notes on my previous birthdays, when they would appear in the living room to say happy birthday with sheepish smiles and thank me for the cake Philippe had given them?

AN OUTSIDE AGENCY was now hiring all new bank staff and I discovered that the agency belonged to CEO. Giving himself loans that he never paid back was one thing, but owning an agency that cut small slices from the already small salaries of his new staff? His petty grasping disgusted me. He often complained of an ulcer, his face crumpling from pain in the middle of meetings, and he seemed more and more feeble, his vibrancy gone. One day he came to work with heavy-framed black glasses sitting stolidly on his face and he looked like an elderly man who had taken his son's cool glasses.

'You don't like them?' he asked.

'Your thin wire rims are more flattering, sir,' I said.

'Maybe when you take over we'll have a CEO who can wear original designer glasses that suit,' he said. He sometimes said things like that, hinting at succession, throwing out little crumbs as if to lure a bird into a trap. But I was already looking away, overcome by a desire to cleanse my moral palate and rinse out my life.

I kept waiting for the right time to tell CEO that I wanted to leave. One day, he asked me to handle a transaction with a private banking client, a new client he had poached from the enemy-friend's bank with an interest-rate offer that made no business sense. The client was always on those magazine lists of wealthiest Africans, but he wasn't half as wealthy as they claimed. He wore a showy watch with the showing-off air of an obnoxious arriviste.

'Omelogor? What kind of name is that?' he asked.

'My name, sir.'

'I've not heard that name before. From where? Rivers State?'

'Anambra.'

'Oh. Igbo girl.' His mouth curved slightly downwards at the edges.

'Do you know what you are doing? I don't want somebody to do a nonsense transaction.'

Maybe he disliked Igbo people, or he resented confident women, or both, or neither and was just one more human being naturally adorned with a nasty streak. But in that moment something was sealed.

I stood up. 'Excuse me, sir. Let me check and see if any of my colleagues is willing to talk to a rude client, because I'm not.'

I walked out, already imagining CEO's anger, how he would shout at me and then scramble to appease the man. And he did, but also his eyes narrowed looking at me, thinking how out of character my reaction was. I had overlooked worse, laughed away a man who told me he could not trust any Igbo banker, shrugged at another who asked for a man because women got nervous at big transactions.

'Did anything else happen?' CEO asked.

'No, sir.' I paused. 'I want to take a leave of absence and go to graduate school in America.'

'Ahn-ahn, because I shouted at you?'

'No, sir, you did not start shouting at me today.'

'So why?'

'I feel that I need a break, to recharge my brain.'

'Okay. We can pay for the executive course.'

He thought I meant one of those overpriced short courses business people take so they can append the names of exalted American universities to their measly CVs.

'I want to do a proper master's,' I said.

'Not that you need an MBA,' CEO said.

'Not an MBA. A master's in cultural studies. I'm interested in pornography.'

'Pornography,' he repeated, and laughed as if it was just one of the strange things I said. 'And you'll come back afterwards and share your newly acquired skills with the bank?'

'Yes, sir.'

He nodded, but he was not a stupid man, and I sensed he could tell that beneath my equanimity tectonic plates were shifting.

Ten

I became interested in pornography after a younger man slapped my breast. Where, I wondered, do we learn what we learn? And how do we learn what we know?

My friend Ejiro was going on and on about younger men, saying, 'You have to try a younger man, twenty-six and below; they really care about pleasing you.'

'Twenty-six is oddly specific,' I said. 'Why not twenty-five or thirty? Does something happen to them at twenty-six? Is it the cut-off age for woman-pleasing?'

Ejiro said, 'I've told you.'

Her younger man had a friend with tattoos running down his arms. Ejiro organized a discreet double date and at some point, he leaned in and asked me, 'Do you want to see my tattoos on my back?'

'No,' I said. Was this a line he used? 'You know tattoos look ugly as you age; they turn greenish grey and look like old algae in a lab.'

He stared at me in astonishment.

'Mine are good,' he said finally.

'As you get older, as you age,' I said.

'Oh.'

'How old are you?' I asked.

'Why are you asking?' he asked.

His asking 'Why are you asking?' meant he wanted evidence of my interest first before we embarked on the potential obstacle of age. I found it sweet. He was twenty-six years old. Just at Ejiro's cut-off, luckily. I was fourteen when he was born. I could have been his babysitter. I almost laughed, thinking this. We drank a lot and he smoked shisha. He and his friend were talking about some celebrities and their cars and watches, and I felt ancient in my boredom. At some point he said, gesturing to the shisha bowl and hose, 'The water cleans it, so it's good for you.'

'No, shisha is ten times worse for you than normal cigarettes. We're killing ourselves,' I said.

He was looking warily at me, as if wondering what he had gotten himself into.

'Don't mind Omelogor, she always talks like this,' Ejiro said. 'Behind that madness, she's very nice.'

I saw him a few more times, to make sure he was not a psychopath, before I asked him to stay.

Ejiro had said, 'They care about pleasing you, they care that you get there', and for this younger man it was certainly true, but it felt strange. He was completely silent, he said no words, his fingers sweeping over my body in a way that made me think of the word 'imitation'. He was re-creating something seen. Suddenly I didn't want it and I didn't want him in my bed. What did I want? The imperfection of the real. There were more practised movements of fingers and tongue. I felt that he was watching himself as his own enraptured audience. I could not peak. I wanted to, if only to make it all less of a colossal waste of time, and then I realized it would be his victory if I did. They do care about pleasing you, but only so they can say, 'Wow, look what I did.' An act of self-praise more than an act of giving. A few dramatic moans, I decided, and then I would ask him to stop. I would say I'm overstimulated rather than I'm bored. I wanted to protect his ego because I liked him and he was sweet and he'd said the day before, 'Look what's happening to my fingers. The skin is peeling back away from my nails. Do you know what it means?' Why did he think I would know why his skin was peeling away from his nails, for goodness' sake? Still, it moved me that he asked. It felt open and soft, as if we might be friends tenderly caring about what happened to each other. I did the second moan and was about to say please stop when he slapped my breast. I looked at him. He slapped it again. My left breast, and it wasn't a soft slap, but even a soft slap would not have reduced my shock. 'Have you gone mad?' I asked him. 'Stop it.' He seemed uncertain, as if he wasn't sure if I meant what I said.

After he left, I turned my TV on to a channel showing mixed martial arts; he must have changed the channel at some point.

'He was watching mixed martial arts,' I said to Jide. 'Is that what the children watch these days?'

'I watch it too,' Jide said.

He was to me simply A Younger Man, an experiment, and because he was sweet, I felt a little guilty to think this way of him. But maybe it was an experiment for him too. While I was in my underwear, he said, 'You look good', and he didn't add 'for your age' but he must have thought it, because I sensed his fascination with and mild repulsion for women older than him.

'Why would he slap my breast? Not caress, slap. Actually slap,' I told Jide.

'If you watched porn, it wouldn't be so strange. That's what they do in straight porn.' Jide was laughing. 'You've been with older men who watched porn when the actors still had pubic hair and when the women were treated a little less badly, so they don't do any of the new craziness.'

'Goodness,' I said, floored, and almost disappointed with myself that I didn't know.

Long before this younger man slapped my breast, my cousin Mmiliaku, Aunty Jane's daughter, told me a story about a belt. Mmiliaku and her husband go to morning Mass on Sundays and then Emmanuel drops her and the children at home and returns to the church for Opus Dei. He doesn't eat meat on Fridays and believes contraception to be a terrible sin. Shortly after they got married, Mmiliaku started saying, 'It's always best to marry someone from your side of the street', because Emmanuel had only a secondary-school education – and a very successful business.

Mmiliaku, drinking Bournvita at my dining table, the mug close to her lips, said, 'Some people cannot reason.'

'What has Emmanuel done now?' I asked.

'He did his normal thing where he just climbs on top of me when I was sleeping. I woke up in pain, and I started pushing him off me. He got angry, so I let him finish. When he came back that evening, I made myself look nice, and after we ate, I started kissing him, touching him, and he pushed me away and said I should stop behaving like a prostitute. I just want us to have enjoyable sex and connect as man and wife. It is terrible, always the same thing: he forces himself into my body when I am asleep. Anyway, later I told him: "Let's try and watch a blue film to see if we can learn." I didn't say it was for him to learn, I said for us, so that he won't say I'm insulting him. He started shouting. "Is that what you do now, watch blue film? Is that how you have become rotten?" Then he unbuckled his belt and raised it and whipped me, three times, a thick leather belt.' She had been teary as she spoke but halfway through she began to laugh. 'He has equipment he doesn't know how to use and he doesn't want to learn. Can you imagine? And he is saying I am rotten.'

'Rotten', that word, 'rotten'. In primary school they said you were rotten if you talked to boys. 'Rotten' was a word smeared in dirtiness and sex and unmentionables all related to sex. Girls were rotten. I never in primary school heard a boy called rotten.

'You think blue film is the way to learn?' I asked.

'Where else will he learn?' she asked.

After Mmiliaku told me this story but before the younger man slapped my breast, there was another reason, and it was the man whose hair I pulled. Arinze, the longest of my emotion-happenings. We lasted eleven months, and I was beginning to think this might finally be the love they talked about. He was clever but not creative; he read widely and brought insight to what others had written, and this for many people would have been enough. But not for him, because what he really wanted to do was create, and so his life became a huffy reaction to this inability to create. Most contemporary novels were trite, he said. He wouldn't read anything published after 1960 and he rolled his eyes at most contemporary music. He worked in an advertising agency as a director and he mocked the commercials his own firm produced. So basic, he said, no imagination. He once gave me a stiff short story he had written and when I told him it was stiff, he said that was the whole point: the telling was supposed to be stiff, to reflect the character who was stiff.

When we first met, he could not cleanly crack an egg. Tiny shell pieces would fall out and I would watch him try to fish them out of the bowl with a fork, looking hapless and focused, and I thought this so amusingly sweet. His determination to make me an omelette in his barely used kitchen with the toaster's tag still on. By the time our relationship ended, I thought it self-indulgent and sloppy: how hard could it be to cleanly crack an egg? What had charmed me at first became what infuriated me at last. Beware the early sources of charm. Sometimes I know as soon as I meet a man what soon will irritate me, but with him I couldn't tell; he was so different, a thrilling mystery I wanted to unmask.

I began to think it might be love when he jerked awake one morning screaming from a calf cramp. He punched at his leg, his face contorted, and I felt the agony of it in my heart. I panicked so much and worried so much. It had never happened before with a man, the sensation of vicarious pain.

'I'm taking you to hospital, we're going to hospital now,' I said, even when it had subsided.

'It's just a muscle cramp,' he said.

For the rest of the day, I watched him, made him tea, asked if I should call my massage person. Maybe I was in love.

It was he who told me, 'You're such a man', because I wanted to be left alone afterwards, to fall asleep in peace. In the beginning, he attempted to hold me, and I would shrug him off, to his confused surprise. Until he understood, and left me alone, teasing me from time to time. *You're such a man.*

And he who said, 'I feel like I don't know you and can't know you. You're unknowable.'

'Everybody in this world is unknowable. We cannot fully know others when we are sometimes strangers to ourselves,' I said, and he scoffed and said could I please not quote poems, even though it was not of course a quote.

He said, also, 'You don't like men.'

'I don't?' I mocked, and suggestively looked at him from top to bottom.

'I mean men as a group, men as a class, you don't like men who aren't your relatives and friends.'

'So do you like random women?' I asked, which was disingenuous, because I knew what he meant but chose deflection, it being easier at the time. 'Anyway you said I'm like a man. So which one is it: I don't like men or I'm like a man?'

'You're dodging,' he said.

'I like you,' I said.

I could have said 'I love you', but he had not yet had the muscle cramp and I still believed I was capable only of the phantom of the feeling and not the real feeling itself. For so long, I have known myself to feel emotions without being inside them, as if to feel it was merely to watch it, myself and the emotions separate things, eternally unable to coalesce.

He liked pornography. He wanted us to watch something together. It took him months to tell me.

'Okay,' I said. I was indifferent; there had been some hastily watched blue films in my teenage years, but they didn't much interest me.

'I thought you would judge me,' he said.

'Why?'

'With your worthy high-mindedness. I mean, look at that,' he said, and pointed at the framed Thomas Sankara quote on my bedroom wall.

The revolution and women's liberation go together. We do not talk of women's emancipation as an act of charity or out of a surge of human compassion. It is a basic necessity for the revolution to triumph.

'I'm not saying it's sophomoric to have words on your wall,' he said.

'Blow too low to be felt,' I said, and we laughed.

We watched it on his laptop, both of us lying on our bellies, our sides touching.

It was not the shadowy scenes with moustached men from the 1980s film I watched at a friend's house in secondary school. I didn't expect it would be, yet I was struck by the good lighting, the tasteful production. We watched in silence at first and then he wanted to know what in the scene I liked. The fakeness of the woman's moaning made me want to laugh, but I saw that he took it seriously and so I did not laugh.

'Why is he squeezing her throat and pulling her hair?' I asked.

He turned to me, looking amused. 'It heightens pleasure,' he said.

'For whom?' I asked.

He turned to me. 'Hey.'

I didn't respond, and because he could tell I was not enthusiastic, he said, 'Let's watch something else.'

'Okay,' I said, and I leaned away, creating a slice of space between his body and mine.

We decided to watch a documentary on television but my mind was still occupied by scenes from the film. 'I remember this boy in primary school saying, "Acting in blue film is shameful but at least you'll be a millionaire,"' I said.

He laughed. 'I was that boy.'

'I was actually a fully grown human when I read something about the industry and how terrible it is and my primary-school self was shocked.'

'Meaning you must have been unconsciously tempted by the millionaire part.'

'Idiot. No, really, it sounded horrible. They pay very little, they coerce women; it doesn't sound worth it at all.'

'Yes, but it's like sweatshops, a part of modern capitalism.'

'Only that sweatshops at least produce useful things.'

He was looking at me. 'You don't realize this industry is the largest global teacher of men? Who do you think teaches men stuff?'

I didn't respond because I didn't want to continue the conversation about porn, and his lopsided smile seemed suddenly unsavoury, as if he had seamy sides to him that I did not know, but I thought of his words, *Who do you think teaches men stuff?*, and I began to feel sorry for men. Can this be said, that I began to feel sorry for men? Some time passed before I set up an anonymous website and paid for analytics and advertising, and in weeks I had men sending messages to me, an anonymous woman who would tell it like it is, but was on their side.

ONE DAY I WAS ANGRY with him. Many months had passed and we had not watched any porn together since; he hadn't asked and I didn't think he would. I was angry with him and my anger had no basis; it was his well-oiled arrogance that had begun to grate. Arrogance in women has the possibility of excitement, because it is subversive, but in men it is always reactionary and therefore boring, especially arrogance of the chivalrous kind, that *noblesse oblige* of the stronger sex. He had a demeanour that said, 'I'm a gift to the world', and it grated. On the day I was angry with him, we were in bed and I looked down at his head, his full head of hair. I reached out and gathered a handful of that short soft Afro, and before I violently yanked at it, I briefly caressed his scalp. I had never thought of pulling his hair in bed; my anger until then was a response to his hubris, but in that moment it sharpened to a singular beam while a handful of his hair was in my grasp.

He jumped, let out a small sound, of surprise and pain.

'What are you doing?' he asked.

'To heighten pleasure,' I said.

He sat up, backing away from me, and in his eyes – incredulous, rimmed with distrust, angry – I saw myself as a crazy person.

'What the fuck?' he said. 'What is wrong with you? You're looking for a reason. You don't need to look for a reason.'

He was getting up, scrambling up, rushing to get dressed and leave. What I missed after it ended: I missed wearing his shirt. I missed those evenings filled with the speed of unfastening and licking and biting. I missed the evenings of happy sexlessness, when we enjoyed being with each other talking, and I missed the laughter, so much laughter; we both once said that a life without laughter is an unlivable life.

He told me, 'I will never forget you. I have never before met a woman who hates wet kisses in the morning before teeth have been brushed.'

When, in the early days, I first turned away from his just-awoken kiss, he asked if something was wrong.

'I dislike wet kisses in the morning before teeth have been brushed,' I said. It was something we laughed about, but it hurt me that he said that at the end. It was deliberate and clever, like him, and he knew it would hurt me that he chose this inconsequential thing to remember me by. I had hurt him, too, with my unfair anger. And so it ended and we took our hurts with us.

Eleven

I tell my friends this might be our last dinner because I don't see how we won't quarantine. I have my full crew, seats brought from upstairs, some perched on the living-room sofa with their plates. Hauwa looks like a patterned column of sheer grace. A peach silk scarf floats over her Ankara print headwrap, the rest of her covered head to toe in the same peach-grey print, and her lipstick is close to the peach shade of her scarf. 'Too much beauty for one person,' I say, and I know she likes me saying that where others can hear.

The biggest presence is Chijioke, who called to say he was in town from Lagos. My friends circle him, unused to him, interested in him.

'If you were not such a fine man, I wouldn't sit near you, I don't know what you Lagos people are carrying,' Chinelo says, and Chijioke laughs.

'How is Lagos?' Ehigie asks.

'Like Lagos,' Chijioke says. 'People are still moving about but a friend of mine has installed a sink at his front door for people to wash their hands.'

'If I was in Lagos nobody would even come to my house,' Jide says.

'You keep saying Lagos, how do you know the thing isn't already here in Abuja?' Edu asks.

'People here don't seem to think that something's afoot, though,' Chijioke says. 'I stopped by in Jabi to see my aunt. When I told her I was going to a friend's house for dinner, she said be careful, and I thought she meant about the coronavirus but she actually said, "Be careful about eating in women's houses." Cracked me up.'

'What is she saying, that women will put jazz in your food?' Hauwa says in an ungenerous tone.

'Ahn, yes o. Women are desperate these days,' Ahemen says. 'And with someone like Chijioke? They will make every love potion there is.'

Someone like Chijioke: a good-looking rich-enough man with no fraud and no bitter betrayed women in his past.

Flirtatiously, Ahemen asks, 'And why haven't you married, Chijioke?'

'I haven't found the right person.' Chijioke looks at me and I look at him, wishing again that I could summon not a mere emotion-happening but more. Finally, more.

'Please can somebody make jazz to destroy this coronavirus?' Chinelo asks.

'They shouldn't have allowed that Italian man to come into Lagos, honestly,' Jide says.

'But it's not as if he was coming from China,' Ahemen says.

'All the underpaid immigrant Chinese workers making designer bags in Italy must have visited home and brought it back from China,' I say.

'I don't understand,' Ahemen says.

'Designers can't make the bags in China because then they can't put "Made in Italy" labels on them. If they put a "Made in China" label, the designer value disappears. So they bring underpaid Chinese workers to Italy to make the bags and when we see "Made in Italy", we think they were made by some quaint, ethically paid family who have been working with leather for five hundred years.'

'Is that a critical tone I hear to the concept of maximizing profit? You no longer sound like a good capitalist,' Chijioke says. I laugh and I notice Hauwa is watching us, speculative eyes moving from him to me and back again.

'They will definitely close borders and impose quarantine, in a matter of days,' Ehigie says.

'What about my ladies' night? I already booked the restaurant!' Chikamso says.

She organizes an occasional ladies' night. Ten or fifteen of us book the good make-up artists to alter our faces, and the good hair-stylists to go from house to house installing frontals and laying edges. Afterwards, we eat at whichever restaurant is the newest or buzziest, a band of glamorous self-possessed women. We go to the lounge in Wuse 2 or the bar in Maitama, to swim in cocktails and dance with one another and say silly things like 'We're shutting the place down!' Hauwa can't come because she doesn't go out late to public places.

'Ladies' night will have to be suspended,' Ehigie says.

'God forbid. Life cannot stop because of virus,' Chikamso says.

'When they say don't touch your face, is it that the virus is already in all of us and then when we touch our face it will infect us?' Chinelo asks.

We laugh but our laughter is full of questions.

Jide says he is not going to talk about this virus at all any more and asks if they know that I know the hotel maid from Guinea who has been in the news and who will finally speak for herself in an interview tomorrow. A prickle of irritation runs through me. Jide is almost swaying as he chatters, his eyes drunkenly reddish, making a spectacle of something he knows I do not want to talk about. I have never spoken of Kadiatou to my friends because I owe her this scrap of privacy. So much has already been left in tatters.

'The maid that said the head of Multilateral Nations raped her?' Ahemen asks.

'She didn't say he raped her, he raped her,' Jide says.

'It was a set-up. Nobody raped the woman. She needs to go and sit down,' Ahemen says.

'Only a fool would organize a set-up that is so amateur,' Jide says.

Ahemen scoffs. 'Why would a man like him need to rape? And rape somebody like her?'

'Handsome men rape, rich men rape, successful men rape. Men rape babies, men rape old grandmothers,' Jide says.

'Maybe he didn't give her the agreed amount. I hope she gets the money she wants. This is all about money,' Ahemen says.

'Ahn-ahn, Ahemen. Did the woman do anything to you?' Chinelo asks.

Ahemen shrugs. 'We have to be honest.'

I look at her and think that it isn't about this particular rape. It is about any rape at all. Ahemen prefers men. In the face of any rape story, she will craft for men the most gorgeous of excuses, and for women her instinct will be distrust.

'Don't forget he is French. They are different when it comes to these things. Many French women support him. Some of them have even come out to say it wasn't rape,' she says.

I think of the regressive poisons of French gallantry. The immaturity at its heart, the backward childishness, rather than childlikeness, which might have had some appeal. I've just read the article signed by some French women supporting him, and the remnants of dispiritedness still lie unsettled in me.

'How do these women know it wasn't rape?' I ask.

'How do you know it was rape?' Ahemen counters.

'Ahemen, Omelogor knows the maid personally,' Jide says.

'So you really know her?' Ahemen asks me, undeterred in her battle, and still breathing her fire; if only the Frenchman could see his dedicated foot soldier.

'My cousin Chia knows her,' I say. I will not dissect Kadiatou for anyone's entertainment.

Chinelo is teasing Lon, whose full name is Lalong Jang: 'You Plateau people have names that sound Chinese. I hope you don't have the virus o.'

'Enough China jokes,' Ehigie says.

'What does everyone think of choking?' I ask.

'Choking?' Chijioke asks.

'This is how Omelogor is always asking us about our bedrooms o,' Chinelo says.

'I like choking but it has to be gentle,' Belema says.

'God forbid choking. Any man who tries that on me, both of us will die that day,' Chikamso says.

'I didn't think I would like this, but it is nice today,' Chinelo says, and I say, 'You like choking today?' but she is pulling towards her a platter of Philippe's potatoes baked in buttery milk.

We are all slack and loosened by drink, teasing and ribbing and laughing.

Jide, you and food!

Omelogor, are you sure that big bum can fit in that chair?

You are mad!

I imagine this banter happening in my circle of non-friends in American graduate school and I begin uncontrollably to laugh.

CHIA SENDS ME a link to watch the interview. Tension weighs down my stomach.

Kadiatou looks pasty, her foundation poorly blended, and I have seen a better wig on her head. The journalist oozes compassion and sensitive, thoughtful nods. She asks her questions with an expression determined to be kind.

Kadiatou is unknowable to her, Kadiatou is a curiosity, Kadiatou exists outside of her imagination. If you put her in Kadiatou's world, she would blindly stumble about. Kadiatou pauses and gestures and pauses and gestures again. Once or twice the journalist finishes a faltering sentence with a word that is not what Kadiatou was looking for, but Kadiatou accepts the word and ploughs on. I imagine producers backstage just before the interview, asking Kadiatou, 'Are you okay? Anything you need?' When they ask, 'Anything you need?' they mean water, ibuprofen, the bathroom. What she needs is a Pular interpreter and an interviewer who understands that immigrants are desperate to raise children who think they have a right to dream, and what she needs is an America that understands this. The interview ends and in the final shot before credits roll across the screen, Kadiatou leans back on her chair, her face drained and relieved, as if she knows she has not done too well but at least it is done.

I think of the journalist's kindness and the raw, radiant power of it. How carelessly Americans wield their power.

THE FIRST TIME I went to America I flew through Frankfurt and at the airport the Germans talked in a normal tone, but on landing in Atlanta the Americans didn't talk, they barked. From the person saying, 'US citizens this way', to the stone-faced person examining passports, it was all one uncivilized tone. It reminded me of how CEO always spoke to his driver in the same shouting tone, whether he was pleased or displeased, as if speaking normally might make the driver forget the steep gradient of power that lay between them. Of course the visa interviewer at the American embassy in Lagos was screaming into the microphone at me, since talking normally was out of the question for them. *You are a potential liability to the United*

States government. I had an American visitor's visa in my passport and money in my accounts and a house and company in Abuja. Why would I be a liability to the American government? Behind the glass, her hazel eyes flashed in response to my insufficient deference. *What exactly is the source of this income? Why should I believe that?* She might not have this kind of rank power ever again and so she was clutching and squeezing it dry. *Speak up!* she shouted. I had never been told to speak up in my life. Slights had always been easy for me to brush aside, as long as I achieved my goal, but something about that moment burrowed deep in the part of me that stored pain. It was the rank stinking power and her rashly righteous use of it, how she chewed my dignity and spit it out just because she could. *Speak up!* The intent was to make me feel small. People paid so much in visa fees and came here timid with hope, only to be humiliated before hearing a no. If she wanted to, she could say no and still leave their dignity intact. Not that I wanted to go to China, but at least with the Chinese you paid only when the visa was approved. *How will a master's degree in . . . cultural studies from an American university be useful to you in Nigeria? What do you know about cultural studies?* Distaste lay thickly on my tongue. Why was I doing this, forgetting I had choices? I could go to the UK or somewhere in Europe. I could go to Canada. I didn't have to stand here like a convict pleading for supervised freedom. And so I cut in and asked, 'Why are you shouting?' She flinched and reared back slightly as if to pounce, and then she pushed the form across the glass and said, 'I'm sorry, you do not qualify for a visa. You can reapply if your circumstances change.'

My circumstances did not change. I merely reapplied a few weeks later, and this time a different interviewer examined my documents, saying little, and asked me to pick up my visa in two days.

I SAW A BAD OMEN in that first visa interview and then in the headaches that started in America mere weeks into the semester. An unyielding band tightened itself around my head, firm and resistant, off and on for weeks.

I had planned to go on weekends to New York to the museums,

as I always did when I visited in the past, but those previous trips felt different, better, as if I'd seen a different country then, an alternate America. Anyway, how was I supposed to look at art with my head in chains? At the student clinic they sent me for a scan. As I slid in and out of the cavernous machine, I imagined myself dying from a tumour growing in my head and I thought: Will my body be shipped back in a coffin or just wrapped up to be more efficient?

I had never thought such morbid thoughts before, but I had also never lived in a place so acutely not mine. The technician's name tag said KOFI. His accent was Ghanaian. I smiled a familiar smile, wanting to say, 'My African brother', but he knowingly evaded my eyes.

'Okay, all done and you did very well, you did great,' he said. If Kofi said this in Accra, his incredulous countrywoman would ask him, 'How exactly did I do well?' At least he didn't say, 'Have a good day!' with that American cheer so transparently false I wondered why they bothered.

I walked out of the building bitter with resentment towards Kofi, because in those moments with me he had made a studied choice. And his not choosing Africa was not choosing me and not choosing solidarity in an unfamiliar world. I called Chia, I was always calling Chia, to tell her about the annoying sellout from Ghana who when he saw me decided to be more American than the Americans themselves.

'*You did very well, you did great!*' I mimicked, in a bad Ghanaian accent.

'You don't know what he's dealing with. Maybe his co-workers are condescending to him and maybe he doesn't want to be an African at work.'

'There were no co-workers there. Just me and him. *You did very well, you did great!*'

'He means you didn't get claustrophobic or scream or something,' Chia said, with a small laugh. She clearly approved of giving mundane praise to people merely because they had done something they were supposed to do which was for their own good. Chia, the American.

The scan showed nothing. At the student clinic a lanky doctor asked how much exercise I did, looking dubiously at my body with all its parts rounder and bigger since I came to America. I said I walked to my classes. Was I eating well? I missed Philippe. Almost every day I ordered curry goat from a Caribbean place, which was tasty but salty and I drank so much water afterwards and still felt thirsty. How many hours of sleep did I get each night and what did I do to manage stress? I said I did yoga, and the lanky doctor was too honest to hide his disbelief. So I smiled and said I had never done yoga in my life. Finally, he said, 'You might benefit from seeing a therapist.' His words made me feel deeply deficient, a lost case, but what would it hurt to try?

Therapy was something I read about in books and it had always had a taint of indulgent weakness. I knew it was different now but it still brought to mind spoiled White people sprawled on a couch. The therapist's office, close to campus, was brightly lit in the afternoon. Two fluorescent bulbs. She wore a swirl of scarves and kept asking, 'Is the light too much for you?' And then she asked, 'Do you feel the burden here or here?' pointing at her chest and at her belly, with a knowing look, as if she would yet fully untangle me. On her window ledge was an orchid plant with fake-looking purple flowers clustered at its tip. I became focused on them. 'Are they real?' I asked, and she said, 'Yes.'

'Is there anything you'd like to tell me?' she asked.

I did not say, 'I came seeking restoration in America and I have not found it.' I should have, but that would leave her with no response for me.

'Whatever you're feeling is valid,' she told me. Valid. It yawned across the room in its blandness, valid; it felt like being given a trophy for effort rather than victory, a recognition you did not really deserve. She said it again and again, *valid valid valid*. It rang disturbingly in my ears like a mosquito and worsened my headaches, and I stopped seeing her. To the ongoing headaches, heart palpitations were soon added. Chia said it was stress from my schoolwork and all those extra classes I packed into my schedule. But the work wasn't demanding at all. It was too soft, like spongy, slippery foam. Everything was about exploring; we were all exploring, always exploring, and we could say we didn't have the answers because we were just exploring, and so we didn't need to boldly risk coming to clear conclusions. Sunk in the miasma of exploring, we cast off clarity. There was little pressure and no real rigour. In the undergraduate class I audited, because the title 'Neuroscience and Emotion' interested me, a student raised his hand and said his paper was late because his dog had an ear infection. I thought he was being funny and we were supposed to laugh, but the professor said okay and asked how the dog was doing. Is this how America became the leader of the world? If Russia or China were about to bomb you, would you ask for more time to clean your dog's ear?

IN MY OWN CLASS of graduate students, I sensed very early that my life was wrong in their eyes. Their quick exchange of looks when I said something, the apartness when we gathered in the coffee area, all tilted away from me as if repelled by rays I was unconsciously emitting. They were all younger, recently graduated; one young man had worked in a non-profit, another started a business in California selling surfing T-shirts. They spoke in tightly bound ways that refused the blurring of lines or the bleeding into each other of different ideas.

When I spoke about my work in Abuja, they exchanged looks, twitchy faces, distant stares, and I came to understand they believed banking was bad; not the excesses of banking, but banking itself. Banking was inherently flawed, a woman called Kaley said to me, *it's inherently flawed,* and I found myself stuttering because I did not know how to make a point that seemed so self-evident to me.

'Where do you put your money?' I asked finally.

'That's not a good argument. I don't have a choice, but it doesn't mean the choices are good.'

'How could the Dutch have done it differently when they invented banking?' I asked.

A woman called Eve said, 'That's right-wing!' Everything she disagreed with she called right-wing, and to call it right-wing was to punctuate it with a full stop. Case closed.

A young man with olive skin often said 'as a multiracial person' before making his point. I did not know what races he meant, and

I was curious to know, but to ask would of course be wrong. He was the star of the class, loops of beads wound around his wrist, his hair a massive halo of curls. The others leaned towards him and waited for his views. He nodded with approval when Eve said the answer to inequality is that the rich must give their money away – not tiny tax-deductible donations, but most of their money.

'Nobody will give their money away,' I said. 'Makes more sense to fix a system that allows people to make so much, instead of expecting saintliness from human beings.'

'Says the person who moves money for murderous dictators,' she said.

I had said some of my clients were politicians, but she had turned it to 'dictator', and 'dictator' apparently wasn't enough, it needed 'murderous'. A toddler increasing the pitch of her unnecessary tears.

'This is not how you create a better world. You don't create a better world by starting with fantasy,' I said.

And to this the mysterious multiracial replied, 'Tell that to all the people who actually changed the world.'

MY FATHER OFTEN SAID, 'Your social register is above average', and I knew he meant I had many friends, maybe too many friends. But in America I had no friends.

There was Andy, the White South African, but he was an aggressively friendly person who was everybody's friend, always asking everyone to come have drinks somewhere, and I thought of him not as a proper friend but as somebody who collected people and who had collected me. Andy made himself my guide, telling me where was best to eat, what bars were good, who was best to talk to and who should be ignored.

He introduced me to a woman named Jerry who spent ages talking with outsize excitement about eating wild mushrooms foraged in the Catskills. And then she said her brother, a rich tech bro, injected the blood of young boys to help him live longer, and she said it mimicking a shudder, but I could tell she was secretly admiring of him.

But Andy did not approve of Chinedu, the Nigerian-American, younger than me, who was doing a master's in international relations and wore a cool puffy coat.

'He's a Federalist Society asshole who doesn't know those folks will never like him,' Andy said, and I felt a flash of protectiveness towards Chinedu. I drifted into Chinedu because he at least felt like a person who was not looking for all that was wrong in me. It lasted a few weeks. He loved Marvel films. He took me to a football game, somebody had given him tickets, and he said he never imagined sitting so close to the great action, while I thought American football was incomprehensible, the field so small it was a joke. Why did the players bother taking breaks? Had they seen a real football pitch? Chinedu became animated when we went to see a movie, and I envied him this ability to feel so strongly about something that brought him only pleasure. I sat beside him in the dark of the cinema, looking at the flashy effects on the screen, the big shiny things, fire and smoke and blowing-up noise. American entertainment had an infantile heart. Maybe it was why American pornography was the most ridiculous, where the men were mechanical, exaggerated, like robots with the programming gone wrong.

ONCE I JOINED ANDY and his friends for a drink at O'Malley's. He introduced everyone but I promptly forgot their names, except for a man with a catchy Irish name, Darragh.

So I smiled at Darragh and said I liked his name.

'Did you get back okay the other night?' Darragh asked.

I stared at him, sure we had never met before.

Andy, fluidly fast-talking, quickly changed the subject and asked if I'd try a beer today.

'You thought I was someone else?' I asked Darragh.

Darragh was blushing and apologizing and I was smiling, curious to know who he thought I was. 'I hope she's at least good-looking,' I was about to say, when Andy cut in and said, 'It's okay, it's okay, let's get you some beer.'

Later I told Andy, 'Don't ever do that again.' And he looked hurt, wounded, terribly wronged, as if he could not believe that I dared to be unsatisfied by his handling of things.

Chinedu smirked when I told him this story. 'That's the problem with these liberal folks. They want to end racism but they can't even talk honestly about it. Try talking to them about the big issues like racism and abortion and next thing you know they're not addressing the issue; they're policing your language, and using buzzwords that don't mean anything, and at the end you're discussing semantics and the real issue is forgotten. With conservatives you can actually talk about what you're talking about.'

'Maybe,' I said, 'but your conservative positions are still rubbish.'

'Like what?'

'Seriously?' I asked.

He was always saying empirical this and empirical that, free market decides this and decides that, and I would say, 'Your problem is you've crammed your class notes but you don't know how people live.'

'The problem is that liberals are not realistic.' His usual retort.

'Unions and regulations and welfare seem realistic as a starting point for a society that works. You need rules to keep a free market free. You can never have a free market if you let companies get too big.'

'See, I don't get offended when you tell me my views are bullshit, even though I know you're wrong.'

'Bravo to you,' I said.

'So let's go all Marxist and give everyone handouts.'

'Marx didn't want people to get handouts. He was all for work. He just wanted the people who actually did the work to get some of the benefits of that work.'

'Still not realistic,' Chinedu said.

He had never been to Nigeria and after it ended, I said, 'You must come to Abuja sometime and stay with me.'

MY ADVISER CONFUSED ME. She looked like the distinguished name that she was, with her long silver hair and her serious face. 'There's increasing scholarship on the horrors of the pornography industry, and how inescapably predatory and exploitative it is, but it behooves us, I think, to pay attention to the sensitivities involved, knowing of course that sex work is work.'

Knowing of course. How did she know I knew, and why should I know, and what if I didn't know? Even saying it like that – 'knowing of course' – gave no room for dissent.

'I'm interested in pornography as an educational tool,' I said.

She smiled thinly, as if to say, 'Now be serious, please.' I was saying I meant the question of where we learn about sex and she was talking again, saying many words, and I kept hearing her say 'liberation'. Everything she said was soft and sank in when touched.

'Liberation? What do you mean? What would it look like?' I asked. She thought I was being provocative but I really wasn't. Sometimes I thought not having gone to university in America might be why things seemed so hidden under layers of veils; no sooner had I peeled one off than others drifted down.

'Of course you know what I mean by liberation,' she said.

Later she said she didn't feel she could support my thesis, with the direction I wanted to take, and recommended someone else I could try working with, but by then I didn't want to work with anyone else. I wanted only to go home.

THE HEADACHES HAD already started when I talked about Uncle Hezekiah in class. I talked about Uncle Hezekiah and about Gideon Akaluka, whose head was paraded on a metal pole around the streets of Kano. Later I wished I hadn't said anything at all, and to the shame I felt for not crying for Uncle Hezekiah, I added more shame for talking about him to a class of Americans heedlessly drunk on their certainties. I made his death something they could trivialize and dig into the dust. It was a class discussion on civilians in civil wars and I should never have opened my mouth; after all, a riot against Igbo Christians in the North wasn't a civil war. It wasn't even one of the big riots, it was much smaller, so small a Lagos newspaper called it a fatal disturbance.

Uncle Hezekiah's beard kept growing even after he was dead, Aunty Jane said. She went to see his body, one of the bodies brought back piled in a trailer, for families to sort through and identify their beloveds among stiffened blood-soaked forms. Uncle Hezekiah was murdered when I was in university, by men who shopped in his convenience store, men he had exchanged greetings with for years. But it was only when Gideon Akaluka, a complete stranger, was murdered, in the police station where he had gone for succour after his wife was accused of using a page of the Holy Book to wipe her baby's poop, that I cried, looking at a grainy photo of the macabre. A head. A human head. I was supposed to cry for my uncle but I cried for a stranger instead.

My words laced themselves together as words sometimes do, and as soon as I finished I wished to take them back. Silence followed. The class was free of fidgeting and small coughing and throat-clearing and looks exchanged. Then the multiracial person spoke.

'There's so much Islamophobia in the world; don't add to it.'

He was leaning forward on the desk, looking at me. His demeanour was all disgust, but it was not disgust for the barbarism of Uncle Hezekiah's suffering, but disgust for me. His eyes held that brand of condemnation made worse by thinking itself gentle and right. I stared at him, too taken aback to respond.

'You're weaponizing your family's loss and that's problematic,' he said.

I looked around the class in that African way that asked, 'Who else is witnessing this with me?' A woman sternly settled her hair behind her ear and kept looking straight ahead. A man was nodding. Many were averting their eyes, too distressed by my crime to even look at me.

I was too stunned to do anything but push back my chair and pick up my bag and leave. If I didn't have liquid rushing in my head and in my ears, if my body wasn't faltering, I would have asked, 'Do you feel nothing else? Are the compartments of your heart not roomy enough?' The professor was looking down at her notes, tapping her iPad pen on the desk, like a biased referee pretending to be fair. It wasn't even that they felt offended; it was that offended was the only thing they felt. Perfect righteous American liberals. As long as you board their ideology train, your evilness will be overlooked. Champion an approved cause and you win the right to be cruel.

I HAD COME TO AMERICA hoping to find a part of me that was more noble and good; I came in search of repair. Because I wanted so desperately to look up higher and be reminded of things I could believe in again, my disenchantment stung. Disappointed disenchantment, or disenchanted disappointment, a feeling with flint at its core, as if a much-loved aunt I ran to for succour had turned to land on my face a series of surprising slaps. My apartment building had a game room and a roof deck and a restful resident lounge, vacuumed twice a day. I walked through the glass doors wishing my insides matched the brightness of that lounge. Misery always had seemed a big dramatic emotion, but I knew now that it was small and slow-dripping, a shallow submerging that felt eternal.

THEN MISERY GREW into rage and my rage became ravenous and had to be fed. I got into arguments that felt so meaningless. I always started them. They were unnecessary and unedifying, but I still started them. No, the Democrats haven't always cared about Africa; both parties don't care about Africa because they don't have to care. What party bombed the pharmaceutical factory in Sudan? What party destroyed Libya? What party meddled in my country's elections and imposed a nincompoop on us? I hoped someone would bite on this so we could drag it out, but nobody did. They wanted me to put my glass down and get up and leave the bar, so they could continue their happy time. 'Race is a construct,' said a badge on someone's shirt, and I pointed at it and derisively asked, 'So how do sickle cell and cystic fibrosis know who to afflict?'

Of course I knew the meaning, that race is not an idea set in stone, and is always about the social setting, as one person in America might be called Black but in Brazil or South Africa be called a different race. When I asked, 'So how do sickle cell and cystic fibrosis know who to afflict?' I added, 'It's not enough. Don't just say that and be smug. Race is a construct but – and there's always a but – race is also the language of health care with real consequences. Black women have more aggressive breast cancers and Black women have bigger fibroids and Black women die more often in childbirth.'

They all stared at me, a gasp suspended in the air but their scorn unhidden in their eyes. The winter layers I wore made me feel muffled; my thoughts were deadened and I could not hear myself.

'That wasn't worth being so angry about,' Chia said later.

'It was.'

'You know depression can show up as anger.'

Depression can show up as anger. America has bamboozled us all. We are all defining our worlds with words from America.

'I don't remember when you last laughed,' Chia said.

'Would help to have something to laugh about. These people don't laugh,' I said.

'You're depressed,' she said.

'I'm not depressed,' I said, and I was horrified to see that tears had gathered and I was crying.

America didn't owe me restoration and yet I felt that it did, as if it had reneged on a promise that was never really made. I drank whisky alone in my apartment and went so often to the liquor store the man at the counter said hi and then said we have a new single malt you can try. I was drinking as I packed up my apartment, and I liked the companionable scent of whisky on my breath. I began writing the only post I ever wrote on For Men Only that was not in response to messages I received, but I deleted it days later, when I was in Chia's house, feeling slightly better, and eating Kadiatou's fonio, which I had never tasted before.

Some Thoughts on My Brief Time in an American University, marginally related to being on your side, dear men.

America is so provincial, like an enormous giant of a man from a bush village who blunders about with supreme certainty, not knowing he is bush because he is blinded by his strength. If you've lived your whole life in a sensible part of the world – that is, Africa or Asia or Latin America – be careful going to America for a master's degree in the liberal arts. Science is fine, and an MBA is fine as long as you are happy to become a parroting robot. As soon as I started my programme, so much I said was wrong but I did not know why it was wrong and they did not tell me because even my asking why was wrong. They expected me to know. Welcome to the world of the Americans of the pious class. We're talking about race in Europe and I mention how Lord Haw-Haw, who was a British Nazi, claimed that Churchill's father had African blood and suddenly somebody cuts in: 'This is an intellectual game for you while Black people are dying!'

I was puzzled. From outside, America makes more sense. They want your life to match their soft half-baked theories and when it doesn't, they burst out with their provincial certainty.

Somebody was reading a novel about the Nigerian-Biafran war and said, 'It's really fascinating, but honestly I'm still a bit confused about why the Igbo people were massacred?' And I said that to understand Igbo people in Nigeria, think of them like the Jews. People say don't trust Igbo people because they want to control everything and they love money and they're too pushy.

A woman said, 'Oh my God, don't say that, you can't compare anything to the Jews.' What do you mean by 'can't'? What in the cultural genetics of Americans makes them think they can decide for the rest of the world how they should think? I never knew that there existed in this world a class of people who feel so securely entitled to the minds of other people.

London was the centre of my childhood dreams and even though I went as a child to Cambridge with my father, I didn't feel I had seen England until I saw London, so as soon as I could afford it, I went, and I was disappointed that the staff at my posh hotel were all Polish and spoke poor English because it wasn't the London I expected.

And an American bursts out: 'How can you be so fascist and anti-immigration and perpetuate a dangerous nativism?'

The professor didn't say, 'Let's be civil.' They love that word 'civil' by the way. But when this White woman was mocking White women for paying Jamaican nannies to raise their White children and I said that was regressive nonsense, women throughout human history have always had help caring for their children, it's the relative or the husband's relative, it's the village, and now it means paying for it, but then so what, the Jamaican nanny is building a small house outside Kingston for her parents – and then the professor said, 'Let's be civil.'

Let's be civil indeed, as if their quiet evil isn't the real incivility. The incivility of quiet evil.

There was this Chinese-American woman talking at a bar about her Chinese parents and how racist they were for not wanting her sister to marry a Black man. She said, 'I've cut them off and I'm mad my sister still takes their calls', and everyone in that godforsaken circle told her she was so brave. I could look through her and see the glow of her sanctimonious soul. She thought she was resplendent in her righteousness, but she was just a person unable to love. They don't know how to love, these pious people, and they don't know love. Even the way they help each other is so cheerless and earnest.

I said I loved Kigali, and they said oh my God it's a dictatorship. But the policemen are trim, the markets are clean, people stand in line, and I am proud of it because it is African and I am African. I asked them – Can you understand that love and pride complicate? They can implicate as well but first you must see how they complicate. But they can't see because their hearts lack eyes. Their hearts are blind. They are so dead to human foibles, these Americans of the pious class. And they don't laugh. I mean

actual laughter, that sound nature made to lighten our
hearts and calm our blood pressure.

One day I mentioned my driver Paul and a woman with a
nose piercing said you mean exploited labour, call it what it
is – all Third World domestic staff are exploited labour. She
was a famous academic feminist but she didn't like women.
She liked only the idea of women. She posted cryptic quotes
about feminism that you were supposed to feel guilty about
but not understand, and vaguely threatening conditions
for how to be a feminist, like if you don't know blah blah
blah about Bangladesh then you're no feminist, if you don't
liberate this and that then you're no feminist. Her followers
loved her for her bitterness, and even if she ever wanted to
let joy in, she couldn't because she would lose the applause.
And anyway it would have to be joy as resistance. Or joy as
a subversive anti-patriarchy project. Never just joy. As joy.

One day we're listing the many horrors of Facebook and
I say, for full disclosure, I just put up an ad on Facebook for
a logistics person for my company in Abuja, someone 35 and
above.

An American bursts out: 'It's illegal to mention age in
job ads!'

Well, it isn't in Nigeria. You Americans need to climb
out of your cribs. You think the world is American; you
don't realize that only America is American. To be so
provincial and not even know that you are.

Twelve

'It's the rich people who go abroad that are getting this
corona,' Paul says, and I sense a sly movement, a forward gesture of
his head, as if to say, 'People like you.'

My mother calls and says, 'Don't use your air conditioner. They
said it spreads corona. Open all your windows.'

My father says, 'Have you stocked up sufficiently on food items?'

He is relieved that Aunty Adaeze and Chia's father have just come back from Paris. 'They're closing borders. This thing, nobody knows,' he says.

'Nobody knows,' I say.

My ixora has flowered into the most beautiful red, like bursting into song. In the kitchen, Philippe is sanguine, drying his hands on a dish towel. He says it isn't serious, this sickness they are talking about, it doesn't affect Africans. And as long as you stand in the afternoon sun every day, you'll be fine.

Chiamaka

ONE

In the middle of lockdown, I felt trapped in my house, with the sensation of my days being erased, not lived through, not experienced. I wandered around from room to room – this house, this haven, where I returned from trips to write in my study with its pastel walls and shaggy rugs. The high foyer, the lingering lemony scent in the rooms, the reassuring off-and-on hum of central air. I liked to sit out on the deck and watch the leaves turning gold in the autumn in the beautiful preserve of trees that my mother called a forest. Now the trees were bearing down on me, their branches hostile and pointy, shorn of leaves. I dreamed of escape but I was too anxious even to walk down the slope of my driveway and check the mailbox. One day I stood by the front door longing for a walk. I had so often walked the nearby trail, lightly and swiftly and pumping my arms, sometimes slowing to savour a bird's orange plume, or a tortoise on its toes, or other small treasures. When I re-emerged on the road, to a friendly wave from a neighbour driving past, I felt flush with accomplishment. So precious now, that simple walk. I looked for long minutes at my driveway, the wilting plants at its edges, the dead grass. I unlocked the door to step outside, to breathe open-air air for the first time in weeks, but I hesitated, thinking of the woman in the news who got the virus even though all she did was crack a window. And she lived in a spacious suburb too. I locked the door without opening it. How could I possibly be both sluggish and restless? But

I was. There were rumblings of an impending end; the protests on television against lockdown felt like gestures of reassurance, of the possibility of an ending.

I worried about Kadi. She was losing weight; the slackening of her flesh aged her. She was the only one whose video calls I still took. She looked thinner on the screen, her clavicles sticking out, her cheeks sunken in. Even though I saw only her face, I sensed the downcast air of her posture. She was suffering. Her face carried so much weight, the weight of unsolvable problems. Her lawyers were coaching her on video calls, the prosecutors were questioning her on video calls. I could barely imagine the intensity of it.

'Is it normal?' I asked Zikora. 'Is it normal for the prosecutors to act as if they're not on her side?'

'I'm guessing they just want to have a watertight case.'

'But should she be feeling so distrustful about them?'

'Chia, I'm a corporate lawyer.'

'It just feels wrong.'

'It can be a lot, but if they do it well it should be an easy win, never mind the rapist's team of star lawyers. If they make it about just that day. What happened that day. It's tough to argue that a minutes-long consensual act happens in extraordinarily improbable circumstances.'

'I know!' Zikora was finally sounding as I wanted her to, her neutral-lawyer cap put aside. Often I imagined Kadi walking down the court steps in a halo, a spark again in her eyes. If only the trial could begin right away.

'Kadi, you know there's a woman in France, a White woman, who said he did the same thing to her,' I said.

Kadi shrugged, uninterested. 'I don't know.'

I watched the woman on television, slim and sensitive, speaking with the courage that truth can bring. She had gone to interview him in an apartment and he grabbed her, and she went from asking a question to wrestling him away, her jeans already savagely undone. She was impressive. I felt a new sadness for Kadi that she had felt herself undeserving of the right to fight him off with her full might.

Omelogor said once that she wished Kadi had clamped down her teeth as hard as she possibly could.

LASHAWN SENT A TEXT to say, *My mom's gone. I can't believe it.*

LaShawn's mother. I spent Thanksgiving with them in my senior year of college, and she told me of her time in the Peace Corps in the sixties; she had travelled across West Africa and loved being in the motherland, except that everyone told her not to chew fufu before swallowing. What was the point of swallowing without chewing?

'What's the point of fufu?' she would ask me each time I saw her after that, and we would both laugh. She introduced me to sweet potato pie. She raised four children in a White town in Georgia and kept them home from school on Martin Luther King Day every year, even though Georgia did not recognize the holiday. Now she was gone. A vile virus determined to wipe away a generation too soon. I called LaShawn and when I heard her voice I burst into tears, saying, 'I'm so sorry, LaShawn, I don't know what to say.'

'She got sick and just died on me, just like that. It was so fast. I can't think of how she got it. We were so damned careful. She died on me, just like that.'

'Oh, LaShawn.'

We think we have time but we don't, we really don't.

MY MOTHER SENT voice notes saying, '*Anyanwu ututu m*, please let me see your face, please.' And feeling remorse for worrying her, my thoughts dark with LaShawn's mother, I went back to joining Zoom calls. As soon as I did, I wished I hadn't. The sense of doom returned. From an untimely apex the world was splintering and fracturing, about to topple, and take with it all that was clear and certain. Bunachi was reeling out thousands of the European dead. Afam said politicians in Nigeria were hoarding palliatives meant for the poor, and I imagined these wealthy people piling bags of rice and cartons of Indomie noodles in their homes while the hungry roamed the streets.

OMELOGOR SAID SHE was worried when I wouldn't take video calls, she knew I wasn't writing, and so she took to sending me texts she hoped would make me smile, teasing me about rummaging in my past.

Don't forget your tall thin white men phase, she wrote. It did make me smile, remembering how Omelogor had studied Luuk's photo and then studied the Englishman's photo and finally said, 'Strange what people like.'

I met Luuk soon after the Englishman, too soon, the weeks after I came back from London so barren that I must have wanted to escape the singular tragic story of my life. I recoiled from memories of the Englishman, banning and shutting down and closing, but memory imposes itself even with photos erased and texts wiped clean. Often, I thought of him at home, revising his manuscript, waiting for his wife to come home so he could give her a cuddle. I imagined her as an un-nurselike figure, a certain kind of Englishwoman: matter-of-fact, Tory-voting, brusque and flinty, a little mannish in style, a person whom you dared not annoy. His book was published not long after and once, with Luuk in London, I saw it displayed in the Waterstones on Piccadilly. I picked it up and then forced myself to place it back on the shelf without looking at his photo on the back flap.

LUUK DID LOOK like the Englishman, very tall and very lean, but I told myself it could not be a transferred attraction, because the resemblance was superficial. Luuk was nothing like him. Luuk was curious, but about things rather than ideas. He brimmed with that mix of information and insecurity so common in men who want to own the latest gadgets. The Englishman would think Luuk vulgar, with his monogrammed travel case and his pampered hair. Luuk would think him faded and forgettable.

'Are you an artist?' Luuk asked me, at an art gallery in Mexico City. I was the only Black woman there, in the high-ceilinged space, sedate paintings hanging on very white walls. I told him I was writing a travel essay about the art scene in Mexico City.

'Who do you write for?'

'I'm freelance.'

'Freelance,' he said. 'My English is not great. My mother tongue is Dutch. I spoke Spanish and French before English. So you must forgive me if I have misunderstood, but freelance means unattached? So you will be free to have a drink with me.'

He overflowed with flagrant, flaming charm. He was too obvious, too much, and yet not unappealing. I said yes to dinner; something to do on my last night in Mexico City. The restaurant had unusual volcanic walls. Luuk pulled out my chair with a flourish, and when I ordered an apple juice he teasingly said, 'You know I meant a proper drink, no?' The waiter spent too much time at our table, entranced by Luuk, laughing at Luuk's jokes. Luuk asked his opinion of everything and listened and nodded and finally said yes to his suggestion: fig tacos to start, followed by a dish made of rabbit. I had never liked the idea of eating rabbits but the waiter was so enthusiastic that I kept silent.

'Do you want to taste?' Luuk asked, and offered me his agave cocktail. I shook my head, amused. How inappropriate to ask me, a stranger, to sip his drink, and yet also how oddly disarming. His manner felt familiar, almost African: expansive, sensitive to status, heedless and harmless in crossing boundaries. He was an executive at a Dutch company, managing a Mexican subsidiary for a year, being groomed to become CEO of the whole thing back in Amsterdam. I would have been mortified to praise myself as he did himself, his words tumbling out as unheeded as the self-praise. He had managed major companies in Brazil and India and Russia and was voted best CEO in all three; he sailed and went deep-sea diving and flew small planes; his golf was excellent and his tennis even better. He was a talker who didn't need a listener, a person allergic to silence, and from time to time my mind wandered away. I remember the moment

I awakened to him; it was not gradual but an exact instant, a singular ascent to affection. He was talking about visiting a commercial apple farm he had invested in and how shocked he was to see fields full of stunted apple trees. 'The trees came up to just above my knees,' he said. 'Trees! Can you imagine? Very unnatural. I didn't want to look at them.' For once, his voice roughened and darkened and it moved me to see how affected he was by the terrible wrongness of stunted trees. Suddenly I wanted to hug him close. There were deep cuts in his life, strained sensitivities, lurking beneath his flamboyance. I knew I would see him again, and again. I felt, strangely, a protective desire to shield and save him.

He was divorced; they had not been married, but after eleven years together he called it a divorce. He took this Mexico job to escape her efforts at reconciliation. Her name was Brechtje. He did not say 'my ex'; he said Brechtje as though I, too, knew her. They had raised her child together.

'It must be difficult for you. Divorce always is,' I said.

'Yes, but sometimes a relationship ends a long time before we say okay it has ended. I felt released finally.' He sipped his drink and repeated 'released'.

'Is that the English word you meant to use? "Released"?'

'Yes, like being freed from a prison that is not so bad but still it is a prison.'

'Oh,' I said.

'You have had this same experience?' he asked.

'No,' I said, because I would not sprinkle old ashes on fresh surfaces.

'I'm very happy to be supporting the galleries here. Otherwise I would not have met you. I was nervous to talk to you, at the gallery.'

'You didn't look nervous.'

He laughed, he laughed as one would expect a self-aware successful business executive to laugh, a lusty satisfied sound. 'You think so?'

'I thought maybe you had a Black woman fetish.'

'Fetish?'

'You were interested in me because I'm Black.'

'Oh, I have a fetish, yes, but it is a beautiful woman fetish,' he said.

I was smiling. It was impossible not to be swept up by the glamour of his flattery. It gave him power, the kind you accede to willingly, and sheepishly. The extravagant courting he embarked on when I returned to Maryland was so predictable it felt improbable. Slender jewellery boxes wrapped in matte paper arrived by signature-required courier; elegant boxes of frozen gourmet food appeared at my door, followed by elaborate arrangements of roses, some so heavy I needed the delivery person to help settle them on my kitchen island. Each time I thought, Oh goodness, what has Luuk sent now?, shaking my head, and yet for the rest of the day I walked around in a cloud of delight. I didn't like roses and hardly wore bracelets, but I felt special to be thought of like this, to live so sumptuously in his mind. I told him I loved lilies and tulips, and he sent an arrangement of heritage tulips, swirly coloured with wrinkled petals, and laughed indulgently when I said I really preferred ordinary tulips.

WITH LUUK I EXISTED in a universe of touch, his palm always grazing my back, my shoulder, my waist. It was not territorial, but softer, an act of wonder, as if to say, 'You're really here.' He was so tall I joked that I had to stand on tiptoe when we held hands. In bed, I faked orgasms, but happily. They weren't coming and so I pretended they did, because I was sure that one day they would. How could they not, with this charismatic man, head nestled between my legs, and arms raised above his head, as though in ever-patient crucifixion. I spent long weekends with him in Mexico City, and sometimes in Monterrey, where he had a second office. He would leave after breakfast, groomed and glinting in his slim-cut suits, and return hours later, looking just as fresh and talking non-stop, full of plans for what we could do. We were always doing – live comedy, a theatre opening he had underwritten, an art gallery he had sponsored, a new restaurant, a gala, drinks and dinner with visiting business associates. He ordered dresses for me, and I would slide them out of their sheaths and say, 'Luuk, I have breasts. This is too low cut', and he would say, 'That's why I picked it. In it, you will be all woman, from head to toe, all woman.'

He glowed with pride, looking at me, but his expectations haunted and hindered me. How does insecurity creep up, and spread and choke your mind like weeds? It flattered me, to be the trophy he liked showing off, but I felt inadequate, the wrong kind of prize. For his annual company gala, I abandoned my braids and got a long wavy weave, spending hours at a salon in Washington, DC, because it felt to me more suitable.

Kadiatou sucked her teeth when she saw it. 'If I have hair like you, never anything else artificial. Weave is for people like us.'

And she pulled off her scarf to rub at her bald temples.

'No, Kadi, I think he will like this, it's mainstream glam,' I said.

But Luuk's face fell when he picked me up at the airport. 'But your African look is the best, the braids are beautiful, I like even more the cornrows.'

I like even more the cornrows. What a confidence tonic a man's words could be. We're told to find it within ourselves, and some people can, like Omelogor, but I viewed myself with more esteem because Luuk liked the way I looked. *I like even more the cornrows.* I wore heels and the dresses he bought, low cut but tastefully so, and I smiled through the surprise of some people who met us, because I was not what they expected for him. In every gathering, he set out to win over everyone, his head bobbing above the room. The appeal of his lithe and sinewy height, the undeniable lustre of his charm, the boom of his laugh. Men liked his directness, how he said 'fucker' when nobody expected it. Women were attracted to him; they signalled possibility, even availability, and made innocuous comments syrupy with other meanings. He flattered and flirted, always lightly, to show that his devotion was cleanly mine. *I like even more the cornrows.* Sometimes the success of other men became a personal affront to him, and he was quick to read meaning into their actions or words.

'He said it's tough with a Fortune 500, the fucker. That's a dig at me. Doesn't he know what net we posted? Just because they are listed higher?' he said, on our drive back from the gala.

'I don't think he meant it that way, Luuk,' I said, consoling.

'Did you see how he shook my hand? Like "I am superior,"' he said.

'No, actually I think he admires you. You're younger than him and you're about to become the big star in Amsterdam.'

'You think so?'

'Yes. And he's jealous that he can't dress like you. Boxy American suits are terrible, but his takes the cake.'

Luuk liked that, and laughed. I knew he would; he noticed men's watches, ties, things. He'd bought his first iPad because one day at an airport lounge, he was reading the pink pages of the *Financial Times* and noticed the men around him were all reading the newspaper on their iPads. And he felt stupid. When he told me this story, I told him he shouldn't have felt stupid and those men probably thought he was a cool contrarian, and anyway you read more widely with an actual newspaper than with the clear-cut sections of apps. So strange how we wade through life's swamps thinking our insecurities are unique to us. If I had been watching Luuk as a stranger from afar, I would not think he cared about using the device which other men had. His excitements seemed considered, curated, like his magpie hoard of watches. 'Like it?' he would say about a new watch. I didn't know much about expensive watches; they all looked the same to me, with their artisanal cluttered faces.

'Very nice,' I would say. 'I think my father has something like this.'

His daysailer was the only thing he owned that wasn't the latest. I liked going because it was the one thing I felt made him shed his self-consciousness, he wasn't watching for other people's reactions, wasn't noticing or comparing. I would watch him, my life jacket wrapped tight, feeling unsteady as I had never been sailing before. His deft manoeuvring, the rippling leanness of his raised arms, and I thought here was a person doing something that brought him pure joy. I thought it made him happy, too, when we stayed in his house in Monterrey, swimming and lounging, the pool unfathomably blue in the sunlight. Or when we sat in his grassy garden in Mexico City surrounded by birdsong. He said 'our house' and he said 'we' and I said 'we' too, and I liked our both saying 'we', even though sometimes I felt myself loitering on the edges of this shared life.

One day he came back from work springy on his feet with childish excitement because the egomaniac company chairman was finally leaving and, in a few months, he would move back to Amsterdam and take over.

'Very soon, when I travel together with you, no more flying commercial!' he said.

I smiled, swinging on the verandah hammock, and wished for him that it mattered to me. His housekeeper Yatzil appeared with a tray. She worshipped him, bloomed under his teasing and his praise, and each day she tried to outdo herself, with yet another fresh fruit plate, another freshly cooked mole sauce. She always looked at me with suspicion-sharpened eyes, as if distrustful of my intentions towards Luuk. I wondered if it was me, or if she would be that way with any other woman. In all the time I spent with Luuk, she smiled at me only once, a short smile quickly sucked back as if she had betrayed herself. She'd brought a plate of fruit, guanabana and mamey and mangoes, and I said, 'Thank you so much, Yatzil. I love guanabana! When I was growing up, we had the trees and we always tried to let them get ripe and soft but also pluck them before the birds could get at them. Sometimes we were too late and we would have to cut off the parts with holes from the birds. This one is so nice and fresh! Soursop, it's called soursop in English.'

Her smile saw me differently, for once, a person with a story, with family and trees in a country, and not just Luuk's woman.

Luuk said, 'Yatzil brought it especially for you.' He was blind to Yatzil's distrust, and was convinced she liked me. I didn't correct him. I didn't mind her dislike, I understood it, but it would upset Luuk if he knew, because he liked things to be as he had decided they were.

HE WAS READING a glossy travel magazine, and he tore out a page, and said, 'This is the place to go this year. They say all the fashionable set is going this summer.'

I mock-groaned. 'Not another top place to go, please.' We had gone to the US Virgin Islands because a magazine said it was the top place to go. He wanted fashionable and I wanted interesting.

'Okay, you choose between these two.'

'No, you choose,' I said. 'Wherever you decide, it has to be after I come back from Ramallah.'

'If you get the visa, no?' he said.

'Luuk! That isn't very hopeful.'

'Well . . .' He shrugged and laughed.

He didn't want me to go to Palestine. 'It's all too sad,' he'd said when I told him I wanted to write about the restaurants and food scene in Ramallah.

'I wonder what it's like, somebody who wants to visit your country has to get permission from another country,' I said.

'Horrible,' he said. He peered at my laptop screen, a YouTube documentary about the Deir Yassin massacre.

'I need to know a bit of the history,' I said.

'Okay. Enough of this. We watch something more uplifting now, okay?'

'I know you don't mean a comedy,' I said. I teased him about liking comedies too much. When he went diving, he took his phone, caged in a waterproof box, so he could watch comedies during long decompression stops. I imagined him deep in the sea watching *Fawlty Towers* as seahorses floated past. Sometimes I felt his life was lived as though in flight from sorrow. He was a restless, jerky sleeper. He woke me often, his body twitching as if in some internal rebellion, and I would hold and soothe him until his movements ceased.

LUUK MARVELLED AT my relationship with my parents. When I talked on the phone with them, he would come by from time to time, shaking his head in amazement. 'Talking for so long? And laughing like this?'

'My mother is such a talker,' I said. 'My father talks a bit too but not like her. How was your dad?'

'He never talked. He preferred action. More efficient, you know?'

'How?'

'This is the best example. One day he pushed my head into a dustbin on our street and told me if I ever got a girl pregnant, he would make me eat the rubbish.'

Luuk roared with that laughter of his. I watched him, thinking about the uses of laughter. Laughter as shield. Laughter as deflector.

'When did he die?'

'Seven years now.'

'Is – was – your mother a talker? I mean, before.' I was stumbling to be tactful about his mother's dementia.

'Even less.' He paused, as if about to say more, before he abruptly changed the subject and asked when his bestie Omelogor was coming so he could finally take her skydiving. It hadn't surprised me how easily they became friends when they met. Omelogor said Luuk was a Nigerian born in a European body, down to his strong cologne, and Luuk smiled, pleased. It was in New York. Omelogor had come for a conference and I was with Luuk on a business trip. We were in Luuk's hotel suite. Luuk got a message saying his wife's friend had passed out while skydiving in Switzerland.

'At one thousand feet!' he said, as if we would understand whether that was good or bad.

'Did she die?' I asked.

'No, she's recovering.'

Omelogor said, 'I don't understand why people jump out of planes.' Which made Luuk laugh. 'You're very direct, no?' he said to Omelogor, and I said, 'Maybe she's a Dutch woman born into a Nigerian body', and Omelogor gave me a look filled with knives.

'I'll take you skydiving and you'll see why,' Luuk said. 'Gravity is very powerful. It makes you know we are very small on this earth.'

'I know that already,' Omelogor said.

At some point she asked Luuk, 'Where did you learn about sex?' The question she was asking everybody.

She had asked Zikora, and Zikora primly said from books, offended that Omelogor had assumed it was from pornography.

'But Zik, we were all curious as kids,' I said.

'I never watched blue films,' she said. She had a puritanical strain, Zikora, and had life gone as she wanted, she might have been extremely conservative, leery of openness.

Luuk's response to Omelogor's question was 'This is not something I have thought of.'

'You must have seen a film or a dirty magazine when you were a teenager,' she said.

'But learning from it? I don't know, maybe I learned from practice?'

Luuk glanced at me, jokingly clamped his hands over his ears, and said, 'I don't remember now!'

WHEN LUUK FINALLY told me about his mother, I remembered how quickly he used to change the subject. I was at the time fascinated by the shifting places of Europe. This town used to be Romanian, now it is Ukrainian or Hungarian; that one used to be in Germany but now is in Poland. The towns didn't move, of course, the borders did, and you could leave your home in one country and return to the same home, many years later, now in another country. Alsace-Lorraine was in Germany after one war and then in France after another, back in Germany during the Second World War and then again in France after it ended. Did their souls sway from side to side? What did they do with their passports? I might want to keep old ones, to make it easier in case the borders shifted again. At a restaurant, I tried discreetly to tell who was a tourist and who was a local bearing the history of two nations. I wandered through quaint villages, past half-timbered houses that looked as if transported from a benign fairy tale; I would feel claustrophobic living in them. Storks had built their tall nests on some of the roofs, piled-high twigs and sticks and grass, and I saw a few of the birds in majestic flight, wings widely spread, gliding through the air. The driver I hired for the day talked endlessly about storks and repeated things he had said before: storks are mute and clap their beaks to communicate, storks are faithful to their nests and not to their mates, in local lore storks bring good luck. I said how charming it was, and laughter erupted from him when I asked: with storks on their roof, did they wake up to see bird droppings splattered everywhere?

Later he slipped out of his tour-guide persona and told me the underground champagne tour was boring and I would get cold. Still, I went, and halfway through I was shivering, made worse by a stomach roiling from the quiche in a quaint restaurant. There was altogether too much quaintness all around. The driver said there was a literary festival in a small town in the heart of the Black Forest, and we drove an hour there, but heard only the tail end of a Slovenian poet reading his ironic poems. Afterwards I walked around the streets; further away from the centre the houses leaned closer together. The locals stared at me with eyes shorn of warmth. There weren't many; I walked past a dozen people maybe. A woman that made me think of a babushka character in a film slowed to look me over, her eyes scanning my head to my feet. I saw one Black person at the literary festival but none on the streets. If there were no Black people here, why were they hostile instead of just curious? Already I had an idea for my article. 'Feeling Black in the Black Forest.' I told Luuk about it, saying, 'I wonder where their view of Black people comes from', and I said this mildly, but redness crept up his neck and he burst out, 'Germany is terrible, terrible! How can you ask where they get this racism? Look at what they did!'

'Well, good thing I didn't turn and walk away when we first met, because I thought you were German. You sounded German,' I teased.

'No!' he said, unsmiling. 'You know where these fuckers killed the highest number of Jews in Western Europe? Holland.'

His expression confused me, a deep disruption of his well-being that I had not at all expected. 'Luuk, darling, I'm sorry. I didn't mean to upset you,' I said.

He shook his head as if to shake away his distraught.

'My grandmother, the mother of my mother, had a Nazi lover during the war. You know of the Dutch women they punished when we were liberated? They beat them and paraded them on the streets and shaved off their hair, and poured sticky black tar on their bodies and all this. My grandmother was one of them. She was pregnant with my mother. Nobody talked about it. I was a teenager when I found this out, after a relative of my father said something rude about my mother.'

I stared at him, stunned, uncertain what to say.

'My brother still says the German lover was not our grandfather. He says it was the Dutch soldier our grandmother was engaged to.

This Dutch soldier died early in the war, in 1940. My mother was born in 1945. Can you imagine? Now we perform miracles in my family.' He snorted and I came close and held him and leaned into his warmth. Was it what made him turn himself into this polished pot of charm, that he grew up with inherited shame? Or was I drawing a too simple line? But much of our lives could be explained by drawing simple lines; we inherit our parents' scars more often than we know.

'Our house always smelled of blood sausages,' he said. 'My mother kept a tidy house and she knitted and she cooked, and all the time the house smells of these blood sausages.'

I did not know how Dutch blood sausages in the 1970s smelled, but when we went to Holland and drove past his childhood home in Haarlem, I imagined the smell of blood sausages in the air.

He pointed. 'The dustbin was just there. The one my father pushed my head into.'

We visited his mother in a nursing home, in a sad room with small windows, armchairs upholstered in faded print. His mother no longer recognized him. She looked blankly at him with her rheumy blue eyes. He gave her a bouquet of tulips and she took them, and placed them on her lap. I wanted to leave the room to give them privacy even if she no longer recognized him, but he said no and tightly held my hand. She was well looked after, her thinning silver hair clean and carefully brushed. I looked at her and imagined her childhood spent in a cloud of shame. Was it a relief to be separated from her mind, unable to remember her wounded past? Before we left, I moved closer and hugged her, and afterwards I wasn't sure why I had. She neither shrank away nor hugged me back. In the car, Luuk's eyes were wet. 'Your African warmness, so touching. I'm so happy I came together with you.'

His sombre tone, the whole visit, had unsettled me.

'"Together with,"' I mimicked him. 'It's so cute how you say that: "together with".'

'Is it wrong?'

'I mean, you could just say "with".'

'Then I will stop saying "together with".'

'No, don't stop, it's very cute.'

———

BRECHTJE HAD BEEN UNWELL, and he wanted to visit her before we left Holland. Did I mind? he asked, as if he wanted me to mind. He suggested what I might do while he was gone: a massage at the hotel spa, or the driver could take me shopping? I trailed my fingers against his cheek and said, 'Luuk, my darling, I don't mind. I think it's nice that you're going to see her.'

'I will tell Brechtje about you. You are not the reason we cannot come back, of course. But she deserves to know,' he said.

I felt almost guilty, imagining this woman Brechtje, dark-haired and curvy and pretty in her photos, and her son who called Luuk Papa, both bereft, still holding on to hope – and now, on his first visit back since he left for Mexico, to hear about another woman in his life. The finality, the blow of it.

'Maybe don't tell her, not now. I can imagine she'll be very upset.'

'She will feel even worse to know you are Black.'

Silence followed, echoed by more silence. I said nothing because I didn't know what to say. His honesty moved me and his honesty disgusted me. What in her layers of humanness, what vital lack, what yawning void, would make her feel worse that I was Black?

'Always she says it's the Black people who make noise on the trains, and she doesn't mind the Turkish or Surinamese so much, but the Moroccan boys and the Black boys . . . You know about Black Pete in Holland? She said these people should stop complaining about the tradition, because the skin is black from the chimney. I was asking, but why do the lips look so big, is that also from the chimney?' Luuk sounded triumphant. He was the story's unstained hero, the righteous one, and that was all that mattered. He couldn't see how I would see it. And what was to be said of his virtue if Brechtje could tell him these things?

'No, I don't know about this Black Pete,' I said, even though I knew, and I changed the subject to suggest we get a couples massage when he came back. Some surfaces I prefer to leave alone because I fear what I will find underneath.

When he came back, he looked drained, a bluish tinge under his eyes. He said, 'She would not stop crying.'

I felt a flash of pity for her and then annoyed with Luuk for telling me this, and other things.

'Luuk, I don't need to know more about Brechtje.'

'I want to share everything with you.'

Now I felt ungracious. Was this not what women wanted, a man who did not build walls? And yet I did not want to hear another word. He wanted to show me the gardens at Keukenhof, and we walked around the landscape's vibrant palette, the flower-rich scents of spring and the flowers themselves, splashes of colour lifting my spirits. In the evening, we met his brother at a restaurant, which felt like walking into softness, with muted piano music and a large cluster of modern chandeliers glistening above. Willem. A flicker crossed his face when we stood up to greet him. Surprise, confused surprise. Luuk had not told him I was African. He said hello and nice to meet you and we ordered wine. We sat by the window, below us the shimmering vista of Amsterdam, miles of lights spread out like spilled jewels. The air between the brothers was mildly charged with malice. Luuk the older and more successful, his brother playing catch-up; he, too, alarmingly tall, but fleshier than Luuk. Willem said he had been to a new restaurant in London last week. Luuk said, yes, he knew the restaurant, not bad, two Michelin stars. No, three stars, Willem said. Their teenage rivalry had ripened but never burst open to free them. Willem said something in Dutch and Luuk replied, his voice a low growl that I had never heard before. Willem stiffened and drank his wine and then turned to me, to dispel their tension.

'Have you had a chance to see our beautiful city?' he asked me.

Why did Europeans do that? They called their cities beautiful, as if you had no choice but to agree with them. I liked Nigeria well enough but I didn't expect others to, and so I could not understand this European conceit. I always said yes and agreed that the city was beautiful, even if I didn't think it was. But something about Willem irked me. After our initial hellos, he had not addressed me, had barely looked at me, and as he spoke to Luuk, he didn't include me in the sweep of his gaze. This sudden interest was incidental and insincere. He merely needed an emergency buffer between him and his brother, and anybody at that moment would do. Even a dog or a cat would do. Something alive to which he could deflect. And I could not help thinking of the woman I did not know, Brechtje, and merging them both in my imagination. They probably got along well.

'Have you had a chance to see our beautiful city?' he repeated, unnecessarily; perhaps he also thought I was slow at comprehension.

'Yes, this isn't my first time,' I said brightly. 'Amsterdam has such a mouldy charm.'

His brows furrowed. 'Mouldy?' He glanced at Luuk, to confirm the English meaning. 'You mean like mould?'

'Yes,' I said.

Luuk burst out laughing and his laughter was a rain of darts aimed at his brother. His brother colored. I felt remorse, and then rebuked myself for wanting to appease this man who clearly had no use for me.

'That was a poor joke,' I said, even though I did think of Amsterdam as a place of mouldy charm: the canals and the houses near them looked as if they could benefit from a vigorous wash. 'The architecture is beautiful. Something so confident about canal houses.'

'Yes,' he said, instantly mollified; he really wasn't the brightest of people.

For the rest of the dinner, Luuk talked and talked, giving Willem a litany of his successes, asking me some details he pretended not to remember while I mostly looked down at Amsterdam's lights. 'Were we in Monterrey or at the retreat in Bermuda when the *Harvard Business Review* list of best-performing CEOs came out?' he asked. I said we were in Bermuda.

On our way back to the hotel, I asked Luuk, 'What did your brother say that made you angry?'

He shrugged my question away. 'Oh, just one of his stupid things. You know, I don't tell him now when I buy a new car because he tries to buy the same car too, and he can't afford it, of course.'

———

ON THE MORNING of our last day in Holland, we took a walk to a café, and ahead of us was an elderly White couple, both silver-haired and slightly stooped. They walked slowly, hand in hand, and then stopped at the same time to look at a shop window. They said little, their faces mere inches apart. They looked at the shop window for a while and then continued walking, his foot rising as hers fell. There was between them a quality of gentle, long-lasting collusion; each knew the other in a way that nobody else in the world did. Watching them, I began to cry.

Luuk noticed my tears. 'Chia? What's wrong?'

I shook my head.

'Is it cramps?' he asked, and drew me close. 'Let's go to this one for tea, something hot? Or turn back so I can give you a back rub at the hotel?'

He had read up about premenstrual dysphoric disorder and on my bad days would make me tea, rub my back, coax me into move-ment. 'Just walk with me around the pool,' he'd say, slowing his nor-mal lope.

'Yes, let's go back to the hotel,' I said, letting him believe my tears were from hormones rather than from the sudden overwhelming melancholy of seeing what I so longed to have and feared I never would. Later, as Luuk and I drove to the airport, I looked out of the window, at the almost provincial calm, the women pushing strollers in the afternoon, on their day off from their part-time jobs. Already I felt the sting of loneliness. I could never be happy here.

We flew to Mexico City and then on to Monterrey. On the plane, a man seated across the aisle looked often at me, a Mexican man with black hair a little too long, a rakish man, his shirt unbuttoned, a scarf wound carelessly around his neck. He smiled at me, like a man eager to shrug off an old life, and I smiled back. I imagined a new life with him, each day filled with excitement's beating heart. We landed and I watched him hug an autistic little boy at baggage claim; the boy's repetitive hand movements, his open innocent face, filled me with shame for daring to long for a man so needed by his child.

'Ready?' Luuk asked, after loading both our suitcases in a cart. He looked quizzical, as if he sensed my new reserve. In the lavish hum of our life together, I had felt like a spectator, sated and satisfied, but a spectator still. We were not at the end but I knew, that day at the airport in Monterrey, that we were almost at the end.

Two

In the final days of lockdown, I lay in bed thinking of all the things I left unsaid throughout the years, and all my futures that never were. Why do we remember what we remember? Which reels from our past assert their vivid selves and which remain dim, just out of reach? I remembered some fleeting encounters so clearly that I wondered if the remembering itself was significant. The Qatari man in London who I met at Harrods, of all places, who said he had come to pick up his sister. 'Hey gorgeous' was his greeting. It sounded so contrived that it was interesting. *Hey gorgeous*. Maybe he thought this was what you said to a woman, a Black woman, you had run into, and then impulsively decided to talk to, at Harrods.

'I just want to let you know, you're beautiful,' he said.

He looked younger than me, his skin unusually clear, as though smoothed all over with foundation. The trendy hip-hop stir about him, his expensive sporty clothes and enormous sneakers should have put me off. But as he spoke, I thought his Arabic accent was the sexiest accent in the world, and I did not want him to stop talking, and I imagined other things said in that accent. He was nervous, moving his big shiny phone from hand to hand. His nervousness enchanted me because it spoke of things unpractised. His sister was upstairs and he asked if I would give him my number, and I said, smiling, 'Go get your sister first', because I wanted to be flirtatious and mysterious. He hesitated. It was the smallest of silences, but in that delay of time came a dawning; I remembered somebody once saying Arab men date Black women, but only in secret.

'Okay, see you in a bit, yeah?' he said, and then added, 'Promise you won't go anywhere.'

He turned to go upstairs and I walked to the exit and out into the street. That hesitation, his brief debate with uncertainty, meant he didn't want his sister to see me. Later I wondered if he returned to roam the halls of Harrods looking for me. What if I had been wrong and he hesitated only because he feared I might leave without giving him my number? Why hadn't I just given him my number, and given it a chance?

And there was the man from Argentina with a Danish surname who I met in Santiago. His craggy face spoke of time in the harsh outdoors; he climbed mountains and played football. At a bar we playfully bantered about the Argentina and Nigeria football teams. 'You're good but we're better,' he said, and I said, 'No we are better, we just don't have organization', and he said, 'Yes, which means we are better.' He was impressed that I knew so much about football.

'I have two brothers,' I said. 'I'll never forget the day Nigeria beat Argentina in the Atlanta Olympics. I felt like I was floating in the air.'

'Jay-Jay and Kanu! I cannot ever forgive that team.'

'Our Dream Team!'

'You must visit Argentina again,' he said. 'I'll show you a game.'

'I've actually been thinking of going to Bariloche, just to see the lakes, but I heard that's where all the Nazis from Germany escaped to. Will I make it out alive if I go?' I teased.

'I'll protect you,' he said, and his knee grazed mine.

We were flirting and I liked the light-hearted air, and wanted to keep it that way, but two drinks in and he became intense, moving too close, his eyes a washed-out grey.

'I am looking at a beautiful woman. A very beautiful woman. You know what we both want.'

'What?'

'You know what we want. You know. Do you want to go to my hotel or I come to yours?'

How quickly the delicate threads of promise turn crude and bristly. A pall came over me. Had I given a wrong signal? But how and when? I was flirting and open, not sure where it would end, waiting to see, but he already saw an end and presumably thought I did too. Everything was spoiled. The bar's dimness had become a shadowy threat.

I said, 'I need the toilet, I'll be right back.'

'I can watch your bag, you don't need to take it with you,' he said.

I stuttered and said, 'Oh, I just need my hand cream.' Had he been menacing? Was he trying to control me, to keep me from leaving? I walked towards the toilet and then cut to the door and left the bar. Later I asked myself if perhaps the failure of that day had been a failure of language – my Spanish was poor, his English was functional, and he paused often to search for words. Had I misunderstood him, and had I missed out?

There was a Kenyan man I met on an Ethiopian Airlines flight. When we boarded in Addis, he asked the flight attendant if she had a pen. His voice attracted me, polite and confident, with that elegance of Eastern African English. I said hello and offered him my pen, and then felt shy and retreated behind my iPad. I had never said hello first, never offered a pen to a stranger. He asked if he could ask me my name, which amused me. 'Is it all right for me to ask your name?' He pronounced Chiamaka perfectly.

'I have never met an African travel writer,' he said warmly. He didn't know whether I was any good and already he was approving. 'We need African travel writers to write about Africa. There are many terrible travel books about Kenya written by people who in this day and age still call Kenya "Kee-nya".'

Why didn't I go to more African countries? I had visited only three. I told him I loved Accra, that gentle city, and Dakar, for its understanding of beauty for beauty's sake, and Abidjan's poise, on an uprise, expanding and spreading, its roads pothole-free. Soon the air radiated with our mutual interest in each other. He said he was a businessman and he dabbled a bit in political affairs, and from the practised modesty in his tone, I sensed he was famous. A thin band glowed on his forefinger. He talked about Africa, how we neglect the riches of our past and we don't sell our glorious myths and we stunt our imaginations.

'We need regional currencies. Imagine what would be unleashed if we had properly structured intracontinental trade and travel . . .'

His words shimmered. They stirred me, and I resolved to visit as many African countries as I could, to do better by our continent. He grew more attractive as he talked, the stately silhouette of his face in profile, his high forehead and high cheekbones.

'Gikuyu culture is very similar to Igbo culture, in so many ways,' he said suggestively, and I welcomed all the possible suggestions in his words. Yet when we landed at Dulles, I hurried out of the plane before him, and rushed down the taxi ramp, as I had not checked bags.

It was not long after Darnell, my mouth still rank from the after-taste of him, and the Kenyan was an academic like Darnell, even though he did not brandish his knowledge, as Darnell did. I should have waited to exchange numbers. Because of him I went to see the ruins of Gede. I would forgo a light-hearted take and do something weighty in Africa, and what better than a thriving African town from the twelfth century. I planned to go to Robben Island after Gede and already I imagined an article about Mandela being a product of a rich cosmopolitan past. The Kenyan, if he read it, would be impressed. The Kenyan embassy had extra checks for Nigerian passports and by the time my visa was out, I couldn't do South Africa too, as their process was even worse. (Later, I decided it was silly to treat Africa differently by writing solemnly of only serious things, and on my next trip, to Zambia, I visited restaurants.)

At Gede, the tour guide, a skinny intense man from Mombasa, led us almost reluctantly through the faded ruins, mumbling and pointing. Three Black Americans, one Jamaican, and one white Englishwoman. The Jamaican was talking about his next trip, to Ethiopia.

'What did you say that was?' the Englishwoman asked the tour guide, pointing at what seemed to me a stump. He mumbled something and the woman asked, 'Are you sure? What?'

'Toilet! Modern toilet!' the tour guide barked, and I jumped. 'You think you invented the toilet? We did in Africa!'

From mumbling to ferocious rage in seconds and he didn't care about our shock.

'We invented the toilet in Africa!' he repeated, and turned to me, his African sister, with a look that said, 'These people.' I nodded in solidarity. I dared not show my amusement. I understood that his anger was for her question and for a thousand other sneers. How long had he led tours in which sun-flushed foreigners wearing linen and sandals challenged what he said? Strangely, it was with the fleeting Kenyan man on the plane that I imagined sharing this story. I would repeat, 'We invented the toilet in Africa!' And we would laugh, intimate, knowing laughter, the kind to be laughed only among Africans.

My clearest memory was the oldest, of the young Indian man in a video shop in Lagos. His heavy lidded eyes, half-closed, as though he was eternally dreaming. He was tall and brown and handsome, his head very full of very black hair, and he was looking at me; I turned each time and caught his eye. Video shops have disappeared because videocassettes have disappeared, but the memory remains, of his eyes, and of the shelves stacked with tapes. There is looking and there is looking; one objectifies and the other dignifies. I looked at him and then hurriedly away, because I had a sudden intense urge to cry. The longing in his eyes, so wistful and wasted. Would he melt away from his friends and come to talk to me? Of course he wouldn't. Omelogor was done with the videotapes she wanted to borrow and said, 'Chia! Let's go!' General Abacha's government had just murdered Ken Saro-Wiwa and we were all sad, but Omelogor was behaving as if she had personally known him, snappy and sulky with everyone. It was just before I left for my A levels in England. Uncle Nwoye was on sabbatical at the University of Lagos and they lived in a small gated house in Ilupeju. They called Ilupeju Little India; on the street corner hawkers sold unfamiliar squashes that only the Indians bought.

'Chia!' Omelogor said.

I left with her, reluctantly, and I wanted to turn back and look at him but I didn't. I never forgot his eyes. We went back to the video shop some days later and I lingered until Omelogor asked what was wrong with me. Years later, in Delhi, the men startled me with their looking, and I thought of the guy with the half-closed eyes in the video shop in Ilupeju. An online magazine refused to publish my piece on Delhi unless I removed the sentence *The men stared at me in a way I have never been stared at before, a hard, barefaced staring, not with harmless admiration but with a darkness that frightened me.* I removed the sentence and they published it.

THREE

Lockdown was over and I walked and wandered outside. Cars on the windy suburban road, a tree aflame with flowers, a trilling in the grass. I walked on the trail and walking ahead of me was a man who stopped briefly to look at a bird on a tree and I thought how wonderful it was to stop on a walk to look at a bird. We were still alert to small wonders. Life might yet be life again. I called Omelogor and told her maybe life would be normal again, and she said, 'Yes, let's dream it into being.'

'Stop laughing at me.'

'I just fired Paul. He's been stealing from me for a long time, but this time I had had it. Why would you open cartons of milk that you're supposed to deliver to the motherless babies home, and take half the contents and seal it back? And he didn't have any real remorse, the idiot.'

Beneath Omelogor's tough tone, I heard a kind of hurt.

'He'll come begging and say "for the sake of my wife and daughter", and you'll shout and shout and then you'll take him back.'

Omelogor snorted. The last time I visited her, before Christmas, Paul always seemed nervy and jumpy, as if on the cusp of committing a crime. Omelogor mocked me whenever I said Nigeria has a smell but it does. Especially Lagos, the smell of layers of rot, clogged gutters and sewage, salty wind from the ocean. This time I thought Abuja smelled of space – wide open vistas, the feeling of generous air, and more of it to breathe. I saw why Omelogor had settled here, Lagos no longer in her plan. She took me to work, showing me off, saying 'This is my cousin Chia', first to her boss, the smallish man she called CEO. On office doors, she rapped, opened and entered, all in one fluid movement, not pausing to be asked in. One of the managers looked up from his desk, annoyed, and I felt uncomfortable to be the reason for her barging in.

Still, he forced a smile, accommodating her. Observing Omelogor's power brought an intense flush of pride: she could not be dismissed or ignored. She roused strong emotions in people – admiration and aversion, envy and devotion – but never the graveyard of indifference. Even those who disliked her listened to her. Her life felt so charmed. The eclectic circle of friends at dinner, some with that ferocious stylishness of Nigerian women that made me dizzy and unsure where to focus, on their impossibly swingy wigs, or on their mask-like make-up with severely drawn brows, or on the clothes, fitted, sparkly, sweeping the floor.

After dinner, they played charades and truth or dare in her living room. They spoke of their domestic help with languid disdain. Halfway through dinner, Ejiro went out to the balcony to roll a joint; they called it Loud. Omelogor once said that at Ejiro's birthday party, waiters circulated every half hour with trays of cocktail glasses, a single white pill in each glass. Every thirty minutes.

'It was almost as if they couldn't bear a moment being under the influence of just themselves,' Omelogor said.

'I didn't know Abuja was so full of drugs,' I said.

'Chia, you make it sound like some kind of den of extreme iniquity.'

'I mean stories like that sound more like Lagos.'

'Well, it's not like people are staggering around here high every day.'

That defensive tone, unusual for her, was because of Hauwa, her friend, her newish friend. The friendship surprised me, such an unlikely closeness, lightweight and heavyweight. There was something of a small bird about Hauwa, a bright-coloured girly bird, quick and pretty, never perching for long enough to be known. I thought Omelogor would find her depthless and uninteresting. But affection always blurs sight. Hauwa was texting her driver to ask him to buy shortbread biscuits. 'I have to send him a picture or you can be sure he will come back with bread,' she said, not the funniest thing but Omelogor laughed a proud laugh, as if to say, 'Look how funny Hauwa is.'

Omelogor had asked if I wanted to come on a day trip to Igboland, to distribute her grants. Of course I did, a thrill rising in me. To be part of my cousin's magical boldness, taking stolen money to redistribute to the poor. ('Couldn't you have called the company something else?' I asked when she first told me about it, and she said, 'A certain level of brazenness should be kept brazen all the way.')

Then she said Hauwa wanted to come, too.

'She knows about Robyn Hood?' I asked, upset, surprised by how upset I was. 'You hardly know her.'

'What do you mean I hardly know her?' Omelogor snapped. 'You think I now can't tell who to trust?'

Anyway, Hauwa did not come with us, something about her husband being back in town, and she rarely went out when he was in town. In Owerri, we stopped at the bank on Douglas road, for Omelogor to get more cash, a high pile of disgusting refuse piled beside the bank building with its modern metallic sheen. One of the tellers recognized Omelogor, their famous expert in Abuja branch, and soon the branch manager wanted to say hello to her. We sat on overstuffed sofas in his office, the tall piles of files on his desk felt ancient, a relic from pre-computer times.

'We actually have two branches on Douglas road,' the manager was saying, and Omelogor cut him short and said, 'Douglas was an English colonial officer who murdered hundreds of Igbo people, and we then named the biggest road in a state capital after him. The enduring stupidity of the colonized.'

'Well,' the manager said, looking bemused. 'You know they don't want us to learn our history.'

'Who is "they"? You think anybody cares enough to invent a conspiracy to keep you away from your history? Go and learn your history. It's not anybody's responsibility to teach you.'

Now he was taken aback. 'Ahn-ahn, are we quarrelling?' he asked.

'Do you want us to quarrel?' she responded, suggestive and combative, and I saw him dissolving before her as men always did. I saw his eyes stray, and his mind collapse into imagination; she saw it too, and later she asked me playfully, 'Should I explore him?'

She was in a bad mood and it had to do with Hauwa, my questioning about Hauwa, but I was not sure how. I was thinking of how to ask her, how to clear the air between us. In the car, after she had given money to eleven women, Omelogor said, 'Hauwa doesn't actually know the details of Robyn Hood. She thinks it's just my money.'

'Okay,' I said, waiting for more.

'You were right to question how much she knows. I shouldn't have snapped. Only you and Chijioke know the details.'

'Okay.'

'You don't like her,' Omelogor said.

'No, it's not that.' I paused. 'Well, there isn't much to like or dislike.'

'Ouch!' Omelogor said, laughing, and the tension was lifted. It was then that she asked, about the manager at the bank, 'Should I explore him?'

That evening she sent him a text asking if he wanted to come to her hotel room, and of course he did, and she emerged in the morning looking refreshed and amused.

'When men say they would have married you, do they ever wonder if you would have married them?' she asked me.

'At least he'll get his two weeks,' I said.

'He lacks intellectual curiosity,' she said and I began to laugh.

'So no two weeks for him?'

Omelogor is made differently. Her short passion attacks fascinate me. But if I lived like that, my heart would be a desert, struck by insatiable thirst, eternally unfulfilled.

'BUT SERIOUSLY, don't you ever dream of an entirely different life?' I asked Omelogor at the end of lockdown.

'Not an impractical one,' she said. 'Although Aunty Jane really shook me when she said my life is empty.'

'It shook you because you do dream of wanting to be known,' I said.

'Chiamaka, stop looking for a partner in your madness. And what does it actually *mean* to be known? You want somebody to study you and cram you like a textbook?'

'Yes, and anticipate me.'

'Anticipate you.'

'If you live your life and die without one person fully knowing you, then have you even lived?'

'Well, I know you fully.'

'It has to be romantic.'

'Why?'

'It just has to be.'

'Your thesis is falling apart. So you're not looking to be known, on principle; you're looking for a heterosexual man who will study you like a textbook.'

'It doesn't sound as nice when you say it like that.'

We were both laughing and I thought of how much I had missed my cousin, how I longed to hug her again.

'I really wasted time with Darnell,' I said. 'His ex was cutting herself, a woman clearly in pain, and he turned it into glamour and I actually felt bad that I wasn't like her.'

'Your voice just changed.'

'What?'

'Talking about Darnell, your voice just changed.'

'Why was he even with me? He didn't even like me. Why be with someone just to be cruel to them?'

'Don't you Americans say that everything is the fault of the parents? Maybe they didn't hug him every night before bed.'

'His family was solid. His mother was lovely and had a hair salon. His father adored him and kept a stable job in the Water Department.'

'Chia, you're not asking yourself why *you* were with him.'

'What do you mean?'

'You're allowed to be victim and something else, not just victim. If you can take some responsibility, if you can say, "Okay, he was cruel but I allowed him to be cruel", then you can also say, "Next time I will not allow a man to be cruel."'

'I've always known I allowed things I should not have allowed,' I said, feeling chastised. 'But it's because I believe that love must ask something of us.'

'That man did not deserve to tie your shoelaces. Remember your Swedish Nazi? How you said your break-up was nice?'

'What? Oh, Johan.'

'Ahn-ahn. How can you have forgotten somebody you said you would marry?'

'I never said that.'

'You did. Until his friend defended the Holocaust or something.'

'I said it was easy being with him. And he is not a Nazi!' I was laughing.

'So you didn't look him up?'

'No.'

'Your dream count is incomplete, then!'

FOUR

Why had I forgotten Johan? The Swedish man with a long torso who looked like a pale European gazelle would, if such a thing existed. I sent Omelogor a photo of him and she wrote back, 'Englishman has permanently changed your spec.'

Loudly I protested but quietly I wondered. After Luuk, and here I was with another tall, thin White man. Johan was blond, with the throwaway air of an adventurer who could live for weeks on a single backpack. He was not made for permanence of any kind, and I felt from the beginning that we were sailing on the surface because there was no option of depth.

'Do you know of the saying that romantic love lasts three years?' he asked, as though to prepare me, even though we barely lasted a year, both of us benignly watching as the seams of our relationship came apart. With him I had a rare moment of feeling known, while walking about fruit and vegetable stalls in a farmers' market, the air smelling of the rightness of imperfect things.

'Which do I like, peaches or nectarines?' I asked him. I could not remember.

'Nectarines. You don't like how fuzzy peaches are,' he said, and in that moment, there was splendour all around.

We met at a book festival in Brooklyn, during a travel-writing panel that turned out to be insipid. The moderator talked about himself for too long, while the panellists sat uncomfortably silent, one doodling on the back cover of his book. Johan was next to me and he whispered, 'Somebody should shut that man up', and I had the sensation of being alone with him in that room filled with people. His front tooth was missing, and each time he smiled I tried not to focus on the square hole. It was from an accident, he said. He had cracked his skull and, after surgery and complications, a lost tooth seemed inconsequential. The accident had shaken him into clarity, and he saw how skeletal his routines were, how he was living like a person waiting to live. He left his culture job at a newspaper in Stockholm, went freelance and began travelling.

'I could have died without having done any of the things I really wanted to do,' he said.

I felt that I understood this sentiment and, therefore, understood him.

He laughed at my jokes and often said, 'You're so funny.' I was not that funny – I could not possibly be, perhaps he didn't know any really funny people – but I basked in this, my image as a funny person, my ability to so easily make him laugh. When we talked of travel, our words came rushing out, eager to share and compare, under the enchantment of a mutual passion.

'Trieste? You went to Trieste?' he asked.

'Yes,' I said. 'I read this Jan Morris book about it and decided to go.'

'Wow.'

He loved Germany and had briefly lived in Frankfurt and Berlin. He laughed when I said Frankfurt was dingy, that there was something in its corners that was past its prime. He was amused that I had gone the year before to Berlin just to rent a taxi and drive around looking at the *Gründerzeit* houses.

'You haven't seen the real Berlin,' he declared.

'Why are the dirtiest parts real? The people in grungy places live there because they have no choice, not because they want to be real. They would leave if they could.'

'But those are the parts that show the real city, the real character.'

'I think I will keep going to the unreal parts, then.'

Johan laughed. I told him there were cities I loved almost as soon as I landed, wide-armed cities I knew I could befriend, and others that left me cold, and still others that smouldered with unwelcomeness to which I knew I would never return.

'Left you cold?' he asked.

'Kraków. Santiago.'

'Loved on landing?'

'London, of course. Colombo. Auckland. Dakar. Rio.'

'Won't go back?'

'Moscow. Sydney. Buenos Aires.'

'Racist much?' he asked, and I laughed.

'I mentally prepare myself for hostility in small places, but sometimes it's in the larger cities that you feel Blackness as this heavy thing that you have to rise above. Moscow was like that. Just not a good feeling.'

'I've never been to Russia.'

'They can't build toilets, by the way; you flush and the thing is still sitting there in the bowl looking at you.'

'Still better than the pit latrines I used in China!' He was learning Mandarin. He wanted to write culture pieces that connected America and China. 'Nobody is doing that. How can your biggest market also be your biggest enemy? They should cooperate. If they cooperate, both of them will benefit and so will the world. But it's all ego, on both sides.'

I said Korea and Japan interested me, not so much China.

'China is the future,' he said. 'Let's plan to go together in the fall? Oh, I know they'll be difficult about visas to Nigerians. I can't believe what you go through with a Nigerian passport. It's kind of crazy.' And he looked at me as if I had given him entry into an exciting new reality.

At first, we explained our worlds to each other, and it was intoxicating, how we peeled back layers and saw our lives anew. Then it became wearying, and I blamed him for not knowing what he could not possibly have known.

'This obligation to send money to people in Nigeria is fascinating,' he said.

'It's not people. I send money to my relatives.'

'It's really kind.'

'It's not kind. It's just what I should do.'

'So it is an obligation,' he said.

'No, it isn't. Not in the way you think of an obligation.'

When he said he had only been in the US for six months, I said, 'Your English sounds so American.'

'Really?' he asked, and a small smile appeared; he was pleased to sound American. 'I learned English from watching American television shows.'

His oozing infatuation with America disconcerted me, how he reeled off the smallest details about American films and American music, especially African American music. He had visited Detroit years ago just because he adored Motown, which was no surprise since his parents said he had been conceived while the Commodores played loudly on the stereo. He lit up talking about Tupac and Tina Turner and Prince, not merely their music but their recording contracts and their relationships, and it was almost perverse that he should know so much of a country he had never lived in. He rarely spoke of Sweden.

'Maybe you're actually an American who lived in Sweden?' I said, and he laughed.

WE TRAVELLED TO Germany together because he was trying to interview a Chinese artist in Berlin. He had lived briefly in Berlin and had friends there, and one of them was having a dinner party. I was surprised by the big house in a self-satisfied neighbourhood of big houses, all groomed greenery and low iron gates.

'Your friend is rich, which means she is not real,' I said, and he laughed and said she had inherited the house, as if it made a difference. His friend, Anna, was a stylish German woman who walked with a cane; slender, dark-haired, wearing jeans, her crisp white shirt almost halfway unbuttoned to her chest, small half-globes of her breasts exposed. She seemed to fit well in the mixed décor of her home, the severe modern sofas and antique chests, the imposing paintings. When she talked to you, she coolly looked you in the eye and held her stare for a little too long, as though she enjoyed the discomfort it caused. The guests were already high-spirited from drinking, all speaking German, around a table spread with cold cuts and cheeses.

Johan said in English, 'Chia is an English speaker, everyone.'

'No, it's fine. I like the sound of German,' I said, which was a lie. The harsh undertones of some German words unsettled me.

'Only English,' our host decreed, watching me. They switched to English and I felt sorry that some of the guests spoke haltingly, slowed by a language not normally at the tips of their tongues. They were telling entertaining stories, louder than I expected, dipping into bowls of thin salted pretzels.

'The German middle-class trajectory of success is you go to school in Berlin, get your first job in Hamburg, and then start a family in Munich, with its spotless river – everyone loves the river,' somebody said scornfully.

'Let's tell jokes!' somebody said, full of beer. Johan told a joke about a conversation he had in India with an airport worker and everyone laughed. I was next and unsure what to say. Why did it matter to me that I amused these strangers? When in doubt, make fun of yourself. I said when I was growing up in Nigeria, I read about bagels in a novel and imagined them to be elegant, like macarons or cupcakes, and how shocked I was when I finally had a bagel in America. My punchline was 'I asked for a bagel, not a dense doughnut!' As soon as I said it, I wished I had told a different joke, more ironic and less folksy. There was scattered laughter.

'Bagel,' Anna said, ruminatively. 'Bagel is a Jewish food, yes?'

She had a kind of high style, an intentional superciliousness lodged inside her self-assurance. She emphasized the word 'Jewish', saying it slowly, at a pace different from the rest of her sentence, and gave it an unearned weight in the sentence. The air swirled as it was not supposed to. Her German accent, her expression, eyebrows slightly raised and lips slightly curled, became a cliché, and I felt myself suddenly plunged into German history. Dizziness coursed through me and the chill of goosebumps spread on my skin. I thought I should press shut my eyes, to make the vertigo pass.

'It's a Jewish food?' she repeated, her eyes on me.

Somebody said yes it was a Jewish food. The chatter continued, as though she had not just asked 'It's a Jewish food?' about a bagel.

Even Johan was indifferent, tipping his head back to drink from a beer bottle. What was her family's story? The walls of the room were unsteady. An abstract painting hung on the other end and seemed suddenly to swell with accusation. Pictures formed in my mind from films and documentaries about Germany during the war, the Nazis in their fastidious uniforms, flawlessly cultured and implacably murderous. Maybe this woman was a recalcitrant granddaughter. Maybe this house had blood in its solid stone foundation. Until we left, I avoided looking at Anna, as if I might see proof of something I preferred not to see.

'How does a person think of a bagel today as "Jewish" food?' I asked Johan as we left.

'I think you've given this an American interpretation,' he said.

I stared at his unshaven face, his blond stubble. I felt upset with him too.

'She made it about Jewish food. Why does it matter whether or not it's Jewish food, that's not what the joke was about, and the way she asked and the look on her face . . .'

'You view this issue in an American way,' Johan said, and I felt he had cut me off. 'It's not the same here. People don't even eat bagels.'

'Really?' I asked. He shook his head and changed the subject, asking if we could go to Kreuzberg earlier than we planned, because the Chinese artist had moved the interview to late evening. I looked at him. I didn't really know him; there was no reason to be surprised. Our break-up was the nicest because it was the lightest. We had not done the labour of learning each other, and so we parted unburdened by resentment, which, to grow, requires knowledge of the other.

THE ENDING OF LOCKDOWN trailed off like a forgotten song. If only life could immediately return to what it used to be. Some bars and restaurants had opened, all hesitantly, the rules changing day by day. Zikora and I met at a restaurant in downtown DC, and sat on rattan chairs outside, under the awning. I looked around, at the three other customers. We were wary and masked; we were beaten down, defeated by a changed world.

'Makes no sense to come in masked, only to then take off the mask and eat and drink.'

'I know.'

Zikora brought out a bottle of hand sanitizer, squirted into her palms, rubbed them briskly together. I did the same.

'Driving here, I saw a police car and I panicked. Just thinking of the early days of stay-at-home when they were cruising the empty roads, stopping the lone disobedient car to ask for proof of "essential worker" status,' Zikora said.

'I heard someone was shot in a Walmart over toilet paper. You would think they would fight over food,' I said.

'We've become our base animal selves,' Zikora said.

'But also our best selves,' I said. 'People helped other people so much. I used to cry watching the people on TV that came out to clap for essential workers.'

Zikora pulled down her mask to reveal a reddish cluster of rashes around her mouth. 'I feel like joining the crazies who don't want to wear masks.'

'Goodness. *Ndo.* Are you putting anything on it? I have this rash cream I got in Colombia.'

'My mother suggested zinc cream, she's always reading about all sorts of things. I think it actually helped a bit. Man, Chia, we lived through a plague. Chidera now thinks masks are normal; he saw one of my old pictures and was shocked and said Mommy is not wearing a mask!'

'I miss him. I miss the sweet sweet smell of him.'

'He loved that puzzle box thing you sent him. You can keep him this Saturday. My mom will bring him.'

'Our hummus place has closed down.'

'So many places have. We don't even know the full damage. We'll see in the next weeks how gouged out we are. Like a coconut somebody scooped the flesh out of and put the shell back together.'

The waiter almost threw our drinks at us, standing too far away from our table, double-masked and wearing gloves.

'Well, he managed not to spill it,' I said, and we laughed. Our laughter lifted my spirits. 'But it's really messed up, working like this, in service jobs.'

'I know. I found this really good online therapy site. But you wouldn't need that, would you, Madam Milk Butter, because normal people spent lockdown suffering anxiety while you were busy looking up your exes and reviewing your body count.'

'My dream count,' I said.

'So how many dreams have you been with?'

'The world has changed and you look back to take stock of how you've lived. And you have so much regret,' I said. I wished I had not used that word, 'regret'. Chidera was almost five and Kwame's parents did not yet know of him.

'Regret is a useless feeling.' Zikora paused and squirted more hand sanitizer. 'So what was the conclusion of your dream count?'

I was playing with my still-full glass, running my finger along the handle. I was reluctant to drink because to drink would be to pull down my mask. 'I should have tried harder with Chuka. I thought that wanting to sustain a relationship was not enough to sustain a relationship. I Googled him and saw his wedding photos and I just felt . . .'

'What?'

'I don't know. That feeling of wanting to go back and do it all over again.'

'You are such a soft and spoiled person, Chia,' Zikora said lovingly. 'Milk Butter.'

FIVE

When Zikora group-called Omelogor and me, and we hadn't planned on a call, I knew it was about Kadiatou, and I knew it wasn't good news.

'The charges will be dropped,' she said. 'They said she's lied about too many things and they can't trust her.'

'What?' I heard my own screaming voice, as though from someone else. 'What?'

'They will *drop* the case? Just like that? It's over?' Omelogor asked. 'Yes.'

'I don't believe this,' Omelogor said tightly.

'They said she lied?' I asked. 'How can they know she lied?'

'Not about the assault. They said there is compelling evidence to support her version of events, but because she wasn't honest and forthcoming about her past, they can't trust her and don't think a jury will trust her.'

'So nobody in that prosecutor's office has ever lied in their lives,' Omelogor said.

'I saw the press release,' Zikora said. 'They're really throwing her under. It's almost as if they're exasperated with her. It's so odd.'

'She didn't lie about the rape but because she lied about something else in her past, a jury of normal people will not believe her about the rape,' Omelogor said.

'But Kadi didn't lie,' I said.

'I'm saying even if she did lie about her past, it means she's lying about everything else? Why can't they just focus on what happened in that room, what she actually accused him of?' Omelogor said.

'What will I tell Kadi?' I asked. I was stunned, unsteady; a thousand dots swayed in my vision and Kadiatou's voice in my head, saying, *He will send people to kill me! He will send people to kill me!*

'There's still the option of a civil case. She will almost definitely win a civil case, and she'll get some money and she can start her restaurant,' Zikora said.

'But it's a shabby consolation prize,' Omelogor said.

'What is?'

'A civil court win. I hate how Americans think money is justice. Winning money in a civil case isn't justice. How can the government drop the criminal charges? Goodness, everybody in America has lost their bravery. So what is their alternative story? If you reject a story, then you should tell us what the real story is.'

'They're not saying her story isn't true. They're saying they can't prove it because of what she's said in the past,' Zikora said.

'But what does the past have to do with what happened?' I asked.

'The prosecutor is just a self-serving coward afraid to do some real work. America is so messed up!' Omelogor's voice was cracking.

'Yes and Nigeria is better,' Zikora mocked.

Omelogor looked almost hurt, as if this wasn't an appropriate time for their baiting. 'Zikora, Nigeria doesn't call itself the land of the free and the brave.'

'I don't know how to tell her,' I said.

'Chia, you need to go and see her. To tell her yourself, before her lawyer does,' Omelogor said.

'Yes, it will be easier for her,' Zikora said. 'I can come by after work.'

'Chia?' Omelogor said.

'Yes, okay,' I said.

And so I called Kadi, an audio call because I did not want her to see my face.

'Kadi, I have to come and see you. I have something to tell you. Zikora found out some information.'

There was an intake of breath, a brief strangled silence, and then she said, 'They will deport me? But Binta can stay. Binta can stay.'

'No, Kadi, it's not that. Nobody is deporting you. I'll see you soon.'

'Okay.'

What did it matter what I wore to Kadi's to tell her? But I changed three times. My dull black-grey dress felt right, sombre enough. Her apartment's entrance smelled of mushrooms. Binta opened the door wearing a white mask and hugged me, our papery masks brushing against each other. Her eyes looked sad, this lovely young girl who should not be cooped up with her mother in a small apartment waiting for justice. I held her tightly for a long moment. Kadi had been cooking, the smell reminded me of my kitchen when she cooked folere. The old wood floors of her apartment had the sheen of frequent scrubbing. Old-fashioned scrubbing, with a brush. Kadi once told me that Amadou joked about how she didn't need to bother with plates in his apartment in New York, he would eat his food from the floor, because it was too scrupulously clean to waste. A clanging sound of a heater. It was warming up outside but the heater was on. The living room sat half in shadow, the windows ungenerous with light, and Kadi was in the shadowy corner, on an armchair, and she was gripping one arm of the chair. A well-worn chair, it looked like something she sank into after a long day at work to watch her beloved Nollywood. A fringed lampshade stood on a side table, looking out of place.

'Kadi,' I said.

'Miss Chia,' she said. She looked wary, and almost impatient; she knew it was bad news and she wanted it done with straightaway. If the air were made of fabric there were crinkles in it. Binta was hovering, her anxiety palpable, as if I could reach out and feel the air thickened from it. I took a deep breath, feeling so utterly sorry for Kadi. After all the interviews she had suffered through, the questioning and requestioning, after it all, to end with this nullity.

'Kadi, they will dismiss the case. They've dropped it. They won't go to court.'

'What does that mean, Aunty?' Binta asked.

Kadi looked puzzled, her brows knitted. 'They dropped it?'

'Yes, it's ridiculous but they said they can't prove your case, but it's also because he has very big lawyers.' I paused, feeling inept. I was not explaining this clearly.

'So no court? No court case any more?' Kadi asked.

'Yes, but Kadi, there is something called a civil court –'

She cut me short. 'So Miss Chia, no court case? They dismiss everything?'

I had a sudden niggling feeling that something was not right, that the rising pitch of her voice was wrong, a stirring energy unsuited for the news. Did she not understand?

'Yes. They have dismissed everything. Nothing will happen now.'

Kadi's eyes flew wide in disbelief, but not in dread; it was that other kind of disbelief, tentative, asking, *Do I dare believe?*

'No court case?' Kadi asked.

'No.'

And then Kadi smiled. I stared as her face changed, like those reverse animations that show a wilted flower slowly returning to bloom. She stood up to her full statuesque height and in a flash she and Binta were in each other's arms, clasped together, Kadi making a sound that was neither crying nor laughter, a low-toned keening.

I felt suddenly limp, my own tension draining away.

'Oh, Aunty Chia,' Binta said. 'She's been dreading the court case. She's been praying that it won't happen. She didn't want to stand there and answer all these questions about her private life, and some-times when her lawyer calls she doesn't answer because she's so tired of practising the questions, and she gets scared when the prosecutors call, and she hasn't been sleeping, she just cries and cries at night.'

Binta was crying now and smiling through her tears.

Kadi paced around the room and then lowered herself onto the sofa, near the window, and Binta sat next to her, holding her hand. I felt that I was observing something remarkable, the unfolding of Kadi, a woman becoming anew before my eyes. How in a moment despair was flung away.

'Oh, Miss Chia,' Kadi said.

My phone was ringing. Omelogor calling, but I didn't pick it up. Later, driving home, I would call her back, the phone barely beeping before her harried voice asked, 'Chia, how did it go? She must have been shattered.' And I would reply, a little triumphantly, 'Actually, no. She wasn't, at all.' But now I let my phone ring. I wanted to savour this moment for just a little bit longer, Kadiatou and Binta, these two thoroughly decent people, mother and daughter, sitting on a sofa holding hands, their faces bathed in light.

Author's Note

Novels are never really about what they are about. At least for this writer. *Dream Count* is, yes, about the interlinked desires of four women, but, in a deeply personal way not obvious, at least not immediately so, to the reader, it is really about my mother. About losing my mother. A grief still stubbornly in infancy, its so-called stages not so much begun as utterly irrelevant, its contours intact and untouched – the confusion and disbelief, the myriad regrets.

When my mother died, too soon after my father, my life's cover was ripped off, leaving behind an unmoored sense of nakedness, a straining and longing to take back time, a desperate addiction to looking away, a terror of acknowledgement, a fear of finality, and, most of all, ceaseless sadness and anger, each sometimes emerging wrapped in the other. Little wonder, then, that there is so much here about mothers and daughters, highlighted by the scene at the end, of Kadiatou and Binta, mother and daughter, beginning anew.

I could not have imagined writing the character of Kadiatou, who is inspired by Nafissatou Diallo, when, in May 2011, I first heard of her, a Guinean immigrant who cleaned rooms at a prestigious hotel in New York City. She was in the news because she had accused a hotel guest – Dominique Strauss-Kahn, head of the International Monetary Fund – of sexual assault. I followed the story closely, even ardently. It touched many flashpoints of modern American life, power and sexual assault, gender and immigration and race. The details had the addictiveness of crude melodrama: the lowly maid, the man who would be president, his arrest on a plane just about to fly off to Paris. And I felt the stirrings of protectiveness, for although Nafissatou Diallo was unlike me in many ways, she too was a West African woman living in America, and therefore familiar, intuitively knowable; sisterly feelings emerged.

My interest had darkened to disappointment by the time I published an essay about the case in August 2011, part of which read:

> When Dominique Strauss-Kahn was arrested in May, accused of raping Diallo in a hotel room, I applauded the American justice system: a powerless woman had reported an assault by a Big Man and the Big Man had immediately been arrested. In Nigeria, where I come from, this would not happen. Neither would it happen in Guinea, where Nafissatou Diallo comes from. Although I cringed at Strauss-Kahn's 'perp walk' – which really should be abolished for all accused persons because it suggests automatic guilt – his arrest reminded me of what I admire about America. Now the case has been dismissed, not because the prosecutors are certain that Strauss-Kahn is innocent but because Diallo is not a saint.
>
> The prosecutors have evidence of a 'hurried sexual encounter'. Diallo has consistently said that she did not give her consent for this sexual encounter. He was a man she had never seen before. She was a woman he had never seen. Minutes after she met him, she was spitting out his semen on the floor. Her colleagues who saw her after the incident confirmed that she was upset. His lawyers have suggested that the sexual encounter was consensual. How does consensual sex between strangers happen in ten minutes? It is not impossible, but it is unlikely and a trial might have clarified this. On television, Strauss-Kahn's lawyer called Nafissatou Diallo 'evil or pathetic or both'. He also repeated 'she lied', and by saying 'she lied' over and over again, as many commentators have done, it becomes an all-encompassing truth. She becomes nothing but a liar. But what did she lie about?

The rest of the essay is similar, my position less than a happy one. Nafissatou Diallo's accusation represented a significant cultural moment

in America, a pre–MeToo opportunity to rethink mainstream percep-
tions of sexual assault against women, especially of those assault cases
upholstered in power. It raised questions about the American justice
system, France's political trajectory, the media coverage of assault, the
interplay of immigration and gender and race. It was, in short, too
important a case to be so shabbily dropped.

I could not stop thinking of the woman at the centre of it all, and of
her West African mannerisms during a TV interview, her voice hushed
as she spoke of being intimately examined in a hospital after the assault.
She seemed certain of her recounting but uncertain of her forced plunge
into public life. Her daughter, she said, had told her, 'Mom, promise me
you will stop crying.' That anecdote; it broke me open and moved me
and lingered in me for years.

With the case dropped, with lawyers publicly calling her a liar, with
no court of law to vindicate her or not, she became, in my imagination,
a symbol, a person failed by a country she trusted, her character muti-
lated by false stories in the press, the fabric of her life forever rent.

The creative impulse can be roused by the urge to right a wrong,
no matter how obliquely. In this case, to 'write' a wrong in the balance
of stories. Nafissatou Diallo had accused a man so well-known and so
floridly in the public eye that it was impossible to reduce him to a single
thing: a man accused of assault. But she became, in the public imagination, the woman whose case against an important man was dropped
because she was said to have lied. An ungenerous, undignified represen-
tation, incomplete and flattening.

Which also becomes inspiration for creating a fictional character as
a gesture of returned dignity. Clear-eyed realism, but touched by tenderness. A relentlessly human portrait, not an ideological one, because
ideology blocks different ways of seeing and art requires many eyes. Especially a recent, peculiar quality to contemporary ideology that seems not
only incompatible with, but opposed to, art, by shying away from the
all too human possibility of contradiction, and reaching answers before
questions are asked, if questions are asked at all.

The point of art is to look at our world and be moved by it, and then
to engage in a series of attempts at clearly seeing that world, interpret-
ing it, questioning it. In all these forms of engagement, a kind of purity

of purpose must prevail. It cannot be a gimmick, it must at some level be true. Only then can we reach reflection, illumination, and finally, hopefully, epiphany.

What is it to attempt to fictionally humanize a person? 'Humanize.' Of course she is human. It is rather to create a character as rumination on what this often-quoted notion of humanizing means. As an idea it is solemn, serious, sombre. But as experience it is messy and unformed, laughter and pain, cowardice and bravery, it is how we let ourselves and others down, how we emerge or don't from our failings, how we are petty, how we try to overcome and strive to improve, how we seethe in our self-pity, how we fail, how we hold on tenaciously to hope. There is grandeur to our humanity, but to be human day to day is not, and should not be, an endless procession of virtue. A victim need not be perfect to be deserving of justice.

(Speaking of virtue, did it matter that the 'lying' linked to Nafissatou Diallo was not in fact about what happened in that hotel room?)

Stories die and recede from collective memory merely for not having been told. Or a single version thrives because other versions are silenced. Imaginative retellings matter. Literature does truly instruct and delight – or at least it can. Literature keeps the faith and tells the story as reminder, as witness, as testament. Stories help us see ourselves and talk about ourselves. As Seamus Heaney writes, citing Neruda on the art of the Dutch Masters, 'The world's reality will not go unremarked.'

But how is this remarking to be done? When I was writing my second novel, *Half of a Yellow Sun*, about the Nigeria-Biafra war, I knew that a generation born after the war and raised in the silence of its aftermath would come to the novel as history as much as art. And while my imagination freely roamed, in tenor and tone, I did not tamper with, or dilute, any consequential narratives of that war. I did not feel that I had the moral right, for example, to make significant changes to episodes of massacres. I could illuminate with detail but I baulked at creating scenes that might change a reasonable person's understanding of the history. To do so would be to debase a monumental history that had disfigured the lives of millions. It would make meaningless the expression 'based on a true story'.

Nafissatou Diallo's recounting of the assault felt sacrosanct. This, the assault, is after all why she became a public figure, a person so widely covered in the news as to inspire a character in a novel. It felt to me that the assault scene as described by her was the seed around which I would weave my imagination. It is the only part of *Dream Count* that I have left as close as possible to Nafissatou's account of what happened. Kadiatou is inspired by Nafissatou but Kadiatou is not Nafissatou. She cannot possibly be, as I do not know Nafissatou Diallo apart from what is in the public domain. Nothing of Kadiatou's pre-American life as recounted here is based on any known fact of Nafissatou's. The post-assault scenes are only skeletally based on facts – we know she went through a hospital examination, and that she had a lawyer, but the shadings and details of Kadiatou's experiences are mine. As is the entire landscape of her emotional life. Imaginative writing fails when it leaves emotional heights unscaled. I do not know how Nafissatou Diallo felt because I cannot possibly know, but I can imagine it in a fictional character's life, and then invite willing readers to join in this gesture of returned dignity.

We know from her interviews that Nafissatou Diallo felt wounded when the criminal charges were dropped. An expected and understandable reaction. But the artistic imagination is also the world of 'what if'. What if, instead of being broken, she instead saw the dropping of charges as an escape from a system she knew was not set up to benefit people like her? What if she saw it as a complicated relief, having been denied justice but also granted the potential of retrieving her life from where it had stayed frozen in the ice of the unknown?

Sometimes, in writing fiction, magical moments float down, characters reveal themselves, revelatory pieces coalesce into scenes, as happened at the end of this novel. It touched me greatly, that ending, gestated in the savage terrain of personal grief and yet so removed from grief.

My mother would, I think, have liked the character of Kadiatou. I imagine her reading this novel and then sighing and saying, with a kind of resignation and fellow-feeling, 'Nwanyi ibe m.' *My fellow woman.*